Praise for Eric Rickstad's
What Remains of Her

"A gorgeous thrill ride of a novel. Eric Rickstad's *What Remains of Her* is a literary page-turner that delves into the sacred and sometimes fraught relationships between fathers and daughters. A young girl's disappearance results in an excruciating journey of guilt, penance, and revelation for her devastated father and her childhood best friend. In Rickstad's hands, what will remain with you is the satisfaction of a story masterfully told."

—Lisa Alber, award-winning author
of *Path Into Darkness*

"*What Remains of Her* is a brilliantly creepy page-turner. A gripping, unsettling thriller electrified by Rickstad's rich and haunting prose."

—Laura McHugh, award-winning
author of *The Weight of Blood*

"Rickstad's best novel yet. With shrewd and crafty skill he spins one taut and chilling psychological ride."

—J. D. Barker, internationally bestselling
author of *The Fifth to Die*

"Dark, claustrophobic, and hypnotic, a classy thriller that will make you sleep with the lights on, if you sleep at all."

—Mark Edwards, #1 bestselling
author of *Follow You Home*

"*What Remains of Her* is chilling and heartbreaking at the same time. A twisty, diabolical read."

—Peter Swanson, author of *All the Beautiful Lies*

And *The Names of Dead Girls*

"Beautifully written with original language and imagery, *The Names of Dead Girls* is a chilling page-turner. The superb cast of characters rings so very true, from the conflicted mom police detective to the troubled Rachel Rath to the anthropomorphic, wet fog. Atmospheric, empathetic, and addictive."

—James W. Ziskin, Edgar-nominated
author of the Ellie Stone Mysteries

"Eric Rickstad is the rare writer who can wrap a dark, gritty story in smooth, poetic prose. If you haven't discovered his work yet, *The Names of Dead Girls* is the place to start. It's a taut, masterful thriller and a terrific read."

—Alafair Burke, *New York Times* bestselling
author of *The Ex*

"A tour de force of unstoppable suspense drives readers deep into Rickstad's dark and haunting world. An out-and-out bone chiller. Impossible to put down."

—Gregg Olsen, #1 *New York Times* bestselling author

"Eric Rickstad has handed us a diamond of a thriller in *The Names of Dead Girls*. . . . Rickstad is a seriously gifted writer, and trust me when I say that this book, from its explosive beginning to its startling ending, will grab you by the throat and not let go. You have been warned."

—Mark Pryor, author of *The Paris Librarian*

"*The Names of Dead Girls* is that brilliant, rare literary thriller: captivating in character, told with precision, and fueled by relentless, mounting terror. A compulsive page-turner that will have you racing to the end even as you dread what's coming."

—Steve Weddle, author of *Country Hardball*

WHAT REMAINS OF HER

Also by Eric Rickstad

The Names of Dead Girls

Lie in Wait

The Silent Girls

Reap

WHAT REMAINS
OF HER

A NOVEL

ERIC RICKSTAD

wm

WILLIAM MORROW
An Imprint of HarperCollins*Publishers*

WHAT REMAINS OF HER. Copyright © 2018 by Eric Rickstad. All rights reserved. Printed in the United States of America. No part of this book may be used or reproduced in any manner whatsoever without written permission except in the case of brief quotations embodied in critical articles and reviews. For information, address HarperCollins Publishers, 195 Broadway, New York, NY 10007.

HarperCollins books may be purchased for educational, business, or sales promotional use. For information, please email the Special Markets Department at SPsales@harpercollins.com.

FIRST EDITION

Designed by Diahann Sturge
Part title art © andreiuc88 / Shutterstock, Inc.

Library of Congress Cataloging-in-Publication Data has been applied for.

ISBN 978-0-06-284331-9

18 19 20 21 22 LSC 10 9 8 7 6 5 4 3 2 1

For Meridith, Samantha, and Ethan
My Loves. My Love.

ACKNOWLEDGMENTS

Thanks to all who've encouraged, improved, and championed my writing over the years. My lovely wife, Meridith. My daughter, Samantha, and son, Ethan, for their smiles, hugs, and joy, and for their love of books and stories. My mother. My sisters: Beth, Judy, and Susan. All of my nieces and nephews: Jaclyn, Jacob, Harrison, Emily, Bryanna, Eric, Willa, Boone, Hailey, and Poppy. Gary Martineau. Libby and Herb Levinson. Todd and Diane Levinson. Allyson Miller. Ben Wilson. Dan Myers. Dan Orseck. Tom Isham. Mark Saunders. Lailee Mendelson. Kimberly Cutter. Anya DeNiro. Rob O'Donovan. John Mero. Roger and Susan Bora. Jeff Racine. Mike and Janice Quartararo. Stephen and Carole Phillips. Eric Weissleder. Chris Champine. Dave and Heidi Bouchard. Jim Lepage. Phil Monahan. David Huddle. Tony Magistrale. Bill and Mary Wilson. Jamie and Stephen Foreman. Bruce Coffin. Matthew Engels. Daniel Nogueira. Lucinda Jamison. Greg Cutler. Paul Doiron. David Joy. Steve Ulfelder. Roger Smith. Meg Gardiner. Hank Phillippi Ryan. Jake Hinkson.

Lisa Turner. Drew Yanno. Tyler Mcmahon. Howard Mosher. Rona and Bob Long. A special thanks to my agent, Philip Spitzer, and to Lukas Ortiz and Kim Lombardini. And to the wonderful and creative people at HarperCollins, especially my editor, Carrie Feron.

From the moment of birth we begin our slow
turning toward death. In that time, live. Live.

—ANONYMOUS

PROLOGUE

The Pit

The pit lay hidden beneath a bewilderment of wild vines and lush undergrowth, concealed amid the shadows of beeches and hemlock, as cool and damp as a fresh grave.

The two girls knelt at its edge, peered down.

Neither girl knew what the pit was for or how it came to be. Neither cared. The pit was theirs; they'd found it fair and square while exploring this part of the woods their parents had forbade them to ever enter. The lure of the woods and pits, and the possible secrets they might reveal, an arrowhead or dinosaur fossil, proved too alluring to resist.

Toads had fallen into the pit. They squatted sullen in the muck at the bottom as crickets sprang and trilled around them. Other creatures had fallen prey to the pit as well, their frail skeletal remains and desiccated carcasses scattered in the mud.

In the darkest corner, a knot of baby snakes pulsed and writhed like a malformed heart.

The girls remained unafraid.

Together, they could brave whatever peril came.

They lay on their bellies now, inched backward over the edge of the pit to hang from its lip, fingers clawing into the earthen edge. Their feet dangled, and their bony arms tensed as they hung straight down beside each other, looked into each other's eyes, whispered *one two three*, and let go to drop the final few inches with horrified shrieks, as if they were plummeting a thousand feet to their deaths.

They squealed as cold mud squished between their bare toes and the gamey, milky, reptilian odor of the snakes bloomed around them.

Their skinny legs stuck out straight as pins as the girls sat at opposite ends of the pit, facing each other, the bottoms of their bare feet pressed against each other as their pink fingers picked away at the earthen walls in search of a remnant mystery of the past. Today, however, there was another mystery to reveal.

Lucinda's heart skittered with excitement. She'd waited *forever* to hear Sally's secret. "Tell me," she pleaded as she slapped a mosquito on her cheek, the insect sticking to her skin with a splat of her own warm blood.

Sally smiled. Her teeth glowed in the murk. A ray of sun lanced down through the thatch of leaves above to light up a lens of Sally's thick eyeglasses.

"Can you keep a secret?" Sally whispered.

What a ding dong question. Of *course* Lucinda could keep a secret, especially Sally's secrets. Didn't they always? That's what friends were for, to tell each other secrets, and to keep them. And Lucinda and Sally were best friends and would always be best friends. Forever. So of course they told each other everything. And the whole entire reason they even came to the pit was for

Sally to tell Lucinda, *show* Lucinda, the secret. But Sally was teasing. And it drove Lucinda crazy when her friend did that.

"Tell me," Lucinda said, "don't tease."

Sally leaned in, still smiling. Except now her smile seemed plastic and freaky, like a smile on a crazed clown doll.

"Why are you smiling like that?" Lucinda said.

"You can't tell, anyone," Sally whispered.

"I won't."

"Ever."

"I won't. I said I won't."

"Promise?"

"Hope to die. Come *on*."

Sally leaned in, cupped a hand around Lucinda's ear, and whispered the secret.

Lucinda yanked away and pushed herself back, deeper into her corner of the pit, her heart knocking. She looked up at the snarl of branches and vines concealing them, listening, eyes darting, searching. Each noise now, each play of shadows and light in the trees high above a threat that sent a tremor of terror through her bones.

From above came the sharp *snap* of a branch.

Lucinda gasped.

"Shhh," Sally said. "He'll hear us."

BOOK I

November 6, 1987

CROOKED

When he first arrived home with a bouquet of black-eyed Susans for Rebecca, and a new yellow dress and coat for Sally, Jonah Baum sensed nothing amiss.

He called out for his wife and daughter and, upon receiving no reply, assumed Rebecca was out running errands and Sally was at a friend's house, as was often the case when Jonah returned from teaching his Thursday sessions of transcendental poetry and Gothic lit at Lyndon State.

A part of him was relieved to be alone. More than a part. He did not wish to face Rebecca. Not yet. And with no one home, he figured he'd get a jump on grading the papers he'd not gotten to while sleeping during his office hours in the dingy, windowless space he shared with three other adjuncts.

If he burrowed deep enough into his work, he reasoned, he might escape the gloom cast over him by his and Rebecca's altercation the previous night. By the dull rock of ugliness hunkered in his gut, he knew his part was lamentable; he'd overreacted to his suspicions, and when Rebecca came home later he'd have apologizing to do, and he'd gladly do it.

How much apologizing, he couldn't say. He'd not seen Rebecca or Sally that morning to gauge mood. With the world still dark, he'd stolen out of his house and into the black cold dawn like a criminal from a crime scene. Whatever Jonah's level of culpability, the yellow dress and coat Sally had wanted, and the cache of Rebecca's favorite flowers he'd picked across the road along the river, would carry him through.

Perhaps, a voice said, *Rebecca isn't home yet because Rebecca does not wish to be home yet.*

Jonah shrugged off the voice and entered the living room, stepped around Sally's menagerie of stuffed animals, preciously arranged for tea around the scuffed coffee table with a matchbook wedged under one leg to level it.

Jonah stopped. The watercolor painting of Gore Mountain hung crooked on the wall. Nothing new. The train that rampaged past on the tracks just across the river from their old house saw to that twice a day. Soon after moving here, Rebecca had learned to place her fragile knickknacks at the rear of shelves to keep them from skittering over the edge from the train's vibration.

The crooked painting drove Rebecca mad, her outrage so disproportionate to the painting's affront that Jonah had once teased that the painting and the train were conspiring to undermine her sanity. She'd slapped his arm, hard: *Not funny*.

No, it wasn't.

Normally, the painting didn't bother Jonah: if he straightened it, it would only go crooked again later this evening when the train rumbled north. But something about the painting bothered him now, and he straightened it with a blush of satisfaction as disproportionate to the deed as was Rebecca's ire toward the painting being crooked.

At the kitchen sink, Jonah filled an empty wine bottle with water and arranged the flowers, most certainly the last blooms of autumn.

Jonah plunked his backpack and the bag with Sally's dress and coat on the table, searched the refrigerator for a Rolling Rock. Realizing he must have drunk all his beer the previous night, he unearthed Rebecca's two four-packs of Bartles & Jaymes, cracked open a bottle, and put half of it down at a go, scowling at its sweetness as he settled in to correct the papers with his blue pen.

Jonah never used a red pencil to correct papers. As a boy, he'd suffered enough of the shaming red graffiti on his own schoolwork, despite his every earnest effort to focus and study hard, despite his empty stomach, and the bullying exacted on him for his high-water jeans and the hand-me-down shirts two sizes too small that he had to tug down at the back to cover his ass crack and the bruises and scabs from lashings. He'd promised himself that when he grew up he'd never demean kids or dismiss their problems as petty. One never knew how deep the secret pains of others cut.

Perhaps he was soft to keep promises made as a boy whose every cell had been replaced by new cells so many times in his thirty-three years that a hundred generations of himself now stood between the boy he'd been and the man he was. He was no longer who he'd once been.

Mercifully.

THE DOLL

Jonah was putting his third wine cooler to shame when he heard the sound from down the hall.

Had it come from Sally's room? Was Sally home?

No. She would have answered when he'd first called out. Unless she'd been playing with her dolls and stuffed animals. Her focus then was so intense it obliterated outside distraction. She'd sit so oblivious in her hermetic imagination it alarmed Jonah, as if she were tuned to an alternative frequency, another realm. Waving a hand in front of her face didn't awaken her to this world. Only shaking her would revive her from her fugue, a measure Jonah resisted at all costs, though Rebecca had been known to shake her back to the present, to reality.

Yet surely if Sally were home, Jonah would have heard her holding court with her stuffies.

So what had he heard? A squeak? No. Not quite. A cry?

He took his wine cooler and walked down the hall, unsteady as an unaccountable apprehension coiled in his chest.

At Sally's bedroom door, his heart twitched. He stared at the sign—SALLY'S ROOM—scribed with blue crayon in his daughter's left-handed scrawl.

Jonah suddenly missed his daughter and wife profoundly and longed for them to be home, now, right now; all three of them together.

He put his hand on the doorknob. The old house's antique glass knobs were among the intricacies that had sold him and Rebecca on the house. Some intricacies, however, had worn thin; what had seemed "antique" had proved old and in disrepair. The beloved leaded windows were sieves for drafts, and most cold nights now Jonah lay awake listening to his paltry savings bleed dry as the furnace groaned without relent or mercy.

Jonah clutched the doorknob, and since the door stuck in cold weather, he shoved a shoulder into it.

Losing his grip, he stumbled into the room as the door slammed against the wall.

Sally was not here. Everything seemed as it should: Sally's rock and mineral collection lay scattered on the floor among scraps of paper on which Sally had scrawled the names and traits of each mineral and rock. The dog-eared *National Geographic* magazines whose pictorials Sally had obsessed over of late—one cover featuring King Tut, another skeletal remains from Mt. Vesuvius, and a third of arrowheads and spearheads—lay splayed open in a toss of sheets on her new, big-girl bed. The cost of the bed had forced a rift between Jonah and Rebecca, who'd argued for a secondhand bed. Jonah, however, had insisted his daughter have what he'd never had as a child.

Jonah sat on the bed and picked up the *National Geographic* that slid to the floor, the headline beside the cover photo of the unearthed skeleton reading: THE DEAD DO TELL TALES AT VESUVIUS.

He set it aside and eyed a stuffie in a tangle of sheets, Ed the elephant. Sally adored her stuffed animals, though lately she'd lobbied for a puppy. Rebecca had explained that maybe when, if, Daddy was tenured, they might be able to get one. Sally had whined until Jonah had said maybe, if Sally were very good, they could find a way to get a puppy.

Rebecca had called him a pushover, said he spoiled her. *You spoil her.* Said false promises were unhealthy. Perhaps. But there were worse things one could do to their child. Much worse. Jonah knew.

Jonah sighed, exhausted from forever having to choose between his family's present wants and future needs. No matter which he chose, the other suffered, with no end to the financial strain. He picked up Ed the elephant. "A puppy shouldn't be a *luxury*, should it?" he asked Ed.

Ed remained mum.

Jonah stood.

Ed tumbled to the floor.

Children's books populated the shelves above the bed. Jonah took down *Blueberries for Sal.* He'd bought it five months before Sally was born, so ready to be a father; yet so apprehensive, with no model on which to base the role.

Rebecca had said, *Do the exact opposite of what was done to you, and you'll be father of the year.*

As he turned to leave the room, Jonah twisted his ankle cruelly on a doll. He heard and felt the pop of a ligament, and a wild anger reared in him as his mind flashed to calculate how much a sprained ankle would cost in medical fees.

He jammed *Blueberries for Sal* back in place, the jacket ripping, and snatched the offending doll and hurled it into the corner.

The doll struck the wall and emitted a meek baby's cry. *Was that the sound that lured me to the room?* he wondered.

A zoo of stuffed animals crowded his feet. He kicked all of them, including Ed the elephant, into the corner as a mean, unbidden thought scorched his brain: *Spoiled. A spoiled brat who begs for a puppy she knows I can't afford. If she only knew how—*

Jonah tried to harness the forbidding thoughts that, when he was under duress, sprang into his mind and, when spoken, threatened the life he'd built: that fragile curio left too close to the shelf edge.

He picked up the stuffed animals, and weak with indignity, rearranged them with care on the chair, thankful his daughter's playthings could never reveal his abuse.

Awake in the Dark

Jonah awoke at the table with a shudder, as if from a Van Winklean sleep. The whole house vibrated as the train thundered past outside. Shadows crawled out from the corners to shroud the kitchen in a smoky darkness. Drooling, his mind muddy, he looked up, surrounded by empty wine cooler bottles, head bludgeoned by cheap booze.

He sat up in the ghostly gloam, perplexed. The kitchen seemed a cold, mysterious, spectral approximation of his house with none of the warmth of home.

What time was it?

He shoved his chair back to stand and lost his balance, cracked his head on the stove handle as he crashed to the floor.

He lay there, bewildered. The plastic owl clock on the wall, with its glowing, shifty eyes meant to be comical, but which now seemed grotesque, showed 6:32. The second hand ticked ominously with the loud metallic snap of a revolver's hammer being cocked over and over again.

It couldn't be 6:32.

Rebecca and Sally should have been home two hours ago. Wherever they were, they were together. If Sally had been at a friend's house, she'd have walked home before dark. She didn't like the dark. Who did? And if she'd been invited for dinner, she'd have called. So she had to be with Rebecca.

Jonah stood, knocking over the chair.

Favoring his injured ankle, he limped to the living room window and pulled back the curtain as though his daughter and wife might be standing out on the front lawn, locked out of the house and waiting mutely for him to let them in.

They were not.

The 1979 Gremlin with the dented fender he'd never had repaired—keeping the insurance check to buy Sally clothes—was parked where he'd left it.

Rebecca and Sally had to be at one of Rebecca's friends' houses, and Rebecca had not called to let him know because . . .

Because she was still bruised by last night?

He tried to remember the specific words said the previous night but conjured nothing but distorted voices, like those of a lingering nightmare.

He dialed Rebecca's closest friend, twisting the long phone cord around his forearm as the phone on the other end rang.

A woman, frazzled, answered: "Martins' residence."

"Laura. It's Jonah."

"Oh."

"I'm looking for Rebecca."

Laura shouted: "Put that down!" Then, her voice tattered: "Sorry. She's not here."

"Was she there earlier?" He twisted the phone cord more tightly around his forearm.

"Haven't seen her. Put that *down*. Jonah, really I—"

He thanked her and hung up and dialed another friend. And another. And another.

No one had seen Rebecca. Or Sally.

Jonah's head screamed from the wine coolers. He phoned the last and least of Rebecca's friends.

"You okay?" the woman said. "You don't sound like yourself."

"I don't know where they are," Jonah whispered, though his voice seemed to detonate in the quiet kitchen.

"They'll turn up. Call Laura Martin. I'm sure—"

"I *called*. I called them all. You're the last." He thought he heard her suck in air.

"They should have been *home*"—he glanced at the owl clock; the only light now in the dark kitchen was the clock's ominously glowing hands—"nearly three hours ago."

"Why are you just calling now?" the woman's tone was laced with accusation.

"I was *working*," Jonah snapped. "I thought—" His arm felt deadened and engorged. He looked down at it. He'd wound the cord violently around his forearm and strangled the blood flow. His hand was a swollen, pulsing, sickly purple.

"I need to go," he said.

The Cost of Fibbing

Lucinda sat on the fireplace hearth, spellbound by the flames, her face all steamy and glowy from the crazy heat, eyelids drowsy as her daddy trucked into the living room donning his sheriff's cap and pulling on his shiny black sheriff's parka. "Lucy," he said, "I need to go out."

Lucinda hated being called Lucy by *anyone*, except her dad. He said *Lucy* different than the other grown-ups who said it in a baby-talk way. Lucinda was not a baby, even if she was the youngest girl in first grade. When Dad called her *Lucy* it sounded like it should sound: a big girl's name.

Lucinda picked up a crayon on the hearth and shielded it with her body so her dad couldn't see, sneaked it through the gap in the fire screen, and flipped it into the fire. The wrapper caught fire, the wax bubbled out in a thin blue stream that burst into tiny flames.

"You're not playing in the fire, I hope," her dad said, yanking the zipper of his jacket up snug to his chin, shadowed with its evening whiskers. Lucinda liked his whiskers, how they tickled her cheek when he kissed her good night and good morning. It made her laugh. Her dad laughed a lot. But he wasn't laughing now. He had a serious look, and his smile wasn't his real smile. It was his fake smile he used when something was wrong but he tried to pretend it wasn't. He was a rotten pretender.

"I'm not playing in the fire," Lucinda fibbed. She felt bad for fibbing, and scared. If her dad caught her in a fib, he would not let her sit by the fire anymore. Yet getting away with her fib made her bubble with excitement. Like she had a secret superpower.

"You better not be lying," her dad said.

As sheriff, part of his job was to sniff out fibs. Lucinda's mom rolled her eyes every time he said: *Haul the lies out of the darkness and slay them with the light of the truth.*

Her dad's face wasn't just serious now; he looked—what? Upset? Mad? She gulped. It felt like food had gone down the wrong pipe. Maybe he knew she'd fibbed. If so, she had to admit it right now. It was better to fess up now than to get caught later.

The fire crackled and a spark leaped through the screen out onto the back of Lucinda's denim jumper, searing a hole in the fabric. "I—"

"You need to come with me. Mom's upstairs with a tummyache and I might be a while."

"Is someone in trouble?"

He tugged his gloves onto his hands. "I hope not."

He walked toward the kitchen door and stood with his hand on the knob, waiting for Lucinda.

Lucinda looked for Baby Beverly, the doll Lucinda took with her everywhere, and who got scared when left alone. Where was she? Lucinda started to peek under the couch for Beverly, but her dad smacked his hands together and said, "Let's go."

Lucinda trudged to the door and put on her boots and jacket, fingers trembling so much with the giddiness of going on a real live police call that it took her three whole tries to tie her bootlaces right.

"Where are we going?" she said.

Her dad opened the door and cold air jumped on Lucinda, made her shiver. Her dad left the door open and was halfway out to his truck, moving fast, the way he did that time they were at the beach and the boy had started to drown.

Lucinda hurried out and shut the door.

At the truck, the driver's door open, her dad stood looking at her.

Lucinda's excitement flew away like a bird, replaced by what she saw on her dad's own face. What had been there all along that she'd tried to name, and he'd tried to pretend with a fake smile wasn't there.

Fear.

PROMISE

The truck joggled over the railroad tracks, making Lucinda's stomach flop, then swung into a yard as familiar to Lucinda as her own yard. "Why are we here?" Lucinda said. This couldn't be the place where someone might be in trouble.

"Don't say anything," her dad said. "Sit on the couch and be a good girl, understand?"

Lucinda nodded. Her stomach felt squashy, the way it did when her parents yelled or she got lost in a store and couldn't find her mom. She should have been happy to be here, but she wasn't. Her dad always went out when the ambulance was called, and she fretted Sally might be really sick.

"Promise me," her dad said, looking at her with a tight mouth. She promised.

He messed up her hair with his bear-paw hand, but the look on his face wasn't playful. It made her want to be home, by the fire. She was sorry she fibbed about the crayon and promised herself she'd never play with fire again, so she'd never have to fib about playing with it.

"I was melting crayons in the fire," she said and braced for her scolding. Her dad opened his truck door, not seeming to hear her. "I won't do it again," she said. "Ever."

The porch light was out, and Lucinda and her dad stood side by side on the porch in the darkness. Her dad tipped his sheriff's hat back with his thumb and knocked on the door, once. Hard. He clasped his hands behind his back and cleared his throat.

"You can just go in without knocking," Lucinda said. "I always do. Mrs. B. says I'm family, and Sally never knocks when she comes—"

"Don't jibber jabber in there," her dad said, lifting his chin to stare at the closed door, his spine stiff, his shoulders square. "Remember about the couch. Stay planted."

The porch light blinked on, and in an instant Lucinda was relieved and glad to be there. She'd been silly to think Sally might be so sick she'd need an ambulance. Dramatic about her squashy feeling. Her mom often said how dramatic Lucinda was. Called Lucinda a— Lucinda could never remember the word. An *alarmist*. Making mountains out of molehills, a phrase that tickled Lucinda though she didn't really get it.

Whatever was going on, Lucinda was happy she'd have Sally to sit with on the couch.

Lucinda's dad had warned her to stay on the couch, but he hadn't said anything about not sitting *with* Sally. Maybe Lucinda and Sally could watch TV with the sound off. Or maybe it would be okay if Lucinda played in Sally's bedroom. The last time Lucinda had been in Sally's bedroom Sally had shown her something scary. Not super scary, but scary enough that Lucinda had giggled to try to show that she wasn't scared at all.

The front door opened and light from inside washed away the rest of Lucinda's silly fears that had started to sprout in her brain. Until she noticed Mr. B.'s face.

He didn't look like he'd seen a ghost: he looked like he *was* a ghost. Like he'd been dead for a jillion years.

Lucinda pulled up close to her dad's leg. Her dad gave her shoulder a squeeze and guided her into the house with his palm at her back.

THE SHADOW OF BEASTS

Inside, Lucinda's dad removed his sheriff's cap and snugged it under an arm, cupped the back of Lucinda's head, and steered her toward the couch. "Remember: stay put."

"Where's Sally?" Lucinda said. "Can't we—"

She stopped. Mr. B.'s face looked so weird, like it was melting from sadness.

"Just sit," her dad said and flashed his fake smile. "Okay, sweetie? For Daddy? Mr. B. and I have important grown-up things to talk about and I need you to be a big girl. If you are, I will forget all about you lying about playing in the fire."

Lucinda's face got wicked hot and she plopped down on the edge of the couch, gnawing a thumbnail as her dad and Mr. B. disappeared into the kitchen, their voices low and spooky.

Why couldn't she just go visit Sally in her room? Even if Sally was really sick, which maybe she was, Lucinda could at least talk to her, unless maybe Sally had something that was catching.

Maybe Sally's in trouble, Lucinda thought.

Lucinda chewed her thumbnail, fidgeted at a very bad thought that rooted in her mind.

Maybe Sally was mad at Lucinda for something and didn't want to see her.

Lucinda could think of nothing she'd done to ever make her friend that mad.

Or maybe Sally had told her parents about the Big Secret in the woods and she'd gotten in trouble for—

Mr. B. shouted in the kitchen, startling Lucinda.

Lucinda peered toward the kitchen, but her dad and Mr. B. weren't sitting at the empty table; all she could see was their shadows shifting on the wall, stretched out crazy, like the shadows of storybook beasts.

No, Lucinda thought, *Sally would never tell grown-ups the Big Secret.* She'd never tell anyone any of their secrets, especially since Sally had sworn Lucinda to secrecy.

Lucinda peeked down the hallway. Light bled from under Sally's door. Maybe Sally was playing with her animals, or the piece of rock they'd found in the pit that Sally swore was an arrowhead, their first real artifact from a dig, even though Lucinda swore it was just a rock. In fact, Lucinda had called Sally stupid for thinking it was an arrowhead. Was that why Sally wasn't coming out? Lucinda's guilt sank in her belly, made her feel like she'd drunk a cup of cough syrup. Or maybe Sally wasn't hiding or mad. Maybe she was reading. She was a super good reader, so much better than Lucinda, and when Sally got to reading, she vanished to her Faraway Place as if she were no longer here at all but in a different space and time.

Lucinda picked at the tender flesh of her thumb cuticle. She wanted *so* badly to slip down the hall and visit Sally. Maybe she could tiptoe down the hall and knock on the door and at least let Sally know she was here, and Sally could join her on the couch.

Lucinda glanced at the kitchen again.

Distorted shadows crept on the kitchen wall.

Slowly, Lucinda stood and tiptoed down the hall, holding her breath as she heard a noise, a tiny cry perhaps, just behind her best friend's bedroom door.

SHRIEK

Jonah strode around the kitchen table. Disoriented. He needed to find his bearings. Rid his head of this lousy static. Time was greasy. It seemed he'd arrived home to an empty house years ago; yet it also felt as if the few hours had passed in a blink.

He'd believed having Maurice come over would put him at ease, that Maurice would provide a reasonable explanation for Sally and Rebecca's absence, console Jonah with his composure, make clear nothing was amiss. That's what friends did. That's what Maurice did. Had always done. Remained composed. Constant. Amid Jonah's chaos.

Except Maurice had questions instead of answers.

"Can you tell me?" Maurice asked again. He stood at the window, trying—Jonah knew—to keep his face as blank as possible, something he'd done since they were boys. The steady, comported older brother Jonah never had, who'd rescued Jonah from his boyhood anger and from a tailspin into petty crime that might have led to much worse.

Jonah shook his head to try to clear it. "What?" he whispered.

"Have you been drinking?" Maurice said, his face pained to have to ask, more so for knowing the answer.

"Maybe a cooler or two." Perspiration moistened Jonah's upper lip. His entire body itched. Felt hived. He wanted to rake his nails into his flesh to make the sensation abate, wanted to lick the sweat away; however, he did not want to call attention to his sweating and agitation. Yet why shouldn't he be sweating? His wife and daughter were missing. His pulse rocketed and he felt dizzy and untethered.

Maurice's calm eyes remained fixed on Jonah's eyes. They did not shift the slightest toward the empty wine cooler bottles on the table. They did not have to; they'd detected them first thing.

"I had a few," Jonah said. "Nothing we don't all do together regularly. Not coolers for us men." He tried to force a laugh. "But beer. We—"

"I'm not judging you," Maurice said. "I'd be the last to do that." He attempted laughter, but it sounded as forced as Jonah's attempt. "You need to know, as a friend, I am here in a law enforcement capacity first. For now. I'm obligated. It's important I point that out. It's critical I get the specifics. I need to know what you know."

"What I know? About what?"

"Your state of mind for one."

"State of mind? Why don't you put out a bulletin to look for Sally and Rebecca instead of—"

"Done. As soon as I hung up with you. Contacted my two deputies. This is a weird one. Professionally speaking. For a missing persons situation. Missing adults, the waiting period is seventy-two hours unless there is a clear sign of criminality. Missing kids, there's no wait. We have both, if they're missing at all, and not just off somewhere. Which likely they are. But if not, we don't know if they went missing together or if Sally didn't come in from playing or something and Rebecca went out looking for her and—"

"Missing persons?"

"That's why you called. Rebecca and Sally are missing."

"No. Yes. I mean. They're not here, but—"

"Do you know where they are?" Maurice's professional air left Jonah cold.

"No."

"Then they're missing. Did you check with friends?"

"I called all around."

"Who?"

"Everyone she knows."

"Is there a chance that there might be . . . a friend that Rebecca has that you don't know about?"

"What— No."

"Of course not. Sorry."

Jonah could not help but wonder if Maurice sensed Jonah's own misgivings. Maurice and his wife had dropped in unexpectedly one recent evening to catch Jonah and Rebecca in a humiliating and intense personal exchange. He wondered what impression that had left.

"Where do you think they might be?" Maurice said.

"I don't know. That's why I called. I need to know. I was hoping you'd come talk sense into me, calm me, tell me I was crazy."

"You're crazy."

The two men grunted approximations of laughter, their normal banter quashed. The eyes of the owl clock shifted, side to side, as if following the volley of Jonah and Maurice's conversation.

"I'd be crazy about their absence too," Maurice said. "I am. I just can't let it get the best of me. I need to maintain my bearings. We both need to. Is it possible they're just in town, running errands, grabbing a bite?"

It was possible. More possible than other scenarios Jonah refused to entertain. But. "I called the stores I could think of. No one saw her. Them. This doesn't make sense." Jonah paced, unable to focus. "What do we do?"

"We're doing it."

"Asking me how many wine coolers I drank?"

"Let's sit and go over this. My two men, their sole priority is to look for Sally and Rebecca. They'll find them. Rebecca probably took Sally somewhere for a treat and lost track of time. They're probably eating pie at the Bee Hive."

"Sally doesn't like sweets. She never did."

"What do you mean?"

"She wouldn't be eating pie."

"You said 'never *did*.'"

"Has. Never *has*."

Jonah swallowed hard to keep down the vomit he felt surge in his throat, his face damp, doughy.

"Sit," Maurice said.

Jonah sat and exhaled a long breath that failed to expel his dread.

Maurice picked up the chair Jonah had knocked over earlier and sat in it across from Jonah, sliding a stack of Jonah's corrected papers out of the way as he eyed the flowers in the wine bottle. He placed a notepad on the table.

"I should be out there, looking," Jonah said. His desire to look for his wife and daughter was a deep magnetic current. He willed himself to remain seated and answer questions that made him feel ineffectual and had nothing to do with where his wife and daughter were or how to find them.

Maurice's eyes flickered at a disruption only he seemed to sense. A vein ticked at the side of his neck. "How many? Wine coolers."

"Four. That has nothing to do with it—"

"Maybe not."

"*Maybe?*"

"We'll find them before you and I are done here. Then we'll all have a beer, or wine cooler, and celebrate our idiotic overreaction over a wife who forgot to call because she and her daughter got caught up in shopping." He straightened, jammed a thumb in the waist of his trousers and ran it around the inside of the band. "But if we don't find them right away."

"What—"

Maurice brandished his massive palm for Jonah to stop. Being shut up triggered in Jonah an innate desire to lash out that he'd developed as a kid. He bit back the urge, having learned long ago such reactions only exacerbated situations.

"If they are not found right away," Maurice said, "there *will* be questions. Brutal. Intrusive. Unkind questions. Aimed square at you. From unexpected angles, by people who don't know you like I do, and who will see you only as a suspect."

The kitchen faded in a fog until only Maurice's face popped out from the murk in garish relief, as if Jonah were looking at his friend through a preposterous magnifying glass, Maurice's spittle lathering, the papillae of his tongue and the pores of his nose grotesquely cavernous. His voice boomed, though his mouth moved with torpor.

Jonah shook his head, failed to clear the fog, a metallic, burnt odor in his nostrils.

"*I* need to prepare you," Maurice said. "Just in case."

Jonah felt a distant pressure on his hand and looked to see Maurice had placed his own hand on Jonah's. "Whatever this is," Maurice said. "We'll sort it out. Together." He retracted his hand and tapped his pencil on his notepad.

Except at the very edges of Jonah's vision, the fog in the kitchen had receded, and Maurice's face reverted to its natural proportions. Jonah readied himself.

"Did you and Rebecca argue recently?" Maurice glanced at the flowers.

Jonah's heart jerked; a shadow slunk by in the other room, at the periphery of his vision.

"You can't hold back," Maurice said.

One thing had nothing to do with the other. Jonah and Rebecca had argued. The nature was the same as always; marital, private, and nothing to do with this. It was a typical, petty, regrettable spat during which Jonah had allowed his insecurities to get the better of him. Again. Overreacted. Again. His MO. He promised himself now: no more beer that might barb his tongue. Not even with Maurice. The fight, the *argument*, wasn't really even about his suspicions, had not started out that way, but about money, about Jonah needing to be more aggressive pursuing a tenured position, even if it meant applying to a community college or a high school. Better to be a tenured big fish in a small pond than an adjunct minnow in an ocean, with no benefits, no health insurance. He'd been angry. Asked Rebecca why *she* didn't help more, get a real job, too, instead of the part-time clerk's job at the Dress Shoppe where she worked so she could gossip and take advantage of discounts on clothes, and where— The argument had nothing to do with *this*. It couldn't.

"Did you?" Maurice said.

Jonah wondered if his hesitation had stamped the truth on his face: *Yes, we fought. Argued. But it has nothing to do with this.*

"No," Jonah said. Because it wasn't a fight. Not in *that* way. He'd not harmed her. He'd never harm her. Or Sally. No matter how upset. "No," he said again, trying to firm up his voice even as it quavered.

Maurice scratched a note in his pad.

"What happened tonight?" Maurice said. "Be honest, as a friend. Did Rebecca take off in a huff with Sally, and now you're worried? If so, we have less to worry about than if you—"

"This is ludicrous, accusing me of—"

"Slow down. I can't accuse you of anything when we don't even know what *happened*. My question isn't ludicrous, considering the chair I'm in was knocked over. And that gash on your head. And the flowers, and"—his eyes flicked to the floor in front of the stove—"the blood on the floor there." He clasped his hands and set them on the table. "Before anyone else gets here, I suggest, strongly, as the closest person I've had to a brother, you tell me the absolute truth. Exactly what happened. You lied about drinking, don't lie about anything else."

"I didn't lie, I—"

"Fibbed. As our girls say. You don't want to lie about this. I'm telling you. If the state police get involved, they will tear you apart. If they catch you in even the most innocent lie, they will smell blood, whether there's blood to smell or not."

A prickling sensation spread across Jonah's face and spidered down his back.

"We did not fight," Jonah said.

"What about the chair?"

"I knocked it over." To convey sincerity, Jonah locked his eyes on Maurice's; but looking people in the eye made him nervous, and he rarely did it. Maurice knew this better than anyone. Knew Jonah was put off by those who looked him in the eye as a cheap tactic to win trust, a ploy out of a Holiday Inn self-esteem conference.

Maurice waited, calmly looking square into Jonah's eyes, straight through Jonah.

Jonah's unnatural attempt at eye contact was alerting Maurice to a counterfeit behavior. But Jonah could not blink first now.

He had nothing to hide.

"When I realized how late it was," Jonah said, his throat dry, "I rose too fast and got light-headed, maybe from the coolers and not eating all day and having been lost in the papers for a couple hours. I lost my balance and hit my head." He was speaking too fast, on the brink of hyperventilating. He touched the gash on his forehead, felt now how swollen and tender it was. A knot of bruised flesh. What the hell did it look like? Had he bled? He'd not realized he'd struck himself so badly.

Maurice must have noticed his wound straightaway, but nothing in his manner or eyes had betrayed it. Had he been waiting for Jonah to volunteer how he'd wounded himself?

"It's the truth," Jonah said.

Maurice stared at Jonah.

"It *is*," Jonah pressed.

"I believe you," Maurice said. "Why wouldn't I? We need to hope others do. Did you check the rest of the house?"

"I went in Sally's room because sometimes she gets so engrossed in a book or her rocks and 'artifacts' it's like she's in another world and she wouldn't know if the train went off the tracks and slammed into the house." He said nothing of the soft cry he'd imagined he'd heard. It had been the doll anyway. Hadn't it? No one had been in the house.

"And?" Maurice said.

"And what?"

"She's not in her room?"

"Why would I call you if she was in her damned room?"

"Did you check it well?"

"It's a small room."

"Under the bed? Behind the door? In the closet?"

Jonah's stomach soured.

"Did you?" Maurice asked. His voice was patient, kind. This frightened Jonah, the tenderness and sadness in his oldest, and only, friend's voice.

"I didn't think to check," Jonah said.

"I better." As Maurice rose, a shriek from Sally's bedroom cut through the quiet house and died with the abruptness of a slashed throat.

Evidence?

Maurice shouldered past Jonah and charged down the hall. Jonah followed.

Sally's bedroom door was shut.

Not a breath of sound whispered from behind it.

Maurice threw open the door.

The room was empty.

No.

A child sat hunched in the far corner like a wounded animal, wedged between the bed and the desk, rocking and sobbing.

Lucinda.

What is at work here? Jonah thought.

From a face slack with shock, Lucinda's lost eyes stared under Sally's bed.

"What is it?" Maurice said quietly, as if to speak at a normal volume might upset an unseen threat in the room. "Lucy?" He stepped slowly toward his daughter.

Jonah remained fixed, though an urge to run coursed in him.

He did not need to see whatever horror was under the bed. If his daughter had been under her bed this whole time—

Maurice approached Lucinda as if she were a feral puppy that might lick his hand or shred it with its needle teeth. He crouched, eyes level with his daughter's eyes.

"Lucy?" he whispered. His squared, lumberjack shoulders seemed to slope now, his commanding stature deflate in the face of his daughter's palpable terror.

Lucinda pointed her slim, quaking finger under the bed.

Jonah's eyes tracked with Maurice's eyes as Maurice pivoted on his heels. Jonah could not see under the bed from his vantage. Did not want to see.

Again, the urge to flee consumed him.

Maurice lowered himself, pressed his cheek flat against the floor, and looked under the bed.

His face was turned from Jonah.

His chest rose and fell with deep measured breathing.

Jonah needed to sit.

Slowly, Maurice lifted his cheek off the floor and knelt again.

He took his daughter's fragile shoulders in his hands.

"Lucy?" he said. "What did you see?"

What was Maurice talking about, couldn't he see whatever was under the bed that had terrified Lucinda?

Lucinda looked at her father gravely. "A . . . spider. A *humungous* spider."

"A *goddamned* spider?" Jonah said.

Maurice wheeled on him. "Watch it," he snapped and turned back to Lucinda, a palm to her cheek. "It's okay. Go back out to the couch. And, stay there, like Daddy told you in the first place. Don't move. Hear?"

Jonah was nearly felled by a terrific envy and loneliness as Maurice spoke to his daughter, as if any ill befalling them was an impossibility, their lives would continue forever, blissful in their normalcy. The fatherly display felt like a malicious twist of a jagged knife.

"Stay put, all right?" Maurice said.

Lucinda nodded, teary, gnawing her bottom lip. "It wasn't *just* a spider," she whimpered. "It was a *monster* spider. Where's Sally?"

"Never mind the spider. Or Sally. Just get out to the couch." Maurice stood and put his hand on her head and nudged her toward the door, patted her bottom. "Go on now."

She inched past Jonah to pad down the hall. Maurice's gaze found Jonah, and Jonah tried a meek smile.

"How'd the hole get in the wall?" Maurice nodded at the hole behind the door. "Looks recent."

"The doors stick. I had to put a shoulder into it. Lost my grip."

Maurice nodded, his gaze fixed on Sally's desk. He picked up a piece of paper that peeked out from under a book on fossils. He looked troubled.

"What is it?" Jonah peered at the paper.

Two crayoned stick figures lay crooked at the bottom of the page. A girl and a woman, maybe. Judging by the hair. Red Xs for eyes. The rest of the page was scribbled in black crayon, except for a bright evening star shining in the top corner.

The drawing unsettled Jonah.

Maurice pulled open the desk drawer to find three more similar drawings. Red crayon was scribbled at the bottom of one page, so the stick figures appeared to be bleeding.

Maurice lifted each drawing by a corner, laid each on the desk.

Jonah reached for the drawings.

"No," Maurice said and picked each drawing up again and slipped each into the pocket inside his jacket.

"What are you doing?" Jonah said.

"Evidence."

"Evidence of what?"

"Why would Sally draw such things?"

"I don't know."

"No?" Maurice said.

"Of course not."

"Why would any kid draw pictures like these?"

"Maybe something scared her."

"Something?"

"Or someone."

"Like? Who?" Maurice said.

"I don't know. A stranger."

"A stranger has been scaring your daughter and you don't know about it? Wouldn't she come to you about it?"

"Of course. I hope."

"Did she come to you? About anything weird? I know Lucinda would come to me, pronto."

Terror raked its claws into Jonah as he thought of a stranger harming Sally or Rebecca. Yet there was a scenario worse than that of a stranger or, even worse than that, of Jonah's irate behavior the previous night being responsible for his wife and daughter's absence. Shame flooded him for even thinking it, and he knew he could never reveal it. Because if it were true . . .

"If these drawings indicate a real fear or danger," Maurice said, "which they may or may not since kids draw a lot of crazy stuff for no reason at all, the state cops will ask which is more probable: a total stranger troubling your daughter enough to make her draw these, or someone close to her?"

"You can't think she drew those because of me?"

"It doesn't matter what I think."

"It does to me. Your turn to be honest. Do you think—"

"I think these are crazy kid drawings. Mildly disturbing, but a hell of a lot tamer than the crap we used to draw. Decapitations, warring beasts. Remember? But. It's not up to me. The state police will filter everything through the spouse first."

Jonah needed to find Sally and Rebecca. Now.

"Let me see one of the drawings. I won't touch it."

Maurice placed a drawing on the desk. Jonah studied it. The stick figures might easily have been asleep under the night sky, instead of dead. Even with the X eyes. And they might not be Sally or Rebecca. Maybe not even female. Maybe they were Sally and a friend. Lucinda. Or the bossy older girls Sally and Lucinda were always talking about being mean. Maybe Sally wasn't scared of being a victim at all, maybe the stick figures were her victims: a fantasy of revenge against the mean girls. This frightened Jonah even more, that his daughter could be the aggressor, even if it were only played out in dark, imaginative drawings. All said, the drawings were works of imagination. No telling what they meant. If anything. But if Rebecca and Sally were not found right away, the drawings *would* put the spotlight on Jonah. Take the focus off whoever it should be on. Jonah couldn't afford that.

"You don't think they mean anything?" Jonah said.

"No."

"Then, maybe," Jonah began, tentative, "we'd be better off if—"

"Do not ask me to tamper with evidence."

"If you don't think they mean anything, and we think we're

going to find Sally and Rebecca safe, the drawings aren't evidence. They're a distraction."

"It's not up to us to decide that."

"You can't let drawings you don't think mean anything be used *against* me."

"They won't be if we find Sally and Rebecca—"

"*If.*" Jonah swallowed hard. "Now it's *if*? I can't have fingers pointed at me. You see that. You said yourself we both drew crazier crap as kids."

"And you thought Sally drew them because a stranger scared her. Now you want to tamper with them to avoid the chance they might be used against you?"

"Used *wrongly*. Waste time. Kids can be scared of anything. TV. Movies. Bedtime stories. Let me have the drawings. They're my property. And even if they point to someone, a stranger, there's no way to tell who they point to, just Sally's potential state of mind, if that."

Maurice stared at Jonah.

"Please." Jonah felt the plaint in his voice, raw at the back of his throat as he pleaded for Maurice to risk his profession.

"I can't destroy them," Maurice said. He drew a deep, unsteady breath, took the rest of the drawings out of his jacket. "But. I can leave them here." He set the drawings on the desk.

Jonah's heart pounded.

"I need to check your bedroom," Maurice said. "Stay behind me. If I tell you to leave, leave. *Immediately.*" He stepped into the hall.

Jonah snatched the drawings, tore them up, and stuffed the shreds in his pants pocket, a twinge of panic and guilt needling him the instant he did it.

THE MAN IN THE WOODS

Lucinda sat on the couch chewing the inside of her cheek.
She was in big trouble. Humungous trouble. She'd fibbed.
Again. First about playing with fire, now about a stupid spider.
Well. She *had* seen a spider, and it *had* been humungous. And she
had thought it was going to bite her. So she hadn't *really* fibbed.

But the spider was not why she'd screamed. She'd never scream
over a stupid spider. Humungous or not, a spider was still just
a spider, still small compared to her. It wasn't like Vermont had
tarantulas. And she knew from books spiders never really bit, except for that one with the funny name. Hermit spider. No, that
was a crab. Rescue spider? *Recluse.* And she could still easily splat
that kind of spider with a shoe. Spiders were just all skin and black
juice, and she'd splattered tons of them in the pit, where Sally had
first told her the secret; told her about the man in the woods.

At the thought of the man in the woods, Lucinda bit down
harder on the inside of her cheek, blood leaking. She pushed her
tongue against the wound, sucked at the blood, hot and salty. She
took a rock from her coat pocket. She'd found it under Sally's bed.

A *rock*. Not an arrowhead, as Sally had insisted, although it did kind of look like an arrowhead. It was thin, with a sort of scalloped edge and kinda sharp edges, but it was soapstone, and soapstone wasn't used for that. At least none of their books and magazines said so. It was talc schist. A metamorphic rock. A pretty swirl of green and gray, the piece of rock felt soft and slippery and comforting in her hand. It was everywhere under the mountains and up in the Gore.

She turned the thin chip of rock in her hand.

She wondered if her dad knew she was fibbing. He'd had that look in his eyes that said, *What are you hiding, what are you fibbing about? When have you ever been scared of a spider?*

All Lucinda knew was she couldn't tell him what had really scared her. She could never tell anyone about the man in the woods. Ever. She'd made a pact with Sally. Friends didn't break pacts. *Everyone* knew that. No breaking pacts. Especially to parents. Sally would be *so* mad. She probably would stop being friends. And that was more important than anything. If Lucinda told her dad what she'd seen out Sally's window, or thought she'd seen, Sally would never ever forgive her. Besides, maybe it had not been him, maybe it had been nothing. Maybe it had been a trick of the light, or a trick of the dark. Maybe what she'd seen out Sally's bedroom window had only been a shadow, a tree, or a branch, or something. It could have been almost anything besides a man.

Lucinda bit her cheek harder.

She could never speak to anyone about him. Ever.

Except to Sally.

Wherever she was.

Where could she be so late at night?

Why was she not here?

And what was taking her so long to come home?

Lucinda squeezed her eyes tight and wished as hard as she could for Sally to come home.

Please, just come home.

She felt something warm in her palm and looked down to see she had squeezed her hand tight around the piece of soapstone and cut her flesh. Not bad, not deep anyway, it was like a thin paper cut, and it stung as blood seeped from it. But she'd live.

THINGS LEFT UNDONE

The door to Jonah and Rebecca's bedroom was shut.

"Is it normally shut?" Maurice asked. "We need to establish a baseline of your normal pattern."

"We don't have a pattern," Jonah said. "It's a door."

Maurice took a handkerchief from his pocket and used it to ease open the bedroom door.

The bed slowly materialized from the dimness, a ghostly Polaroid image.

Jonah choked on his breath.

On Rebecca's side of the bed—which Maurice must have deduced from the creams and lotions on the bedside table—the comforter and sheets were tousled in a heap. On Jonah's side—evidenced by the poetry chapbooks, lit mags, the hardbound *Poe's Collected Works*, and an empty bottle of beer on the table—the comforter and sheets were undisturbed.

It was obvious only one person had slept in the bed the previous night; plainer still who that person was.

And wasn't.

Maurice silently observed the room as if he were a museum visitor absorbing a tableau of ancient man. The silence seemed to jab a bony finger at Jonah: *Where were you last night?*

Maurice, using the handkerchief, flipped the switch on the wall to the left.

The room remained dark.

Jonah sensed an odd aura to the room, something wrong in the room. With the room. He could not pin it down.

"The ceiling light burned out," he said. "I haven't had a chance to fix it."

He'd had plenty of time. The bulbs were in the hallway closet five steps behind him. It would take thirty seconds to replace the bulb. Yet for weeks the light had remained dark. It was one of his many daily failings at upkeep that nagged him and exasperated Rebecca. Every time she came into the room at night, she'd hit the switch and—darkness. She'd stay mum, but in the milky hallway light Jonah would spot the infinitesimal flare of her nostrils as she stepped around the bed to click on her bedside lamp. Jonah intended to change the bulb. He just . . . he got immersed in his dissertation after dinner, working maniacally, and forgot. Which was more important: a damned lightbulb or his PhD needed for tenure?

Maurice stepped deeper into the room. "Where'd you sleep last night?" he said as he clicked on Rebecca's lamp, using the hand-kerchief.

The harshness of the 150-watt bulb Rebecca preferred brutalized Jonah's eyes. He winced; protozoan spots danced in his vision as Maurice worked a thumb along the inside waistband of his trousers.

Jonah had slept the night on Sally's floor, awakened beside her in the morning. After the argument and several more beers he'd checked on Sally, lain on the floor beside her bed to rub her back. He'd fallen asleep, as he had scores of times. As had Rebecca. That he'd slept through the night on the floor was a consequence of his exhaustion from slaving over his dissertation, and the argument.

Come morning he'd woken and crept out of the dark room, never actually seeing Sally, just a lump of blankets, under which he'd assumed his daughter had slept. Where she *had* to have slept, because otherwise—

He shut down the corrupted thought.

"I slept on top of the covers," Jonah said, the lie coming to him in an instant of self-preservation, not wanting his sleeping on Sally's floor to be anything more than the . . . *pattern* it was. For himself and for Rebecca. "I got done working late and didn't want to wake Rebecca. The comforter makes me roast anyway. So I slept on top."

Maurice stared at him.

Jonah wondered if the unkind words he'd said to Rebecca had caused her to leave on her own with Sally. Not *leave* forever. Just for the evening. To cool down. Find perspective. It was more palatable a narrative than others, and his mind snatched the seed of it, let it germinate into plausibility, flourish into certainty. Fact.

One place he had not called to track down Rebecca: the Savoy Cinema. Sally and Rebecca adored movies; perhaps that's where they were. Perhaps Rebecca had taken Sally to a movie to cool down. If so, they weren't in peril. They were safe. That was all that mattered. He thought about telling Maurice, *yes*, we argued. And, now that he thought about it, that was why his wife and daughter were gone: *Rebecca is taking time out with Sally to recalibrate. They've gone to the movies. They'll be through the door any second.*

You can go. Call off the search. Leave me to welcome my wife and child back with gratitude and humility, and in the privacy we all deserve. No need to humiliate me more than I already am.

Jonah opened his mouth to speak, and would have, except Maurice, who stood at the opened closet door, looked back over his shoulder at Maurice, face fraught, and said, "What the hell is this?"

Twisting the Truth

I told you," Jonah said to the state police detective who sat across from him at the kitchen table. "And him." He nodded at Maurice who leaned against the counter behind the detective.

Maurice seemed to be taking the detective's blunt manner in stride, and more than once he had given Jonah a look: *It's formality, humor him so we can find the girls safe sooner rather than later.*

"Tell me again. Why the rifle the sheriff found in your closet was recently fired." The detective, wiry and anemic, pencil-scratch mustache and an odor of wet suede about him, jotted in his pad.

"I was sighting it in," Jonah said. "Deer season starts soon."

"Avid deer hunter, are you?" the detective said.

Maurice cut a doubtful look at Jonah.

"I wouldn't say that," Jonah said.

"What would you say?" the detective said. "Not many people take up hunting in adulthood."

"I just took it back up. I hunted as a kid." Jonah nodded to Maurice. "He can attest to that."

Maurice nodded, face grim.

"And you just decided to take it up again on a whim?" the detective said.

"I don't do much on whims," Jonah said.

"Hmmm," the detective said.

Jonah's every word, every action, seemed a mark against him. All of it suspicious. One of a thousand cuts. "I felt that old urge, and, frankly, free meat in the freezer never hurts with the cost of groceries these days."

"So you have money troubles?"

"I wouldn't say that."

The detective scribbled a note. "And the head wound?" He tapped his pen against his own forehead.

"As I told Maurice, I got up too fast, lost my balance, and hit my head."

"And the dented wall in your daughter's bedroom?"

A cop strolled past the kitchen doorway toward the front door lugging a hard case. He'd been dusting the house for fingerprints. Insane. No stranger had taken anyone by force from the house. Nothing was out of sorts, if you dismissed the hole in the wall, the knocked-over chair, and Jonah's head. All easily explained, as Jonah had done twice already to Maurice and to the detective. But the detective did not seem to take Jonah at his word.

"Sir? The hole in the wall of your daughter's room?"

"The floors are old, you can drop a marble in the middle of any room and it rolls to the corner. The doors catch so you have to push with force. I pushed too hard and the door got away from me. I explained all this."

"You must have pushed pretty hard."

"The door got away from me." Even as he said it, a part of Jonah started to doubt if that was how it happened. If he was remembering it wrong. It all seemed long ago. His head shrieked with pain; he needed aspirin but was afraid if he took some he'd be asked why he needed it, why he had a headache, as if it wasn't obvious.

He eyed the cigarette pack pressing from the inside of the pocket of the detective's white shirt. The shirt was wrinkled and its neck had what TV commercials called Ring Around the Collar, which sounded like a child's playground game to Jonah. The detective's ring finger was bare. If the detective wasn't married and had no kids, how could he possibly understand Jonah's disorientation and anxiety?

"When are you going to start looking for my wife and daughter?" Jonah asked.

"We are as we speak," the detective said.

"I've called neighbors," Maurice said. "We'll put together searches, starting tonight. However long it takes. It won't take long. People are lined up to help, Jonah."

He came around behind Jonah, hovered protectively, faced the detective. "We done here?"

"No," the detective said. He stared at Jonah. "Where'd you sleep last night?"

Jonah had already lied to Maurice, because where he'd slept and why were private affairs. There was a difference between privacy and secrecy. He was not hiding wrongdoing. "On my bed."

"The arrangement of the sheets—"

"*On* the bed," Jonah said. "Not *in* it." Did this detective not *hear*? Was he not aware of words having *precise* meaning? God, the detective was like one of Jonah's freshman students. "I came to bed late and did not want to wake my wife. So I slept *on* top."

The detective jotted a note.

"Now are we done?" Maurice said.

The detective looked at Jonah. "If you want to clarify any-thing—"

"Like what?" Jonah said, no longer able to brook the insinuations. "What would I want to clarify?"

"I wouldn't know. Disagreements. Anything that would make us think perhaps"—his eyes drifted to Maurice and back to Jonah—"your wife has left with your daughter of her own accord."

A theory that had just earlier comforted Jonah now sounded ominous coming from this detective. Jonah wanted to hoist him-self up and tell the detective off, but Maurice put a hand on Jonah's shoulder and said, "I think he's cooperated fully and could stand the benefit of the doubt here."

"You're a sheriff, not his attorney," the detective said.

"I've known him all my life. I can vouch for him."

"Vouch? You're not *elected* sheriff to *vouch* for *anyone*. This isn't membership to a country club we're talking about here." He jerked his head for Maurice to follow him to the living room.

The two men stood near the couch, where Lucinda sat gaping as the detective hatcheted the edge of one palm into the open palm of his other hand to drive home a point. His mouth twisted out words Jonah could not decode. When he finished his remonstra-tion, Maurice nodded compliance, head bowed. Jonah had never seen Maurice come to heel so readily and with such abject defeat.

The detective clapped Maurice on the shoulder, glanced at Jo-nah without acknowledging his presence, and departed out the door.

Maurice, his back to Jonah, looked down at his shoes, flexed his fingers at his sides. He turned and walked back into the kitchen, collapsed in the chair opposite Jonah, shed his sheriff's cap, and scratched his head above his ear where premature silver glinted against his black crop of hair.

He looked vanquished. He gazed at the ceiling, as if unable or afraid to look Jonah in the eye. Dark bruises marred the flesh beneath eyes extinguished of their innate, alert confidence. He looked as if he might weep, something Jonah had never seen him do. "Sometimes," he whispered, "this job . . . That detective has zero official authority over me. Still, state police treat me like a mutt to muzzle and chain to a tree."

This glimpse at Maurice's feelings of inadequacy were similar to those Jonah felt toward tenured PhDs at Lyndon State.

"I appreciate you going to bat for me," Jonah said. "Vouching. I—"

Maurice waved him off, looked at him square again, and shook his dourness with the act of donning his sheriff's cap. "It won't mean squat if we don't find Rebecca and Sally. Things like this. From what I studied back at the academy while you were wooing the It Girl with your poetry, an unsolved missing persons case can stick to a man. Never go away."

"We'll find them. Right?"

"Right."

With a deadening heart, Jonah wondered if he believed this, that they'd find Rebecca and Sally safe; and he understood that whatever was about to happen in the days ahead, even if Rebecca and Sally walked through the door in the next minute, the life he'd built up was about to be torn down, as he'd always known one day it would be.

And it was all his fault.

BOOK II

The Eye Shadow Girls

All of a sudden, grown-ups were *everywhere*, raising a racket as if there was a party going on, except to Lucinda their faces looked all wrong for a party, too sad and stunned and fretting, and they spoke too fast, as if they all had the most important thing to say, yet no one was listening to anyone.

From the couch, where she sat crushed between two doughy women sour with BO, Lucinda spied her dad through the kitchen doorway. He stood stooped over the kitchen table, shaking his head, hands planted on either side of a gigantic map he'd spread out and kept from rolling up on itself by setting a Campbell soup can at each corner. He jabbed a stout finger at the map and stared up at each of the three men in green jackets, state police, Lucinda knew, who stood around him, his eyes big, like, *Listen up. This is Important.*

The men nodded as Mr. B. walked in circles behind them, smoking a cigarette. Lucinda had never seen him smoke, and figured it was because he never had smoked, not because he tried to hide the habit, as Lucinda's mom did. He pinched the cigarette as if it were an insect that might spring away, and he waved smoke from his face and winced. He was a funny man. He made Lucinda laugh, and Sally roll her eyes. But he didn't look funny now, so Lucinda couldn't laugh, even inside herself, secretly, like she normally did at grown-ups.

Lucinda recognized faces of grown-ups from town, many smoked cigarettes, without wincing, the ceiling fogged behind a hovering shroud of smoke. None of the grown-ups noticed her. She felt if she jumped up on the couch and shouted *Where is Sally?* no one would hear her, and no one would answer her. And Lucinda wanted an answer.

Everyone was here because Sally *wasn't* here. Sally's mom wasn't either. And nobody knew where they were. They were just—gone. Except everyone was acting like if they didn't find them this very second, they never would find them. Which of course was the stupidest thing. Mrs. B. was a grown-up. So *she* knew where she and Sally were. Of course she did. There was no need to get hysterical, a word Lucinda's dad used when Lucinda's mom was mad, which only made Lucinda's mom madder.

More grown-ups jostled into the house, flashlights grasped in tense hands. Even Lucinda's mom was here, though she stuck with the other women, and drank ginger ale from a can to settle her upset stomach.

Lucinda's palm smarted where she'd sliced it on the stone. The cut wasn't bleeding anymore, but Lucinda sucked at the flap of skin because it felt good.

The people who came and went left the front door open, and the house grew cold with the autumn air. Some women had a busy shine in their eyes, as if they were glad to have something *important* to *do*.

It was the same look the mean fifth-grade girls got when bossing around Lucinda and Sally at bake sales. The Eye Shadow Girls who were forever brushing their curling-ironed hair and glossing their lips with Bonnie Bell. Always bragging. Their smiles too sugary. When the Eye Shadow Girls caught Sally and Lucinda giggling and putting their fingers down their throats, pretending to gag at them, the Eye Shadow Girls would screech: "This is important! *Homemade* baked goods only at our sales." Brownies from a box would spoil it all. Except that's the only kind of brownie Sally and Lucinda ever brought. And everyone loved them; they sold out fastest and, boy, did *that* make the Eye Shadow Girls even madder. Which only made Sally and Lucinda giggle more. Because. Well. It was fun to make the Eye Shadow Girls mad. Because they were so mean and they deserved it.

Lucinda had asked her mom why the girls were so mean, and her mom had said they were jealous. What a fib! The Eye Shadow Girls weren't jealous of Lucinda and her buck teeth and her freckles that looked like someone had splattered her face with mud puddle water, and her knobby nose to match her knobby knees and her knobby elbows, and her ribs showing like an old washboard, and her dull straight brown hair. She got why maybe older girls would be jealous of Sally, with her dark, phantom eyes like she was looking at you from another planet or some other time, long ago. Like she was a different creature. Sally had an odd-duck, yet lovely face. And was *so* tiny. The tiniest girl in her class, by a ton. But she didn't look sick and weak, like that deaf boy in the special class. She was tough. If any of the big girls were ever jealous of Lucinda, it was because she was friends with Sally. Maybe the Eye Shadow Girls had ESP and could read her and Sally's minds, and knew about their plans, and *that's* what made them jealous and mean, because they knew Sally and Lucinda were best friends for real and were going to be best friends for real, always. Not fakes, like the Eye Shadow Girls. Lucinda and Sally *knew* they were going to have lockers next to each other in junior high. Knew they were going to be archaeologists, or those scientists who found dinosaur fossils. They'd love to be the first to ever find dinosaur bones in Vermont. Or bones or artifacts of some lost people. Girls could do anything. If they worked like twice as hard as boys.

The Eye Shadow Girls, for the most part, stuck their noses up at Sally and Lucinda, smirked and ignored them. But once, Betty Lansing got *really* mean. Scary mean. Sally had called her stupid and Betty had hauled back and slapped Sally's face. Hard. So hard it sounded like a beaver tail smacking water. Sally had looked at Betty in shock, but Sally hadn't cried. Not Sally. No way. Betty had this ugly look on her face, eyes squinted up like a pug's, breathing hard through her nose, fuming, like if she were a cartoon smoke would blow out her ears, like she wanted to do more than slap Sally. Like she wanted to k—

Lucinda coughed; the cigarette smoke in the room was like breathing school bus exhaust. She felt sick and so tired and just wanted to be in her bed, asleep.

One of the doughy women got up with a wheeze, and a boy sat next to Lucinda in the woman's place, the couch cushion caved where she'd sat. The boy was an older boy, like old enough to almost be a teenager. Maybe he even was. She'd seen him around. A loner. His face was inflamed and gross with pimples and he smelled weird. Like he'd been sleeping and sweating in an old sleeping bag for days. Eddie something. Eddie Barnes? Eddie Baines?

"You okay?" the boy said.

Was he talking to her? Older boys never talked to girls Lucinda's age, or at least never to Lucinda.

"You okay?" the boy said.

He *was* talking to her.

She didn't know what to say. She'd never said anything to a teenage boy.

"Something's happened," Eddie said and wedged his fingers into the tattered hole at the knee of his jeans. "She's your friend, right?"

Lucinda nodded. How did he know that? How did he know her?

"I wonder what's happened," he said. "Something's happened. Whatever it is."

"Why are you here?" Lucinda said.

"I'm going to go look for her. My mom and dad want me to help look for her. And her mom, I guess." A man pushed through the crowded room and put his hand on the boy's shoulder. The boy stood and took a flashlight from the man's hand and disappeared out the door with him.

It had to be way past Lucinda's bedtime, which was neat; she'd never stayed up so late, but the night was going on *forever*. There was nothing to *do*. Why wouldn't anyone let Lucinda look for Sally? She hoped wherever Sally was it was more fun than here. She thought for a second maybe Sally was in the pit, but the pit was a secret and Sally would never show it to her mom. Why would she? Women around Lucinda chirped about "praying" and "strength" and "hope" and needing to get out "full force, bright and early." All while their eyes shifted over at Mr. B., narrowing, like he was one of those shoplifters Lucinda's dad had told her about; how obvious it was that they were up to no good. It made Lucinda mad because she liked Mr. B.

Lucinda felt suffocated and needed air.

She stood, wobbly, her head feeling like a helium balloon, as if it might float up to the ceiling. Through the swarm of bodies she glimpsed the queen of the Eye Shadow Girls, Betty Lansing, who must have sneaked into the house with her mom.

Lucinda thought she'd throw up for real seeing Betty in this house, Sally's house. Sally would die.

Betty's eyes burned into Lucinda, and she was showing her teeth, like a mad dog; but when Betty's mom bent down to tell Betty something, Betty's face went all sugary sweet with a fake smile. It seemed everyone had a fake smile, and Lucinda wondered why no one except her seemed to notice it.

DESOLATION

He'd lain in fields with Rebecca, in the ether of dark and humid summer nights, young, both of them, so young; her hand in his, the pulse of blood beneath her tanned thin wrists, God's own salve on his broken soul as they'd gazed up into the dark and spectacular void. She: everything he was not. Self-possessed. Stable. Balanced. Worthy. Who was he to hold her hand? A boy once so enraged over another boy being selected to leave the Boys' Home with new parents that he had taken a rock and ground a nest of baby birds into gruel. How could a woman love a man who'd had that in him, even as a boy? What dark magic was at work that she should love him? Save him? What cruel trick? What abominable sacrifice was being made? He'd trembled at his fortune, and at the knowledge that a day would come when he'd pay for it. Stars ripped across the black night sky as if tearing through a dark curtain to let God's light seep through from the other side. Shhh, she'd said. You're with me now. Shhh. You're safe. No one will hurt you again. He'd carved poetry from his pain. Put himself into her. All of himself. But. Now. Now she'd vanished, and he'd returned to the muck, to his original state. Everything else proven false. Undeserving. You are born what you are.

Jonah fell off Sally's bed with a groan, grabbed at his collarbone, believing he'd awoken in the forest. Believing he was the boy he'd been, in another life, and had not yet lived his life to this moment, had a chance yet to rewrite his years.

He thought of the parents he'd been born to but had never known, for whom he had no memory, though he imagined them as kind people. Gone early, those who'd conceived him. Just him then. Alone, even among others. Traded like a stray from house to house, never a home. Never part of a family. Always apart. Passed among adults who spoke at him, never to him. *Shut up. Sit up. Stop it.* A piss-soaked horse blanket for a bed on the bare, cold, lumped earth in the back of a decrepit toolshed. Bedbug bites and sores. Welts. Cuts. Bruises. A boy. A *child*. Helpless. Voiceless. Even when he screamed and raged.

He'd fled, once. At Sally's age. On a brutally cold autumn day. In just his underwear. While the *Couple* had lain passed out on their couch. He'd splashed through gullies and crashed through woods for what seemed miles, until, depleted, he'd fallen to the forest floor to let the ferns and moss claim him. A fawn.

His naked flesh scratched and torn, eyes burning and shot hollow, he'd lain on his back beneath sumac set ablaze with autumn. The leaves the most spectacular sight he'd ever seen. The cold, hard ground had hurt each knuckle of his puny spine, raised in relief beneath skin gone cadaver blue with the cold. Still, he'd remained on his back to marvel at those leaves. A sign. Proof. He was free. Free of them.

A sweet tang of autumn decay had swum over him.

He'd listened. No sound from the brush had come. No bawling of voices like a pack of hounds gone lunatic for fugitive scent. Just. Sweet. Silence.

Until that clattering. He'd known that sound, and his heart was decimated by it. The Couple's junk truck. It could not be. *Could not.* He'd run *so* far. *So* hard. *So* long. How could he be near a road? How could they *know* where to begin to look?

He'd shrunk down as small as he could make himself, trying to will himself invisible, collected his knees up in skeletal arms.

The clattering had risen, closer.

He'd quaked like a tiny forest creature afraid for the branch's snap beneath the predator's weight, pressed tight to the forest floor as though to make himself part of the earth. Breathless. Eyes watching, watching. The jalopy clanked on the washboard road, so close the squall of dust it kicked up had sifted down and coated his bare body.

The wind rose. Tree limbs bowed to it. Dry leaves cycloned as if possessed by spirits. He could not tell what was the sound of the wind and what was the sound of a pursuer in the underbrush. From somewhere distant and unconnected from his unfolding story came the chaotic hilarity of crows.

The truck had clattered again, moving away, the sound of its sputtering engine growing pale.

He'd listened and watched until his eyes felt about to crack, listened and watched some more.

They were gone.

He'd sobbed and sobbed and, finally, he'd slept.

In his sleep, that quiet darkness of temporal death, no fists pummeled his flesh, no hard mouths pressed against his, no hands plied, no dank cellar or piss-soaked horse blanket served as bedding. There was only the warm womblike darkness and the distant merciful softness of moss beneath body.

And a dream of God.

Until that cruel hand clutched his frail collarbone, broke it.

He'd yowled like a dog set afire.

"Bellyacher. Think you got it so bad you gotta run off? We'll show you bad."

They'd shown him.

For years, they'd shown him.

Jonah groaned from where he lay on the floor, touched his collarbone, felt the hard abnormal spur beneath his fingers. Felt his ribs. In just a few days he'd shed the pudge he'd carried since his teen years, melted away as panic and fear mounted. He dared not look in a mirror to see, or to meet, the defeated eyes he knew awaited him.

He sat against Sally's bed and listened for his daughter and wife, the house so quiet he could hear dust settling about him, dust of their dead skin, detritus of shed flesh. Each breath now poisoned with absence.

Throughout the night, as he'd drifted, he'd awakened again and again to what he'd believed was their voices in the house. Their footfalls. Their laughter. Their crying. It was not them, only memory, past joys mutated into present torment.

If he'd known Sally and Rebecca were dead, he'd have joined them. Gladly, and with great relief. But he did not know. And without certainty, his purgatory of despair knew no end or bounds, perpetual anguish beyond loss. It was as if his daughter and wife had never existed, as if he'd willed them out of existence. Made them less than ghosts. Less than memory. Figments.

Throughout the night, too, he'd tried to remember the argument more clearly, but nothing new surfaced, and as night had bled into dawn again, and no word had come from Rebecca, he agonized over the notion that he'd said or done something to, finally, drive her away, or—

—worse.

The thought wormed in his brain again, too grotesque to follow to a conclusion.

He shoved it out of his mind and stood, gamely, shuffled to the kitchen.

The cops who'd been here during the night were gone. The house desolate. Again.

The black-eyed Susans were dead and dried as straw. He did not touch them, feared they would disintegrate to dust between his fingers. The yellow dress and coat sat in their box on the kitchen table, waiting, dust settling, the sun through the window fading the bow.

Where are my daughter and wife?

He needed to get out and look for them. He'd yearned to look these first days, but Maurice had encouraged him to stay at home with the trooper or the deputy who'd been in the house nearly every moment, in case Rebecca or Sally called or returned. The phone was tapped, the house nearly always under surveillance by a deputy or trooper who sat in a parked car across the road in a pull-off near One Dollar Bridge. A TV van parked beside it. No police officer was inside the house now. Jonah could slip out and search for Sally and Rebecca. Where, he didn't know. The cops couldn't stop him, even if they were here. Follow him, maybe. But not stop him. It was his daughter and wife who were missing, after all. If he wanted to search for them, he damned well would.

The parasitic reporters would stick to him. Each move he'd made and not made in the past days the media had spun into a web of implication worthy of suspicion. When he didn't search, they speculated: Why isn't he searching? What could be more important than looking for your wife and daughter? One rag wrote about his weight loss: "He's shed domestic flab for the fit look of a bachelor on the make."

Let them follow, he thought.

Enough waiting. Enough impotence.

He grabbed a coat from the entrance closet.

A knock came at the door, startling him.

COME WITH ME

O n the other side of the pebbled glass window, a dark shape shifted.

Jonah opened the door to find Maurice, who appeared washed out and twitchy from sleeplessness.

"I'm on my way to search," Jonah said.

"Let's go inside." Maurice tossed his head toward the TV van parked across the road.

"Do you have—"

"Inside, please."

Jonah shuffled inside and collapsed on the couch.

"How you holding up?" Maurice said.

"Can't sleep. Can't eat. Can't work. I've taken leave from my job." Jonah's throat felt grated raw, and his voice came hoarse from repeating the same words ad nauseam the past days, and from having taken up cigarettes, a habit he'd thought he'd left behind in his teens.

Maurice sat on the arm of Jonah's favorite chair, the tattered recliner with the duct-taped arm. "You need to stay here," he said, "in case they show or call. Or someone else calls."

"The media is saying that by not searching I look—"

"Ignore them."

"It's not like I go looking to read the papers or watch TV. It's just *there*. With twenty-four-hour cable news, the newspaper at the door, I can't escape it. One newspaper ran a photo of me in the yard lighting a cigarette, with the caption FATHER AND HUSBAND ENJOYS CIGARETTE WHILE WIFE AND DAUGHTER REMAIN MISSING. *Enjoys*."

"Ignore it."

"I need to get out and help."

"Have you thought more about any reasons Rebecca might leave you, take Sally on her own?"

As no evidence had been discovered in the first days, the theory that Rebecca had left Jonah and taken Sally of her own accord had seeded itself, though Jonah sensed Maurice knew something, possessed other theories he was holding back.

"I could give a million reasons she'd be mad, but not that mad," Jonah said.

"Give me a couple. You never know."

"*I* know."

"Cough 'em up."

"The usual. Money. My being years late with my dissertation. No tenure. You were right."

Maurice looked confused.

"Things change when you're married," Jonah said.

"I did warn you," Maurice said. "How you ever wooed her with poetry, I'll never know."

"Neither will I."

Any other day, the men would have laughed at the improbability of Jonah winning over Rebecca. Instead, Maurice nodded grimly. "I don't know how to say this, except straight. I need you to come with me, to the station. There are questions that need to be asked."

"Ask them here. I'm going out to search, no one can stop me. Ask if you're going to ask."

Maurice sighed. "Do you have life insurance on Rebecca?"

The blood drained from Jonah's face.

"They know you do," Maurice said.

"So why *ask*? Do *you* have insurance *on* Julia?"

"My wife's not missing."

"Get out."

"Jonah."

"Get out. You come here like a friend then trap me?"

"You *know* that's not it."

"Rebecca and I, *we* had insurance. *As a couple.* For Sally. That's what responsible parents do. The beneficiary is *Sally*, on both policies. So if they're thinking there's—"

"What if you and Sally were to pass, would it go to Rebecca?"

"Of course."

"And if Sally and Rebecca—"

"Get out. Or I swear."

"You want me out, force me out."

In their teens, Jonah and Maurice might have come to blows several times except whenever Jonah had charged at Maurice, Maurice had simply wrapped Jonah in a headlock and insisted Jonah breathe and gain control himself, not let his emotions rule him, ruin him. Warning Jonah that one day they would destroy him, if he let them.

"Julia and I have a policy," Maurice said. "*I get it*. But. The state police, they have questions. Questions I've tried to put off. I can't anymore. I'm giving you a heads-up on this insurance thing, even if it's shit. So you won't be surprised and react like you just did. With anger. Because if you do, you'll hang yourself."

"And you're doing me a favor, by asking yourself?"

"I've done favors for you all my life."

It was true, he had.

"And you me," Maurice said. "I haven't forgotten. You can take my asking questions any way you want. But I'm here to help you. You have to believe that. When we find Sally and Rebecca, none of this will matter anyway."

Jonah's pulse calmed. They would find them. They had to find them. He had to see his wife and daughter again. How could he go on otherwise?

"Just come with me to the station, where I can ask the questions so it looks like I'm fulfilling my official capacity and not working to help you, make it look good for the staties," Maurice said. "Be glad I'm the one asking this go-round. Some other new developments have come up, and—"

"New developments?"

"Come with me. We'll sort it out."

"Okay. I'll go. I'm going crazy here."

"No more crazy than usual."

THE UNTHINKABLE

A half hour later, Jonah sat in a stiff, unforgiving chair in Maurice's office, the door shut behind them. Maurice sat behind his spartan desk, facing Jonah. Wire reading glasses that Jonah had never seen sat balanced at the end of Maurice's nose as Maurice's eyes raked over papers in a manila folder. The eyeglasses aged Maurice a decade; perhaps it was the past few days that had aged Maurice. Jonah felt he'd aged fifty years. No, not *aged*, but died and awoken to an anomalous, somnambulant life.

Jonah gazed at a water stain on the peeling ceiling of the office, decorated sparingly with cheap prints of northeastern songbirds. Several cockeyed birdhouses Maurice had built in his basement workshop sat on shelves, one perched on the desk beside the folder.

"What are these developments?" Jonah asked, on edge.

Maurice glanced over Jonah's shoulder, at the door. He took a deep breath. "We know you're in financial trouble."

Jonah's fingers dug into the chair's arms. "I'm not. We're not."

"You are."

"No more than anyone else."

"A bit."

"I'm an adjunct at a state college, for Christ's sake, and Rebecca refuses—" He cut himself short.

"Refuses what?"

"Nothing."

"It's okay to be upset with her even if—"

"I'm upset you're going through my private finances."

"One: *I'm* not going through them. I got myself looped into it as a favor from the state police. A generous favor. Two: your private life is over. Even if Rebecca and Sally are found sunning in Miami with cases of simultaneous amnesia—it's over. You need to tell me the truth. All of it. Here. Now. You're all alone without me. You realize that, I hope."

Jonah wondered what would happen if he left, dismissed this affront.

Except, Maurice was right: Jonah was alone. The women who had flocked to his house with casseroles were Rebecca's friends. Not Jonah's. And they remained on the porch, timid as they handed their baking dishes to Jonah as they peeked behind him into the house, as if he might have his wife and daughter in there, tied to chairs or stuffed in a trunk. Before all this, he'd met colleagues on occasion to play bass in a band of rotating musicians, or for some backgammon and a few pops. But these were not friends. They did not know him. The only people who knew him were Rebecca and Maurice. Besides them, Jonah had always been, comfortably, a loner. All he'd ever wanted, needed, was Rebecca's company, and when he'd finally won it, he'd exalted in it. Since then a family with her was all he'd wanted. It was still all he wanted. His family.

"So what if it upsets you that Rebecca doesn't work more?" Maurice said. "No one is going to crucify you for it. I'm not. I know how she could be. Difficult. What wife isn't? What *husband*? *I'm* a *monster* to live with. That's nature. Things are said. Things we never expected to happen, happen. It's life."

Jonah did not like where this was headed. He rubbed the heel of a palm on the arm of his chair. Sweat trickled down his back. Maurice knew how Rebecca could be. True. And he knew how Jonah could be. Had been. His temper. Maurice also knew Jonah had worked hard to stymie it. For the most part. What Maurice did not know was that Rebecca had acted distracted and nervous lately, out of sorts, and Jonah did not want him to know. It was the last thing he wanted anyone to know. Because— He tried to rid his mind of the toxic thought. Her behavior was, in a word, suspicious.

"We both know she has a hard time sometimes," Maurice said. "Can be . . . dramatic. Some might say troubled."

"*Troubled* is going too far. And it's not her fault. I don't want that getting out, it has nothing to do—"

"Let me finish. The state police believe you played a role in your daughter and wife's disappearance."

"I'm not going to sit here and—"

"What is it you *don't* get? Why won't you let me *help* you? You're your own worst enemy. Impatient. Stubborn. That temper. This is goddamned serious, Jonah. You are in serious, serious trouble here."

"But I—"

Maurice tossed the folder at Jonah, papers fluttering to the floor. "You don't want to help yourself, I can't help you." He rose and started to leave the office.

"Wait," Jonah said. If Maurice left now, Jonah would have no one. He'd be as alone as the day he was born. "Sit. Please. Okay. Sit."

"Can I finish?" Maurice said.

Jonah nodded.

"There's not a cop besides me—not a soul in this town—who believes your hands are clean. And they're approaching this case that way. Possible double *murder*. Of your wife and child."

Jonah had known that as the spouse he was a suspect by default. But to hear it spoken like this— He couldn't breathe.

"Take your time, calm down and focus," Maurice said. "Before I leave this room, we need to come up with a theory that does not include you. I know you didn't do what they think. But I can't help if you don't let me and won't let me posit alternative theories for them to investigate."

When he was able to breathe again, Jonah said, "What about a boy from Sally's school. Or one of the mean girls who are always—"

"Maybe if it were just Sally missing. But you think a boy or girl overtook them both, tricked an adult somehow, and—" Maurice shook his head. "We've interviewed every teacher. Every coworker. Every person we know she's come in contact with in years. There's nothing firm. We're interviewing the few possible kids. That takes time. It's delicate. Their parents need to be present. But I doubt there's anything there." Except there *was* something; Jonah had seen it in Maurice's eyes when he'd mentioned teachers, hadn't he?

Maurice tapped a pen on the birdhouse on the desk. "This is *killing* you. Me too. But . . . You're lying. Come clean so I can clear you of something you didn't do."

"What is it you know?" Jonah said. "What are the cops thinking? I want to tell the truth, but I don't want my private life that has nothing to do with this to come out."

Maurice lifted the top off the birdhouse, fished out a handful of Red Hots, shook a few into his mouth. "The state cops think something ugly had happened between you and Rebecca, and Sally got involved and— Something happened. I've told them no. No way. You didn't do it. Couldn't. I told them, if anything, you had a fight and Rebecca took off with Sally. But they don't believe it. Because how far could Rebecca get without a car? There's a rare outside chance she took Sally for *some air*, say, and ran into someone of a nasty element and— You see how slim those odds are? A lunatic just passing through Podunk, Vermont? And Rebecca and Sally haven't come back. Haven't been *seen*. To the state cops, that leaves you. They know you've lied to them. So they don't believe a word you speak."

It took every iota of self-control for Jonah to sit and listen, but what Maurice said made sense. How could Jonah fault the police for thinking it was him? What were the odds that Rebecca and Sally had met a stranger between town and home? Then again, this sort of thing—women and girls vanishing—happened across the world, every day, didn't it? Dark stars aligned so poor souls collided with cruel predators.

"I have a theory," Maurice said. "One that clears you, but that I hate to imagine. First, though, you need to admit you fought. It's obvious. Even to someone who doesn't know you like I do. If you don't tell the truth about the simple things, the police will hound you and never look elsewhere. Tell the truth. For your daughter and wife."

Jonah exhaled, trembling. "Okay," he said. Perhaps, he thought, it would feel good to come clean on that end. Perhaps it would help. "We fought. But it was *nothing*." He stopped, suddenly certain he'd made a mistake, been tricked. Had he been brought here to be asked questions and helped by a friend or interrogated by a sheriff? Did he need a lawyer? He'd been solicited by attorneys out of state, but not entertained them. And no attorney in the region had approached him, perhaps afraid to appear as an ambulance chaser. Besides, Jonah hadn't been charged with anything.

Yet, a voice said.

"Did it get physical as the state police believe? In any way at all?" Maurice asked.

"Of course not."

"Because. I've seen her go after you, remember, and it's—"

"That happened *once*. She was exhausted and coming off the flu. Sally had been acting up and exacerbating things, and then you and Julia stopped by unexpected. And—"

"It was embarrassing. Just to see it. But I know from domestic calls, this stuff most often isn't isolated to a single event."

"It happened *once*."

"But it was just last week. What am I supposed to tell the state police detectives? How am I supposed to vouch for you, for *her*, if the state police continue to press me as your close friend, press *Julia*, for God's sake, about the state of your marriage? Because they are pressing, and so far we've told them nothing. Given them nothing. Julia can hardly stand the pressure. She's distraught, too, and will crack. We can't have that. I can't."

"Rebecca had every right to lay into me."

"No one has a right to hit anyone."

"*Hit?* She *slapped* me."

"Your face was gashed when we got there."

"It was nothing. You don't know the whole story."

"I *need* to know it. The detectives outside that door, they plan to know it. That night Julia and I stopped in, Rebecca was like a different person. I saw it. Even Julia saw that. It scared her, Rebecca's behavior. So. One last time. Tell me. Did things get out of hand, did she get, how would you put it? Volatile? Antagonistic? Did her mood escalate? Did she *slap* you? That fresh cut on your head, was it really from a fall against the stove? If she gave you that gash, you were in your right to defend your—"

"This is *insane*," Jonah snapped.

A noise came from behind him, the doorknob turned behind him.

"We're *fine*," Maurice said toward the door.

Jonah wondered: What had Julia and Maurice sensed that night Rebecca had launched into him? Had they sensed what Jonah had started to sense, what had always been his gravest fear and nightmare, from the very first in marrying her: that sooner or later she'd tire of him, see him for what he was and start to look—

"You see how easy it is for even me, your friend," Maurice said, "to agitate you. Did Rebecca trigger that side of you? That rage? God knows, *I know*, your anger comes from a world of shit you grew up in that's hard to shake."

"We were kids. You can't hold those times against me." Jonah squeezed the chair's arms. He wanted to smash the chair to dust. His heart wailed.

"I don't hold it against you," Maurice said. "Shit. I was worse, and I was from the good home. I know what you kids go through. That's why Julia and I adopted Lucinda. So she wouldn't have to go through it. But *they*—" Maurice eyed the door, leaned in, colluding. "They don't know how bad you had it. They'd never believe the shit you survived. And if they *did*, they'd scoff at you for using your childhood as an excuse. I won't scoff. Because I *know*."

"*What do you think I did?*" Jonah said.

"*I* don't think it. But *they* believe it. Tell me about the lies you've told, all of them."

There was only so much Jonah could tell Maurice. Would tell anyone. He *had* sensed a shift in Rebecca, a tension, a distance, and that night just before Julia and Maurice had stopped in unexpectedly, Jonah had merely joked with Rebecca about his apprehension, perhaps subconsciously testing the waters, and she'd swung a backhand at him so her engagement ring slashed his cheek, her reaction so instantaneous and intense he'd known in an instant his suspicions were misplaced. She'd not intended to cut him, just meant to swat him away. And she wouldn't have reacted so volatilely if she'd not been genuinely wounded by his insinuations, innocent of them. She would not have lashed out at him again in front of their good friends when Jonah had later made an offhand comment about men—successful, grounded, centered men; real men—coming into the store where she worked.

Wouldn't she? a voice said.

"Is she still on medication?" Maurice said.

Jonah recoiled. The only thing worse than the state police believing he'd murdered his wife and child was the intimation that his wife was ill. Unstable. Rebecca *had* missed a few days of her medication a week earlier, but only because she'd had the flu. She'd been her normal self even when off the medication. Jonah believed the medication disturbed her more than aided her. "Of course she's on her medication."

Maurice shook his head and frowned. "You need to stop. We took the prescription bottle from the bathroom and ran the dates. She's been off her medication for at least ten days. If she—"

"*You need to stop. That's who needs to stop.*" Jonah pounded his fist on the birdhouse that sat on the desk, crushed the roof and sliced his hand on the splintering wood. The edge of his palm spurted blood. He cupped his bleeding hand to his shirt, extracted a long sharp shard of wood from his flesh.

The office door began to open.

"Keep that door *shut*," Maurice shouted. He addressed Jonah. "You just *keep* lying. About fighting, medication, insurance."

"I get *nothing* from insurance if they've disappeared. And I wouldn't want it. It's hardly a motive for—"

"You'd get the money. It would take seven years but—"

"Jesus Christ. I can't even imagine that. I can't even imagine *this*." He waved his arms around. "Any of this. What are *you* not telling me. Why don't *you* come clean and tell *me* the truth? There's something. I can tell—"

Maurice propped his elbows on his desk and leaned toward Jonah. "Take a breath. Okay. In confidence? As friends here? The state police know something happened the night *before* you called me, the night before the girls went missing."

"I've come clean. Rebecca and I argued."

"That's not it. For starters. You lied about sleeping on top of the comforter next to your wife." Maurice's voice was calm, quiet. Controlled. Everything Jonah was not. "Forensics *prove* the comforter and sheets and pillow cases were freshly washed, yet none on your side had a single hair of yours. Plenty of Rebecca's hairs, even though she slept on the other side. If you'd spent even ten seconds on that bed, we'd have evidence to prove it. Instead we have evidence that proves you didn't. Proves you lied."

Jonah's mouth hung open. How could one tiny, innocuous lie amount to so much?

"You've forced them to ask: *If he lied about that, too, what else did he lie about? Where did he sleep? If he slept at all. With who? And why would he lie?*"

"Jesus Christ. I slept in Sally's room. Comforting her."

"From what?"

"Just. Comforting her. Like any other night."

"This wasn't any other night. It's the last night anyone's seen your family. And the next morning. You went to campus *abnormally* early. A janitor saw you."

"I woke early. I was stiff from being on the floor. I wanted to get out of there. I needed space."

"From what?"

"Just. Space."

"Did you see Rebecca and Sally in the morning?" Maurice said.

"I didn't want to wake them. I brought home flowers and a dress and coat to apologize later that day, for God's sake. Why would I do that if—"

"You didn't kiss your daughter good-bye?"

Tell the truth, Jonah's mind screamed.

"No. I sneaked out."

"Then—" Maurice drummed his fingers on the top of the birdhouse. "How do you know Sally was home? That either of them was home that morning?"

"Of *course* they were home."

"How do you *know*, if you didn't see either of them?"

"Where else could she have been? I didn't physically see Sally. I didn't kiss or touch her because I didn't want to wake her. But I saw a heap of blankets. It had to be her."

"And you didn't see your wife. The state police . . . they don't think either one of them was there in the morning. They think that whatever happened to them, whatever caused their disappearance, happened the night *before* you called me. The night you've now confessed you argued."

Confessed? Did Maurice believe him, or not? Was he here to free Jonah or to trap him? "That's *impossible*. I fell asleep in Sally's room with her asleep in bed. If anyone had come in the night . . . or . . . No. They had to be home when I left in the morning. They had to be. What aren't you telling me? Goddamn it. *You* stop holding back. What do you know? What do the police know?"

"Sally never *showed up* at school the morning you sneaked out."

"What?" Jonah said, floored.

"And *you* didn't call in her absence, and Rebecca didn't either. This being a small town, no one was concerned. Until after the girls disappeared. We got a call from a person in administration who found it suspicious."

Jonah felt weak with nausea and bewilderment, not just at Maurice's revelation, but at a memory that struck him cold. The afternoon he'd come home. The crooked painting. It had seemed odd. But he had not known why. Now he knew. It was odd that the picture was crooked at all that time of day. If Rebecca had been home any time after eight A.M. when the morning train had gone through, she would have straightened the crooked picture after the rumble of the train had skewed it.

Maybe she *had* left the house before eight o'clock, and *nothing* had happened in the night. His daughter and wife had been home. They had to have been.

"You've been withholding information from me," Jonah said.

"*We've* been withholding information? Sally *never* showed at school and Rebecca was not seen in town by anyone. The only thing the state police can conclude is your wife and daughter disappeared the night before you called me, an evening about which you won't tell us anything helpful."

Us, Jonah thought. So now it's *us*: Maurice and the state police.

Jonah stared at the cut on his hand from smashing the birdhouse, his shirt sopped with blood. He took a deep breath. "Why don't you believe me?"

"I do."

"You keep making it seem like you're interrogating me, and I know you're holding back, hiding something."

"I am holding back."

"Tell me what it is. Please, tell me."

"I know you didn't do it. But knowing that, and knowing the odds of a random encounter whether Sally and Rebecca fled your home or were out for a stroll, what does that leave us with?"

Jonah tried to swallow, but couldn't; his throat felt choked with sand.

"I know you'd do anything for Rebecca, anything," Maurice said.

"Of course I would. She's my wife."

"Anything to protect her, or her memory."

"Of— What?"

Maurice cleared his throat, picked at a piece of wood that had broken off the birdhouse. "I believe you've been lying and hiding things since the start because you're protecting Rebecca, or her memory, and protecting your own part in this for arguing with her, pushing her. Maybe not consciously, but subconsciously, maybe you're in denial, because God knows I'm in denial and have skirted around it here for an hour trying to find the guts to say it straight. You're lying because deep down you believe the same thing I do, whether it happened that night while you slept, or in the morning after you sneaked out early." Maurice gritted his teeth as if trying to swallow poison. "Rebecca has harmed herself and Sally."

Jonah stood, rippling with rage. "No," he said. "I don't know how you can even think that."

Except Jonah did know how Maurice could think it, because it had been the very thought that had wormed in Jonah's brain over the past days and as recently as that morning when he'd startled awake in Sally's room; a thought he had shoved away, repressed, for being too macabre to entertain. The same thought Maurice had voiced aloud.

Rebecca harmed herself and Sally.

Because you *pushed her to it.*

No, a voice said. *They're out there. You must believe that. You must find them. You will see them again. One way or another.*

WISHING

Lucinda sat on the edge of her bed and rocked, eyes squeezed shut. Wishing wishing wishing. Wishing school wasn't canceled, because it would mean Sally was home. But school was *still* canceled, to allow every grown-up and older student to look for Sally.

Lucinda was so stupid.

She had been so sure Sally wasn't missing and that all the grown-ups were being silly, worrying so much. Lucinda had been wrong, and now she couldn't even think the word *missing* without emptying her heart. Each second Sally was gone, Lucinda felt more scared, and lonely. And guilty. She hadn't told her dad about the man in the woods and wondered if she should have.

She shivered thinking about it.

But . . . A secret was a secret.

And if she told her dad, she'd have to tell him she'd been in the woods where she was never ever supposed to go. He'd be so super mad. And if Sally came back, Sally would be super mad that Lucinda had given up their secrets and ruined their hideout.

Lucinda held the shard of soapstone from Sally's bedroom in her palm as she gazed out her window, shut her eyes to feel the warmth of the sun through the glass. Her dad was out there somewhere, leading a search.

Lucinda opened her eyes at a noise.

Her mom stood in her doorway. She was having trouble putting her coat on after coming home to take a long nap and make a zillion sandwiches she'd had Lucinda pack in a cardboard box earlier, for the searchers. She tugged a hat over her ears, her coat crooked. She'd buttoned it wrong. She looked dazed, a sleepwalker. She did not seem like herself or look like herself. None of the grown-ups looked like themselves anymore. They looked like sick twins of themselves, their eyes red and lost, faces pale, hair a mess. Maybe it was good. Maybe it meant the grown-ups were working so hard to find Sally that they did not have time for sleeping or eating. Her dad sure didn't have time.

"You buttoned your coat wrong," Lucinda said.

Lucinda's mom stared at Lucinda as if she didn't know who she was. "What?" she said. Even her voice wasn't her own voice. It was all scratchy and raw.

"Your coat," Lucinda said. "It's buttoned wrong." She tried to put a sunny sound in her voice. But it didn't work. It sounded flat and fake and stupid. She was just as fake as everyone else.

Her mom glanced down at her crooked coat and shrugged.

A knock came on the foyer door downstairs, and she disappeared from the doorway.

Lucinda slipped the soapstone in her pocket and sneaked to the top of the stairs to see her mom greet a woman who'd come to watch Lucinda while Lucinda's mom went back out to search.

Lucinda did not want to be home alone with a stranger. She did not want her mom to go. She did not want any of this. She wanted things back the way they were before, when everyone was who they really were. Including herself.

The woman, cheeks reddened from the cold, plucked off her silly furry earmuffs, her cat-eye glasses fogging up. She sniffled and wiped her leaking nose onto the arm of her parka, took off the parka, and slung it on the peg by the door. It took Lucinda a second to see that the woman was a friend of her mom's who worked at the post office. Her hair was collected in a ponytail and she didn't have on her usual purple eye makeup. On her slight frame her rumpled sweatpants and sweatshirt sagged. Even from the top of the stairs, Lucinda could smell the woman, a weird sour smell like that of a load of wet clothes left too long in the washer.

Lucinda's mom picked up the box of sandwiches and slipped past the woman and out the door, saying, "I don't know when I'll be back."

Then she was gone.

The woman sat at the card table in the living room and sorted puzzle pieces Lucinda's mom had dumped out but never started to organize or assemble.

"Want to help?" the woman said. "Puzzles keep our minds busy." She peered up. When she smiled, it looked as if her face might shatter to bits.

Lucinda didn't feel like doing a silly puzzle. She scuffed off to her room and sat on the edge of her bed and looked out the backyard window again.

In the yard, the tire swing at the edge of the woods twisted from its tree branch in the breeze. Lucinda's dad had put up the swing two summers ago, after Lucinda's adoption was final. The swing looked as sad and lonesome as Lucinda felt.

Lucinda and Sally had played on the swing every day that summer, spinning on it until they thought they'd throw up. It was the best thing ever.

They never played on it anymore. Sally had said they were too big for it, even though Lucinda had still wanted to play on it. Now, Lucinda felt sorry for the swing. Even though it was dumb to feel bad for a hunk of rubber that couldn't feel anything. But she felt sorry for not playing on it just to prove she was big, even though her dad always said, *Don't be in a hurry to be big. You spend the rest of your life wishing you were little again.*

She did not know what he meant. Who would ever want to be little? She and Sally had worlds to discover, treasures to unearth. Yet she did not feel so big now. Did not want to be big. She wanted to crawl into bed between her parents and snuggle in, safe and warm. Except both of them were out in the cold, searching for her friend as if she were lost treasure herself.

Out the window, past the woods, rose a hill where Sally and Lucinda liked to sled. The hill was super steep, and Lucinda and Sally weren't supposed to sled there. Their parents said a boy had been killed years ago when he hit a tree. Lucinda and Sally agreed the story was made up, like the story of the bottomless talcum mine shafts in the Big Woods.

Dark shapes crawled like bugs over the hill. The searchers. They inched across the hill in a line. What if Sally wasn't found? What was Lucinda supposed to do then? She'd never make another friend like Sally, could never sit next to Sally's desk without Sally at it beside her. What would the school do with Sally's desk and chair? Would they just let some other kid sit there? They couldn't do that. It was Sally's desk. Would they leave it empty? Would they take the chair away to leave a big hole like the one in Lucinda's belly?

Lucinda couldn't stand the thought of it. Just couldn't. She had to do something. She had to find her friend.

For the zillionth time, she wondered if she should tell her dad about the pit and the man in the woods. Maybe Sally was in the woods. In the pit. Hiding. Maybe she'd gone there to hide. Or . . . maybe . . . she'd been taken to the pit. Lucinda didn't know if Mrs. B. was with Sally or not, but maybe it was worth checking the pit.

Tell your dad, a voice said.

No. She couldn't. Not yet. She'd go and check the pit herself. Somehow. If she found anything, she'd tell her dad. Right away. If she didn't, she would keep her secret, as Sally would want.

We could slip out your window now, the voice said. *Drop onto the garage roof and onto the back porch. Sneak through the woods, make our way along the creek, to the covered bridge, then up into the woods.*

But how would she get back in the house without being seen by the woman downstairs? Even if she tiptoed in through the back sliding door she'd get caught. And what if her mom or dad found out she was gone? She didn't want to worry them. Not now. She wanted to be good; yet she wanted to find Sally more.

Maybe, the voice said, *we could sneak out at night.*

She knew the way. She had a good flashlight. She could do it and not ever get caught, and maybe help. Maybe find Sally.

Tonight, the voice said, *we'll go tonight.*

Home Free

Lucinda lay awake beneath her bedcovers. The wind wailed at her window. Tree branches scraped against the glass like ragged fingernails. It was almost too scary to go into the woods. Almost.

Under her sheets, she shined her flashlight on the map of the woods she'd drawn with crayons in a sketch pad. She was a good map drawer. She and Sally drew tons of maps in their notebooks. Maps and diagrams of their dig sites, of the pits and the woods. She ripped the page out and folded it up and sneaked it into the pocket of her bib overalls she'd put on after her mother had tucked her in.

She peered out from under her covers. Her alarm clock said 12:32. It was the latest she'd ever been awake, yet she was alert, all shaky with excitement. And fear. She thought of Sally and drove the fear from her head.

She eased the sheets off and placed her feet super quiet on the floor.

The ancient floorboards sighed.

She listened for the sound of footfalls announcing her parents coming to check on her.

She heard nothing but the screech of the branch on her window.

She turned slowly to look at the window.

A hand tapped at the pane.

She jumped back.

No, just a branch.

She eased closer to the window to sneak a look outside. Her warped reflection gaped back at her. She cupped her hands around her eyes and pressed her nose to the window. The glass was cold. The night was black, no moon, no stars. Only the white snow gave off any light, a ghostly glow.

She glimpsed movement, a person hunched over at the edge of the yard, by the woods. She pressed her face tighter to the window.

The tire swing rocked in the wind.

She'd been certain it was a person. It wasn't. She was giving herself the willies. She needed to stop it. She needed to be brave, to think of Sally, pretend Sally was right there with her. So she could do this, find her friend.

She slipped her coat on and zipped it slowly, the sound loud in the silence. She just knew it was going to wake her mom and dad. If they were even asleep. It seemed no one slept anymore. She put the flashlight in her coat pocket.

Knowing that opening her bedroom door slowly made the hinges squeak, she flung it open fast, poked her head into the hallway. No light came from under her parents' bedroom door.

She slipped down the hall toward the stairs, past the photos of herself on the tire swing and of her and her parents during holidays.

The top stair tread was loose, creaky and dangerous. She'd

tripped on it more than once. She stepped over it and tiptoed down the stairs.

At the bottom, she headed for the kitchen, where her boots sat lined up near the door to the outside.

In the kitchen, she stopped.

The cellar door stood cracked open and light seeped from the basement. Lucinda stared at the light, looked at her snow boots squatting in the foyer. All she had to do was go ten more steps and put the boots on, sneak out the door, and she was home free.

A sound rose from the cellar. A voice.

Lucinda crept to the cellar door and stole a look.

At the bottom of the stairs, Lucinda's father sat on a stool at his workbench, his favorite place when he needed to think about his sheriff work. He built and painted birdhouses down there too. Or tried. The houses always came out odd and lopsided. Lucinda didn't mind, she liked them that way. Because they were her dad's. The birds seemed to like them too; they built their nests in the houses her dad put in the yard every spring.

Her dad wasn't working on birdhouses now. He sat slumped on the stool as he spun the handle on the bench vise and shook his head, muttering as if trying to rid his mind of horrible thoughts.

He was worried about Mrs. B. and Sally, and Mr. B., but he tried not to show it to Lucinda. To anyone. The day before, Sally had overheard her mom telling her dad, "You have to do something to help him."

"I'm *trying*. This is a nightmare," Lucinda's father had said and hugged her mom who shook from sobbing.

Lucinda needed to get to the pit; yet her dad seemed so alone.

She wanted to go down there and give him a big hug.

If she did, he'd put her back to bed and she might not get

another chance to sneak out. She was torn between her friend and her family. Both needed her.

Her friend needed her more.

She crept over to her boots by the door and tugged them onto her feet.

Her hand was on the doorknob when she heard a lone sob rise from the cellar.

Lucinda stole back to the cellar door.

Her dad was down there, pinching the brow of his nose.

She'd give him a hug then head to the pit, somehow, later.

She shed her coat and started down the stairs.

Normally, her dad would have heard her first step on the top stair. Not tonight.

At the bottom step, she said, "Daddy?"

Her dad whirled around on the stool, startled. Then he smiled, though the smile didn't match his sad eyes. "Sweetie. What are you doing? It's late."

"I had to pee," she fibbed.

He cocked his head the way he did when he knew she was fibbing but he didn't care that she was. "What is it, sweetie?" he said.

"Sally," she whispered. She suddenly wanted to tell her dad the truth. "I know what happened."

Her dad's eyes got big, as if he might get sick, like when he'd eaten bad fried clams in Maine. He stood and took her shoulders in his hands. "Know what, sweetie? Tell me."

"It's my fault."

"*No.* Don't *ever* say that."

"I should have told you."

He swept her up in his arms and hugged her. She hadn't let him pick her up in a long time. She was too big for that. But she was glad he picked her up now. Glad he still wanted to pick her up. He wiped dirt from her boots, the cellar's dirt floor muddy from the rainwater that had leaked in before the rain had turned to snow. "What are you doing dressed, and with boots on?" he said.

She'd forgotten the boots, shrugged.

"You can't be down here," her dad said. "It's filthy. Your allergies." He was right. Her nose and eyes were already crazy itchy.

"It's my fault," she sobbed.

"Shhh. No. What happened has nothing to do with you. Nothing."

"I should have told you about the man in the woods."

Her dad's body stiffened. He held her out away from him, looked her in the eye. He looked scared. "What man?" he said.

"The man in the woods, watching me and Sally."

"In *what* woods *when*? What are you talking about, sweetie, a man, what man? Did you recognize him? Did he approach you? Did he *hurt* you?"

Lucinda believed if she undid her fib maybe she'd somehow get her friend back.

"He didn't hurt us. He never came close."

"What'd he look like?"

"We never saw his face. Just movement in the woods. Green pants and a green shirt. I only saw him once, but Sally told me about him. He was her secret. She'd seen him a bunch. She made me promise to never tell. But . . ."

"You're not supposed to be in those woods," her dad said. "If you fell into one of those old mines—"

He hugged her so tight she couldn't breathe.

"Daddy," she said, "you're hurting me."

He relaxed, looked at her, his eyes sharp. "If you tried real, real hard, do you think you could remember anything about his face?"

She shook her head. "I never saw it." She sucked strands of her hair into her mouth. "Am I in trouble?"

"No. No. Of course not, sweetie. No. Never. This. It could help. You could help."

"But I fibbed. I didn't tell you, and Mom says leaving something out is the same as lying. And maybe if I had said something right away, Sally wouldn't—"

"Don't think that. You told me now. Maybe we can find this man."

She nodded, but still felt like she had eels swimming in her stomach. "Do you think he did it?" Lucinda asked. She didn't know what "it" meant, but for the first time thought maybe something really bad had happened to Sally, and she wasn't just lost. "Is Sally dead?"

"I—" Her dad seemed about to cry. He looked away toward the corner of the cellar to hide his face from her. He cleared his throat and looked back at her. "Some people. They do bad things. That make no sense to other people, who would never do them. And they make things up in their head that make those bad things seem okay. But they're not okay. I want you to think. This is important. It could help." He looked super serious now. "Did you get even a glimpse of the man's face or anything else that might help?"

"Nuh-uh."

"You sure it was a man? Could it have been a boy? From school, maybe spying on you?"

Lucinda had not thought of that. Sally had called the person a man so Lucinda had thought it was a man. "Maybe. I saw boots. Like men's work boots, but they could have been boys' boots. Boys wear the kind men wear at the Grain & Feed, but they never lace them. They wear the tongues hanging out because they think they look cool. But it just looks really stupid."

Her dad smiled. A real smile.

"These boots were laced. But. Girls wear them too. A couple older girls in school. Eye Shadow Girls."

"Who?"

"Mean older girls."

"Are you sure it wasn't just your imagination? It's okay if it was."

Lucinda thought how she'd believed for certain she'd seen someone outside Sally's bedroom a few nights ago and had screamed, and her dad and Mr. B. had come running. But afterward she'd thought maybe she hadn't seen anyone at all. And just earlier tonight she'd thought she'd seen someone out her own window but it had just been the stupid tire swing. Hadn't it?

"In my work," her dad said, "we need to be as sure as possible. It's okay either way. Whatever you say. Maybe there *was* a man, or a boy, but he was just a hunter or hiker and not someone following you."

"Maybe."

"How did you know he was following you?"

"That's what Sally said."

"Does she ever make stuff up?"

"Sometimes. I guess. Yeah. But—"

"Did she ever act scared?"

"Sometimes."

"Did she ever show you drawings, of scary things?"

"Nuh-uh."

"Or tell you she was scared?"

"She's always telling scary stories. About the mines and pits. But she isn't actually scared. She'd tell me if she was."

Lucinda thought hard, back to that day they'd peeked over the lip of the pit. All Lucinda had seen through the leaves were work boots and a flash of green pants. Unless the green had been plants or leaves. Which, maybe it was. But. She had seen boots, hadn't she? She was sure of it. Almost sure. It was more confusing than ever.

Her dad must have known she was confused, because his voice softened. "Did you think it was a man when you saw what you saw, or did Sally tell you it was a man?"

"Sally told me. We heard a branch snap. Loud. And I *saw* it. Them. The boots at least. I swear, Daddy. I'm almost a hundred percent certain." She wondered if she would have thought the movement in the trees was a man if Sally hadn't said so. Sally made things up. Sally read so many stories she sometimes seemed to think they were real. It was fun, most of the time. "It was a man," Lucinda said. "It was."

"If a man was following you, why on earth didn't you tell me?"

"Because you'd find out we were playing by the mines. And I knew how mad you'd get. Are you mad, Daddy?"

Her dad looked like he was going to cry again. "No, sweetie. Never. I'll take you up to bed. You want to ride on my shoulders?"

"Aren't you going to go look in the pit?"

"Not in the dark, sweetie."

"But she might be *there*."

"Why would she be there now?"

"To hide. Or if maybe the man in the woods took them there."

"I see."

"I'm serious, Dad. She might be there!"

"I'll check in the daylight. Promise."

"But she'd be so scared there at night. And if she's been there this whole time . . ."

"She won't be scared if her mom's with her." He tried his best to smile, but he seemed to know it was no use and gave up. "How about that ride on my shoulders?"

"Yes, please." She was so tired now. So sleepy. All of it felt like a dream. An icky dream.

Her dad hoisted her up onto his shoulders with a groan and took her back upstairs and stayed with her in her room until he was sure he was asleep.

Except she wasn't asleep. She was pretending.

Because she knew what she'd seen.

Almost knew.

And if Sally was in the pit, she would be scared at night, for real, because the one thing she hated was the dark, even if her mom was with her.

And if Lucinda's dad wasn't going to take Lucinda seriously and go help Sally, that meant it was still up to Lucinda.

She needed to sneak out, help her friend.

But her eyelids were so heavy, and soon sleep overtook her.

SMOKE

Jonah fell off Sally's bed and slammed his head on the floor as he awoke from a dream in which Sally told him everything was going to be okay, all he had to do was remember her. When he reached to touch her cheek, she'd dissolved into smoke and he'd fallen from the bed.

A soft knock came from down the hallway, at the front door.

Jonah wrapped his bathrobe around his naked body and sat up against the bed. He did not wish to answer the door. He did not want to face anyone. Face any more questions and accusations or theories about what he, or worse, his wife, might or might not have done. He could not stomach another bout of interrogations.

The knock came again.

Soft. Delicate.

The knock of a girl.

He got up and rushed to the door, nearly tripping in his slippers.

He flung open the front door.

She stood there, smiling shyly, and Jonah's heart broke.

I'm Not Sally

Lucinda," Jonah said. He wrapped his bathrobe tighter and glanced out at the road. No deputy car or TV van was out there yet this morning. "What are you doing here?"

"I miss her," she said. Her tiny voice quaked. She was on the edge of tears. Jonah's own grief now seemed a frivolous indulgence in the face of the girl's anguish. How cruel these days must have been for Lucinda, whom Jonah had all but forgotten existed.

"Can I come in, Mr. B.?" Lucinda said, chewing her hair.

"I don't know. I—" He felt nervous bringing her into his home. The place was a wreck with laundry and stale food and strewn newspapers.

"I have to tell you something," she said.

"Let's sit out here on the porch swing," he offered.

The morning air was brisk, but it did little to wake his slumbering and befuddled mind, the dream of Sally lingering. The morning's glary, soupy gray light seemed to alter his depth perception.

Jonah and Lucinda sat on the swing, each at opposite ends. Her feet did not quite reach the porch floor.

A woodpecker flitted toward the three trees Jonah and Rebecca had planted when Sally was born, a tree each for Sally, Jonah, and Rebecca.

"Did you get off the school bus here?" Jonah said.

"There is no school today."

"What day is it?"

"Wednesday, Mr. B.," Lucinda said, giving him a queer look: *You're so silly.* She glanced at his bathrobe. "Wednesday afternoon."

"But there's no school?"

"School is closed because people are searching."

"Oh. Of course it is. Of course they are." Strange. He'd thought somehow it was Sunday morning.

Lucinda stretched her legs from the very edge of the swing and pushed with her tiptoes to rock it, then sat back.

"Sally saw a man in the woods," Lucinda announced.

Jonah jolted, turned to stare at her. His heart thundered.

"What do you mean?" he said.

"We both saw him, Sally and me," she said. "In the woods. I know we weren't supposed to be there. But—"

"What are you saying? The woods? A man in the woods? What man? Who? Tell me. Please, you need to tell me." Somehow he'd moved closer to her without realizing it and now found her frail shoulders clutched in his hands. She glanced at his hands, winced. He loosened his grip and got up, knelt to look her face-to-face. "You need to tell me," he said. "And your dad. Everything." A man in the woods, following the girls. This had to be linked to the disappearances, didn't it? This was the suspect they needed. The person to find. He needed to know where his wife and daughter were. He needed to know if they'd been taken, or—he needed to know why and how they'd disappeared. Who was to blame.

"I did tell my dad," the girl said, "but I don't think he believes me."

"*I* believe you. All that matters is that I believe you."

"I can *tell* you believe me. I thought you might want to come with me to see her."

"See her?"

"Sally, in the pit."

Jonah stood, light-headed; his head swam and his heart skittered, seemed about to give out. "What pit? Sally, what are you talking about?"

"I'm not Sally, Mr. B., I'm Lucinda."

"Lucinda, right. I know. I *know*. Lucinda."

"Me and Sally found it. The pit. Near some of the old mines."

"But what man? You've got to tell me, *what* man?" Jonah loomed over the girl. Why had he not been told about this? Why had Lucinda kept this from him? Why was he always in the dark, goddamn it, why hadn't Maurice informed him of this development? "When did you tell your daddy?" he said.

"Last night."

"Okay." Jonah needed to call Maurice right now and find out if there was anything to this. "Tell me more about the man."

"I never saw his face, or much except for his boots, or what I thought were his boots. They must have been. I heard a branch snap. I saw boots. But Sally, she saw him a couple times when she was in the woods alone. It was our secret. He was. And the pit. We knew we'd be in big trouble for being in the Big Woods." Lucinda continued to prattle on about the man, or what she thought was a man. With each passing second she seemed less and less certain of what she saw, and Jonah needed her to be sure. Certain. Absolutely certain.

"I'm going now," Lucinda said, hoisting up her backpack. "I

packed cheese and crackers and brought a thermos of milk. You want to come find Sally with me?"

"I better call your dad first. Is he out searching or—"

"No." Lucinda shot up. The swing rocked and caught her in the knees, knocked her down. She popped up, face pinched with a child's obstinacy. "He thinks I made it up. I *know* he does."

"You stay here," Jonah said and marched inside to use the phone. As he dialed the phone, he glanced out the kitchen window to see Lucinda darting out of the driveway and into the road, beelining for One Dollar Bridge.

What Are We Going to Do?

Jonah hung up the phone, tugged on his barn boots, cinched his bathrobe belt tight, and chased after Lucinda.

Lucinda had fled across One Dollar Bridge and was almost out of sight where the road began a steep climb toward the Gore, toward paper company wilderness, and the old talcum mines.

Running, Jonah cried out after her.

Lucinda charged onward, clumsy in her boots but faster than Jonah, who was winded, what scant energy he had left from his days of grief flagging rapidly.

Up ahead, Lucinda dodged off the road, into the woods. With the snow, however, there was no way for her to escape. Jonah could easily track her.

He trudged up and up the road and found her tracks and began to follow them into the woods.

The woods were dark and still beneath the ancient hemlock and spruce. But Jonah had been wrong. Tracking Lucinda would not be easy.

Snow was scarce beneath the old conifers, most of it heaped

on the massive bows above him. It took Jonah a while to find Lucinda's slight tracks in the skiff of snow, and he was slowed by having to go around a labyrinth of blowdowns that the girl was small enough to pick her way through and out the other side. Up and up she climbed, like a nimble cat.

Yet for Jonah, the going was slow, arduous, and the cold air needled his lungs.

He tracked her for what seemed an hour, the frigid air stinging his bare skin beneath his robe. Lucinda's tracks were angling toward the old mine shafts and he feared for her, and for himself.

He stopped now and again to hear nothing save the wheeze of his lungs. Several times, he lost her trail and had to backtrack. Gasping, he rested against a hemlock. He considered heading back, getting Maurice. But he'd gone too deep into the woods, and pushed on.

Up ahead, she cried out.

Jonah tried to pick up his pace.

A snowshoe hare sprang from beneath a young fir and loped away in a whirl of snow.

Jonah pitched forward, the snow deeper, Lucinda's tracks easier to follow.

She cried out again.

She was close. Very close.

He searched the woods, tracked her prints in the snow until they brought him to a snarl of impenetrable branches.

He started to go around when she called out again.

She was in among the tangle.

Beneath it.

Jesus.

"Here," she whimpered.

Jonah yanked away brush to reveal a pit in the earth.

He knelt and held his hand down for her.

"I'm okay. Snow crashed down my stupid neck and I screamed," she said. "It's cold! This is where we were when we saw him."

"Come out of there," he said.

The look on her face grew guarded. "You come down, I'll show you. He was in the bushes. But . . . It's so different in the snow. Nothing looks the same. It's like another world."

"Sally, please. Come on out of there. Okay. Stop this."

"I'm not Sally, Mr. B., I'm Lucinda."

"I know. I *know*."

The wind kicked up and snow cascaded from the branches onto Lucinda's face. She cried out, wiping at snow and spitting. She began to sob and held up her hand to him.

Jonah reached down and helped her out, then collapsed beside the pit.

Lucinda sat down beside him, sniffling. He slung his arm around her, drew her close. He shivered, his bathrobe damp from melting snow, his skin cold, nearly numb. What could he do to help this poor girl? What could he say to salve her wounded heart when he could barely get out of bed or bring himself to eat more than bread that had gone stale? When would any of this end?

Lucinda huddled closer. "I thought for sure—" She sniffled. "I'm so stupid."

"You're not stupid," Jonah said. "You're sad." *Sad and desperate, like me. Like all of us. Desperate to return to the lives we had.*

"Is she ever coming home?" Lucinda wiped her nose on her coat sleeve.

"I don't know. I hope so," Jonah said, peering around the dim woods.

"Why did this happen?"

"I don't know."

"It's not fair."

"No. It's not. It's cruel."

He pulled her tighter to him.

"What are we gonna do without her, Mr. B.?"

"I wish I knew."

She peeked up at him. "I'm never going to give up. I'll look forever and I will never ever stop. And never ever forget her. Ever."

"Of course not." He wiped a tear from her cheek. He needed to shuck off the negative thoughts, for her sake. "Hey. Enough doom and gloom. She could be back at the house right now while we're sitting here being stupid and mopey, right?"

"You really think so?" Lucinda chirped.

"Why not?" he said, and believed it for a heartbeat before despair returned.

She hugged him just as terrible pain exploded at the base of his neck and he collapsed on his back.

He looked up just in time to take a fist to his face.

Sorry

L ucinda shrieked.

Jonah felt himself jerked to the cold snow by the collar of his bathrobe, the robe falling open, his vision obliterated by snow and by blood gushing from his cut eyebrow.

"What are you doing?" a man's voice bellowed. "What are you *doing*?"

Jonah struggled to sit up, wiped the blood and snow from his eyes, pulled his robe closed with his numb hands.

The man towered over him.

Maurice. Glowering. Taut with menace. "What are you doing with my daughter?"

"She—"

"What are you doing here, Daddy?" Lucinda said.

"Getting you. You took off and I asked around and someone told me they'd seen you by *his* house. But you weren't there and neither was he—" He took a labored breath, sweating, shaking with anger and fear, hands on his hips. "I was looking around the yard and an old woman walking by said she'd seen you run from

the house, looking scared. And he"—Maurice glared at Jonah—
"was chasing you in his robe."

"Maurice—" Jonah began.

"Shut up. I'm talking to my daughter." Maurice addressed
Lucinda. "What'd he do to scare you?"

"Nothing, Daddy. I wanted to show him the pit, but he didn't
want me to. He went to call you instead, to come get me. But I ran
off. And he chased after me because he was worried about me going into the woods alone."

"He didn't scare you? Or hurt you?"

"*Daddy*. It's Mr. B. He would never hurt me. He's our friend."

"Why did you want him to come here?"

"*You* didn't believe me, that Sally might be here. You wouldn't
come."

"Sweetie." Maurice went to his knees and held his daughter's
cheeks in his palms. "Of *course* I believed you. I came here at daylight, before the new snow fell. There's nothing here, sweetie. No
sign of whoever or whatever you saw. It will be hard to figure out
who it was if you didn't see a face, if it had anything to do with
any of this at all. But if it does, Daddy'll find out. I will find out."

Maurice stared at Jonah on the ground. Then held out his hand.
Jonah took it and got up, brushing snow from his tangled bathrobe, hugging it around him and tying the belt tight. He could
barely feel his legs they were so stung with cold.

Maurice looked off into the woods, shaking his head. "This
whole damned thing. What a damned mess."

"Daddy, those are bad words," Lucinda chimed.

Maurice patted his daughter on the head, tucked her close to
him as she hugged him. The act pained Jonah to see. He'd have
swapped the rest of his life for one more hug from his daughter.

Maurice looked at Jonah. "I'm sorry," he said. "Not just about this. I never took the time to say I'm sorry. For what's happened. The girls disappearing and me pressing you for answers, *truths* that don't matter a lick in the scheme of things. I know you didn't have anything to do with it."

"This man the girls saw, we need to follow up on it," Jonah said. "He's got to be—"

"Do you believe it?"

"It's *something*. We can't just dismiss it. We wanted theories. Now we have one. Until we can prove otherwise, I believe it. We need to believe it, look into it; the police, you, need to follow up."

"We've got nothing, even if he is real. A pair of brown boots. Green pants. It eliminates no one."

"We have to try."

"I will. I will. I promise."

"He exists," Lucinda said. "And he's still out there."

Maurice sighed, hugged his daughter tight. "I wish I could wave a wand and reveal him, or whoever it is, and put an end to all this for everyone."

No Wand

There would be no wand to wave. Nothing to reveal. No man to find.

There would be no suspect charged. No arrest made. No trial. No conviction. Without bodies there was no murder or proof of a crime.

There was only absence.

And speculation. Brutal scrutiny. Unholy persecution. Unwarranted suspicion. Of Jonah.

After a spell, no TV van or police cruiser parked across the road from his house. No one visited. No one called. He had nothing to live for except the return of his wife and daughter, and with each breath that eventuality grew less likely.

What savings he had were depleted by the end of his first workless year. He'd tried to return to teaching but could not focus. Could not engage. He'd wanted to, wanted to immerse himself in the work he'd loved, distract himself if only for fifty minutes of class a few times a week. But he couldn't. The questions in his students' eyes, the curiosity, the suspicion, might have been bearable, and faded with time. They were young. Curiosity and intrigue part of their makeup. But his last day on campus came when he'd dragged himself in early to try to work away from home, and heard, from just outside the door of his shared office, two colleagues in dialogue:

"You think he did it?"

"Let's just say, he's a strange bird, that one."

Jonah had left and never returned.

What money he earned from odd jobs went straight to paying the mortgage and taxes. As torturous as it was to remain in the house, he dared not leave in case they returned. He sold the old Gremlin to pay bills and bought an even older jalopy truck.

All this time, he searched for them, his wife and child, on his own. He wandered every hill and field and ditch and riverbank what seemed a hundred times. He searched in the day and night, all night, calling their names, pleading to the darkness to give his wife and daughter up to him, hoping that in the night's silence his voice would carry farther and reach them, their voices would carry farther and reach him.

He found only more silence.

He searched for the man in the woods, too, for a sign or clue of him, that he existed. At times in the nighttime woods, Jonah sensed he was being followed in the darkness. By someone who knew something. Someone who had caused all this. No one could be trusted, perhaps even himself. He ranged deeper and deeper into the woods, farther and farther up into the mountains.

On one search he stumbled upon an abandoned miner's cabin, tucked up in treacherous terrain.

Despite not believing in an entity found in any books written with a man's hand, he'd done his praying. Prayed for their return. Begged for it. Their safety, at least.

His prayers and pleading and weeping were met with the same response: silence.

He offered himself in their place. Wept for forgiveness for what he could not remember. Pleaded for it not to have been his wife's hand in this. To spare her memory, he considered confessing to the crime, committed in a spontaneous rage. He would gladly pay for it to save his wife's name. But he could not lead the police to any bodies.

The money ran out; the mortgage went unpaid. The bank foreclosed. Took ownership. But they'd never sell the house. People did not move to Ivers from other places; people left Ivers for other places. And no one in town would ever buy this tainted home.

He took the yellow dress and coat he'd bought Sally, photos of Rebecca, his books of poetry and science and short stories, and what few other cherished belongings would fit into a trunk and drove the truck up to the Gore and settled into the deserted miner's cabin, where all he asked for was to be left alone to wait for the miraculous return of his daughter and wife.

BOOK III

November 6, 2012

25 Years Later

Sweet Ache

Jonah stood on the stoop out in front of the Grain & Feed, his shoulder pressed to the post, worn boots crossed at the ankles as he scraped a wooden match along the rail and touched its flame to his fresh-twisted smoke, inhaling deep and deeper still, eyes closing as though he were dreaming of better times past, though there were no better times past of which to dream and none to come that he knew.

No credit, Lucinda had said when Jonah had asked to put supplies on his tab. Supplies he needed. He only risked venturing off the mountain and into town when it was a matter of need. He had not been to town in nearly a year, only to hear from Lucinda: *No, Jonah, sorry.*

Sorry. And she'd looked away as if she had not known him. Her dismissive tone stung him deep. Lucinda, of all people. Today, of all days, to reject him, as if he were a stranger, and they did not share a past; as if she'd forgotten what day today was.

The ancient anger rampaged in him now, a hot magma wanting to rupture from within him, consume and destroy him. It made him feel mean toward the very last person who deserved his rancor. Until she'd sent him out. No credit.

He shook the match and flicked it to the dirt where it trailed a dismal tendril and died. He drew another long pull of smoke, his diaphragm going taut to stoke that delirious lust, the delirium ignited in the brain and piqued in the blood bettered only by the sweet godless filling of lungs gone as black and as foul as sun-rotted meat.

He spat. Picked at a bit of tobacco stuck to his tongue tip. Couldn't get it. Spat. Clawed at it. His anger besting him. His hands shook from Lucinda's betrayal. That's what it was, a betrayal. Never mind the humiliation of being denied credit in front of onlookers who eyed him sideways.

Squatter. Lunatic. Murderer. He heard their thoughts, saw it in their eyes every time he was forced to come into town. He wasn't deaf. Wasn't dead. Not yet. After all this time, those who remembered the Disappearance still looked askance, whispered to one another from behind cupped hands. Afraid. That's what they were, he'd decided. Afraid of his life lived apart from them, and afraid of their own viciousness and suspicion, judgment and self-made calamities. *We know what you did. We know.*

He heard their thoughts, registered the suspicion in their eyes.

They knew nothing, these people who'd shaped him into a monster stitched together from rumor and breathed to life with fear when he was only an old man now, worn down as river stone, as alone now as he'd been entering this world. *He'll do it again, one day.* That's what Jonah saw in their eyes and heard in their thoughts: *He'll do it again, one day.*

What fear could do. He knew better than any of them. How

many of them knew a pain that altered the color of your blood from the red of life to the black of death.

A woman in a red wool coat skirted around him now on the stoop and eyed him with the look of one gauging the length of a rabid mongrel's chain.

"What?" Jonah snarled. "What?"

The woman scurried away like a frightened squirrel.

Jonah flicked his smoke to the dirt where it lay burning.

Let it burn, he thought, his anger, his pain, welling in him.

Let the whole town burn to the ground.

THE GORE

Up in the mountains, Jonah tucked his old truck into the woods off the dirt road and hiked up into the Gore; up through the glacier-scored hollow, where he alone dwelled with the few solemn bears that sought their winter retreat in the lightless reek of the talcum mines, amid the gloom of the few colossal hemlocks that had escaped the saw's tooth and whose monumental size seemed now less majestic for their survival than sorrowful for their scarcity elsewhere.

In a clearing, he knelt, his heart heaving as it did every time he knelt here.

Every day.

He brushed twigs free of the two flat stones he'd set in the hard earth and chiseled crudely with his own hands years ago:

Sally
March 11, 1980-19—

Rebecca
October 15, 1953-19—

He took his cap off and fell still.

A creek trickled over rocks nearby.

He laid his palms on each of the stones, remembering.

He rose with effort, a quick catch in his bad knee, continued on, pushed deeper into the wilds.

Now and again he stopped. Hacked phlegm. His breath rattled like the wind in dried milkweed. What was once done without effort was now an endeavor of will against a body that was ready to quit.

The cabin lay inked in shadows beneath the hemlocks, unseen from the rutted trail running through the undergrowth like a scar.

His head howled and his blood roared as he stepped inside the cabin. He needed to quell his anger, stanch it before it overtook him. He needed to find the one photo of Rebecca he'd taken here, calm himself with her visage.

He rooted for the photo among his bookshelves, tilted from tectonic shifts and made of stacked bricks and old wood planks.

No credit.

He tore through warped drawers and flung papers and nails and dead batteries from them as if he were a bear tearing apart a log, drunk for honey.

Where was her photograph? He'd not looked at it, not dared the anguish, in ages, but now he needed to see it, see her face. See his wife's face.

He yanked free a drawer. Tipped its debris on the card table and spilled his hands round in the ruins as a miner fingers a tumble of pebbles in search of that hunk of godforsaken gold.

Where was her photo? Where had he put it? Why was it not here? There.

There it was: her photo.

Rebecca.

He picked it up and fell to his knees and stared at her image, faded despite his keeping it stored away to prevent her becoming all the more a ghost.

The scream of blood in his head quieted to the flutter of a moth's wings. He looked at her face and trembled. So long ago, yet he trembled. Yet he could smell her. Yet he could hear and feel her every breath on him. See her. Still. The sweet ache persisted with the sense that if he turned around he'd find her standing there behind him.

His breathing ebbed as her photo calmed him.

He returned the photo to the drawer and stood so calm among the ruins he'd cast about himself it was as though he'd died in taking in her image, and his stupid soulless body had yet to know enough to fall limp to the wood floor where it belonged.

If only he'd the courage.

USELESS FACTS

Lucinda stared at the envelope in her tremulous hand, still unable to bring herself to open it, afraid the letter inside might not say what she hoped, the ink of its fateful return address smudged by sweat where her fingers and thumbs had worried it. She'd fielded unfavorable replies so often in years past, she wondered why she'd bothered this time.

A voice startled her.

Lucinda looked up from the envelope as Ed Baines speared a hot dog from the steamer with his jackknife blade and plopped the sorry dog on a paper plate beside a jar of opaque vinegar, in which floated pickled eggs that looked like odd organs left to cure in formaldehyde.

"What's that?" Lucinda said.

"Jonah, I never seen him so riled," Ed said. He grabbed a hot dog bun and with his stubbed fingers wedged the dog in it, dribbled relish on the dog, and bit down, half the dog gone with a bite.

Lucinda slipped the envelope under the cash register drawer and set to counting grubby ones and fives from the day's scratch lotto ticket haul, wetted her thumb between each bill and counted aloud. Recounted. She penciled the lottery tabulation in a leather-bound ledger then packed the bills into a vinyl bag, zipped the bag snug, and slid it back under the cash drawer. She did not want to talk about Jonah. She'd not seen him in going on a year when he'd entered the Grain & Feed earlier. He'd looked poorly, though not as poorly as her father, and she felt sick for turning him away.

She slipped out from behind the counter, a clipboard pressed to her hip, and walked down among an aisle of screws and bolts, nuts and washers, slid out each flat metal drawer. She fished her fingers through the metallic machined pieces that kept the world from flying apart, her lips moving with arithmetic precision. The cool, smooth feel of the bolts and washers slipping between her fingers comforted her. With a pencil stub, she calculated the inventory.

"I feel awful about it," she said, her voice sounding as injured as her heart felt for wounding Jonah, and, let's be honest, wound-ing herself in turn. Refusing him credit was not business, it was personal. For Jonah, and for her. It was shameful.

She tried to blame her behavior on the fact that she'd just dis-covered the envelope in the mail as she'd spied Jonah and his cart of supplies behind a customer on whom Ed waited. She'd been so fixated on the envelope that she'd hardly glanced at Jonah as she'd said, "No credit, Jonah, sorry." Dismissed him. "It's me, Jonah," he'd said, as if his decline in appearance and hygiene left him un-recognizable to her; as if Jonah, dear *Mr. B.*, could ever be unrec-ognizable to her. "I know. No, Jonah, sorry," she'd said as she'd started to peel the envelope open with the edge of her thumbnail.

The look in his eye. She'd betrayed him, the one person he trusted, the only person he spoke to beyond perfunctory com-munication with other store clerks. He'd stood there stiff with humiliation, smoldering with rage, then stalked out of the store. She'd been cruel. She despised business. The necessity of it. It made her behave in ways against her nature, or what she felt was her nature. Which was why she'd been so anxious when she'd seen the envelope in her mail. Perhaps she would get a reprieve from the Grain & Feed for a spell, if she could arrange it, and if the letter inside the envelope proved heartening.

"I can't just let him keep charging and never paying. Can I?" Lucinda said, cringing at her attempt to justify her actions. She could afford it; it wouldn't have killed her or her meager bottom line to help Jonah. Of all people. That counted. He counted. Still, there came a point, didn't there, when business was business and enough was enough? The store was not a gold mine. More a money pit. Changes needed to be made if it were to even survive. Still.

"Can I just let him keep charging?" she repeated.

Ed shrugged.

Lucinda swung the clipboard toward the front corner of the store to the side of where she stood. "I'm gonna bust out that wall," she said. "Clear out this front area, put in a bay window. Give customers a place to sit with their coffee. Maybe get a rack of bestsellers. Paperbacks. Wi-Fi for the iPad crew. I need cash flow for that," she said, though the plans might now, perhaps, be rendered moot by the news in the envelope.

"Good luck with Wi-Fi here, Sisyphus."

Ed, Mr. Hyperbole. It was only Wi-Fi; how hard could it be to get up here in the shadow of Gore Mountain? "People like that," she said. "Just to sit. Drink coffee. Read. Let the sun on their face through the bay window. Offer up maple syrup and aged cheddar." She liked it, when she had time. It had been ages since she'd just sat and read for pure pleasure. Her only reading of late was for her archaeology classes at Lyndon State, classes in which she'd felt as conspicuous among the nineteen year-old students as a plastic fork in an Ice Age excavation site. Much as she enjoyed the class's introductory texts, she already knew most of the history, techniques, and biographies on the syllabus and probably could have taught the class herself based on her private studies over the years; she'd certainly offer a wider breadth of texts than the classes offered, which consisted of texts written about men by men with names such as Arthur and Rudolph and Oscar. Famous male archaeologists, no doubt, men she respected, even revered, and whose work and contributions to the field were legend and undeniable. Still, she'd hoped in a college-level class to read more than brief mention of pioneer Kathleen Kenyon, and of Mary Leakey— the first *person* to discover the hominid *Proconsul* skull of an ape ancestral to humans, and the *Zinjanthropus boisei* skull—who was relegated to a few brief paragraphs and referred to as the *wife of* Louis Leakey. Why was no man ever referred to as the *husband of* . . . ? Lucinda wondered.

Still, Lucinda felt fortunate. If she were not obligated to read for her classes, she'd not be reading at all. Her time for herself had dwindled these past months in proportion to her father's deteriorating health, her need to be there for him. The time she gave him strained her time elsewhere, here, and at home with Dale. She wondered how she would be able to leave her father if the letter said what she hoped it said. She wondered what Dale would have to say about the letter too. She'd kept him in the dark about applying. For good reason it had seemed.

"Coming to that, is it?" Ed said, startling her. "Maple syrup and cheddar cheese."

He swung his hand toward the far wall and said, "Bring in some biscotti and croissants and whatnot while you're at it. Hazelnut coffee. The fancy stuff. Might's well go whole hog. Just don't get rid of these good dogs." He popped the rest of the hot dog in his mouth and burped, thumbed a dollop of relish from the corner of his mouth, prepared a second hot dog. "Jonah sure was hot."

Lucinda wished Ed would let it go about Jonah.

"Why he needs supplies for a new shed way up in there is beyond me," Lucinda said. "He's too unwell to be up there alone. He should just move down to town. Where it's safe. That's what I say."

"Jonah doesn't care what you say. What anyone says," Ed said. "I were him I would never step foot in this town. Would have set off for Alaska years ago. Now *there's* a state for such a man. And it's not a shed he wants to build. It's a smokehouse."

"Shed. Smokehouse," Lucinda said. "He's got his old house right in town. Rough as it is. He could squat there as easily as in the Gore, no one would say a word." All these years later, and Lucinda refused to look at, did not dare to look at, Jonah's old house, whenever she drove by it; yet, here she was expecting Jonah to *live* there.

"I doubt he wants to step foot in that place ever again. Which is why he hasn't," Ed said.

A customer ambled over from the aisle of awls and mauls. Malcolm LeFranc. A steer of a man. Mustachioed Frenchman. A tree cutter among generations of tree cutters. On the counter, he set a Timber Hookaroon, then brought out a wad of cash with fingers greased black.

"If you're talking about Jonah," he said, "he's got more to worry about than credit. I told him just earlier when I was up near his cabin that we're going to be logging up there in the Gore. Come spring. It's foregone. Right up to his old shack. And right on through it. That's private forest. He's squatting. Has been all along. It didn't matter any when we didn't want the trees for money. It matters now that we do. And I can tell you, Jonah, he's got his back reared and teeth bared. He won't go easy. That man is going to go the hard way."

Ed rang up LeFranc and counted his change.

"It's the act of building not what's built," Baines said. "That's why Jonah wanted supplies."

LeFranc rolled his eyes and exited the store.

"Makes an old man feel vital," Ed carried on. "Jonah's got nothing of import to do with his days." *Import?* Who did anything of real import with their days, and where did Ed get such words? Lucinda wondered if Ed, single and forty, sat around at night trying to figure out where he could shoehorn his dictionary words into everyday conversation, or if the words just flew into his brain and out his mouth all on their own, in the moment. Tracking inventory and stocking shelves, busting out walls to make a coffee nook, where was the import in that? It all seemed a distraction *from* a life of *import* or at least the life she'd once imagined for herself, so many years ago.

Her girlhood dream to escape Ivers and pursue archaeology or paleontology had disappeared with Sally and— Hell. She couldn't even claim her dream had vanished with Sally. Who could say if she and Sally would have even remained friends. Many girlfriends in grade school became strangers, if not nemeses, by junior high. Lucinda's dreams may well have gone by the wayside even if nothing had ever happened to Sally and the two girls had remained friends. One thing was certain: the natural course of their lives had been stolen from Sally *and* Lucinda. The disappearance had rendered it impossible for Lucinda to live the life she'd been *meant* to live. For years, Lucinda had clung to her friend's memory, heard her friend's voice and laughter, spoken to her, not just in her head, but aloud. She'd shared her secrets with Sally as if Sally were still here, because it *felt* as if she *were* still here.

Yet, on her darkest days, as Lucinda entered the hormonal perdition of adolescence, Lucinda had resented Sally, who was always spoken of in a reverent tone, as if she'd never disobeyed her parents to explore the Big Woods, urged Lucinda to join her, or promised Lucinda to keep secrets, *lies*. In her most immature hours, Lucinda had wished she, Lucinda, had been the one who had disappeared, thinking: *Sally's probably enjoying her* perfect *self wherever she is.*

In her early twenties Lucinda had wondered if she'd used Sally's disappearance, and hope for her return, as an excuse not to leave town. She'd felt as stuck as George Bailey in her favorite old movie, *It's a Wonderful Life*. Except Lucinda had no guardian angel and no inclination to jump off a bridge. And, really, she was not stuck at all.

She'd visited New York City in eighth grade for a 4-H trip to see dinosaur skeletons at the American Museum of Natural History and found, instead of a land of tall glinting buildings of silvery promise, one of gray, drab streets, narrow and sunless, the air stinking of sewage and sweat, a humid mealy air that stuck in her windpipe as flocks of people shouldered past with manic hurriedness. It was a city where all things were possible, including men who lay on steam grates, faces sooted with cab exhaust as they mumbled to the people who stepped over them.

The trip had caused her to appreciate home, faces she knew. Faces that knew her. As she'd taken on more responsibility at the Grain & Feed, she'd told herself there was worth in helping those she knew with what they needed to get their jobs done and that if she left, she'd miss it here. True. What was also true was that she'd not dared pursue a dream Sally could not live. She'd told herself exploring for Algonquin and Revolutionary War artifacts in the nearby fields and riverbeds was enough to sate her, rationalized that if she'd not pursued her dream when younger perhaps there'd been a reason for her staying not yet made clear. A purpose. Import.

This reasoning comforted her.

Until a few years ago.

She'd been on one of her Sunday hikes, bushwhacking on the other side of Strange Mountain in search of stone cellars rumored to be of Celtic origin, when she'd seen it: white against the dark earth. She'd gone to her knees and picked at the soil around it, brushed it away to reveal bone. Cupped like a bowl. The crown of a cranium. A child's skull. A slender shaft of bone too. Straight as an iron rod. Yet delicate. Frail. She'd been certain of what she'd found. Sally.

She'd returned with her father, who'd called the state police to meet at the site.

The bones proved human. A child's. A male child's. At least two hundred years old. Likely Native American. Abenaki. Quite a find, though not the find she'd believed it to be. In that moment of discovery, however, Lucinda had regretted each ill thought she'd ever had toward Sally, and wished it had been Sally's remains. At least then, the days of not knowing would be over.

"Old women can garden," Baines prattled now. "Cluck their tongues at one another. A man needs to keep doing in his old age, build, like Jonah does, to feel worth a damn."

"You men, horseshit. And you'll never see me garden or cluck."

With a new hot dog dressed with red relish, Baines bit down as he ambled toward the door and tipped his half dog at Lucinda as though making a point, though he had no point to make, just relish dribbling down his wrist.

He opened the door.

The cowbell clanked overhead.

"You think I was too harsh on him?" Lucinda said, the answer clear as spring water.

"He was riled."

"You don't think he'd do something?" Lucinda said, fearing for Jonah what she'd always feared, that he'd end things one day. Just give in. For years she'd worried that Sally and Mrs. B., their remains, *would* be found. And with that discovery, Jonah would have no reason then to continue a life without . . . import.

"Jonah wouldn't do anything to you. You're a daughter to him, a—"

"I don't mean he'd do something to me, but to himself or to, I don't know. *Someone.* He was so *angry.* If he ever went and did something . . . because of me—"

"If Jonah does *something*, that's on him. That's a fact."

"I could have continued his credit. That's a fact."

"World's just full of useless facts," Baines said as he exited the store.

Lucinda opened the cash register drawer. She took out the envelope and tucked it into her jeans pocket, wedged it next to the fragment of soapstone whose edges had been worn down by her worrying fingers over the past twenty-five years.

No

Jonah fetched his .30-.30 carbine rifle from the corner of the cabin and levered its action. He worried his thumb over the hammer, worn so smooth he needed to be mindful not to let it slip and fall, fire the rifle accidentally.

From a shelf above the woodstove, he took an oil can and a hank of flannel shirt, ambled onto the porch where he sat with the carbine across his lap.

The afternoon had fallen cold. The season had turned and there wasn't any turning it back.

Jonah curled his palm to the rifle barrel, feeling its length as a finish carpenter feels a hand-turned spindle for imperfections. Cold. Always cold. Even in the hot guts of summer. That steel. He smoothed his palm over the walnut stock, wood grain like lines of a topographic map.

He'd killed a lot of deer with the rifle, but sensed this year's deer would be his last. This winter would be his last. If Lucinda could turn on him, what was left?

Nothing.

He ran the oiled rag over the carbine's receiver, worked it inside the action, inspecting the black. With time, things grew only dirtier.

How easy it would be to put the rifle muzzle to his forehead and use a stick to pull the trigger.

How many times he'd imagined it.

Legions.

Each day's urge stronger than the previous day's urge, for going on ten thousand days.

Yet he couldn't.

Didn't dare.

He got up and drank spring water percolating from a nearby ledge. At his ramshackle smokehouse, he jiggled a screwdriver set in the broken handle, opened the door, and took stock: a lone rack of jerked hare meat. He brushed away mouse droppings and grabbed a chunk of hare and sucked on it.

He took up the rifle and sneaked under the hemlocks' dark canopy, searching the woods for a flick of a white tail, twitch of an ear, the horizontal animal darkness among the vertical tree world.

Jonah knelt at a track in the muck, the dewclaws set deep, toes splayed. A good buck. He'd seen it three months ago, in the green summer fields, antlers in velvet. Others had seen it; the young men tooling back roads in pickup trucks. They'd come up here soon, scouting for the buck they knew would head into the beeches for mast. If Jonah had his way, the deer would be jerky by then.

Jonah's knees clicked as he rose and picked his way down along the brook, the brook's music masking his noise.

He left the brook to work the edge where the spruce met beeches, skirted above a mess of blackberry cane, and leaned against a beech trunk shattered by lightning.

He watched the blackberry cane, motionless. His mouth grew dry. His feet cold. The winter wind watered his eyes.

Down below, in beech whips, a flick of motion. He squinted. Blackberry cane leaned in the wind.

Another flick.

A deer, bedded down? He'd shot more than one deer in its bed. But he couldn't make it out clearly.

His eyes were spent. Like the rest of him. Buck or doe, he'd shoot it. One shot. He couldn't afford anyone to hear more than one shot before the season started. He didn't need a game warden up here. He didn't need anyone up here.

Flick.

He squinted.

Whatever it was, it was in the thicket, hard to sneak a shot in there. He moved his head the slightest to gain a new angle. *Flick.* Deer. Or coyote? He'd eaten coyote. He'd eat it again.

He shouldered the .30-.30, rested his elbow on his knee. He pressed his cheek to the stock and eyed down the barrel, took an easy, long breath. Let it out.

He set his thumb on the hammer. His heart beat. His eye caught movement. Low to the ground. His finger curled against the trigger.

Flick.

Damn if he could tell what it was. Meat, that much he knew. He worked the hammer back.

His thumb slipped on the worn hammer. The hammer fell.

The rifle bucked. Roared.

His ears rang and the sweet biting odor of cordite filled his nostrils.

Nothing moved.

He scrambled down the ridge, his hip aching.

At a blowdown, he looked around. He could see nothing.

Where had it—

He saw.

Beneath the sprawling nest of branches and vines.

A pit.

Like the one from so many years ago.

Was it the same pit?

No, he was too far up in the Gore for it to be. Wasn't he?

Whatever he'd shot was at the bottom of the pit.

His heart drummed as he pushed back the fallen limbs and creeping vines. Thorns clawed at his hands as if to protect what was down there.

He peered into the pit, and reeled backward.

No.

He looked up through the crowns of the trees high above where turkey vultures carved an arc in the sky.

He looked back down.

It was still there.

She was.

Impossibly.

A child.

A girl.

A naked, bloodied, dead girl.

WHAT HAVE I DONE?

What have I done? Jonah thought as he leaned against a tree, panting.

He'd broken the simplest of rules: Never aim a rifle at a target of which you are unsure.

And now this.

This . . . girl.

How could such a young child have found her way up here? And why? *Nothing good drove her here*, a voice said. *Not like this. Naked and torn.*

He looked at the girl, the same size and age as Sally had been when she'd gone missing. Had Sally ended up in the woods somewhere up here, she and her mother? Had they been chased to such a place? Were they still out here, fallen into a pit like this, or into an old mine shaft? Or had they been taken to some faraway place? Were they still being kept somewhere, alive, wondering why they had not been found? Or had their end come swiftly? All his years of searching, even to this day, had led to nothing.

He paced around the edge of the pit.

He'd killed the girl.

Shot her.

What was he going to do? How would he explain why he was even in the woods with a deer rifle when it wasn't deer season for another week?

He knelt at the pit, head pounding as he imagined her parents when they heard what Jonah had done to her, to their lives.

He could not bear it.

He sat against a tree with the rifle, ejected the empty shell, leaving the hammer cocked. A live round ready to fire. He wedged the rifle between his knees, pointed the muzzle at his face, grabbed a stick, and placed it against the trigger.

Closed his eyes.

What was that?

A whimper. Soft and low. A soft cry, of the kind he'd heard long ago, in a different life. In Sally's bedroom, that last night.

He eased the rifle's hammer down, set the rifle aside.

He peered over the edge of the pit.

The girl stirred. Jonah saw now where his bullet had struck a sapling near the lip of the pit. He'd not shot the girl; though knowing this did nothing to allay his shame for firing the rifle.

The girl had been injured some other way. Her left thigh was a knot of raised, bruised flesh, her bare back livid with welts.

His back tensed with the memory of such meanness exacted against the flesh.

Who did such a thing? Too many people. He knew.

Another thought, just as terrible, struck him.

"Hey," he whispered. "Hey."

He had to get her out of the cold and snow, or she surely would die out here.

The girl remained still and soundless, cowered like a tiny forest creature, alert to the predator's presence. Her face was turned to the side, and her hair, cut ragged, as if with a piece of broken glass, draped in her eyes.

"Hey," Jonah said. He'd not been so near a girl since Lucinda had taken him to a pit just like this. Perhaps it was the same pit. He could not be sure.

He lowered himself into the pit, its edge coming to his chest. The girl cowered into the corner.

He touched her shoulder gently with his fingertips. She tensed and hissed at him. Her skin was cold, corpse gray. He needed to get her inside. Now. Or she'd die. She might die anyway, if hypothermia had set in.

"It's okay," he whispered.

The girl coughed, a sound like seeds shaken in a dried gourd. Her rib bones were set in stark relief beneath her blue skin. She rolled over, nakedness revealed fully to him.

He looked away, embarrassed, and stared up to see vultures scribing circles in the sky.

He slung off his coat and covered her.

She wailed and cradled her head with her arms to expose a thatchwork of lacerations on her wrists.

"Okay," he said and moved the jacket to lay it gently on her shoulders.

The girl cried out with pain.

Jonah pulled the jacket collar up round her neck. "Can you get up?"

She stayed put, face hidden in her arms.

"Okay. Here," Jonah said. He slipped his hands under her arms to lift her. She wailed.

He didn't want to hurt her or scare her more than she already was, but he had to get her out of this pit.

Okay.

With his palm, he rubbed gentle circles between her shoulder blades—Sally had liked that—then scooped his hands under her.

She kicked, beat her balled fists at his face. He took the blows, his nose bloodied.

"Easy," he said, then counted three and stood with her. His legs buckled and he bit his tongue against a pain that set his hips on fire. He lifted her up and laid her on the ground outside the pit.

She popped up and, despite her wounds and poor state, started to flee.

With a groan and complaint of joints, he climbed out of the pit and chased after her.

She tripped and fell and he scooped her up and set her down before him, holding her shoulders gently, her face hidden behind her ratty hair.

"Don't run. I'm here to help you," he said. "Understand. You will die out here alone. I'll take you inside. Warm you. Feed you. You run and I can't find you, you'll die. You will die without me."

The girl made no sound or movement, but she did not try to run.

Jonah squatted in front of her. "Climb on my back," he said, trying to keep his voice calm and soft.

He looked back at her, over his shoulder. "Train's leaving. I got warm food at home and a fire and blankets."

She said nothing, still would not look at him.

"Do you *want* to die out here? Is that it?" he snapped. He'd not meant to be so harsh, had meant it as playful, a tone Sally understood as teasing.

Her hair fell to the side as she glared at him.

Those eyes.

He—

The girl was climbing onto his back, hooking her arms about his neck as she held fast.

He rose, unstable; planted his feet wide.

Those eyes.

He took a step.

He knew those eyes.

And another step.

They were Sally's eyes.

Now You See Her

Jonah set the girl on the cabin porch and lay on his back beside her, exhausted, his lungs feeling punched through with holes. He shut his eyes.

When he opened his eyes again, the light had changed. The sky had darkened. He'd slept, as he had done at the kitchen table so many years ago while correcting papers.

He bolted upright, cramped and sore. Cried out. "Sally!"

The girl was gone.

ALL BUT FORGOTTEN

Lucinda sat on the fireplace hearth enrapt by the fire; its heat crawled up the nape of her neck, yet did nothing to warm her. She needed to tell Dale about the letter, which she'd finally dared read just before heading home. Yet she wanted to soak up the news a bit herself first. Soak it up and let it be for her alone for a spell, before the *good* news brought conflict. It would blindside Dale and, as much as he would be pleased for her, it would uproot his life too. She had one week to accept or decline, to discuss it with Dale, even if she already knew her answer. The letter, folded and wedged in her jeans pocket, felt hot against her skin.

Now, instead of telling Dale about it, she said, "I feel awful about Jonah. He was always good to me. I've waffled all day about it, unable to focus. In the end, I feel awful."

"It's Jonah's choice, how Jonah lives," Dale said as he sat at his desk sipping his black coffee. How he could drink coffee in the afternoon and evenings and not be wired all night, Lucinda had no clue. He set his mug down and swung a desk-mounted magnifying glass in front of his peering eye, then, with fastidious precision glued a steering wheel to the aluminum replica car's steering column. The car, according to its box, was a BB Korn Indianapolis 1930s Tether. Whatever that meant. It was smart and sporty, though; one of those old, silver, roofless one-seaters in which drivers wore round goggles like those worn by biplane pilots. The replica was remarkable in detail, composed of hundreds of pieces made of stainless steel, brass, leather, and real rubber tires. Dale had a dozen of the replicas on display in his tiny real estate office in the back of the house.

He turned on a swan-neck light above him, lighting his desk with the brightness of a surgery theater. He was always cautioning Lucinda against her worrying, and she braced for it now. She did not perceive herself as a "worrier." But to Dale, any worrying at all got a person nowhere, achieved nothing. It muddled one's thoughts instead of clarifying them. It wasn't as though he didn't care about Lucinda's anxiety about Jonah. He just didn't understand it. Her.

She wished he cared less and understood more. Caring was like worrying: What good did it do? It didn't lessen pain, dull heartache, or salve grief. In the days after Sally had gone missing, every adult Lucinda had known told her how they cared for Lucinda, loved her, yet it had not comforted her, or brightened her; it had often darkened her. Made her feel more alone. *Understanding*, that was the more important of the two. It was what men missed in the equation, *understanding*. And listening. If they could only manage these two easy concepts. Mr. B., Jonah, he understood. That morning he'd followed her to the pit, helped her out of it, and sat beside her in the snow, he'd cared. Of course. Yet more importantly, he had understood. It had eased Lucinda's heartache, if only in that moment.

Lucinda still wondered on occasion about the man in the woods, who he was and what had become of him. Had he been just a hunter or hiker, or had there been something more nefarious about his presence in the woods? Instead of diluting her memory, the years had intensified Lucinda's clarity and certainty, that what she'd seen were a man's boots, and that the way they had crept through the woods, the owner of them had been looking for Sally and Lucinda, or, at least, Sally.

Sally, a voice said.

"*Christ*," Lucinda said.

Dale looked up from his work. "What?" he said.

That's why Jonah had been so deeply wounded. Today marked twenty-five years to the day of Sally vanishing. With plans of remodeling the store consuming her attention, Lucinda had lost track of the days, the date, until now. Lucinda had shunned Jonah on his very worst of days. Guilt rode her, not just for how she'd treated Jonah, but for forgetting the day. *I'll never ever forget her. Ever.* That's what she'd promised the day she'd taken Jonah to the pit to look for Sally.

"If you'd seen him at the store," Lucinda said, not wanting to broach the anniversary with Dale.

"It's Jonah's choice," Dale said again.

"Still."

"There's no still." Dale scrutinized the mounted steering wheel through the magnifying glass, grumbled. Tweaked the steering wheel.

"Still," Lucinda said again.

Dale smiled. His state of Zen appealed to Lucinda most days, though at times, as now, it grated her. She wished he could just let her be upset. What her friends labeled in Dale as calm and centered, mature, Lucinda saw as impatient with her emotions. He seemed to always counter her with *the other side of the coin*, the positive side. He seemed at times to goad her into being argumentative by trying to bring her back to center when she did not want to be centered. She wanted to feel her anger, or sorrow or guilt, or whatever else she wanted to feel.

"You're not responsible for Jonah," he said.

"He's been through so much. You don't know."

"That was a lifetime ago."

"*His* lifetime. It's still his life. It's in him. In me. As if time has not passed. Sally and I. We were like—"

Dale stood and sat beside her on the hearth, put his arm around her shoulder. She slipped her hand in her pocket and felt the letter with her fingers. "I should just shut up sometimes," Dale said.

She leaned into him. "I feel hard," she said. "I never wanted to be a hard person. It doesn't wear well on me. I need to get up there and find his cabin and apologize." She wondered what had happened to the girl she'd been, the one who'd felt sorry for no longer using a tire swing, or who tried her best not to fib. Here she was in a single day shaming Jonah, faulting Dale for being patient and level, and clutching a letter in her pocket that could change her life, Dale's life, yet she remained mute about it. A lie of omission. A fib.

Lucinda slipped out from under Dale's arm and stood, grabbed a bottle of wine from the mantel and poured wine into a glass.

She wandered to Dale's desk and admired his handiwork. His dedication to this precise work reminded her of her father's birdhouse hobby, too, the hours he'd labored in the basement designing new models for varied species of birds, tinkered and perfected, or tried to perfect. Having something to focus on had been his own balm for whatever regret churned in him after the disappearances, and after her mother's unexpected death not even two years later. She supposed now her father's failing health had one silver lining: he was too busy dying to worry anymore about a case that had ruined his dearest friendship and had haunted him all these years as the case he failed to solve. If Lucinda were honest, her father had been slowly dying ever since it had become clear he'd never arrest anyone for the crime and had not done enough to clear his friend's name and end the suspicion Jonah endured to this day and, it seemed, would follow him to his death, perhaps beyond.

The meticulous care and steadfast patience it took to piece together the replica of the car was not unlike what it took to reconstruct artifacts, or a skeleton from an excavation site, Lucinda imagined. Except with artifacts and bones there was no picture on a box and no diagram to guide you on how the pieces fit and what the object or skeleton looked like. And you would almost never have all the pieces, the work would almost always remain unfinished.

Lucinda sat on the couch with a sigh.

Dale sat beside her.

"It'll be all right," he said.

"You always think everything's going to be all right."

"Isn't it?"

"No."

"Why not?" He put his hand on her shoulder.

"The world doesn't work that way. "

"Who says?"

Sally says, Lucinda thought and remembered being outside Sally's bedroom door the night Sally had disappeared, thinking, *swearing*, Sally had made a noise behind the door just before Lucinda had opened it, only to find Sally was not there.

"Why so quiet?" Dale said. "What'd I say?"

"It's not you." *It's the date, and Jonah, and the demands of the store, and the letter*, she thought. The letter. Dale was right; perhaps some things did work out. Just not everything. Or the ones you wished for most.

She downed her wine, her mind troubled, emotions flayed. The letter seared the flesh of her thigh from inside her pocket, branded her.

"I think I'll hit it."

"It's early."

"I'm sapped," Lucinda said, exhausted from the afternoon, yet knowing she'd not sleep all night.

WHAT'S WRONG WITH YOU?

Where had the girl gone?

How had she slipped away so fast? How long had he dozed? Darkness had claimed the woods.

The old fear crackled down Jonah's spine.

Jonah stepped to the edge of the porch. "Hey," he said, his voice projecting but calm. He did not dare scare the child. "It's cold and dark out here. It's warm and light inside. I'm harmless. I swear."

He could not blame the girl for hiding, but she'd never survive the night in the cold woods.

He had to cajole her out from wherever she hid.

Jonah squinted, but the woods were lost to an endless blackness as dark as the eyes of the girl herself.

He turned back for the door to go inside and grab a flashlight.

There. Through the window, he saw her. She lay asleep on his sunken, moldered couch, curled on herself like an infant whose muscle memory is still informed by the womb. So still she might have been—

No, he thought. He hurried inside and took a wool blanket from a chair; a funk of mildew and body odor stirred into the air. Dust motes cycloned.

He stared at the girl, to make certain she was not some imagining of his dotage. Her pale temples pulsed with life.

She was there. Real. But too still. Too quiet.

The backs of her hands were gouged from thorns and caked with dried, black blood, her lank body pale and knobbed. He had to get her warm.

He slipped a pair of his old socks onto her cold feet, pulled them up to her knees, covered her nakedness with the blanket and watched her chest rise and fall in her sleep. He laid a palm on her forehead. It felt hot.

She needed clothes.

He gazed at the door to the back room of the cabin. He had not been back there in twenty-five years.

He went to the door, opened it.

The wooden trunk sat at the center of the otherwise empty room. He stared at it but could not bring himself to move farther into the room, closer to the trunk.

He shut the door. Joints stiff, he walked back to the couch herk-a-jerk, like an old-time wire piano man, and sat and watched her in the ring of light cast by the flashlight.

Her eyes. What did all this mean, to find her where he had, in a pit. On this day.

A voice said: *You were sent to me.*

Then: *Ludicrous.*

Yet the thought persisted, as clear as spring water.

She'd have died in the night if he hadn't found her. The coyotes and crows would have claimed her. There was no one else up here in these woods who could have found her, and the woods and mountains up here went on for miles, tens of thousands of square acres. Yet he'd been the one to find her. No one else. He alone.

The hunters would soon come, the loggers after that. Searchers. Someone had to be missing the girl, someone had to be searching for her. He and the girl were not safe here. She was his to protect now.

We need to get away, he thought.

Stop, the voice urged. *She's not yours.*

His fleeing with the girl was a cruel, insane thought. He knew the girl's parents were at that moment in anguish, from the torture of unknowing. *Why didn't you bring her to town straightaway?* the voice prodded. *Why did you keep her?*

I didn't keep *her. She needs warming up. I brought her here to save her.*

You kept her for yourself. What kind of man keeps a girl? What's wrong with you?

Nothing was wrong with him. The girl was on the edge of death, needed warmth to keep her from going hypothermic. And now it was dark. She, and he, needed to rest, to sleep and eat and gain their strength. He'd return her in the morning and gift her parents the relief he'd never known. What harm would a night make, what difference?

He knew when he returned her in the morning the authorities would prod and slice him with questions. They'd ask how he of all people had come across this girl, so close in age and size and appearance to his daughter that . . . *Identical,* the voice said.

The police would ask:

Why did you keep her overnight?

Why is she naked?

How did she come to get those wounds?

He'd tell the truth: he'd found her that way, naked and despoiled, and had needed to get her to his warm cabin straightaway. They'd want to know why he'd not brought her to town after she was warm and out of danger. He'd tell them it was dark by then, and he didn't dare navigate the woods in the dark.

Why not? You know the woods as well in the dark as the day. Couldn't you make your way to the truck with a flashlight?

He'd tell them his vision wasn't what it once was and it was easy to get off the trail at night. A grave risk with the talcum mines. He hadn't wanted to take that risk with her.

Still, they'd press. And each of his answers would bring more questions, be sensationalized and dissected.

Perhaps, even if she would not speak to Jonah, she'd tell the authorities what had happened. Corroborate Jonah. Perhaps not. She'd not said a word. She was traumatized and frightened. She might confuse events. A strange old man in the woods. With a gun.

It mattered none.

Jonah would suffer the questions for the sake of the girl, though it wasn't true that he worried about the mines in the dark. He knew where each mine was located, dark maws open to depths nearly bottomless. He'd tell the authorities his only thought was to get her warm and keep her safe. This answer would not sate them. No answers would ever sate them. To the law, the only correct action was to have taken her at once to the sheriff. And what would they have said then, when he'd brought her in beaten and naked?

He'd been doomed to this fate since he'd found the girl.

Naked.

He would have to get the girl dressed come morning. He did not dare try to do it now. He did not dare to touch the girl; but come morning he'd look in the trunk to see if the yellow dress and coat he'd bought lifetimes ago still existed, or if time had returned them to dust.

WARNED

"Gretel! Where you at? I find you. You'll be sorry. I swear, you will this time."

Arlene Driscoll stared at the empty closet with the blinking eyes of a toad. The girl wasn't there. Arlene slammed the door, wincing against the stink of soiled panties heaped in the corner. These kids, this one in particular, weren't worth the meager pay the state offered to house 'em, just weren't worth the trouble.

The girl was in first grade and she still couldn't control her bowels. Well, she could clean her own panties or go without, maybe then she'd learn, if she had to clean them herself and smell it. Rubbing her nose in her mess sure hadn't done nothing so far.

Arlene stomped down the hall, beer slopping from the plastic cup she gripped in her hand.

"Look now what you made me do! Spilled on my good jeans. You're making me miss my show!" Arlene licked at the beer suds on her wrist. The girl was maddening. She acted like a baby. Hiding. Moping. Whining. She was way too old for this crap.

I'm too old for it, Arlene thought as she stormed to the front room and watched her TV show and chugged what was left of her beer.

"Three hundred fifty!" she shrieked at the TV. "You're all over-bidding, you buncha jackasses. That recliner ain't worth a dime over three hundred bucks."

The show host exulted, "You all overbid!"

Jackasses. Arlene blinked hard as if she'd just snapped awake. "You better hope I *don't* find you," she shouted at the girl she could not find.

She looked behind the chair where the girl sometimes hid herself, even though she'd looked there twice already and the girl wasn't there now anymore than she'd been there the first two times. Arlene swung open the door to the cellar and yelled down, "If you're down there you better come up. I'm not going down there this time. Come up or I'm going to close this door and lock it and you can just stay down there all night. Maybe learn something this time. How'd that be? I mean it. I'm gonna give you to three.

"One.

"I'm not playing.

"Two.

"All right then.

"Three!

"Don't cry say you wasn't warned, because you was."

Arlene slammed the door so hard the casing split. She threw the deadbolt and poured herself another beer, slumping on the couch to watch the tube.

She shuddered at the thought that the girl had run off. If the girl had run off, Arlene would face far worse from Lewis than that brat had ever faced.

The game show host shouted: "You all overbid!"

"Jackasses!" Arlene shouted.

Each and every one. Jackasses.

What was wrong with people?

Over the Rainbow

"She's gone," Arlene said to her husband, bracing herself to be struck. "I told you I looked everywhere."

"How in the hell did you lose track of a girl?" Lewis said. "What were you doing that you could do that?"

"Nothing. Watching my game shows."

"That's not nothing. That's something."

"It's not my fault. One second she was here, the next second she wasn't."

He clenched his fists, face red and gnarled. "Lucky for you, I ain't got time to straighten your ass. We gotta find her. They find out, they'll take her. We'll have to look 'round the woods in the dark somehow."

"What about calling the sheriff to get a dog here?"

"You *are* as dumb as you look."

Arlene winced. How had she ended up joined to a man just like her daddy, after all those girl years she'd spent crying in her bedroom hating her daddy and swearing over and over and over, *promising herself*: Never. Never ever ever ever. Now. Here she was.

And the girl. She'd run off just like Arlene had always wanted to run off. Smart girl. Brave girl. Give the girl that. She was smart. And brave. Smarter and braver than Arlene ever was. Arlene, who knew she herself could be as mean as a pit bull and as ugly as a rat with her ugly mean thoughts, shutting the door to the cellar on the poor girl when Arlene thought she was down there, just so Arlene could watch her game show in peace and *teach* the girl something. Teach her what? Teach her how to be mean as a pit bull and ugly as a rat? Arlene had wanted to stop herself from slamming and locking the cellar door, but she couldn't; the mean part of her was too strong and it bullied the good part of her from acting the way Arlene knew in her heart she should act, the way God expected her to act. Just like it always did.

Many times in the past weeks she'd wanted, truth be told, to go down in the cellar and grab the girl and take off with her. Use the girl's bravery for her own. Escape. Leave and never come back. But she'd been too scared. Of Lewis. And . . . And what? Scared she didn't know what to do next. Where would she go? What would she do? She had no money. She had no one to turn to. No other family. No family at all. A mean man and a girl who wasn't even her own blood, lucky for the girl.

And now that the girl was gone, Arlene hoped the girl'd get away for good. Arlene rooted for her. And if the girl did come back, if they found her, Arlene would never treat her so bad again. Never yell. Never hit. Never put her to bed hungry. Never lock her in rooms. In the cellar. Never let Lewis get after her again. Never. Never ever ever. She promised herself then and there, promised over and over again.

"What're you mumbling on about over there? You even listening to me?" Lewis barked.

Arlene blinked.

"No sheriff," Lewis said. The spittle on his chin made him look like a retarded dog, Arlene decided. A dog someone ought to shoot and put out of its own damned misery, or at least to spare others from its bite. Same look as her daddy always wore. And now she wished she'd run away. Oh Lord she wished. Her whole life was one long unfulfilled wish for running away to another life. Any other life. Some long-lost distant life and dream, over the rainbow.

Lewis slapped her face. "Earth to Arlene. No sheriff till we look and got a story if we don't come up with her quick."

"It's so cold already," Arlene said. "Poor thing. If we get the sheriff here and—"

"*Poor* thing. She'll manage. Poor *us*."

Lewis hoofed it to the edge of the overgrown yard. "Where you at?! Come on out. We ain't mad," hollered Lewis, who was always mad.

Arlene decided then that if she found the girl, she'd hide her. And if she didn't find the girl . . . Well, she didn't know. But she felt she might curl in a ball and die for all the wrongdoing she'd done the girl. And she needed to right it. If she could. *Lord, give me the chance*, she thought, *and if we don't find her, I'll take a willow branch and lash myself bloody for you, and the girl.*

Lewis stepped into the woods where the night shadows were long and deep. "You'll eat your supper cold."

Arlene sneaked in behind Lewis. *I could take an axe*, she thought, *and strike him in the back of the head and he'd never know. It'd be done.*

Lewis pushed deeper into the dark woods.

A branch whipped back and gashed Arlene's face.

She shrieked.

"Lucky that's all you get," Lewis said.

Trees. Nothing but dark trees. And rocks. "We ain't going to find her in this," Arlene said. "Not if she don't want to be found. We need to get help for her sake—"

"I'll go see Aulden 'bout his dog. He's killed a few bear behind that dog," Lewis said.

"I'll call him," Arlene said.

"Leave me to it. You fucked up plenty already," Lewis said and knocked her to the ground as he shoved past.

Arlene lay on the cold ground, not getting up.

Not daring.

ASLEEP OR AWAKE

Jonah started awake in his chair. The cabin was so dark and cold he felt at first he was still a boy exiled to the back shed for peeing his bed. More and more he thought of those days: boyhood without a childhood. Here, in the dark, he might have been anyone, of any age, in any time. He might have been an animal. Or a bird. Or dead.

He felt his face.

No animal.

No bird.

Not dead.

Not yet.

He was relieved to no longer be that boy, but dismayed to still be the man whose first thought upon waking, as it had been for twenty-five years, was: *Where are my wife and child?*

Where's the girl? a voice said.

The *girl*.

He'd forgotten her. He had dozed again, without realizing it. It seemed he could not remain awake.

He did not remember where he'd set the flashlight. His entire body ached, a dull humming throb of pain. He swam his hands in the dark, mole blind, navigated to where the lantern sat, its metal cold as the devil, his old, cold fingers hard-pressed to work its pump. He got a wooden match and struck it, gravedigger's breath in the match glow. He worked the pump. The mantle pulsed with greenish light, *whooped* into a bright glowing orb.

He cupped his hands around the warm glass.

Better.

The girl. Where was she?

He wondered if he had dreamed her. No. He could hear her mumble in the dark beyond the lantern light's arc.

He carried the lantern over. There. There she was.

Good.

Good.

She lay on the couch. The blanket had slid down off her; he pulled it up to her chin, then stoked the fire in the woodstove.

Fire lit, he gently rubbed the girl's feet, cold even in his socks.

With her feet warmed and the woodstove heating the cabin, he killed the lantern and sat again in the dark, preparing in his mind to return her home.

The darkness and his exhaustion were so complete as the woodstove's heat washed over him that he did not know if he was awake or asleep. Alive or dead.

Find Her

You *lost* her?" Aulden said.

"*She* lost her," said Lewis, glaring at Arlene.

They stood at the yard edge in the dark and cold.

"Hadn't you better call the police?" Aulden said.

"Asshole sheriff'd probably just call you for your dog."

Aulden's redbone, Ms. Rose, whined at Aulden's feet.

"I don't know about this," Aulden said.

"*I* know. I'll pay you."

"With what? Dirt?"

"What you want?"

"Don't want anything."

"Bullshit. We all want something. Name it."

"Help building a new ice fishing shanty. A six-holer."

"I can swing that."

"You pay for the wood."

"*Wood and labor?*"

The screen door swung open.

The two men looked up.

Arlene stood in the doorway, Coke bottle held by a pinkie finger shoved down the neck. No more beer. Never ever ever.

The girl's likely froze to death, Arlene thought, and Lewis's acting the ass. She finished her Coke and tossed the bottle into the woods.

"Wood and labor," Aulden said.

"Christ. Fine."

"You got anything with her scent on it?" Aulden said.

Lewis yanked something from his pocket, slapped it in Aulden's hand.

"Got anything else?" Aulden said.

"It doesn't get any more scent than that."

Aulden put the soiled panties to Ms. Rose's nose. "Find her." His nose wrinkled at the foulness of it all.

Vanished

Flashlight beams bobbed in the darkness, and tree branches jumped out at Lewis and Aulden as they searched, and Ms. Rose bayed.

Down ravines and across creeks, the two men scrambled, their breathing emphysemic as Ms. Rose was drawn on by a scent their human noses had long forgotten how to detect.

Lewis stopped. "Mutt's nose better not be twisted."

"Rose is less a mutt than you. She's got papers."

"How'd that girl'd get this far. What in hell got into her?" Lewis spouted.

"I wonder."

Lewis slipped the tip of his tongue through the spaces where he ought to have had teeth but didn't. "She's run farther than a coon."

Up ahead, Ms. Rose fell quiet.

"Let's go!" Lewis bellowed.

They trudged on, the cold night air metallic with coming snow.

The woods as dark as the other side of the moon save for the flashlight beams cutting swaths ahead.

They followed behind the light, as if the light knew where they were headed.

"Where's that mutt? Call her!" Lewis squawked.

"Ms. Rose!" Aulden called.

Lewis crouched, flashlight tilted under his chin to cast his face into a ghoul's mask. He picked up a twig and snapped it as if to trip a switch in his brain that would allow him to reason out a plan. No plan came. No reason, either.

Ms. Rose bawled in the distance.

They came upon Ms. Rose, each man sweating like a spooked horse. Ms. Rose paced, burrowing her nose into the leaves as if she were a truffle pig.

"Where is she?" Aulden said.

"Find her, damn you," Lewis said.

"Don't curse my dog."

"Hand me them panties."

Aulden handed them to Lewis, who pushed them into Ms. Rose's snout. "Find her!"

Ms. Rose wagged her tail.

"Useless bitch!" Lewis said.

"Keep it up, I'll knock out the rest of your teeth," Aulden said.

"Well, how in hell can she have her scent then not have her scent?"

"Wait." Aulden walked away, circling ever wider around Lewis, Ms. Rose in step. He swung his flashlight beam. Rocks and stumps jumped out from the darkness and were eaten again by it. Ms. Rose fell into a lazy walk beside him until they came back to where Lewis stood.

"It's like the poor thing just vanished," Aulden said.

"Poor thing?" Lewis said. "What about me? We don't find her we lose four hundred a month." He swept his flashlight round, frantic, but it did not make the girl appear.

Preparing

D awn came. Brittle.

A patter on the tin roof like that of dancing mice. Sleet.

The girl squatted like a bush child on the corner of the couch, eyes locked on Jonah's.

Those eyes. Sally's eyes. He felt as if his heart would give out from looking at them, and from the pain he'd be unable to endure if he had to give up a sight he'd lived to see again for the past twenty-five years.

Drive her to town. Now. To the authorities and her family, the voice said. *Bring her back. Right now.*

No. He had to wash her first. Feed and clothe her. She was not an animal, some stray dog he'd found in the woods.

Her hunger and hygiene and nakedness be damned. Take her back now; wrap her in the blanket and take her back before it's too late.

He looked at the girl gnawing the ends of her stringy hair as if trying to eat it. Her grimed, abused body. Hair caked with mud. No. He needed to tend to her first.

Liar.

And it was a lie. He did not need to, he *wanted* to care for her, consequences be damned. He did not want to give her up.

He wanted to keep her.

"You need to eat," he said and seared salt pork in the cast-iron pan atop the woodstove.

Her eyes tracked him.

He brought the pork to her on waxed paper.

She sniffed, curled her lip.

He picked up a piece.

Took a bite.

"Mmmm," he said. "Mmmm."

A phantom smile haunted her face. But the girl would not eat. Her dark eyes slayed him with emotion he'd not known in ages. He wanted to hug her, pull her tight to him and comfort her. Protect her.

The voice said, *Careful. She's not yours. Get her home.*

Her eyes seemed to examine each crevice of his weathered face, a look in them and a tilt to her head as though she were trying to conjure a memory.

He slid the pork toward her.

"Eat."

She picked up a piece, nibbled it.

"There. See. Good." He felt the long-dormant rush of parental pride.

She spat out the pork.

Sally didn't like salt pork, either; she picked the smallest speck of it out of her baked beans.

"Not the best meal," Jonah said. "Let's get washed."

The girl eyed him, mud-streaked face quizzical. Her hands crusted with dirt.

Outside, he filled a tin bucket of water at the spring, then brought it inside and warmed it on the woodstove, soaped up a ratty towel.

Sally loved to be bathed, even as an infant in that cheap little plastic tub Rebecca had received as a shower gift. When Rebecca squeezed water from a sponge onto Sally's tummy, Sally had drummed her heels and pumped her fists, wriggled and gabbled, dark eyes gleeful, her face breaking into that wondrous toothless smile. "She's babying out!" Rebecca would exclaim. "Our water baby!"

The girl scratched at her scalp. Jonah parted her hair with his fingers. Lice teemed, and red, raw sores polluted her pale scalp.

Jonah wiped at her face with the corner of the towel. A faint smile again passed on her face.

"Warm. Nice," Jonah said. He placed the warm towel on the back of her hand. "We need to get you all nice and cleaned before we take you home."

She shook her head with violence, as if to break her neck.

"Nice. Warm. Clean," Jonah said. "Mommy and Daddy will say what a good girl you are."

She shook her head again.

He handed her the towel. "You're right, you can do it. You're a big girl."

She rubbed the towel all over her face, water running into her lap.

"Behind the ears. We don't want potatoes growing back there," Jonah said.

Her ephemeral smile glimmered. Paled.

"The neck," he said. "Good. An old pro. I'll leave you be." He went out to the porch.

The cold mountain air was bracing, yet the sunshine filtering through a break in the clouds caressed his cheek with its warmth.

He closed his eyes and turned his face to the sun. Its heat drummed lightly on his eyelids. How unfathomable that the sun's heat reached across ninety-three million miles to warm his face. Ninety-three million miles. How mystifying its life-giving heat. How impossible its very existence. How mad. How miraculous.

He listened to a raven's clotted call. Listened to the melting snow drip on the wood steps. Breathed in the biting scent of spruce and hemlock. How was it people believed in heaven? What place could be more wondrous than here? For the first time in decades, he sensed wonder, felt a compulsion to translate what he felt into words. To write a poem.

A voice said: *If the sun's light and heat can reach across ninety-three million miles in eight minutes to warm your face, why can't your daughter return to you from across twenty-five years? To be made flesh again.*

He jolted as if he'd touched a live wire.

The voice was madness.

Yet the impossible and miraculous sunlight continued to reach across the universe to warm his face and light the earth, grant the world life.

He coughed, hacked up phlegm.

Red blood stained the white snow.

From far below in the beeches, the calamitous din of a revving engine rose.

An ATV.

Jonah froze.

Listened. The ATV was down in the beeches. Where he'd found the girl.

Were they coming to search up here already?

I told you to take her to town straightaway, the voice said. *They'll never believe you were going to bring her back if they find you up here with her.*

Panicked, he hurried inside.

The bucket was knocked over and the girl stood in a puddle of soapy water, sucking on the corner of the soaked towel.

The sound of the engine rose outside.

Jonah grabbed his rifle from the corner. Cocked the hammer.

The sound of the ATV died.

Whoever was driving the ATV would have to hoof it from there. It was no more than a half-hour hike, if one knew of the skein of a trail leading to the cabin.

"Stay here," Jonah said to the girl.

She frowned.

"Stay," Jonah said. "I'll be right back."

Her eyes shimmered, wet.

"Please," he said.

Outside, Jonah sat in his old chair, rifle on his lap, and waited.

The sun was gone behind the clouds now.

Snow was falling.

The skin on his arms prickled.

The engine did not start again.

Whoever had driven up was still out there, somewhere.

He clutched the rifle tighter in his cold hands.

Sally

Jonah jarred awake, mind cobwebbed with memories and dreams. A pale ghost stood beside him, a slight luminescent hobgoblin with dark lost eyes.

Jonah's mind ached as it lingered in the netherworld and he saw himself sitting at the edge of the pit with Lucinda, his arm around her, holding her as she sobbed; her father charging from behind to knock Jonah to the ground, beating on him as if he believed Jonah meant Lucinda harm. Then the image was gone. No, not gone. There, yet invisible, dust in a bar of sunshine vanishing with the drawing of the window shade.

A ghost hovered at his periphery.

Not a ghost. An angel.

The girl.

How had he gotten out here on the porch? He didn't remember. Couldn't remember. The ATV. He'd come out to stand guard, protect her. And he'd dozed. Failed her. Why could he not stay awake?

The girl sucked on the corner of the towel he'd given her and nodded at his feet. The rifle had fallen from his lap, with its hammer cocked. It could have gone off. Killed him. Killed her. Could still go off if not lifted carefully.

He eyed the rifle.

She reached for the rifle to help. Her small hand clutching at it. Near the hammer.

"No," he said.

She reached for it.

"No," he shouted. "Leave it, damn it."

She cried out and covered her head with her arms.

"I'm sorry," Jonah said. "Sorry. It's dangerous." He tried to bring calm to his voice. If she'd picked up the rifle before waking him . . .

She sniffled, curled away from him, face hidden.

"It's okay. You're not in trouble. Daddy's not mad. Okay. Just. Don't touch. I'll get it, go on in."

She sucked on the corner of the towel.

He grabbed the rifle, swung the muzzle away from her, eased down the hammer.

What do you think you're doing? the voice said.

"Who are you?" Jonah said. "Tell me your name."

The girl looked at her hands.

"You must have a name," he said. "We all have names."

She sucked on the towel. Why would she not tell him?

"You must have a name. Pretty one, I bet," he said.

She stared at him unblinking.

"I have to call you something. I can't just call you 'girl.' That's silly, right?" Jonah said. "If you won't tell me your name, we'll have to pick one. Yes?"

Her dark eyes seemed to take in the question but revealed no answer as she remained voiceless.

"We'll have to give it thought," Jonah said. "I had a daughter once, Sally. A long time ago. When I was someone else. She looked so much like you, it's scary."

TROUBLE

Lucinda stood on a ladder taking the measurement of a shelf above the hot dog table when the cowbell above the Grain & Feed's door clanked.

She turned and saw them: trouble from the hills.

She watched them.

They demanded watching, those two.

Ed, sitting on a stool behind the register, saw them, too, and stood.

But Arlene and Lewis did not go about their usual meandering with eyes glancing at the fish-eye mirrors, shifty hands going to and from their pockets, the way Lucinda's father had warned her in regard to shoplifters when she was a girl.

Instead, they marched to Lucinda's ladder.

Lewis looked up, drank in a good full look of Lucinda's belly where her sweater had ridden up. Lucinda tugged the sweater down and stepped off the ladder to address the couple. Lewis was a short, wiry, grotesque little man with the sallow, jaundiced skin of a lifetime chain smoker. Arlene was scrawnier than he was, yet not frail. Hard. Bone hard.

"My girl," Arlene blurted to Lucinda. "She's gone missing. You gotta help us, Deputy." Arlene gulped down a deep breath, her eyes bright with fear.

Girl. Missing. Lucinda felt her own breath catch.

"Our girl," Lewis corrected. "*Our* girl."

"You gotta find her. That's your job, you gotta. Someone's took her," Arlene said, her breathing sharp now, a pant.

"Slow down," Lucinda said.

"They took her," Arlene said.

"And you better goddamn well find her, you're the deputy, after all," Lewis insisted, but his voice seemed glassy and practiced to Lucinda's ear, bereft of empathy.

Ed wandered out from behind the counter.

"Slow down. There must be a reasonable explanation," Lucinda said, though there did not need to be a *reasonable* explanation for a young girl to go missing. She knew too well.

"You're deputy. Do something," Lewis snorted.

Deputy. It was true. Lucinda *was* deputy. Part-time deputy. Not even part-time. And that only because her father had been sheriff, and the town had elected her as a write-in candidate for deputy believing she'd wanted the position. Which she had, on the level of her believing everyone had an obligation to perform a civic duty. But she didn't handle crimes, let alone serious ones, what few instances that there were in Ivers. She handled loose dog cases. Breaking up parties of underage drinkers at the lake. Collecting roadside donations for the fire department on the Fourth of July. Not this. She had no experience with missing persons. No professional experience. Still, she squared her shoulders, alert now to the magnitude of the situation, to the knowledge that this moment would not come again. She had to memorize everything that was said. Had to record it in her mind and had to say the correct words and make the correct decisions.

"They took her through the window like they do on the TV. You're the deputy. I been calling your boyfriend sheriff, and he ain't nowhere to be found like usual." Lewis grunted like he'd been gut punched.

"He's not her boyfriend," Ed said.

They all looked at Ed, who added, "Not anymore."

Lucinda took out her cell phone and brought up the app for recording.

"What're you doing with that thing?" Lewis said, his hot breath foul, the stench of an old damp sock.

"Recording us," Lucinda said.

"What in hell for?" Lewis said.

"For the record."

"What record?"

Lucinda did not know if Lewis was demonstrating his habitual, genetic belligerence or was being defensive for a reason. She pressed the red record button on her screen.

"The *official* record," she said. "Now. How do you know someone took her?" Her voice was clipped. Official. Assured. Her dad's sheriff's voice. It came to her instinctively as she tapped into all the years she'd witnessed her father's tactics and command. Confidence, or the appearance of it, was essential.

"She's not in her goddamned room is how. She ain't anywheres," Lewis said. "So. What else coulda happened?"

Lucinda could think of many things, the things she'd tried never to think of in regard to Sally. Cruel, debasing things. *Everything will be fine*, she told herself. *This girl will be found safe. She has to be. This cannot happen again. It will not.*

"Have you looked for her?" Lucinda said.

"Are we retarded?" Lewis said. "We looked. Everywheres. She's nowheres."

"Could she have wandered off maybe, when you weren't—" Lucinda paused. She needed to select her words with judicious precision. Arlene's angst appeared genuine. Her nervousness, too; she kept cutting her eyes toward Lewis. Lucinda continued, "Could the girl have slipped away when you were maybe too busy with something else and maybe lost track of time?"

"I guess," Arlene said.

"Could she have run off?" Lucinda looked at Arlene and ignored Lewis to test his reaction.

"Now why in fuck would she do that?" Lewis said.

"We put her down last night," Arlene said, her voice flat. Rote. "She was there, then this morning she ain't."

"I'm a glorified crossing guard," Lucinda said, wanting them to underestimate her interest. They seemed circumspect, and this behavior did not sit well with her. She did not trust this couple to come into her store and leave it without trying to steal, and she certainly didn't trust them with this story. "I'll call dispatch to get the sheriff to meet us, but let's the three of us head up there now. We can't spare a second in this cold if we're going to find your daughter."

"Alive?" Arlene said.

At all, Lucinda thought as she went behind the counter and unlocked the safe, removed from it her holstered 9 mm and her badge.

She buckled the holster around her waist and tucked her badge in the pocket of her EMS parka she shucked on and zipped.

"You really need that?" Arlene said, eyeing the sidearm.

"We'll see," Lucinda said.

THE WINDOW

Lucinda shifted her Wrangler into four-wheel drive as she turned the Jeep up Dead Crow Hill; the bare trees bordering the road stood dark and skeletal against the white, virgin snow. Ahead of her, Lewis's Cobalt whipsawed on the muddied road, rooster tails of slop geysering out behind it to splatter the Wrangler's windshield.

Lucinda turned on the wipers and windshield fluid as she wondered if Lewis was sending muck onto her Wrangler on purpose. How he lived up here through the winter with a two-wheel-drive car, Lucinda did not know. She snowshoed up this way often. The road came to a dead end another mile past Arlene and Lewis's place. Beyond that, ancient logging roads served as ski and snowshoe trails when the snow fell. She'd tried her hand at cross-country skiing, but she fell too often and disliked having to trounce uphill with awkward skis splayed in a herringbone fashion that made her feel like a waddling goose. Yet she liked when the skin of her cheeks tingled from the bite and brace of cold fresh air; she liked the bright blue clarity of the sky on a clear, sunny morning following a fresh snowfall. She liked the silence of the woods broken by the sharp crack of branches. She liked when she jumped a hare from where it hid beneath a young spruce to erupt in a squall of snow. So she'd traded skis for snowshoes. The rhythm of legs and arms and poles, in time with her breathing, calmed her. It beat running, which had always pounded her joints and ankles and given her shin splints. And it did not feel like *exercise* of the kind girlfriends endured, indoors, on a *machine*, or on a mat. She disliked contortions. She wanted steady forward, fluid movement, through the woods, in the fresh air, through space and time. She longed now for just such an afternoon in the woods to clear her chaotic mind.

She'd be having none of that today.

She pulled the Wrangler into a yard behind Lewis and got out in front of a double-wide stripped of its siding, particleboard exposed beneath loose flaps of black Tyvek paper that snapped in a gust of wind like fantastic bat wings. The fresh snow in the yard was as smooth as cake icing; not so much as a mouse track marred it, though here and there slats of the vinyl siding jutted up from under the snow.

Lucinda wiped at her dripping nose with the back of her hand. The cold morning air needled her face. Branches clattered in the wind as snow filtered down through the trees in silence. Arlene shuffled near Lucinda, arms wrapped around herself, her jacket too thin for the cold. Lucinda was struck with a sudden pang of sympathy for Arlene. The woman who, until now, Lucinda had frankly dismissed as *trouble from the hills* appeared genuinely distraught and, Lucinda saw as Arlene gnawed her bottom lip and stole nervous glances at her husband, afraid too. Lucinda had an urge to put an arm around Arlene and console her and tell her all would be okay. Except Lucinda could not do that. She was here to investigate a possible crime. A serious crime. Not here as a citizen or a neighbor. And, until cleared, Arlene and Lewis were suspects, just as Jonah had once been a suspect, was *still* a suspect to many people in town.

Twenty-five years to the day, Lucinda thought, and a girl goes missing. Lucinda wondered if the girl, like Sally, had disappeared for good. Had she been taken, or run off, or had Lewis and Arlene done something and were trying to cover up their crime by calling Lucinda out here? Lucinda did not know which scenario most benefited the girl. A child alone in the woods in this cold, overnight, would come to a slow, grim end. Lucinda shoved the thought from her mind. The missing girl deserved Lucinda's resolve and focus. Lucinda needed to be attuned, see with clear eyes and think with a sharp mind, listen with attentiveness and suspicion. She knew from her father's experience with Sally and Mrs. B. the toll such cases exacted from the parties involved. She had one aspect going for her in a way her father had not: she knew to brace herself for the possibility of this case not going well, the girl never being found, even as she told herself, *You will find this girl. You must find her. Alive.*

"I thought you said you looked everywhere for her," Lucinda said, looking Lewis straight in the eye.

He glanced at Arlene. "We did."

"There's no tracks in the snow."

Lewis licked his mustache. "I meant everywhere *inside*, not everywhere in the world. And, yeah, there ain't no tracks, so that means she was took before the snow flew, or during it."

Could be, Lucinda thought. *Or not.*

"We yelled a bunch for her, but never heard nothing," Arlene said.

"Which window is hers?" Lucinda said.

Lewis pointed. "That one there."

Lucinda took out her cell phone. One bar. She dialed Kirk's work cell. She'd deleted his home and personal cell numbers long ago, though they were still etched in her memory. She'd called dispatch twice to try to get word to him, to no avail. When his voice mail picked up, Lucinda said, "It's Lucinda. Same message as earlier. Wherever you are. Get to Lewis and Arlene Driscoll's place on Dead Crow Hill, as soon as you get this. We got a missing child." She wondered if she should call in the state police. She thought about it. But it'd take a half hour at least for them to get up here, if a cruiser was even in the region. No. She'd take a look first. Time was paramount.

"Stay put," she said to Lewis.

"It's my house," Lewis protested.

"Stay," she said again.

"What am I, a dog?" Lewis said.

"Come with me, please," Lucinda said to Arlene.

The double-wide stank of cigarette smoke and of rancid milk. The stench of lives unkempt.

Magazines—*Entertainment Weekly, People, Us, Guns & Ammo, Survivalist*—lay scattered among a litter of soda cans and potato chip bags and cigarette butts snubbed out in pie plates and coffee mugs.

The mounted head of a bobcat stared down from the paneled walls, the taxidermy work so tragic the animal's bared teeth looked pathetic and comical instead of fierce.

A flat-screen TV the size of a garage door overwhelmed the room from the wall opposite.

"Where's her room?" Lucinda said.

Arlene rubbed her snubbed nose with the palm of her hand then jabbed her chin toward the narrow hallway. "Last on the left."

"Stay here, please," Lucinda said.

Lucinda crept down the hall as her skin pricked with an appreciable drop in air temperature. A cold draft. A breeze. She stood in the bedroom doorway. One dirty twin mattress draped by a dirtier gray blanket atop it lay askew on the floor. Clothes heaped and scattered. Not a toy in sight. Not a pillow. Self-disgust quivered through Lucinda as she remembered the legion of stuffed animals and dolls she and Sally had owned as girls, and how both she and Sally had constantly teased for more. They'd acted so deprived and neglected. Normal girls part of decent working-class families, having no perspective of or respect for the luxuries of ordinary life, of real poverty. A sour reek rose in Lucinda's nose. The window was cracked open, a skim of snow drifted on its sill. Water puddled on the floor.

Arlene stepped behind Lucinda. "You can't be here," Lucinda said. "Go back to the living room."

"That there's the window she was took from," Arlene said.

Lucinda stepped into the room.

Arlene made to follow.

"You need to stay out," Lucinda said. "This is a crime scene." If Kirk didn't show in the next five minutes, she'd call the state police. Perhaps she should have called them straightaway. Perhaps she'd made a mistake. This was not in her purview. She'd never handled anything close to this professionally, and her mind kept tripping back to memories of Sally's empty bedroom the night of her disappearance. She closed her eyes to clear her thoughts, opened them, focused again on the present. She stepped to the open window. Arlene remained in the doorway. "Have you touched anything, the window or sill?" she whispered over her shoulder, not sure why she was whispering.

"No," Arlene said, her voice meek.

"Was it like this when you found it?"

"Damn right," Lewis's voice said. Lucinda turned as Lewis stepped into the room, his chin thrust out and chest puffed up, as much as it could be at least.

"Get back in the hall," Lucinda said.

Lewis ignored her. "You can see it's too high for a squirt like her to get out of herself," he said.

"Step back in the hall," Lucinda said. "In fact, I need you to leave the premises entirely."

"It's my house," Lewis said.

She stared at Lewis, his eyes feral, jumpy. Lucinda feared what she might find in this house; if it was anything as mean and nasty as what she saw in his eyes, she was not sure she'd be able to bear it, braced for horror or not. "It's not your house anymore," she said.

"The hell it ain't."

"It's a crime scene. *My* crime scene. You leave now or I arrest you for interfering with the duties of a law enforcement officer. For starters. How'd that be?" Lucinda set a palm on the butt of her 9 mm, her heart kicking as she steadied her breath and her eye.

Lewis fished a toothpick from his shirt pocket and stabbed it between two foul teeth. He elbowed Arlene in the ribs behind him as he stepped back into the hall and spread his stubby arms wide, dramatic. "How's *this*? This okay?"

"You're still in part of my crime scene," Lucinda said. She looked around at the floor, deciding to prod Lewis. "Any toys missing?"

"We look like we're made of money?" Lewis said.

Lucinda thought about the gargantuan TV in the other room.

"You didn't hear anything?" she said.

"*Like?*" Lewis said.

"Like anything. The window opening. Like your daughter crying. Or screaming."

"If I'd a heard screaming," Lewis said, "you'd be looking at the asshole's body shot dead on the floor instead of an open window."

A car pulled up outside.

Lucinda looked out the window to see Kirk unfold himself from his cruiser, situate his sheriff's hat atop his wave of hair, and affix the strap under his jaw as he looked at his reflection in his cruiser's window.

He looked up at the house now, hands on his hips. Part of his shirt was untucked.

"Your boyfriend's here," Lewis said. "A real cop."

"Out," Lucinda commanded and herded Lewis and Arlene down the hall.

Lucinda pushed across the lawn toward Kirk, her breath billowing in a cloud, boots squeaking on the snow as she felt Lewis glaring after her, the nape of her neck burning from his gaze. She fought a shudder.

"You look good," Kirk said as his eyes slid over Lucinda, the shiver that ran through her a reminder as to why she avoided him and made sure the times she met with him were for official meetings only, with the dispatcher and Vern Ross, the other deputy, present.

"We have a missing girl," Lucinda said.

"Not even a 'Hello, Kirk, you look good too'?"

"She's seven years old," Lucinda said. "She's been out since last night."

"Okay," Kirk said.

He smiled, raising dimples in his stubbled cheeks. The wind tugged at the crop of black hair that peeked out from beneath his sheriff's cap.

"They say someone took her," Lucinda said.

"What do you say?" He hooked his thumbs in his holster belt, the leather squeaked.

"I've never believed a word they've spoken before this," Lucinda said. "But. Stranger things have happened."

"They sure have." His slate eyes sparked. "Remember—"

"I'm sure I don't," Lucinda said, though she was sure she did. His attitude only reinforced her decision to delete and block his personal numbers on her cell phone.

Lucinda strode back toward the house, her blood hot in her face despite her distaste for Kirk's actions.

Kirk sauntered his way past her, tucking in his shirt. Lucinda followed. "Stay out," he ordered as he passed Lewis and Arlene. Lewis heeled. At the porch, Kirk jerked his thumb at Lucinda. "You too. I alerted the state police. You should have already done that."

"I—"

"I'll take it from here and fill the staties in when they get here."

Lucinda nodded, her face flushed at being dismissed, and at her own failing to call Kirk out on his sad come-on moments ago. Her anger deepened with her knowing that if she had flirted back, played along, she would not have been left out here, literally in the cold. Kirk would have invited her in with a smile. But if Kirk thought she was going to succumb to his flirtation so she could be involved professionally—or that she'd otherwise obey and stand on the sidelines as punishment for not playing his game—he was mistaken. She would be involved in this case because she would involve herself. She'd find this girl, for the girl's sake. And for Sally's. And Jonah's.

Kirk entered the double-wide, the storm door slapping shut behind him.

Lucinda stood out in the yard, composing herself, yet not certain how to proceed.

"We need to find her, fast," Lucinda said to the falling snow, out of concern for the girl, and out of a selfish concern for herself too.

Right then, though, she decided what would benefit her and the case most was to see the person with intimate professional knowledge of such cases, someone who knew her and police work best, even if he was at his least. Her father.

CRAZY YOUNG

Lucinda parked her Wrangler on the quiet street outside the house and got out. Snowflakes licked her eyelashes and melted, water droplets slid down her face. Hot and itchy from wearing her coat in the car, she unbuttoned her jacket to let the cold air work its way into her. Still, she felt overheated.

"Okay," she said and took a deep breath.

Though her visits to see her father were a daily routine, the visits themselves were anything but routine. Each visit left her fraught with anxiety. She never knew which father might await her: the father with a crisp mind or the father lost to confusion.

She walked up the gravel drive, past her father's caregiver's Corolla, her father's old truck parked beside it, its tires long flat. Her father would be pained to know his truck tires were flat, and the birdhouse that had hung for countless years from the beech tree in the front yard had fallen to the ground months ago and now lay buried beneath the snow. He'd be upset to learn the front porch steps were caked under snow and had not been shoveled or salted in the meticulous manner he'd seen to for decades. So she never told him of these things, even on those days he knew where he was. Who he was.

The side door off the kitchen opened straightaway when Lucinda knocked, and Dot stood before her, smiling. *Did Dot ever not smile?* Lucinda wondered. No one should smile so much, so *loudly*; it was unnatural.

"You know you don't have to knock, dear," Dot said.

"I guess not," Lucinda said.

"Yet you always knock." Dot smiled. "Come in. He's having a good morning."

Lucinda stepped inside the living room of her childhood. Except it wasn't. Not any longer. She was no longer a girl. A child.

The room lay shadowed, window shades drawn, lamps unlit. The light of her childhood gone.

"It's always so dark in here," Lucinda said.

"If I open the shades, he flies into a tizzy. Finds plenty of energy to grouse."

"I don't understand this behavior," Lucinda said.

"I don't know if that's possible," Dot said. "Or healthy trying. He's at a place none of us can understand until we arrive there ourselves." Dot smiled. Lucinda wondered how Dot could make such a statement when she had not "arrived" in the place she spoke of yet either. Bless Dot and her bromides, but Lucinda resented them and her for trying to make simple what was complex and emotional for Lucinda.

The house smelled of mothballs and medicine. The air was still and stale, hot as a greenhouse yet so dry it made Lucinda's skin itch. She shed her jacket and hung it on the coat tree that had stood in the same place for decades. Affixed and dutiful. Lucinda waved her hand in front of her face to move the still air, afraid she might pass out from the heat.

"You grow used to it, believe it or not," Dot said. "Runs up the oil bill, to keep it so hot. But I guess that's neither here nor there."

Lucinda stamped melting snow from her boots onto the mat. Same old mat on which she'd stomped her boots ten thousand times, ten thousand years ago. Half her childhood she'd needed to be reminded to wipe her feet, her mother calling out from the kitchen, *Don't tread mud in here, wipe your feet!*

Her mother would not call out today.

What Lucinda would give to hear her mother call out once more. Hear her voice. Just once more.

Everything. She'd give everything.

"You okay?" Dot touched Lucinda's wrist. Smiling Dot.

"Sure," Lucinda said, though she wasn't. She was unsteady of mind and spirit. The shadow of regret still hung over her for treating Jonah so poorly; she needed her father's help in matters of this missing girl, though he likely could offer none; and then there was Kirk, and the needing to be in proximity to him if she wanted to work the case. She'd not mention Kirk to her father. He despised Kirk. Lucinda could not fault him that, though she had when she was young.

Focus on the girl, she thought. *And on the new days to come for you.*

"He's in the kitchen," Dot said.

On her way through the living room, Lucinda passed photos of her father and mother, photos obscured by the murk of the room, but whose images remained clear in her mind; her favorite photo of herself and Sally, arms tossed around each other's shoulders, gap-toothed and hysterical with laughter as they ran a three-legged race. The photo had been taken during the summer they'd found the pit in the woods. Lucinda stepped closer to the wall of photos. The photos were faded from the sunlight that had once filled this room, photos of another time, another life. A world of pigtails and water sprinklers. Barbecues and beaches. Puppies and proms. Braces and birthdays and boyfriends. Much of which Sally had missed.

The people in the photos stared out at her, eyes pleading for her to free them and let them live again. *Please, let us live again as we once were. Young and happy. Alive.*

She needed to find this missing girl, alive.

She needed to go see Jonah at his cabin and make amends. Extend his credit to him while she still owned the store. She would do both. She would.

Lucinda looked at a photo of Sally captured in the perpetual act of making a wish just before she blew out candles on a cake. Eyes squeezed so tight, wishing, wishing. She was always wishing. The two of them, always wishing.

"I can't," Lucinda said, startling herself.

"What, dear?" Dot said.

"I don't know," Lucinda said. She did not know why she'd spoken aloud, to whom she'd spoken, or what it meant.

Dot squeezed her hand and guided her into the kitchen, which was lit by a fluorescent light above the ancient gas stove.

Her father gazed at Lucinda from his side of the kitchen table where once he had sat to shine his black work shoes each morning as he left for his rounds as sheriff before he headed to the Grain & Feed. He'd often said the state of a man's shoes spoke as much about the man as the firmness of his handshake and ability to pay his debts. Now his feet were so tortured by gout that even loose paper slippers pained their tight, swollen flesh. His sunken face was leached to translucence. His breathing whistled through the tubes from his nose to the oxygen tank beside him on the floor.

Lucinda touched her fingers to the doorframe of the living room, where pencil marks had measured her height over her first seven years. Her mother had been the one to keep track.

Lucinda kissed his bald and mottled head. "I hear you're having a good day," she said, trying to inject good cheer in her voice as she sat in the chair beside him. This, *this*, was a good day.

Dot left them to be alone.

Her father patted Lucinda's hand and tried to speak, his voice so pale she could not decipher what he said. She leaned in closer.

"You," he wheezed. "Tired?"

"I'm okay," she said.

"Worry." He labored to swallow, smacked his dried lips. "About you."

"That's a good one."

"Father. Always. Worries."

He smiled. Teeth stained. Lips bloodless. Eyes flat. Dry. Jaundiced.

"A girl went missing," Lucinda said and wished she hadn't. It was her problem, not his, and he was not fit enough today to bring up the sorest of his memories.

"Murdered," he mumbled.

"We don't know yet."

"Killed."

"She's just missing right now."

His eyes fogged.

Outside, the wind gusted, causing the vent above the stove to flap.

"I'm helping find her," Lucinda said. She wanted to ease into asking him about how to handle herself in this situation, what to look out for and what to guard against when working with the public and the state police. "What— I don't trust the parents. Foster parents."

Her father winced. "Can't find her. Won't ever—" His trembling fingers worked at his pajama top buttons.

"We'll try."

"Can't find them. Failed. All my fault." His body shook.

Lucinda did not know why she'd believed her father might be able to help her. Despite the reality of his health, she could not help but think of him as confident and capable, still able to give her advice. It was engrained in her, despite the evidence to the contrary before her. She regretted agitating bad memories of guilt and failure. She placed her hand on his frail hand. "Okay, Dad. Okay."

His breath whistled hollow in his chest.

"I'll find this girl," she said.

He shook his head, weak. "Young. Crazy young. You're so young."

She was losing him. "I worry someone close to her has—"

"Peace," he rasped. "Find it."

His eyelids fluttered as his head lolled to the side.

She clasped his hands in hers.

His eyes opened, dim yet present.

"I—" She could not continue this thread. It disturbed him too much. "I got a letter," she found herself saying as she took the letter from her jeans. She unfolded it. "I've been accepted, for an internship. I'd about given up I'd applied so many times to so many teams. Maybe they just got sick of me and gave in."

He stared at her as if he did not understand the word, intern.

"It's volunteer. I'm one of just five amateurs to join the dig, in Newfoundland."

"Canada," her father said. "She's not in Canada."

"Me. I'll be in Canada. I hope. I have to get word back to them one way or another. Within a week." She'd planned to email her response, her acceptance, to the Newfoundland Archaeological Society this morning, until the girl had gone missing. The off-site study and preparations for the dig started in a month. The interns were expected to be a part of the entire process, needed to be present from the start. It was a ten-month commitment. She'd need to buy gear and clothing, bring Ed up to speed and train him to take over for her responsibilities, work with the contractor to facilitate the remodeling sooner, or scrap it all for now. Maybe she'd sell the store. She hated even thinking such a thing in her father's presence. Maybe— She did not know. Damn it, there was too much to keep straight. But she'd need a couple weeks minimum to do all she needed to prepare to leave. And she had yet to tell Dale, who would not be able to join her.

Above all, there was the girl. If she did not find the girl in time, Lucinda would have to decline the acceptance she'd waited to get for years.

"Tell me. More," her father said, his eyes clearing.

"It's prestigious. Exciting. There's no way of knowing if the dig will pay out, but the site may contain the remains, or at least artifacts, of Vikings. It may be the first evidence ever of Vikings being established so far south and west in North America. It'd be a historic find. Even if we find nothing, no artifacts or remains, it'd be an experience of a lifetime. Sally would have loved this. Maybe even more than me."

Her father took her hand in his, his flesh cold, the skin cracked and calloused.

"Find peace," he said.

She squeezed his hand.

"Before. Devil finds you," he said.

"He's slipping," Dot said. She'd entered the kitchen quietly. "He's been talking of God and the devil lately."

"What does it mean?" Lucinda said.

"Nothing. They all do it. When the end nears. We all do it."

Just a Few More Minutes

Jonah eased the truck down the old mountain road, the girl curled up under a blanket beside him on the bench seat. He'd wrapped her in an old shirt of his, unable to bring himself to look in the old trunk for the yellow dress.

No one had been on the road yet, and the unmarred snow lay as pristine as it had fallen.

High above, turkey vultures carved circles in the sky.

As he descended down from the Gore, Jonah fished a cigarette from his jacket pocket, pushed the lighter into the truck's dash.

A deer leaped in front of the truck. Jonah pumped the brakes. The girl did not budge as the deer, a yearling buck, stood in the middle of the road staring at the truck. Its coat was winter dark; its hot, living breath steamed in the frigid air as it tapped a front hoof, shivered so it shed water in a rain of silver droplets, then loped into the trees. Gone, a ghost.

The lighter popped from the dash.

Jonah lit his cigarette. The glowing coils of the lighter warmed his face, the tobacco crackling as he inhaled. He let the smoke leak from his mouth and nose as he started on down the road again.

The girl sneezed in her sleep.

Jonah cranked his window down and flicked the cigarette out into the snow.

The river valley lay in front of him, fields blanketed with snow. Silver maples and alders clumped at the riverbank, branches coated in a skin of ice so dazzling the branches appeared crafted of blown glass.

Decrepit barns sat out in the snowed fields, boards blasted pewter by generations of wind and rain and snow. Woodsmoke uncoiled from chimneys and hung low in the valley as cows stood out in the fields, their dumb gazes following the motion of the truck as they worked their cud.

Coming to One Dollar Bridge, Jonah slowed the truck. A weather-worn sign was nailed to the bridge brow: $1 FINE FOR TRAVELING FASTER THAN A WALK ON BRIDGE.

The truck trundled onto the bridge, the world going dark.

The girl whimpered. Jonah put a hand on her shoulder. So many nights Sally had endured ear infections and colds, and he'd taken his turn rocking her, doing his best to soothe her, though it never felt like it was enough.

The truck bounced over railroad tracks as the snowy dirt road turned to plowed pavement. Jonah parked on the side of the road for a moment, where once a state trooper cruiser and TV crew van had parked. He looked at his old house. He'd not been inside it for twenty-five years. No one had, far as he knew.

A town plow charged up the road, its yellow lights busy, sand fanning behind it as snow flew from the blade.

A sheriff's cruiser pulled to the stop sign on a side street, a block down from Jonah, then pulled onto Main Street and headed away from him, toward the old rectory that served as the sheriff's office. Jonah waited to see if the cruiser would swing back his way.

It didn't.

Nerves calmed, Jonah pulled down the street a few blocks and drove into the Gas-n-Go parking lot, parked at the side of the building. He knew he should take the girl to the sheriff immediately. But he wanted to get something for her. A gift. What would it hurt? He knew they'd ask, *You stopped at the Gas-n-Go? Why would you do that?*

Because he was hungry. And because. Well. He didn't want to give the girl up just yet. He couldn't tell them this. He couldn't tell them that he could barely stand to part with her. She'd found him for a reason. He felt it. He knew it. But who would understand that? He didn't understand it himself. He was not certain he even believed it, or just *wanted* to believe it.

You're senile, the voice said. *Sentimental and superstitious.*

No. This girl, those eyes. Jonah had found her, in a pit. His mind carouseled around one continuous thought. *What does it mean?*

Why does it have to mean anything? the voice said. *Fool. Give her back.*

He would. But he was hungry, needed coffee, and a few more minutes with her. Just a few. And to give her a gift by which she could remember him. When he turned her over to the authorities, he was going to face an arduous day. *Days.* He wanted to let these last few minutes soak into his marrow. Enjoy them.

They're not yours to enjoy, the voice said.

He pulled the blanket up to her chin, marveling at her. Then he got out.

He shut the door with a soft click and stood and watched her through the window. When he was certain she would not stir, he walked into the store.

BLIND

The woman at the register looked up.

Her name tag read: MARNIE. HERE TO HELP.

"Morning," she said.

Jonah nodded. "Pack of Zigzags and a pouch of Gambler," he said and picked up a coffeepot beside the counter, poured some coffee into a paper cup, took a sip. It tasted like boiled puddle water, but it was hot.

He browsed an aisle, took a pack of beef jerky, looked at the price, and put it back. He picked up a can of salted pork and wandered into the next aisle.

A young man with a bandanna on his head entered the store and shouted, "*Marnie.* What's shaking? Gonna get your slut on tonight?"

Marnie glanced toward Jonah uneasily.

The young man slapped money on the counter. "That's for the petrol. See yah tonight, sweet stuff."

"Maybe."

"Maybe ain't in my vocab," the young man said.

"It's in mine," the cashier said.

As the young man headed out the door, he shouted back, "That's some crazy-ass shit about that little girl!"

Jonah watched the young man charge across the lot past Jonah's truck, hop into an old Firebird, and haul ass out of the lot, tires spitting snow.

Jonah set the salt pork on the counter. The cashier placed the rolling papers and tobacco beside it.

"What's that about a girl?" Jonah said.

"The one that was abducted," the cashier said.

Abducted.

"The one all over the TV and radio and internet?" the cashier said when Jonah did not immediately show recognition.

"I don't have a TV," Jonah said. He didn't know what the internet was either, though he'd heard Lucinda speak of it a time or two. He swallowed dryly. He should have put the truck radio on to get a sense of the story, see if there were updates, who the girl was and what her situation had been. Her parents had to be insane with worry, and here he was buying a parting gift.

"Selfish idiot," he whispered.

"What?" said the cashier.

Of course, the story had to be all over the news. *Maybe,* he thought, *just maybe, when I bring her back I'll be seen as a savior.*

Never. Abducted. You're the prime suspect now, the voice said.

"Abducted?" Jonah said.

"Right from her window. So they *say.* Who knows what's the truth on the tube. You're smart not to have a TV. I only have this one at work. A bunch of nonsense. Every idiot wanting their voice heard, thinking their opinion is more valid than the next bozo's. Never mind the idjit opinions and speculation on social media. None of it's *news.* And that *couple.* Who had the girl."

"Poor parents."

"Foster parents."

Foster parents.

"*He's* downright nasty," the young woman said. "I've seen him in here barking at her, the poor little girl, and at his wife. Wife barks her share. In self-defense, from what I've seen. Seen him swat at her more than once. Looks at them both as if—"

Jonah glanced out the window at his truck.

"How do people like that even get a foster kid?" the cashier said. "And apparently they've had a whole slew of them."

"She's not theirs," Jonah whispered.

"What?" the cashier said.

"Nothing." Was it the girl's foster parents who had abused her and driven her away or abandoned her? He'd imagined good parents facing the nightmare of their lives. Jonah searched the newspaper rack at the counter.

"Sold out," the cashier said. "You know it's all the buzz when a newspaper sells out these days. So many theories. Experts. Everyone a judge, jury, and executioner. If she wasn't taken, then maybe they, the nasty foster parents, you know. Maybe they did something. If she run off, she'd have come home by now; it's too cold to be out there. What's the world coming to?"

The world isn't coming to anything, Jonah thought. *The world spins just as it has always spun. Blind to our tortures.*

"Let me ring you up," the cashier said.

"Hold it," Jonah said.

He hurried down an aisle and eyed a pile of coloring books and crayons and colored pencils. He hesitated. Grabbed a coloring book and flipped through it. Put it down. Grabbed another, paged through it. He felt the cashier's eyes on him. A coloring book. The parting gift. How would it be perceived by the law? Every action scrutinized. He set the coloring book down and swapped it for a notebook and a pack of crayons. He walked up and set them on the counter.

"Coloring are we?" the cashier said and cocked an eyebrow.

"Cheaper than carpenter's pencils."

Jonah glanced out the window at the truck.

The cashier's eyes followed his.

He brought his eyes back to her.

She rang him up.

Jonah dug in his pocket for a few grimy bills and handed them over, his palms sweaty as she counted back the change.

Outside, the cold air and mean bright sunlight stunned him. The world tilted. He looked down the street toward the sheriff's cruiser parked in front of the old rectory.

He hurried to the truck, jumped into it with a groan. The girl lay still. When he touched her shoulder, her flesh was as cold as a marble headstone. He drew the blanket tighter up around her and turned the truck's crank.

Nothing.

Shit.

He looked out the windshield at the store window to see the cashier looking out at him.

He turned the crank again.

Nothing.

Turned it.

Nothing.

C'mon.

The girl moaned in her sleep.

"Shhh," Jonah said. "Shhh."

He looked up.

The cashier had the store's door open and was staring at him.

Jonah fumbled with the ignition key.

He turned the crank.

Nothing.

He covered the girl with the blanket, trying to minimize his movement. His heart thrummed as fast as a grouse's drumming wings.

"You all right?" the cashier shouted and stepped outside of the store.

Jonah rolled down his window.

"Yeah," he said, trying to keep his voice low. He did not want to wake the girl. Could not wake her. "Truck does this. Stubborn."

"I can relate," the cashier said. She came down off the steps toward him.

He licked his lips and turned the crank. The engine caught and stalled.

The cashier strode toward him, halfway to him now.

He turned the crank again. Come on.

The truck started. Idled.

"See there," Jonah said.

The cashier stopped a few feet away. "Looks like you're all right."

"Looks like," Jonah said.

The cashier stared at him, as if committing his face to memory, then turned back inside.

GIVE HER BACK

Jonah crept the truck down the street and eased past a crowd of cars parked outside the rectory. State police cruisers; six TV vans. Six times the number of TV vans than twenty-five years ago. Where did they all come from? Maybe it had to do with what the cashier had said about online and the internet.

Jonah spotted Lucinda speaking with the sheriff. Jonah had forgotten she was, technically, a part-time deputy, a position she'd inherited against her will, or so she'd confided in Jonah when she'd first been a write-in candidate. She could have refused the post but hadn't. A glorified crossing guard, she'd claimed. *Whatever happens around here that a deputy is really needed anyway?* she'd let slip, her face reddening with mortification as she'd apologized to Jonah for her stupidity. *I didn't mean—* she'd said. *Of course there are times.* Jonah had told her not to fret. If anyone had been affected more deeply by Sally disappearing than Jonah, it was Lucinda. Young people, it was claimed, weathered trauma better than adults because their minds are more malleable and they lack perspective to know the severity and permanence of a situation.

But Jonah had witnessed Lucinda's devastation and bewilderment when she'd finally understood her friend was likely never coming back. Her scars were deep and did not know the bounds of time, despite the good face she put on it now as a young woman. Anger bit into him at the thought of Lucinda sending him from the Grain & Feed.

As Jonah drove the truck slowly by the crowd, no one paid him any mind.

The girl moved to sit up on his truck seat. Jonah put his hand on her head. Her scalp was dry and crusted. Scabbed. Lice. Thick with lice.

He pulled his hand away.

"Be still," he said.

What are you doing? the voice said. *Pull over. Drop her off.*

What was he going to do, drop her off in front of reporters and cameras? The recluse suspected of murdering his wife and child twenty-five years ago? Was he just going to open the truck door and say, *Here she is, I* found *her.* A girl they believed had been abducted.

He couldn't.

You have to, the voice said.

Jonah drove past, thinking. His jaw hurt, his *mind* hurt. What to do, what to do, what to do? He considered dropping her off somewhere safe yet private, without being seen. But what if she could speak and she described him to law enforcement. That was worse, surely.

Even if he gave her back safely and he was cleared of wrongdoing, he could not return her to those "parents," to a system that had failed her and would fail her again and again. He knew that system. He knew it.

At the Grain & Feed he turned the truck around and started back the way he'd come.

He drove past the crowd and caught a look at a couple engaged with the sheriff. The scabby little man stabbed a finger at the sheriff's face. The woman shrieked at the sheriff, face distorted.

With one glance, Jonah knew the man and woman were the girl's foster parents, knew what they were capable of doing, and why the girl had been in the woods.

End it here. Now, the voice said. *Drop her off, explain the facts. The truth.*

The truth. How had that served him in his past life?

If she had been lost to good parents, he'd pull over now, speculation and persecution be damned. He'd be ecstatic to give her back to parents with whom he shared a miserable bond of a child missing.

But to give her back to these people. To this system.

The woman and man barked and howled at the sheriff, spittle flew from their mouths.

Jonah pulled the blanket farther up over the girl and drove back through town, past his old house toward the covered bridge.

The girl jolted awake, sat up, rubbed her eyes with balled fists before Jonah could get a hand on her. She stared past him out his side window.

"Home," she said, her voice soft as bird down.

"You want to go home?" Jonah said.

You're mad, a voice said. *Take her back to the cabin and it will be the end of you.*

The voice was right. There would be no explaining it, despite how reasonable the argument he made to himself. Once he took her back up to the cabin, he destroyed any legal defense for himself. But this was not about doing what was *legal*.

This was right. For her.

For you, you mean.

They would not stay at the cabin. They would go back so he could regroup, figure out what to do next, where to go next.

"Home," she said.

"Lie back down," he said. "Rest."

She looked out his window.

"You want to go back?" he said. "To your foster parents?"

She shook her head furiously. No.

"You want to be with me?" he said.

Whatever her answer he'd abide.

She nodded. "Home," she said.

"Okay," he said.

And he knew then that upon buying the crayons he'd never intended to give her back.

Nothing You Can Say

Lucinda had never liked the old rectory, now serving as temporary sheriff's office. The place smelled of candle wax and furniture polish, and despite its vast windows that spanned from floor to ceiling, shadows lurked, as if the dark woodwork itself swallowed up the room's natural light.

Lucinda walked into what had once been the old parlor, now the sheriff's makeshift office, to find Kirk with his feet up on his desk.

Lucinda's father would never have taken such a lax posture working such a case, or no case at all. A man with his feet on his desk was a man too smug for his job, a man beneath his station.

Kirk gnawed at a Lucky Spot breakfast sandwich, same as he'd eaten each morning going back sixteen years to when he and Lucinda had dated, the first time around.

They were good sandwiches. Joe at the Lucky Spot slathered his homemade biscuits with maple syrup then griddled them. Used a thick wedge of aged cheddar. Bacon from hogs raised at High Meadows farm. Eggs. Gooey yolks as orange as an Indian paintbrush petal. But to eat one every day proved an appetite un-checked, an adolescence never outgrown.

Kirk sucked yolk from his thumb.

The sandwiches were the first food Lucinda and Kirk had shared after she'd given herself to him. She despised the term, *given herself*, but that's how it had felt. She'd succumbed. Her first boy. The only boy, she'd thought, dreamily envisioning a future with him.

They'd sat at a booth at the Lucky Spot and shared a breakfast sandwich. Not saying a word, relishing the secrecy of what they'd just shared in the empty apartment above the hardware store Kirk had been painting before the next tenants moved into it. When their eyes met, he'd smiled an easy and unguarded smile. A kind smile. And she'd believed she'd tapped into a part of him no one else got to see. The *real Kirk*. She'd felt giddy with pleasure for drawing this side out of the Tough Boy, proving his toughness was an act masking a soft side she alone had the power to conjure.

Kirk looked at her now and licked his fingers. Smiled. That smile. The devil in it.

"What are you doing here?" he said.

"I'm the deputy sheriff."

Kirk sniffed, licked at yolk at the corner of his mouth. "What do you plan on doing? You don't have any experience in this sort of thing."

"More than you."

"How's that?"

"Sally."

"I mean legal. The law. Investigation. You can't be nosing around and certainly can't be going out to crime scenes on your own."

Nosing around. Christ. It was his MO, though, and it did not surprise or anger her; it was as expected from him as a grunt was from a hog. His nonchalance, however—this infuriated her. His indifference to the urgency and seriousness of the missing girl was inexcusable. He should have been up on his feet coordinating, delegating, investigating.

"I was at the crime scene because you were unreachable. When you're supposed to be reachable at all times. The parents tried to locate you."

"I was on a call. I got to their place quick enough. You, though, you shouldn't have gone inside the place, you could have contaminated it."

Lucinda bit her tongue as Kirk reached in the bag and took out a sandwich.

"Remember these?" He smiled. All the hardness in his face melted like winter ice on a spring day.

"What are *you* doing in here like this?" Lucinda glanced at his boots propped up on the desk.

"Mentally preparing for the press waiting in the other room," he said and set his feet on the floor. Slid the sandwich across the table toward her. "One won't kill you."

She poured a cup of weak black coffee into a Styrofoam cup. Kirk got up and stood too close to her.

She moved away.

"Child Welfare'll be here pronto," he said. "I can hand that over. Think you can handle it? I need to put heads together with the troopers on the search and the real investigation. You can do background."

Background.

"I thought you'd handle the press and I would support the state police with searches," Lucinda said.

"Don't throw a tizzy. You will help. But I can handle these two things at once."

Lucinda glanced through the doorway at reporters and camera operators talking and prepping for questions in the adjacent room.

"I'll handle Child Welfare," Lucinda said. "Then help with search coordination. I can handle two things at once too."

"I knew you'd see it my way." Kirk winked at her on his way into the other room.

Lucinda did not know what to expect or what to ask the Child Welfare liaison. Her only experience with foster care was her own personal experience. Her parents had been her sole foster parents since she was five days old and adopted her at five years old. They were her true parents, no one else, and she was fortunate to have their love and kindness, could not relate to the experiences some children in the foster system endured.

She wanted to do her utmost in the meeting with Child Welfare, do whatever was asked of her role as deputy, even if it was Kirk manipulating her with his authority. Her father had always said *respect the chain of command, if not the commander.*

She'd abide by that, for as long as she was able anyway. This was not 1987. She was not her father. And her father had never had to report to the likes of Kirk. If he had, he may have made an exception to his mantra.

The best approach to the meeting with Child Welfare, however, would be to simply listen. Her father had said to listen to those who know more than you, let them speak first and the appropriate questions will come. Lucinda was beginning to appreciate the pressure her father must have weathered when Sally and her mother had disappeared. Especially with his friend as the prime suspect for a time. What a nightmare. No wonder it had taken its toll on both men. Especially Jonah. First chance she got at personal time, she needed to get up to see Jonah at his cabin.

Dale came up from behind, giving her a start.

"Where'd you come from?" Lucinda said. "You scared me."

"Through the back. Private powwow with Kirk?" He nodded through the doorway, to Kirk patronizing the press.

"We were discussing the girl," Lucinda said.

Dale wrapped his arms around her from behind.

She took his hands from her hips and stepped from his embrace. "I'm working." Did any man she knew respect the bounds of professionalism?

"Looked like you were having coffee with him," Dale said.

So there it was. Jealousy. She did not have the time for it.

"I have an interview with Child Welfare," she said.

Kirk rambled into the room, locked eyes with Dale.

"Sneak in the old back door, did we?" he said. "How's the insurance racket?"

Dale didn't correct Kirk, who knew damn well Dale was a realtor, respected by both buyers and sellers, a rarity for the profession.

"Real estate," Lucinda said. Lucinda had met Dale two years ago when she'd been looking to buy a small home for herself. He'd not been her agent, but when he'd overheard her speaking to his colleague at the office, he'd said, "I know the perfect place for you." Lucinda had resisted rolling her eyes. Of course a realtor knew the *perfect place.* Didn't they all? *It just came in, I haven't even listed it yet,* he'd said. *You're lucky.* Lucinda had rolled her eyes then. Yes, *lucky me,* she'd thought. She'd waited for this agent who claimed to have the perfect place to hoist himself up from his desk and horn in on the sale. Take advantage. Instead, he'd given the agent Lucinda was working with the address and handed over a folder and a set of keys. "If it's not the one for you," he'd said, now preoccupied with his computer screen, no longer looking at her, "you're out of luck in this town." He'd said *this town* as if he'd been the one living here his whole life, and Lucinda was a newcomer, instead of the other way around. As if Lucinda hadn't known the town as well as him.

The place Dale had suggested hadn't been *perfect*. It had been better than that. Perfection didn't exist, anyway, and its approximation was dull, plastic. However, the house was *just right*, as Dale had been on his and Lucinda's first evening of bowling and pizza together after Lucinda had closed the deal on the house and insisted she buy Dale a beer for directing her to a home she had not even known existed in her small hometown.

"Right. Real estate," Kirk said now. "Sell the land out from under us locals."

"That's not what I do," Dale said.

"Right. Well. This room is for official business only," Kirk said. Dale looked at Lucinda.

"It is," she said.

"Using it for coordination. Lots of coordinating to do," Kirk said. "Lots of late hours ahead."

"I'll see you at the house," Lucinda said to Dale.

"I'd like to help search," Dale said.

"Get over to the grange hall then," Kirk said. "With the rest of the volunteers."

"I'll see you later," Lucinda said. "I have something I want to talk to you about."

Dale made to kiss Lucinda; she offered her cheek. She did not feel comfortable with affection on such a somber case as a missing child.

"Got it," Dale said and went out the door.

"Sensitive," Kirk said.

A woman entered the room, fur earmuffs slung around her neck as she plucked a stray hair apparently shed from the frizz of gray hair on her head, her eyeglasses steamed up when she breathed. She reminded Lucinda of a woman she'd known in the past, but Lucinda could not place the woman in her mind.

Kirk nodded and sauntered out to address the reporters.

The woman removed her glasses and lowered them on their chain, clasped a binder against her chest.

"Deputy," the woman said.

Lucinda nodded. Yes. She was. Not a crossing guard. A deputy sheriff, working the background of girl who was missing, and quite likely the victim of a serious crime. "And you're?"

"Maxine Fields."

"Have a seat," Lucinda said. "I poured coffee."

"I refrain from caffeine."

As she sat, Fields opened the binder and looked at Lucinda as a mother might look her child in the eye before explaining a hard fact of life. It set Lucinda on edge, made her feel remotely culpable for some vague sin she could not recall committing. To calm herself, she took her notepad out of her jacket pocket and perused it for a solid question to put forth.

"Let me shed some light," Fields offered, as if sensing Lucinda's uncertainty of where to start. "Let's see. Gretel Elizabeth Atkins. That's a name given the missing girl by the state. We estimate she is roughly seven years old, though by her physical appearance and her mental and emotional makeup due to trauma, she would pass for perhaps four or five years old. Her date of birth is unknown. Place of birth, New England, as best we can narrow it down. Her biological parents are unknown. She was abandoned outside the hospital Emergency Room in St. Johnsbury at around two weeks old, give or take a month. She weighed five pounds, thirteen ounces. Her parents never turned up. No one ever turned up. There was no record of a regional birth to parents that fit the girl's stats during a two-month time frame. Child and Family Services checked across the river in New Hampshire. No records there either. Or western Maine. Or eastern upstate New York. She must have been given birth to privately. A teenage mother. Likely. Happens every day. Gretel is a mystery, as if she appeared out of thin air."

The information took Lucinda aback. She'd thought with the girl being in foster care there'd be troves of information on her.

Fields glanced at the binder.

"Her first foster folks were good people," she said. "Very good people," she stressed, as if to make certain Lucinda understood that the parents who subsequently ended up with her were the anomaly, and not the other way around. "But the father lost his job and they had to leave the state. She, Gretel, lost out.

"After that," Fields continued, "she was a ward of the state for a time. Then she got taken in by a couple who"—she paused—"who abused the system. The woman proved to be an alcoholic. She blacked out while Gretel, who was eleven months at the time, fell out the open window of the second-story apartment and into the bushes below. Gretel broke both legs. She still has a limp. There was, it seems, brain trauma, though the extent is unknown as she's still developing. If it'd been a sidewalk she fell onto instead of bushes . . ."

Lucinda shifted, uncomfortable. The more the woman spoke, the more grateful Lucinda felt for her own parents; and guilty somehow too. How did she deserve such a good home and parents while another child did not? The truth was that "deserve" played no role. It was the luck of the draw. Fate.

"Aren't foster parents screened?" Lucinda had told herself she'd refrain from asking questions until Fields was finished but could not help herself. She knew nothing about how the foster system worked. Or failed to work. She assumed many foster parents were loving, generous, well-meaning people. As her own parents had been. Why, then, did she have an instinctive distrust of foster care?

The woman did not answer Lucinda's question. "It gets worse, I'm afraid," she said. "Her next foster situation." She paused again. This was difficult for her, a personal embarrassment, an affront; it seemed Fields took failings of the system personally. "They, unfortunately, passed the girl around," Fields said.

"I don't understand," Lucinda said.

"They shared her . . ."

"But . . . she's seven," Lucinda said. She felt as if she might be sick. She thought of Sally, who'd disappeared at about the same age as Gretel. Even when Lucinda had finally understood Sally was likely never coming back, and had become aware of the epidemic of sad crimes against women and children, she'd never imagined Sally in such a situation. She'd always kept Sally safe in her mind, comforted and protected, still with her mother, at least. Or she thought of Sally and her mother as, simply, *gone*, *vanished*, as if they had gently, peacefully dissolved. Lucinda shuddered. Coffee acid ate at her stomach.

Fields flipped a page in the binder. "I'll spare the details, unless you'd like—"

"Leave the binder. I'll dig deeper as necessary. Who does this kind of stuff?"

"More people than you care to know," Fields said.

"How can they fool the system meant to protect the kids they harm?"

"The system's made up of people. Well-intentioned, hardworking, overworked, fallible people. Sometimes they, we, *I*, miss things."

Lucinda wanted to be angry with the woman, ask her how *anyone* could *miss* things? Yet Lucinda felt no anger toward the woman. Only empathy. Even if Lucinda had been angry, lashing out served no end. Her father had spoken of the need to compartmentalize the viciousness of the world, to keep it locked up and at bay so one could continue with one's work, one's life. Lucinda needed to do that now, focus on finding Gretel.

"I've seen worse," Fields said. "Much worse. Fortunately the likelihood of PTSD for the girl is negligible. That's the one blessing of acts like this happening so young. The young brain isn't built to create long-term memories. This type of abuse, however, may stay with certain victims. It seems to almost molecularly alter them. The mind may not remember, but the body does."

Fields closed the binder.

"I don't know what to say," Lucinda said.

"There's nothing one can say," Fields said.

I Live Here

Jonah parked the truck off the road to the Gore and got out, gasping for breath, trembling. There was no going back now. No one who would understand his justification for keeping the girl. They'd think he'd taken her from her home, they'd believe it like they believed in God.

Jonah pulled his coat collar up against his cold neck. The temperature had dipped. A wind kicked up. It threshed the treetops, the branches clattering. Vultures arced in the sky over the distant trees over near the cabin.

A blue jay heckled him from a spruce branch as he scrambled around to the passenger side to retrieve the girl. He had a grip on the truck's door handle when he heard it.

An ATV.

Throttling up the road behind him.

The girl looked at Jonah through the truck window. He put a finger to his lips, shhhh. Motioned for her to hunker down.

She did.

She'd run off for a reason, and she wanted to stay run off. They would leave together. Start fresh. Soon. Very soon.

The ATV gained on him, the deafening blat of its exhaust and reek of its toxic fumes polluting the still mountain air. The rider was fat, bearded, a slow look in his eyes.

He brought the ATV to an abrupt stop and slung mud and snow on Jonah.

Jonah stepped toward the ATV.

The rider gawked at him. "Hey," he said.

Jonah said nothing.

"Know where there's trails up here?" the rider said.

"No trails. Not for those things."

"No trails?" The rider torqued the throttle. The engine revved. The tailpipe puked exhaust.

"That's right," Jonah said.

"Maybe I'll just make my own trail then." The rider revved the engine louder and spat a wad of chew into the snow.

"You don't want to be doing that," Jonah said.

"Why's that, Pops?"

"I live up here."

"You own the land?" The rider pressed a thumb to the side of one nostril and blew snot out of the other nostril, slung the snot from his fingers. "I don't think so. We're gonna log up here. The whole mountain. Come spring. Knock 'your' cabin flat with a skidder."

The logging company would be relentless, pressuring him. The searchers would find their way here too. No place was safe. He would not be here long anyway.

"It's not spring now," Jonah said. He wished he could see his truck behind him, see if the girl was keeping herself hidden. If she so much as peeked over the edge of the window . . . "And I don't want to hear those things."

"Well, Pops, if you don't own the land, you don't have a say now, do you?"

"Do you own it?" Jonah said.

"How's that?"

"Do *you* own it?"

"No." The rider blew snot out of his other nostril.

"Then since neither of us owns it, but one of us lives on it, I'd say the one who lives on it has more say than the one who doesn't. Wouldn't you say?"

"Listen, Pops."

"I ain't your fucking Pops."

"I ain't hurting nothing."

"You're hurting my fucking sensibilities."

"Your what?"

"My fucking sensibilities, my aesthetics, my peace of fucking mind." Jonah's blood was hot with rage. His teeth ached with it.

"I don't know what—"

Jonah stepped in close to the rider. "Listen to me," he said. "You listening? I am telling you just once."

"Jesus," the rider said.

"Jesus doesn't have a say in this. I did my praying once when it counted most and—I'm telling *you* this once. Turn that fucking contraption around and do not come back up here. Not ever."

"You got no fucking right."

"Right? Right don't matter. Only what I'm about to tell you matters. You come up here again, I will shoot you fucking dead."

The rider blinked. "Hey. Listen—"

"You listen. What I say is the truth. Sure as you sit your fat ass on that fucking thing. You come up here again, I will shoot you dead. But first, I will wound you, so when I come over to you and look you in the eye as you lay on the ground blubbering and confused about how it ever came to this, you'll know it came to it because you didn't fucking listen when you should have, pretty much I guess how you've lived your whole useless fucking life."

The blood sang in Jonah's veins now. Magma blood. He'd kill the man. He would. He was nearly blind with rage he could not suppress.

The rider revved the engine.

"Get the fuck out of here," Jonah said.

The rider scowled, but he engaged the ATV and backed up and drove off.

Jonah watched the ATV ride back down the road out of sight, standing there until he could no longer hear it.

Then he sagged to his knees with relief, choking for air. The rage had overcome him so swiftly, he'd felt he might black out.

ONLY ONE OPTION

He had to get the girl away.

Jonah paced in the cabin, his thoughts frenetic and conflicted, a kaleidoscope of confusion and doubt. No matter how he worked it, the best thing, for the girl, was to take her away, someplace safe, with him, with someone who understood. But where? He could not afford even a fleabag motel, yet he could not stay here. It would not be long before someone connected the date of his daughter's disappearance to the date of the disappearance of this girl, or the logger on the ATV came back with more loggers.

"What are we going to do?" he said.

The girl pulled the blanket around her.

He sat in the chair. The warmth of the stove washed over him, a gauzed drowsiness webbed his mind and slackened his jaw. He could never have imagined this is how his life would turn. It did not seem like it *was* his life at all, as if he had never, from day one, had any control over it.

How many lives make up a single life? he wondered.

She sat blinking at him.

What were they going to do?

One step at a time, he thought. The girl had to be starving. He'd start there, by getting food in her belly. She'd need to be well nourished for a journey. And dressed. He could not be taking her around wrapped in a blanket and a grimy shirt.

He boiled a pot of oatmeal, added evaporated milk to it. He smacked a box of brown sugar gone hard as stone on the edge of the woodstove and stirred the brown sugar chunks into the oats, set the bowl and spoon beside her.

She didn't touch it.

It was hard to get Sally to eat when she'd set her mind against it. By the age of three she knew all the ploys: reverse psychology, games, dares, the claims that eating a certain food meant she was a big girl, or would make her jump higher or run faster; none of them worked.

"I'm not doing the airplane thing," he said. "You're too old for that. If you don't want it, I'll eat it."

He took her bowl away and began to eat the oatmeal. He was famished. His empty guts churned.

She frowned.

He pushed the bowl to her.

She shoveled the cereal into her mouth with her fingers, ravenous, feral, not taking a breath. Finished, panting, she threw up all over herself and sobbed.

"Oh," he said, searching for a towel. "Shhh. Easy. Easy. There's no need to cry."

But, of course, there was every reason to cry.

So he let her.

"We'll clean that right up. It's nothing we haven't done before. Then we'll see about making a plan for getting us out of here," he said.

Don't Touch a Thing

Lucinda took a deep breath, nervous; she'd never been comfortable in a crowd, let alone speaking in front of one, or leading one. She was distrustful of them, the mob, how the seeming safety and invisibility offered by the crowd could bring out the worst in the individual, even when people gathered for a common good. She had an uncle and aunt who lived in Buffalo who went on guided tours to far-flung destinations, spent weeks with strangers busing from site to site as a tour guide recited the same facts about the locale as the guide had done the day before and would do the day after. Lucinda could think of no worse way to spend time than with strangers holding brochures and wearing headsets, unless said tour was done on Segways.

The crowd looked up at her with expectation. Most of the faces she knew. Neighbors and customers. Other faces were foreign. She took note of them. The state police detective who'd charged her with this responsibility, for this quadrant of the search, had told her to keep a keen eye out for suspicious persons and behavior. To her, in this circumstance, everyone was suspicious. She remembered with a chill the looks of suspicion the women had given Jonah in his living room the night Sally had disappeared.

"You've each been given your maps," she said, her voice sounding strange to her ears, too high pitched. "As well as a description of the girl. She's roughly seven years old. Brown hair and very distinctive, deep, dark eyes." *Like Sally,* she thought. *Her eyes are like Sally's.* "She may have a limp. She's shy and quiet. Speaks very little. It's not known what she's wearing, if anything. She's about forty-three inches tall and fifty pounds. Skinny. Some of you will search along Logger Brook, others in the fields behind the schools, or the woods along Lye Brook and Beaver Meadows. Your map reflects the area you'll cover, outlined in red. We plan for each area to take five hours."

The faces peering up at her glanced down at the maps held in cold hands.

"We'll take a lunch break—sandwiches and bottled water and fruit will be provided—then go on. We ask that you choose a partner, someone to stay by you. We'll work in a line with each other as we go. Stay within arm's reach of each other and go at the same pace so nothing is overlooked. Those in Logger Brook will be led by me. Those in the school area will be led by the sheriff, and those elsewhere will be led by state troopers Halcomb and Bender, who will speak in more detail in a moment and take over the responsibilities of the entire search, which goes far beyond where we will be looking in our group."

Lucinda nodded at the troopers who stood off to her side, hands clasped behind their backs.

"What are we looking for?" a woman asked.

Lucinda glanced at the troopers. Trooper Halcomb stepped up, and Lucinda stepped aside.

"You are looking for everything and anything that at all looks out of place. Clothing. Tracks in the snow. Blood. The girl herself."

"Alive?" a man asked.

"Let's hope. If you find something, anything, do not disturb it. Do not touch it. Blow the whistle provided you, and the leader will take it from there. Just blow the whistle. That's it. Do not under any circumstances touch what you find. Any more questions?"

"You don't think she's alive, do you?"

"I've no idea. I hope so."

"You think she was taken?"

"I'm afraid that is the most likely scenario."

In Vain

Lucinda searched with the others. She searched the hills and fields and woods around Logger Brook Wildlife Management Area. The rivers and creeks and swamps. She helped scour the frozen turned fields and tumbled stone walls. She found scraps of filthy clothes, the pink and inert plastic arm of a baby doll, a deer carcass ravaged by vultures, its intestines slopped out across the snow, its guts swollen and fermenting with its own bodily gases. She found rusted license plates and broken lawn furniture, bottles and cans. Every scrap she and the others found of any possible significance was tagged and bagged. They found bones and hair from the corpses of dogs long disappeared, most just off dirt roads where they'd been struck by cars and lived long enough to crawl off into the woods and die alone.

They found no girl.

They found no sign of the girl.

Or whoever had taken her.

And she had to have been taken.

Arlene and Lewis's double-wide was searched and investigated thoroughly by forensics, who found evidence of extreme neglect and emotional and psychological abuse by isolating the girl in the basement. Arlene had confessed that this was Lewis's way of *setting the girl straight* when she *needed to learn respect*. But there'd been no sign that physical violence, at least of the sort to cause external bleeding, had taken place in that house.

Lucinda slogged through the bogs, picking her way among the alder and poplar of upland woods in grim silence alongside sober-hearted and tired-eyed fathers and mothers who seemed stunned yet also secretly grateful it was not their own child they sought out there in the unforgiving cold. She could see it in their eyes: What if. What if. What if.

Students searched, glad for the day off, oblivious to the gravity of their task, some older kids that Lucinda had learned from the case-file interviews had mocked the missing girl for being sent to kindergarten in pajamas and sent back home for head lice. Kids who'd called the girl Larva because her face was so pale as to be nearly translucent, and Alien Eyes because her eyes were so otherworldly dark.

Lucinda found herself on a hillside, walking with others in a line, and realized she was searching Dead Boy Hill, where she and Sally had once, long ago, secretly sledded against their parents' wishes; the hill where, from her bedroom window twenty-five years prior, she'd watched a search party look for her friend, wishing she could be part of it, wishing she was old enough to join them, to help. Wondering how on earth she, the world and life could possibly go on without Sally. Yet she had gone on without her. Life had, the world had. One sad second at a time. She stopped and looked up across the shallow valley of a stream to her old house, where her father now likely sat in his kitchen chair. She wondered if he was at the window watching her as she had watched him all those years ago, wishing he could be a part of it, help. She could see her old bedroom window, the one from which she'd watched that day as she felt hopeless and helpless about her friend, her mother standing in Lucinda's bedroom doorway, beleaguered and beaten down by the events, her coat buttoned all wrong. "Where are you," Lucinda whispered now. "Where are you?" Not sure if she meant Sally, for whom hope had been abandoned so long ago, or Gretel, for whom hope still remained, however slight. Or both girls.

"We'll find her, have hope," a woman near Lucinda said, Lucinda not realizing she'd spoken loud enough for anyone to hear her.

"Hope?" a man beside the woman said as he twirled his whistle around a finger on a string. "In this world."

"God works in mysterious ways," the woman said.

"He's mysterious all right, I'll give him that," he said.

"Please," Lucinda said.

The man's scoff upset others around him. "I know how these things work out."

"You haven't seen this one worked out," the woman said.

"What do you think we're going find after she disappeared with no coat or boots in this cold? Think we're going to find her having a picnic? Think she even left on her own? Someone took her."

"Please," Lucinda said. "Stop it. Or leave."

At dusk, the pale winter sun slipping beyond the hills and the snow cast in blue, Lucinda and the citizenry of searchers disassembled with nothing of consequence discovered to reward their bleak work.

They scuffed back to their cars and trucks parked at the school and along the dirt roads, kicking snow from their boots and blowing into their stiff-fingered hands wanting nothing but to go home. To be home.

Some waited for their engines to warm, others did not, wanting to depart as fast as they could. All of them were gone before darkness fell, as if they might be trapped there, lost themselves, if they did not flee now, while they could, in what light remained.

As the troopers headed back to their state barracks and Lucinda made for home, Kirk stepped over to her. "Hold up a minute."

"I should get going," she said.

"Should, should, should." Kirk took her by the wrist.

She looked at his fingers around her wrist. His grip strong. As ever. She pulled away.

"I'm tired," she said.

"That sounds a lot like I've got a headache," he said.

"Is this how it's going to be?" she said. "You acting liking this."

"I'm not acting."

"*Being* like this."

"Don't get pissy."

"This is *work*. You understand. Work. That's the only reason I'm around you. That's why, when there is no real work, when it's day-to-day small-town stuff, and not serious work like this to be done, I am *not* around you."

"Come back to the rectory, we'll work. Go over things. Have a drink to end a tough day."

"The girl is probably *dead*," Lucinda said. "I respect that even if you don't."

FIRE

Lucinda stared into the fire as Dale handed her a mug of tea.
She let the mug's warmth seep into her fingers. Her face felt
blistered from being in the cold all day. Her soul reduced to embers. They'd found nothing of the girl. No trace. Someone had to
have abducted her, just as the parents claimed. She did not believe
them, not in her gut, but she had to follow the evidence, or lack
thereof, too.

"Understand what?" Dale said as he sat beside her on the hearth.
"What?"

"You just said, 'I don't understand.'"

She'd not realized she'd spoken her thoughts.

"What don't you understand?" Dale said.

She'd been thinking of Kirk. She did not understand him, his
need to press, his disregard for professionalism and attempt to
take advantage to get close to her, ignite an extinguished ember
of attraction.

"I don't understand this about the girl," she said.

She gazed at the fire. She remembered putting household objects into the fireplace in the old house and lying to her father about it. Perhaps that's what it came down to with Kirk, a juvenile yet engrained behavior: he liked playing with fire. As naive as she'd been, he had been her boyfriend at sixteen. Except it hadn't been love, only a tsunami of hormonal urges that mutated into potent emotions and compulsive behavior she'd outgrown, and Kirk had not. "He says if they're not found right away, odds are almost zero that—"

"Who says?" Dale said.

"Kirk."

"Ah."

"Don't say it like that."

"How *should* I say it?"

"Should, should, should," Lucinda murmured. She did not know why, or even *if*, she was antagonizing Dale. Perhaps it was to do with her letter. She still needed to tell him about it; time would get short. The stress made her feel pent-up and cornered.

She sipped her tea. It warmed her throat, but by the time it reached her stomach it was cold and of no comfort. "How does a person just disappear?" Lucinda said.

"She'll turn up. She's somewhere," Dale said.

"The snow. It covered everything. Wiped it clean. I felt so guilty today. Or not guilty. I don't know. Strange. Weird. At moments, out there, searching for Gretel today, I kept thinking of Sally."

"Normal enough."

"It distracted me from my job."

"It will probably help you do your job in the long run. Your concern, your attachment to both cases."

"I kept imagining I was the one to find her, safe. Gretel. I imagined I was the savior. It felt wrong, to fantasize about being the heroine instead of just finding the girl and—"

"It's human nature. It's in our DNA to—"

"Don't sum it up. I'm trying to tell you how I felt."

He sighed. It reminded her of the sound a dog made when it had been scolded. Why was she thinking such thoughts about Dale? They dismayed her. Were unlike her. She did not *feel* this way about him, so why was she *thinking* this way about him? She reached in her pocket. Peeked at the letter.

A log on the fire toppled, a cyclone of sparks sucked up the chimney.

"Here the girl is, missing," Lucinda said. "Or God knows *what*. And I'm thinking about what it means to me. Envisioning me as a hero. It seemed cruel."

"You're not cruel, you're—"

"Ask Jonah how cruel I can be. I need to get up there, to his cabin and apologize."

"What are you fidgeting with?" Dale said.

"Hmmm?" Lucinda said.

"In your pocket, you keep fidgeting with something."

She'd worn the letter at its creases so much it was going to fall apart.

"Nothing," Lucinda said.

"What's the nothing that you can't stop peeking at?"

"It's—" She was going to say *private*, but there was no such thing, or shouldn't have been, when you were planning to get engaged. Yet she was not so naive to believe Dale or any other person did not have private thoughts, failings and doubts they kept to themselves.

"Whatever the bad news is in that letter, you've worn it on your face since you got it," Dale said.

"Bad news?" She laughed. "Quite the intuition you have there."

"Quite the secretive way you have of peeking at a letter that's all but lighting your pocket on fire. And I'm not the one with the grim face because of it."

"It's not because of the letter," Lucinda said. "Or, it wasn't."

She fished the letter out and unfolded it and handed it to him.

Dale read it, his face inscrutable. He'd make a good criminal, Lucinda thought, with that poker face and ability to keep calm in tense situations. He looked up from the letter. "Vikings?" he said.

"Maybe. Most of these types of digs—"

"You must be thrilled."

"I am. I was." She took the letter back from him. "I'm not sure what to do."

"Accept it."

"I want to, I was going to email my confirmation of commitment as soon as I got it, but I wanted to talk to you first, and then the girl went missing. I can't leave until I find this girl, one way or another."

"Kirk can handle it. Well. Maybe not. But the state police detectives can, and—"

"I won't feel right. Abandoning the case. Abandoning her. And she disappeared twenty-five years to the day Sally disappeared."

"You think they're linked?"

"I don't know."

"Why did you want to talk to me about the acceptance?" Dale said. "You must have applied with the expectation to go if you got accepted."

"I didn't expect to get selected. I submitted a bunch of applications before I met you and before my dad got real bad. All of them rejected me."

"This one didn't. So. Send your confirmation. Find the girl. Then take a break for a bit. You'll need it."

"It's not exactly for a bit."

"You could use a few weeks off. Slaving six days a week at the store, you deserve—"

"It's not weeks. It's months."

Dale scratched his cheek. "As in? Two?"

Lucinda shook her head.

"Three?" Dale said.

"Ten."

"Some of it must be remote, off-site," Dale said. "You participate from here, with Skype or—"

"It's all up there, in Canada. I'd leave in less than two weeks."

Dale stood and walked to his desk, picked up the BB Korn replica, turned it in his hands pretending to be taken with a detail. "Not something you can do quickly or from a desk," he said. "Digging up bones."

"If there are any to dig."

"Did you apply for this before or after I moved in here?"

"After."

DRAWINGS

J onah needed to keep the girl busy while he shaved and washed
before leaving. Once they got on the road, he could not be di-
sheveled, filthy, and stinking. It would draw attention. He'd need
to blend in, and he'd need to get rid of his truck as soon as they
made it to another state. He didn't know how he could do that
with no real money. He had access to the life insurance money. It
had sat in his bank account for the past eighteen years. He did not
know how much. Plenty. But he did not want to touch it. Swore
he'd never touch a penny, not for anything. Yet he could never
have imagined this scenario. He wondered if he could withdraw
some of the money and leave town while the girl was believed
abducted, without raising suspicions. How soon before he was
tracked?

Jonah set the crayons and notebook on the table in front of the
girl. "I bought them for you. As a parting gift. But we won't be
parting now. We'll be *departing*. You like them?"

She nodded.

"I was going to get you a coloring book. An old man getting a coloring book. Can you imagine what people would say? Sixteen colors in that box. That's a lot more than I ever had. You color while I wash up, then we'll go."

She fiddled with the crayon box.

He spilled the crayons out on the table and spread them around. "All yours," he said. *Go on*, he thought. *Have fun*.

She picked up the yellow crayon. Set it down. Picked up a purple crayon. Set it down. As deliberate as ever with her artistic decisions.

She picked up the red crayon and held it. Touched it to the paper.

"I'm just going to be right in there." He pointed at the door to the back room.

She drew a line with her red crayon.

"Okay then," he said, relieved. He picked up a bucket of soap water and a washcloth.

In the small back room, he levered his suspenders down off his shoulders and pulled his wool sweater over his head, hair crackling with static. He removed his flannel shirt and a T-shirt yellowed at the pits, thin with wear. He bent with a grimace and took off his boots, wool socks, pants, and long johns.

His stench rippled off of his pale, sagged flesh.

He scrubbed and rinsed until the bucket water turned foul. He toweled off and dressed, his T-shirt so rank he left it on the floor. The long johns too.

He looked down at the trunk. He'd not opened it, or even been in this room, for twenty-five years.

The hinges squealed as he opened the trunk lid. The fusty odor of mothballs made his eyes water. There it was. The yellow wool dress sat on top of the clothes. Folded just so. Still as yellow as a dandelion. Just as he remembered.

He closed the lid and left the room. Standing behind her, he looked down at what she had drawn. Ferocious, maddened red lines. Driven so hard into the paper the paper had torn.

"No," he said.

He snatched the drawing from the table. Stick figures. Sprawled near the bottom and scribbled through with violent hacks of red and black crayon wax.

He ripped up the drawing and threw it in the woodstove.

"Why did you draw that?" he said.

She pulled away.

"Tell me," he said.

She shrugged.

"Why did you draw that?"

Her fingers peeled dead chapped skin from her lips to reveal tender living flesh beneath. Pinpricks of blood seeped, blood as red as a rose in the rain.

"Don't do that," he said.

She took her fingers away and sucked on her lip.

"Why did you draw that?" he said. "Please tell me."

She pulled at her lip. Blood seeped.

"Stop. You're hurting yourself."

The girl recoiled with a sob.

"Sorry," Jonah said. "I'm sorry. I'm sorry."

He grabbed a wedge of honeycomb from a cabinet and handed it to her.

"Chew. It's honey inside. It will help your lip."

She bit the honeycomb and rubbed leaking honey on her lips.

"Why did you draw that, sweetie?" he said. "Were you hurt?"

The girl nodded.

"Who hurt you?" Jonah asked.

She shrugged.

"What about your mother, was she hurt?"

The girl shrugged.

"Did she hurt you? Did I ever hurt you?" Jonah asked.

She scrunched her face, shook her head.

"Did your foster parents hurt you?" Jonah said.

Her inky pupils shone. Meniscus trembling, yet no tears spilled. How could such a young child be so practiced at stanching emotion?

He put a finger under her chin.

"You're safe with me. I won't let anything bad happen. Now. Please. Tell me. Why did you draw that picture?"

"Saw."

"Saw what? Where?"

She pointed at her head.

"In your head?" he said.

She nodded.

He pulled out the chair and sat down beside her.

She chewed on the honeycomb. The honey flowed down her fingers.

He studied her eyes. Her face. The mouth was wider. Her hair was darker. But the eyes. If the sun could warm him from . . .

He should never have burned her drawing. It had looked so similar, it had scared him. But perhaps the drawing wasn't as similar as he'd thought. Just a damaged child's dark imaginings, or memories. She surely had her own share. He picked up the red crayon.

"I shouldn't have burned it. It was pretty. Can you draw another? Just like it?"

She shook her head.

"You'll get more honey," Jonah said.

She shook her head, jaw set. Obstinate. *Like her mother*, a voice said. He wanted nothing more than to hold her. He ached to do it. Then, he'd know. And she would too. But he couldn't hold her. He couldn't risk it.

"Why can't you draw me another picture?" he said.

"Can't see."

"Can't see who?"

Jonah hurried to the drawer and rooted around for a photo. He showed her the picture of Rebecca. "Her?" he said and set the photo down. "You mean her?"

She snatched up the red crayon and scrawled on the photo, obliterating the face in violent strokes.

Jonah snatched the photo back, slapped her hand.

She shrunk away, a tiny star collapsing into itself.

"I'm sorry," he said. "That picture is important to me. Give me the crayon."

He reached for the crayon in her hand. She pulled it to her chest and shook her head.

"I'll give you another color," he said.

A single drop of blood leaked from her palm.

He was in over his head. He'd waded too far out into troubled water and been caught in a riptide, was being pulled into the deep with no way to get to shore.

There was only one way to know if the drawings were the same, or merely similar. Compare them to the originals, which were in a pair of pants at the old house. No. He could not return there. Could never go back there.

He reached for her hand.

She shook her head defiantly.

Blood dripped on her shirt.

"Stop," he said. "You're hurt. *Damn it*, Sally. *Stop.*"

The drop of blood had congealed on the card table.

He put his finger to it.

Not blood. Red wax. She'd squeezed the crayon so hard she'd melted its wax.

Her face went calm, beatific.

Eyes clear.

He tried to cup her chin in his hands. She yanked it away. It would take time. But she was safe now. Is that what she'd meant when she'd said "home" as they'd crossed the bridge? That this was her home, where she wanted to be. Or . . . they'd been passing the old house when she'd said it. She'd been looking out the truck window past him.

At the old house.

"Who are you?" he said.

"You know."

"Who are you?"

"You know."

"Why are you here?"

"You," she said.

"Me?"

She nodded. Smiled.

"You found me," she said.

THE YELLOW DRESS

She opened her hand to reveal a pool of greasy clown's red, a poor man's stigmata.

"Messy child," Jonah said. "I got something pretty for you. Let's forget the crayon and the third degree. You want to look pretty for our trip? Prettier? You've always been the prettiest girl on the planet."

She smiled. Wiped her palm on her pants.

"Let's clean up that hand. Then we'll get you pretty." He led her to the back room where he lifted the trunk's lid.

She sucked in a breath and her eyes sparkled when she saw her yellow dress.

Jonah smoothed his palms over the dress, its wool soft beneath the hand. How long he'd looked for a warm dress that would not itch, Sally's soft child skin so sensitive, so easily rashed. Of three big-girl dresses in the shop in town Sally had preferred this one, and its matching boucle coat. Her little-girl taste so odd. So old-fashioned. That of an elderly woman from a time long before her own. As if she—

He pressed his palms onto the dress. The odor of mothballs potent, odor of the forgotten.

He lifted the dress up to display to her.

Her face lit up.

"Mine," she said.

"Yours," he said.

She reached a hand for it.

"Feel it," he said.

Her chapped fingers worked the wool as she pulled the dress to her cheek.

She eyed the matching coat from the trunk. The coat hem frayed. Mice had been at it. *How had that happened with the trunk shut tight, damn it?* He closed his eyes to calm himself. He would not sabotage this precious moment.

"See," he said. "They match."

"Mine," she said.

"Yes, yes, yours."

He searched the trunk, found tights. A tiny tank top. A hat and scarf. The perfect outfit for starting fresh.

"Put them on. I'll leave you be. You'll wear them on our new adventure. I've waited a long time for this."

She nodded.

"We'll have to get real food too," he said. "Canned sardines and smoked pike won't suffice. We'll stock up on your favorite: mac 'n' cheese. You like that, right?"

She nodded.

"I'll be outside the door. Get dressed, sweetie."

He stood outside the door, looked around the cabin, *looked* for the first time in the years he'd been up here. A shack. A sixteen-by-sixteen-foot inhabitance of cobwebbed timbers and sagged plank flooring, of tattered shades drawn across windows opaque from woodstove smoke. A countertop soiled with mouse droppings. The pong of earth and wet wood. The culmination of his days. A trunk of clothes. A drawer of photos. A heart hardened to quartz by the pressures of grief and unknowing. Dark, dank, cold, lifeless. Every day, every moment he'd carried his wife and daughter with him and wondered.

The world had pressed on. Not lost a breath for him. He'd been washed ashore on a barren, desolate island.

But now. He had her. He felt like some amphibious creature who'd lain under the earth's dark cool mud to survive an Ice Age now, finally, in retreat. He was slow and dumb to the ways of a new world. The bright light of the day pained his eyes, but his face warmed as he pushed up through the muck.

A wail from behind the door startled him.

Jonah tossed open the door to see her cowered in a corner, pointing at the trunk.

"What?" he said, kneeling in front of her. "What is it, sweetie?" She trembled. "Spi-der."

"I don't see it. It's gone now," he said.

"No."

"You scared it. You're okay now, sweetie. I won't let a spider hurt you."

She reached up and hugged him tight, pressed herself to him, whimpering. He clung to her, embraced her, finally, her warmth warming him. "You're okay." He let her go and looked at her.

She'd put on the dress. It was lovely, and even lovelier on her.

"You like it?" he said.

She nodded.

"Your shoes are somewhere too. When we get away, find another town, I'll buy you more new clothes. For our trip. But I can't take you to town with me to get supplies," he said. "I can't risk you being seen. You'll be good here, stay put, if I leave for a bit?"

She shook her head so hard her face blurred, and he worried she'd break her neck.

He took her by the shoulders. "Stop that. If you're seen, they'll take you. Do you want that?"

She shook her head.

"I'll be back before dark. I'll be as quick as I can, and I'll get the woodstove going before I leave. You'll be warm. You can color. I'll bring back coloring books. I'll bring back a couple stuffies. Ed the elephant. Yes? Maybe a favorite book." *And the old drawings*, he thought.

She shook her head.

"You want to be together?" he said.

She nodded.

"Then I *have* to get our supplies, food and clothes, and fuel up the truck, alone, without risking you being seen and taken away."

He stood, put his coat on.

"*No!*" she shrieked.

It was no use. He couldn't leave her. He'd get two steps out on the porch and she'd lunge after him or, worse, she'd go after him too late and lose herself again in the woods. Yet, he couldn't risk her being seen in town.

There was one possibility. He did not like it.

"We'll wait until dark," he said. "But when we get to town, you *have* to stay in the truck, under the blanket. You *can't* come into the stores. You can't look out the truck window when I am inside the stores, can't make a peep. Because—"

"I won' peep."

"Promise."

She nodded.

"Okay. We'll wait for dark."

Venom

The cabin lay tattooed with shadows; the fire sputtered. Jonah fed firewood into the stove, again, as he had for years. His life an endless loop of the same tired beginnings. A path too worn. A life of aborted trajectory.

No more. That life was over.

"Let's get that coat on you," he said.

He held out his hand.

She hesitated, took it.

Her hand was warm and soft, and so small. Her grip strong.

He took her to the back room and got the coat. From the trunk, he dug out a pair of rubber boots, dried and cracked, and shut the lid and had her sit on it.

He handed her the coat and she slung it onto herself then clawed at her scalp. He made a note to pick up RID at the store.

"Warm," he said. "Let's get boots on you."

He picked up a boot and tipped it upside down. A sprinkling of mouse leavings spilled from it. He reached his hand in to straighten the lining and a startling, heinous pain bit into the web of flesh at his thumb. He howled and tossed the boot. A spider latched to his flesh, its brown sac abdomen pulsing. *"Fucking Christ,"* Jonah hissed and smashed the spider to brown juice and grabbed his wounded hand. The girl shrank from him, eyes alert with terror.

"It's okay. It's dead," Jonah said.

A fierce pain lit his hand and fire streaked up his arm; the muscles twitched. What creatures this world unleashed. A spider waiting in the dark of a boot. A memory of a spider flared in his mind and died out.

"All gone," he said, sweat washing from him. He tried to flex his hand, the joint and muscles stubborn and rigid, as if set upon by rigor mortis.

He ground his teeth against the pain as it spread and pulsed in his jaw. His heart felt as if it might burst from pressure.

Sweat dripped from his forehead, spattered on her.

"Let's see if they still fit," he said, his voice sounded odd, his jaw fizzed with a remote numbness.

She dipped her toes in the boot and he slipped it on.

"Perrfect," he said.

Cinderella's glass slipper.

He took hold of the laces best he could, fingers unable to grasp fully, and pulled. The laces turned to dust in his hand. He blinked back sweat, a hot sting in his eyes.

"Let's trry the otherr." His cotton tongue disobeyed; his voice, a muddied river.

He slipped her foot into a boot. Perrfect.

He stood. The room listed. He reached out to steady himself.

She was there, next to him. Keeping him upright. Her arms wrapped tight around his waist. He put his good hand toward hers. The bitten hand sang with pain at the center of his palm and his fingertips quivered. His heartbeat was too weak and too fast.

She took his good hand. "Okay," she said. "You okay."

He wanted to take a flashlight with them but he'd be unable to hold it in his injured hand and didn't dare go into the woods among the mines without holding her hand with his good hand. They'd have to muster in the dark.

"I knoww the waay," he whispered. "I knoww the waay."

They ventured onto the porch, his hand in hers and her hand in his. He stood with his legs far apart to steady himself.

Rags of snow seeped up out of the darkness at the knuckles of tree roots. He let his eyes soak up what light the night would give.

"Holld my hand tiight. Don't let go."

She gripped his hand.

"Careful," he said.

And they stepped off into the dark together.

ONE MISSTEP

Jonah crept with her in the dark woods, led by the sound of spring water tumbling toward his truck. He needed to advance with care. The gaping entrances to the abandoned mines waited in the dark; one wrong step, a step to oblivion.

He negotiated roots and rocks; he could not afford to break an ankle. His flesh around the spider bite felt flayed open, alive and crawling with a raw, fiery itch as pain rampaged from the wound. He was glad the darkness hid it.

He stopped to rest, pickled in sweat. His hand felt as swollen and leaden as a water-soaked baseball mitt. He wanted to cut off the hand. Take an axe to it.

The sound of the spring water sliding over the rocks was too distant. He'd strayed. He could not see her in the darkness but could hear her calm breathing beside him.

She squeezed his good hand as he reached out with his wounded hand, felt a rock ledge. Cold. Soft. Powdery. Soapstone. Talc. They were among the mines. Chasms of death.

The phantom wingbeat of an owl swam overhead in the blackness, the *whooph whooph* like the rush of blood to his head.

You old idiot, you've stolen a child, the voice said. *And now you've killed her.*

This was wrong. All of it. Every second since he'd found her. Kept her. They'd die out here. Or be discovered. He'd go to jail and she'd be taken God knew where.

"Trry," he whispered.

It was no later than 7:00 P.M., but it felt like the depth of night when those who are awake know that whatever befalls them is of their own making. Paralysis overtook him. He could not move. "Hellpp," he whispered to the darkness.

"What wrong," she said. Her voice quiet, unafraid.

The owl swam. *Whoooph whooooph.*

"Nothiing," he said. "Justt. Hold my hand tiight. Don't let go unless. If I faall, let go. Don't move till liight."

He waited for his pounding heart to subside. It didn't.

One tentative inch at a time, he picked along in the dark, moving toward the whisper of running water, crawling on his knees, feeling with his enraged hand for the lip where rock fell away to nothing. Hand in hand, they traversed the slippery vein of ultramafic rock embedded in the harder granite, the schist treacherously slick beneath his boots.

He felt a soft bed of moss beneath his aching palm and stopped and sat her beside him to allow her some rest. He shivered, feverish, on fire. His mouth dry as powdered bone.

They sat in the dark. Invisible to each other. He listened to her breathe.

How'd he gotten so far off track?

A creature clabbered over the rocks in the darkness. She drew closer to him.

"Rraccooon," he said with no way of knowing.

She drew closer still.

In the dark, he wept.

"Okay," she said. "You okay."

He stood. A boot heel skidded on a greasy wet rock. He was falling. "Lettt go!" he cried.

She did not let go.

He crashed on the rocks, his wounded hand crushed under his hip against an outcrop. The dark night cracked open with silver lightning in his head.

He vomited, lay there panting.

"We go," she said.

He moaned and rolled onto his side, off his ruined hand. He stood as she held his hand tight.

The gurgle of the creek grew louder, closer.

"Thiss waay."

They hiked through a frigid pocket of air as they crossed the creek. He stopped. Listened. There. Clouds parted and through the trees the moonlight shone in the truck windshield.

He collapsed against the truck. He fished a rolled cigarette and box of matches from his jacket pocket.

He could just see her pale face in the moonlight. He handed her the box of matches.

"Liight them?" he said.

She dumped the matches in the snow and opened his truck door, then went around and opened hers, got up and into the truck.

She latched her seat belt.

She fished the keys from his coat pocket and worked the key into the ignition.

The truck started with a backfire.

He turned on the overhead light and glanced down at his hand in his lap.

Holy fuck.

He shut off the light quick.

"Bad spider," she said.

He didn't know how he was going to drive. Slow, he reasoned. Easy.

He backed up the truck, his neck stiff as he looked over his shoulder.

He drove down among dark trees. The headlight beams swam in a black soup. Truck hit a rut and pitched and rocked.

"Seat belt," she said.

He reached for the belt but could not bring it all the way across.

She reached over and latched it.

The truck lurched along road. Sweat bathed his hot skin, but he heard her teeth chatter. "Turn that dial for heat." He'd forgotten how many responsibilities there were to keep in mind with a child; at the forefront the yielding of the self to another.

Haunted House

As he crept the truck down into the valley, he felt a pressure against his arm. She'd slumped against him, asleep. Snoring. His trousers were wet with her drool. He dared not move to wake her.

He eased the truck over the railroad tracks and turned into the yard of the old house and killed the engine and the lights.

He'd not fully looked at the house since he'd left that day. He looked now, the place ghostlike in shadows cast in the dim moonlight. Shutters crooked. Missing. The shed roof collapsed. Of the three trees he and Rebecca had planted Sally's first spring, only two remained as mature trees, the other fallen over. Dead. His tree.

She awoke. With his good hand he took a flashlight from the glove box.

"Home?" she said.

"Shhh," he said.

"Home?" she said.

"Once," he said.

He opened the truck door and stumbled out.

A truck clunked over the railroad tracks with a racket, drove past without slowing.

"Go up to the porrch," Jonah said. "I need to parrk out of siight."

"Don' leave me."

"I'm not gonna leeave you."

She whimpered.

"Hop back iin then," he said.

They got back in.

"Seat belt," she said. She already had her seat belt on.

"We're not going far," he said.

"Safe," she demanded. Stubborn as ever.

"Hellp me," he said. She helped put the seat belt on and he parked the truck out of sight from the road.

Puzzle

He stood with her on the porch in the darkness and looked toward the town. He could just make out the glowing sign for the Gas-n-Go and the Grain & Feed and other businesses and shops far down Main Street. People inside going about their business. Their lives. People he used to know; people he thought knew him. He bit back his bitterness.

The porch swing swayed gently in the breeze. How many evenings he'd passed here, rocking, dozing, waving to neighbors as he'd corrected papers.

"Swing," she said and looked at him, hopeful.

"Too colld," he said.

"Spring."

"Okay," he said, though they'd be long gone on the run by spring, or he'd be locked up and she'd be lost to him forever.

The door was unlocked, and its hinges cried as he eased it open.

The ammonia reek of animal piss gagged him. Dust eddied in the flashlight beam as another odor of spore and rot emerged from beneath the piss stink. A rush of cold dead air brushed past him. Sweat dripped in his eyes. Nausea roiled in his guts. She sneezed as the flashlight beam cut a pale swath along a pine floor lacquered with dust. His old chair with duct-taped arms revealed itself from the dark. Tattered by rodents. Foam innards home to nesting mice. A wooden leg chewed so badly it had broken and the chair leaned, the motion of falling over suspended in time.

The flashlight beam lit up the couch, the couch ransacked by night creatures who'd feasted on the fabric and burrowed in the guts of it to expose the wood frame and wire springs beneath.

Jonah shut the door behind them, the room so quiet he could hear the dust settling.

He swung the flashlight on the television, its green screen dusted and cracked. Rabbit ears cobwebbed, yet otherwise as they'd been, waiting these years to again perform their common magic of converting invisible signals into moving images.

He stepped among a strewn tea set and the remnants of decomposed stuffed animals and stopped. Dizzy.

The watercolor painting of Gore Mountain hung askew on the wall.

The train had stopped traveling through town more than a decade ago. It could no longer upset the painting.

Jonah handed her the flashlight. "Poiint. Riight heere," he said.

She did, illuminating the painting in a circle of light.

He pressed a fingertip to the lowered left corner of the painting and nudged it. He eyeballed it. Tapped the top right edge.

He took the flashlight from her. Magazines lay strewn on the floor and coffee table. *Harper's, The Smithsonian, Poetry, Paris Review, Ploughshares, Ranger Rick.*

The owl clock on the wall showed one minute to twelve. The second hand dead.

He moved into the kitchen, welcomed by the blooming stench of ripe feces.

Raccoon shit coated the counters.

On the table sat three place settings. The inside of the glasses clotted with spider webs. A dead spider lay in the center of a plate. His plate.

Jonah sat at the table.

Something was missing. Something left him hollow.

The scent of them, Rebecca and Sally; it was gone. Every trace. Nothing lingered but the tang of shit and piss and death.

Haunted house. His house.

"Home?" she said.

"No."

He walked down the dark hall, the creak of floorboards beneath him. The wallpaper had peeled in sheets from the horsehair plaster, as if shedding dead skin. Curled sheaves lay on the floor, brittle as dead leaves.

He came to her bedroom door, shut by him that last day. Still shut.

SALLY'S ROOM. Her handwriting faded.

He turned the knob and opened the door.

"Stayy herre."

"Don' leave."

"Staay in the doorr."

The flashlight shone on the twin bed, forever unmade. The books on the shelf above the headboard encased in dust.

He sat on the bed edge. Her first big-girl bed. Her only big-girl bed. His bones hurt. A deep, marrow ache. His bitten hand twitched. He dangled the flashlight so it lit up the floor at his old boots, the laces frayed. Steel toes peeked out from leather. Canvas trousers worn smooth at the knees.

I disappeared with them.

He shone the flashlight along book spines. There. *Blueberries for Sal.*

He brushed cobwebs from the book and slipped it from the shelf. The jacket was still torn from his outburst of anger. He flipped through the pages, as dried and browned as ancient scrolls. He took the book and stepped to her tiny desk. Over the back of the chair were slung his old chinos, left here one of the nights he'd slept on the floor, hoping for her return.

He dug around in the pocket.

The pieces of paper were dried and faded, yet decipherable. The pieces large enough to put back together.

He lay the pieces on the desk, and started to arrange them into an approximation of the original drawings.

"Puzzle," she whispered, startling him. He'd not heard her enter.

"Yess," he said. His vision swam.

"Mine," she said. "Like mine."

"Yess." Like hers. Not exact, though. Not what he could recall from memory anyway. He'd burned her drawing in the cabin too hastily.

He tucked the pieces in his jacket pocket, shone the flashlight toward the corner. Glimmering eyes shone. Stuffed animals piled on the chair in the corner, where he'd stacked them after kicking them so cruelly.

His abdomen clenched with shame.

The pile moved. An animal jerked to life, teeth chattering. Bared.

No. A rat. It slunk from the pile, long naked fleshy tail trailing behind its bloated body as it scurried past him.

Jonah knelt at the stuffed animals, several reduced to mealy piles of stuffing. Their glass eyes stared at him across the years. What had they seen? What did they know? No less than him. Maybe more. He stroked the cheek of a fuzzy elephant, the velvet fur sloughing off at his touch.

He moved a rag doll out of the way, picked up the elephant, white foam pellets leaking from split seams. He pressed the elephant to his cheek. Smelled it. The odor of mold, the world breaking down. Dust to dust. He buried his face in the elephant and breathed in, a moan rising up from within him.

"Ed," he said. "Ed."

A hand touched his shoulder.

She stood there, her eyes level with his, lit up in the flashlight glow. She held her arms open and he leaned into her, wrapped his own arms around her, and pulled her close.

She patted his shoulder as he convulsed.

When finally he pulled away, he handed her Ed and the book.

She hugged them to her chest.

Ed's pellets spilled onto the floor where they jittered in a frantic motion, drawn toward and pushed away from each other with static electricity that spat momentary blue sparks before the beads stilled.

"You liike Ed?" he said. He took a deep breath to fight off vomiting; his engorged hand felt as if it were being boiled in grease.

She took his hand and they walked out of the room together.

He shut the door quietly and leaned his forehead against it, closed his eyes. He pressed his palm on the sign: SALLY'S ROOM.

"Thirrty-twoo," he whispered.

"Thirty-two?" she whispered.

"Years. Old. That's how old she'd be."

"Who?"

"You know."

He walked down the hall and stood outside his and Rebecca's bedroom.

He put his hand on the knob as he stood in the dark, drowned in the quiet dread of the house. Laughter rose from down the hall. Sally and Rebecca's laughter. A warm rush of longing flooded him.

Then, the laughter was gone, alive only in him.

He let go of the doorknob, unable to bring himself to open the door, to bear the emptiness behind it.

Outside, the wind was up. The cold worked fast and deep on him.

He started the truck, cranked the heat as she put on her seat belt and his. He looked at his bitten hand, looked away, repulsed and terrified.

He pulled the blanket up around her.

"Lock yourr doorr," he said. "Coverr uup."

She pushed the lock down and hunkered under the blanket, pulling it to her chin.

"Safe," she said and smiled.

"Saafe," he said. He hoped.

SHOPPING

The parking lot's lamps for Ivers Grocery scalded Jonah's eyes.

"Staay dowwn," he whispered. "I'll bring a treeat."

He parked in the spot farthest from the door and kept the engine running.

Her hand appeared from under the blanket and worked the button on his seat belt latch to free him.

He got out and stood with the truck door open and looked around the quiet lot.

"Staayy," he said and shut the door.

A boy sauntered past toward the store, eyeing Jonah.

Inside the store, Jonah squinted against the harsh fluorescent lighting, objects pulsating. His stomach rolled. He'd never been in this big grocery store, but she needed real food, nutritious food, fruits and vegetables. Protein. Except to gas up the truck, he would not dare to stop once they were on the road. He slipped a hand basket over his swollen arm to keep his good arm free.

In the produce section, he inspected an apple. Found a soft

brown spot. Set it back, choosing two before he moved off to get vegetables. Broccoli. Green beans. He drifted toward the bananas, seeming weightless, as if gravity was weakening its pull on him.

"Excuse me?" A woman in a ski parka gaped at him.

"Hmmm?"

"You need help?" She nodded at his hand, wincing.

"Spiiderr," he said with a mouth full of wet sand.

"I've never seen a hand look so—"

"Spiiderr." He slunk away, swamped in sweat.

Cereal. Fluorescent lights ticked and spat. His head floated.

The cartoon colors of sugar cereal boxes turned his stomach, yet he chose a box. Her treat. Pop-Tarts too. Brown sugar and cinnamon. Her favorite.

At the back butcher counter, he gawked at packaged, luminous red meat that pulsed beneath its plastic wrap, drowned in fake, dyed blood.

A boy in a white apron slathered with blood edged over to him.

"Got reeal meeat?" Jonah asked. The pain in his arm awakened, livid, as if he'd been excoriated. He was going to pass out. The kid at the counter said something.

"Reeeaal meeeaat that woont give daaughter caancerr." His jaw ached. Seized.

"Cancer?" the boy said.

"Juust. Give me steeeak."

The boy grabbed a steak, weighed and wrapped it. As he handed it to Jonah, he said, "Holy crow, mister. What'd you do to your hand?"

Jonah staggered off in search of aspirin. He needed to sit down. Lie down. Sleeeep. He tried to focus in the medicine aisle. He'd never seen so much medicine. More of everything. More of the same. More of nothing.

He reached for the generic aspirin, knocked the bottle to the floor. He grasped another bottle, dropped it into the basket. He needed . . . What was it? For her head? He stumbled along. Dropped a box of RID in the basket.

He found coloring books and slouched his way toward the checkout line.

The checkout girl gawped. "You all right, sir?"

The world turned liquid. "Rrring meee."

"You need help, I—"

"Rrring. Meee."

She rang him up. "Twenty-eight, forty-eight."

From his pocket, he tossed down three rolls of quarters and reeled toward the exit.

"Sir," she called after him.

Outside, he gasped in the fresh, cold air.

He stared across the parking lot. Could not locate the truck. Had he left the door unlocked? The engine running? He had. Anyone could snatch the truck. Her.

Sick. Needed rest. Sleep.

He spotted the truck, away from everything. So far away. The exhaust pipe chugged smoke. He leaned against the store wall and dropped the bag of groceries as he closed his eyes.

"Jonah?"

He opened his eyes, as if awakening from a coma.

A woman came at him.

"What on earth—"

Lucinda.

"What happened to your hand, Jonah?"

He tried to gather himself to speak clearly. "Spiderr. I wass in the trunk getting—"

"Trunk? Getting what?" She touched his hand to better get a look. He tore it away from her and shrank against the wall. God, he wished for an axe to lop off his entire diseased arm.

"I was going to come see you," Lucinda said.

He needed to escape.

"I'm sorry," Lucinda said. "That business with your credit. I was wrong. I sent you out of the store like a stranger. That's—"

He stared past her, at the truck, not hearing. Not caring, only wanting to flee. To get to Sally.

The truck. He saw movement inside it. Sally was up and was staring over at them through the back cab window.

"—you have to do something about that hand. Jonah?"

"Why I'm heere. Aspirin."

"You need more than aspirin. You look terrible. You sound . . . wrong. You need antibiotics at least. There's something really wrong. How long ago were you bit?"

Nausea ate his belly, his gut one monstrous bubble of gas about to burst.

Leave, the voice said.

"We're getting you to the doctor," Lucinda said.

"Noo." He pretended to look her in the face but looked past her, at the truck. At Sally at the window.

A car pulled in and slung its headlight beams across the truck, illuminating Sally's ghostly face.

"Let me help you. I told you. I'm sorry," Lucinda said. "After what happened with that girl, it's put things in perspective."

Jonah bridled. "Giirrl?"

"The lost girl. Terrible things like that, they put things in their proper light—"

He stared at Sally. *Get down. Get down.*

"That hand can't go unattended," Lucinda said. "If you won't let me help, promise you'll get it looked at." She stared at him. The look of a woman determined, unshakable as a snapping turtle latched to your leg. "Tonight. Go see Dr. Vern. I can call ahead. Or go with you. Let me help you to your truck."

She reached for his grocery bag on the ground.

He snatched up the bag in his good hand, cried in pain.

"Jonah," Lucinda said.

"I'll go, alone," he said.

"To Vern. Tonight. Promise me if I leave it in your hands."

"Nothiings ever been *in my handss.*" He stared at her, under-standing now what before he had not. "*Aany of our handss.*"

"Go see the doctor—"

He adjusted his grocery bag, and with his back to her shoved the coloring book down inside. "I'll live."

She peeked in the bag. He pulled it tight to him.

"I'm sorry," she said.

"Go. Colld. I'll come to the store, charge a bluue streeak. Freeezing."

"I'll see you?"

"Yess."

"I'm sorry."

"We're aall sorrry."

She left him and he watched her enter the store.

He lumbered toward the truck, swallowing down puke. Sally peeked out now, just the top of her head and eyes showing.

At the truck, he looked back at the store.

Lucinda stood inside, looking out the window at him.

He opened the truck door. "Dowwn."

Sally covered herself with the blanket as he dumped the bag inside.

As he pulled the truck out, Lucinda watched him go.

He drove toward the mountains, in the opposite direction of the doctor, of everyone. There would be no escape from town to-night.

He'd be lucky if he made it back to the cabin alive.

Light

Lucinda pulled out the metallic tongue of the tape measure and walked it back from Ed to the wire rack of postcards that customers looked at but never bought. "Fifteen feet two, two and a half, inches," she said and yawned.

She'd lain awake in bed all night thinking about the missing girl and her encounter with Jonah.

"Back up to the chicken wire rolls," Ed said.

Lucinda let the tape go. It whipsawed and crackled, snapped into its case like a tin tongue into the serpent's mouth.

"Ouch." Ed sucked at his thumb where the tape caught him. "When's the wrecking ball, anyway?"

Lucinda felt a tug of regret for her duplicity, for not coming clean with Ed about her possible absence for ten months and what that meant for the future of the place, if the place had a future at all for her, or anyone.

"We going to stay open while they renovate?" Ed said.

"If I even do it. I don't know. If I even stay open at all."

"That's a bolt from the blue. I thought you were excited about the renovations. What is all this? What else are you going to do if not run this place?"

"I'm capable of more than this."

"I meant, do you have something in mind or—"

"I got accepted, to a thing. A dig. In Newfoundland. But it's a ten-month commitment. I'd need someone to manage the store, take over my role, while I'm away. You've been here a dozen years, I know that you've wanted more. I was thinking—"

"I've been thinking, too," Ed said.

"That's beyond your pay scale."

"I might get my grandfather's old workshop in working order."

"Now *that's* a bolt out of the blue," Lucinda said.

"In my spare time," Ed said, as if sensing her concern that she'd be left high and dry. "Just to see if I take to it."

She knew this wasn't true, even if Ed didn't. He would leave the store and never look back when he found he was good at his grandfather's craft of building custom Finnish hot tubs. "You'll take to it," Lucinda said.

"I'd still be able to try to help you out even if—"

"It's not your responsibility."

Ed grabbed a bottle of Moxie from the cooler, cracked it open. "He was famous for his hot tubs, my granddad," Ed said. Lucinda was familiar with the story, but she did not interrupt. Ed was trying to redirect the conversation, and pride rang in his voice; good pride. Pride for someone else's accomplishments. "He went to Finland. By ship. He was in *Yankee* magazine. *LIFE.* The Grocery still has the faded magazine spreads on a bulletin board."

"I saw Jonah at the Grocery last night," Lucinda said.

"Since when is he in town at night? And at the Grocery?"

"He looked horrible. A mess."

"That's breaking news."

"I mean. Really sick," Lucinda said. "His hand looked grotesque. So swollen it didn't even look like a hand. Purple, blistered, and seeping a yellow fluid. A recluse spider bit him."

"Jesus. That's serious."

"I told him to go see Vern and he swore he would; but I checked with Vern this morning and he hadn't seen Jonah. I should have forced him."

"You can't force Jonah to do anything."

The cowbell above the door clanked. Marnie from the Gas-n-Go strode in clapping her hands and blowing into them and knocking her boots together to clop off the snow, her face florid from the cold. She wiped at her runny nose.

"Greetings," she said.

Ed took the tape measure from his pocket and played with the tape, pulling out a length and letting it snap back.

"I hoped to see you here," Marnie said to Lucinda.

"Our haul of wood pellets is due in tomorrow if—"

"No, no. As deputy," Marnie said. "I saw something strange last night. I was driving by that old abandoned place, by One Dollar Bridge, and I saw a light on inside."

"Couldn't be," Ed said. "Place hasn't had power since—"

"A flashlight," Marnie said.

A light? In Jonah's old place, Lucinda thought.

"Did you see anyone, the person using it?" Lucinda said.

"I wanted to stick around. But I was looking for my dog, Jelly Belly; she got loose and I was walking around looking for her. I saw it for certain. I came back to the house after I found Jelly Belly.

She was over behind the Covered Bridge Diner, eating slop around the Dumpster, she likes all that fried food, like I don't feed her enough already, but Jelly Belly she—"

"What was at the house when you got back?" Lucinda said.

"Nothing. The house was dark. But with this girl missing, and me not ever seeing a light on in that house in all these years. And just seeing that old guy in the Gas-n-Go recently."

"Jonah was at the Gas-n-Go?" Lucinda said.

"I didn't even know that's who he was, until the boob tube at work aired an old piece about him, about his wife and daughter. I can't believe anyone believes that about him. He's always been respectful the few rare times he's come in. Quiet. If nervous. Bought his tobacco and rolling papers, and crayons this time and—"

"Crayons?" Lucinda said.

"For something he's building. He said crayons are cheaper than carpenter pencils."

Outside, the town plow charged past on Main Street to heave a wave of snow onto the sidewalk.

"I just thought it was odd," Marnie said, "and you might want to look into trespassers or whatever. I'd rather tell you than the sheriff. He kind of . . . I don't know . . . creeps me out."

Lucinda took her barn jacket from a wood peg by the door, pulled on a wool cap, and shoved off into the morning snow and cold.

FALLING

Jonah lay on the couch, head propped on a pillow he'd not re-
called placing there himself. Slack, immobile, body poached in
sweat. Vision swampy. Tracers of pain flared through each vein,
each capillary. He opened his eyes. Slits. Saw a semblance of her
face through the quavering air as she came and went, yet he felt
her always present. He shut his eyes again and fought the nausea.

A cloth, cold and damp, pressed to his forehead.

His putrid hand soaked in a bucket of warm salt water.

How did she know what to do?

He drifted.

Dreamed.

*Home, the sun pouring through the breakfast nook in the kitchen,
the smell of bacon and eggs and coffee, daughter on his lap giving
him a peck on the cheek, her arms wrapped about his neck loosely
and a round pink face so full of love and innocence gazing up at him
it was all he could do to leave her and set out into the world for a
day of work. She was there, too, Rebecca, standing in the doorway
to the hall taking them in, her husband, their daughter. Her face,*

too, shining. Glowing. The kitchen saturated with sunlight, growing warmer, brighter, until it blinded, caught afire and burned them all to ash.

He started awake, weeping.

A hand touched his cheek.

He took it in his and held it there.

"Sally," he said. "Sally."

And he was gone again.

Falling.

Endlessly.

Discovery

Lucinda stalked down the snowed sidewalk, face flushed, bare hands jammed in her jacket pockets. She stopped fast at the sight of a face staring at her. For a second, Lucinda had thought the photo on the Missing Person tacked to the telephone pole was of Sally. Those dark eyes, the paper wet from snow, cried black ink down the image of the girl's face. It was not Sally. It was Gretel. But, the resemblance. That odd, sweet face. It betrayed none of the abuse inflicted upon the girl, as if she knew that to betray it would bring more upon her. And those eyes. So dark. *We'll never find her*, Lucinda thought. *Not alive. Not now.* "Whoever did this to you, whoever has taken you," Lucinda whispered. "I'll make sure they pay for it."

She hurried onward. Snow drifted down silent from dark, smoky clouds as if it were the ashen fallout of a forest fire. The morning light was sleepy. A gaggle of boys stalked the sidewalk, launched snowballs at a stop sign, making a competition of it. *You'd never see girls do that*, Lucinda thought. A girl's inclination toward competition was more subtle but perhaps more vicious too. For the first

time in years, Lucinda thought of Betty Lansing, the meanest of
the Eye Shadow Girls who had taunted and frightened Lucinda and
Sally. What had become of her? Not long after Sally's disappearance, the girl and her family disappeared, too, not like Sally and
her mom had, but moved out of state somewhere, and Lucinda had
never seen Betty again.

A truck from High Meadow's dairy backed up into the side
street to the loading dock of Ivers Grocery. Lucinda remembered
milk and eggs left in the milk box on the porch. Gone now. That
personal touch. Vehicles eased up and down the street, slush
shooshing. Wipers thwacking. Pickup trucks. Tradesmen.

As she passed Rosie's Hardware, Edsel, the owner, nearly
knocked her over as he trundled a dolly loaded down with sacks
of ice salt.

"Sorry there, Luce," he said. Jowls rubbery as a St. Bernard's.
"Gotta get the salt out for the customers. Town oughtta salt the
walks better. But I can't complain. Selling this stuff like water in
the desert."

Lucinda passed the Lucky Spot, the place mobbed, vehicles
parked out front, idling, wisps of exhaust trickling from shivering
tailpipes.

She crossed Railroad Street and kept going until the sidewalk
ended.

At One Dollar Bridge, she stared across the street at the old
house. In the covered bridge's rafters pigeons purred. Their droppings spattered the old boards. She looked down at the stream
running under the bridge. Clear. Cold.

She looked for trout finning, as she'd done with her father as a
girl, but her eyes were unpracticed and she could not see any trout.
In the summer, kids jumped from the bridge roof into the deep

water. She'd done it. It had always been done and seemed it would always be done. She looked for a moment longer for a trout and crossed the street, stood in front of the old house.

She'd not been in there since she'd sat on the swing with Jonah the day she'd run off to the pit, so long ago.

Stunted maple tree seedlings sprouted from the moss she knew carpeted the roof beneath the snow. The chimney was cratered where bricks and chinking had loosened and fallen out over the years. A tree lay dead on the lawn. How much effort went into the upkeep of life. The work it took just to maintain. She walked up the driveway, the asphalt in rutted upheaval from decades of freeze and frost and thaw, freeze and frost and thaw.

She stopped and stared at tire tracks, nearly erased by new snow. The tracks led from the driveway around to the back of the shed.

She followed the tracks to where a vehicle had parked.

A wide vehicle. A truck? SUV? Someone *had* been here.

Lucinda circled the area where the truck had parked. Boot tracks, reduced to indistinct depressions under the fresh snow, led from where the vehicle had parked to the house.

Lucinda followed the drifted tracks to the front steps. One track was definitely that of a child. Another track an adult's. Squatters? she wondered, with the cold coming? No. The house, as far as she knew, had not been disturbed all these years. She only knew one squatter. And he was up in the hills. She tried the knob, surprised to find it unlocked. She let herself in, as she had so often, so many years ago as a girl, when she was yet untainted by the world's wickedness.

My God.

Her breath left her at the ammoniac stench of animal urine.

Every toy, every glass and magazine sat right where it had been that last night, the place in decrepitude now from time's passing, slow and steady and unstoppable.

Animals had laid waste to the place; feces soiled the carpet and wood floors.

Decades of sunlight washing through the windows had leached color from the wallpaper and furniture, now gone a ghostly pale.

Lucinda tried to breathe, coughed in the dry dust of the place. She'd have sat down in the couch to gather herself as the crush of memories stampeded her, but the couch was befouled with clots of animal hair and scat, and it reeked of piss and musk.

In the kitchen, three place settings sat on the Formica tabletop, each plate still waiting to be used.

Lucinda could almost hear Sally squealing with glee from her room: *Is that Lucinda at the door, Mommy! Let her in! Let her in!*

Lucinda trailed down a hall littered with peeled wallpaper and animal scat and came to stand at a closed door. The faded sign: SALLY'S ROOM.

Lucinda opened the door. The room lay as quiet and still as a held breath. She shuddered and felt nearly overcome with an urge to flee. Her presence seemed a violation of a place sacrosanct. Unease settled in her bones.

A pile of stuffed animals lay heaped in the corner, the creatures reduced to scraps of fur and puffs of stuffing, real animals having cannibalized their faux kin.

She knelt by the animals, overcome with sorrow. Sally would be distraught to see her animals in such a pitiful, unloved state. Lucinda picked up a doll, one of its button eyes missing. "Baby Beverly?" she whispered. It reminded her of her own Baby Beverly. Except her Beverly had both eyes. How she'd cherished

Beverly. She'd taken her everywhere so she would not be alone and afraid. Where was she now? Packed away. In a box, likely. In a dark lonely attic or basement. Lucinda could not even say where her doll was, if she even existed anymore; yet she had a desire to see her again, as strong a desire to find her old, childhood doll as she had to find this missing girl.

She looked at a photo on the desk, the doll dangling by its pigtails from her fingers. The photo was of Sally. A school photo. Lucinda blew dust off it, an archaeologist piecing together past civilizations. Those eyes. So dark yet bright, it seemed a sacrilege they could ever be extinguished from the world. Life in them. Not just Sally's. Life itself. Wanting out. Filling you with itself.

Lucinda set the picture down and looked at a cork bulletin board, coloring book pages pinned to it, as pale now as Lucinda's father's sickly skin.

She pulled a thumbtack out of the board to free a page. A giraffe, its purple body and yellow mane faded.

Stopped.

She stared at the bulletin board, the coloring-book page falling from her hand.

"What the fuck," she whispered.

No

Lucinda reached for what her eyes saw but her mind did not believe.

Her fingertips touched it, pulled away.

A child's drawing on a piece of lined yellow paper, long hidden behind the giraffe picture.

Stick figures. Two of them. On their sides, hand in hand. One larger than the other, with long dark brown hair. Like Sally's mother's.

One smaller, with pigtails. A girl.

Eyes X'd out.

Red slashes across the necks.

All around them, scribbled red crayon. Dark, ragged. Furious. The paper torn from pressing. Blood. Pools of angry blood, so deep and waxy it seemed to be wet. Hovering above the figures, in a black scrawled sky, an evening star. The arms. The legs.

"Christ," Lucinda said.

She looked at the bulletin board.

At all the other coloring book pictures.

She lifted up one of a bumblebee.

No.

One of a rainbow.

No.

Of a cat.

A puppy.

Horses.

She tore them down. Behind each page hid another drawing, each more gruesome, more graphic and angry than the last, of things no child could know unless they'd lived it, or glimpsed its potential within another person.

She stared at the drawings, heart racing so hard it was as though the valves were stuck wide open, her blood a wild, hot torrent.

She was too hot. She reached to clutch the desk edge for balance, but her fingers would not obey. The rag doll slipped from her weakening grip to hit the floor with a dead thud and a mechanical cry: *Help me. I'm hurt.*

Darkness descended.

BOOK IV

Darkness Coming

Cold. Stiff. The light peculiar. An orange glow pulsed and strobed.

Where was she?

Lucinda gained her knees with a groan. Her jaw and her left eye pulsed with pain.

A bedroom.

She was in a bedroom.

Sally's bedroom.

She looked out a window. The setting sun's orange light glowed on the bedroom walls.

Lucinda looked at the stick figure drawings on the bulletin board.

A chill rippled through her. How had Lucinda not known about Sally's drawings? She felt a stab of petty girlhood resentment. How could Sally have kept these drawings secret; she and Sally were best friends. They told each other their secrets and kept them.

Lucinda tucked the drawings in her coat pocket. She did not know what they meant, but they disturbed her. The tracks in the snow and someone having been in this house upset her too. She considered telling Kirk but decided to sit on the development, for now. The house appeared undisturbed, and the snowed-in tire and boot tracks were useless as evidence.

She picked up the doll and squeezed it.

No sound came.

She squeezed it again.

Nothing.

What had she heard it say? *Help me? I'm hurt?*

She squeezed its belly. Its face.

Silence.

She'd heard it. She'd swear. She had heard it cry out. Her old Beverly doll had not been able to do that.

She dug her fingers into the doll. Pierced its cloth with her fingernails and ripped the doll open. Pulled out its stuffing.

Nothing. Empty. No voice box.

Her jaw throbbed. Her eyelid spasmed. Her vision wouldn't focus. It was as if she were seeing through the film of a dusty window. With the room growing dark, she dropped the doll to the floor and fled from the house; she could not get out of there soon enough.

A KNOCK AT THE DOOR

Jonah tried to prop himself up on his elbows, dazed, brain fogged, the cabin shadowed. He peered at his hand, soaking in a bowl of warm water. The swelling had subsided, some. He thought. Maybe. No. No, it hadn't. The purpled palm remained numb and monstrous, the fingers ballooned, taut skin inflamed and chafed, rimmed with salt from the soaking solution.

She'd done it, soaked his hand.

She sat now, hunched at the card table, scribbling.

Jonah sat up, a wave of nausea forcing him to slump on the edge of the couch. *Breathe*, he thought, *breathe*. He hung his head between his knees. Then he planted his palm on the couch arm and tried to stand, lame and feeble. Famished. A salty thirst begged to be slaked.

He needed to leave with her, but he could not venture in the woods in this state, risk the mines in the dark. His energy would flag well before he got to his truck, and he'd never get far driving before sleep or sickness took him. One more night of rest. That's all they needed. Then, they were gone.

He stood behind her at the table, hands on the back of her chair to support himself, his body humming with fatigue. She had a coloring book open and was working away at a horse.

A scrap of notepaper lay beside the book, colored completely black.

"Pretty horse." He pointed at the blackened notepaper. "What's that?"

Her face pinched.

"Nighttime?" he said.

She shook her head, her eyes dark. Black.

He saw she'd drawn another stick figure, lying in the grass. A girl. Or a woman. She'd scribbled red crayon all over the girl and was coloring everything on the page above the woman in black.

"Why are you drawing these?"

She shrugged.

"You must know. Tell me. Who is it?"

A knock pounded at the door.

Jonah gasped: the last breath of a drowning man before he went under for the last time.

She looked up.

Jonah placed a hand on her shoulder. He hadn't heard an ATV.

The knocking pounded on the door. Louder. Insistent.

The girl whined.

"Shhh," he whispered. "Shhh."

A shadow crossed by the front porch window.

Jonah moved in front of her to block her from sight.

Someone peered into the grimed window, a shadowy figure. A man. It disappeared from the window.

The knock came again.

"The back room," Jonah whispered. "*Go.*"

She stared at him.

He picked her up from the chair and hauled her to the back room and set her on the trunk. "Stay here. Understand? Don't make a peep. No matter *what*. And don't come out. If you do, they'll take you and I'll be in big trouble."

She nodded.

The knocking came.

He kissed her forehead then left and shut the door behind him. He took the drawing and coloring books and hid them under a plate, looked around for more evidence of Sally. Saw nothing.

A fist pounded on the door.

Jonah took deep breaths, trying to wake himself, prepare himself. He grabbed the rifle from the corner, cracked the door open, and peered out.

Nostalgia

Lucinda peered at her face in her Wrangler's rearview mirror. She looked like she'd been pummeled with a length of firewood. Cheek gashed. The bruised flesh around her eye, purpled and swollen; it glistened like mica. She pressed her finger to it, hissed in pain.

She got out of the Wrangler and scooped snow off the top of her father's mailbox and pressed it to her tender cheek. The bone ached. The cold snow stung her skin, yet she kept it to her face until it melted. Snow swirled in a dim fan of lamppost light far down the street. If not for the lone pale light from its kitchen window, her father's house would have been lost to darkness.

Lucinda picked her way up the iced driveway, holding on to the side of the vehicles to make her way without falling.

She knocked on the side kitchen door, heard the skid of a chair backing up from the table, footsteps. The door opened.

"Luce," Dot said, "I thought— Oh, your face, darling, what happened?"

"It's nothing."

"I've seen nothing. That's not it."

"I fell on the sidewalk."

"They ought to salt those walks sooner with the taxes we pay. Come in."　\

The kitchen was hot from the oven being on and smelled good, of baking dough. Of roast chicken.

Her father sat in the chair in the corner, his chin tucked to his chest. Asleep or dead, it was impossible to tell. It would be the latter soon, for certain.

"Sorry I'm late," Lucinda said.

"A fall like that. You should be home. Resting. Having a stiff drink with your man. I'd be. Nice you came by at all after such a spill."

"He's my father," Lucinda said. It was true; Lucinda ought to have been here hours ago for her daily visit, and she wanted to be here now; but she'd not come just to visit.

"I hope my own kids come around as much as you do when my clock winds down," Dot said.

Lucinda sat beside her dozing father, his breath so faint it was a wonder it was enough to keep him alive. Lucinda took a tissue from a box on the table and dabbed drool from his lip.

"He have a good day?" Lucinda asked Dot.

"He did."

Lucinda touched his cheek lightly with the back of her hand. She took his hand in hers. "Dad," she said.

Her father lifted his chin. Blinked and looked at her. His eyes brightened. "Lucy," he said.

"How are you?"

"Just . . . dozing. Happy now. You're here. Happy to be . . . awake."

"You want to stay?" Dot said. "I made a chicken potpie for myself. It's a frozen store-bought. But a good store-bought. Far as that goes."

"I just want to see him." Lucinda eyed the cellar door. "Speak to him, in private, if I could."

Dot nodded and left the kitchen, wiping her hands on her apron.

"Dad," Lucinda said. "I need you to look at something. Can you do that?"

"My eyes work okay, today." He grinned, his face hollowed out, the skull pronounced beneath his skin.

Lucinda slipped her hand in her jacket pocket and took out one of the drawings she'd found in Sally's room. She held it up to show her father. His fingers squeezed her fingers, tight.

"What is it, Dad?"

"Where—"

"I found these in Sally's room. There were a bunch."

"Why did you bring them?"

"I wanted to see what you thought about them. I think she was scared. I think she was scared of the man in the woods, more than she ever told me. I mean. *Look* at them."

He didn't look at them, he looked away.

"Too long ago now," he whispered, his voice as frail and brittle as his bones.

"It's not too long ago. It's never too long ago. And. There's a missing girl, *now*. And I think . . ." Lucinda did not know what to think. She had no concrete theories. But the drawings, they set her on edge, set her mind to trying to draw connections. Connections between what? Gretel and Sally? Sally's mother? "What do you make of these drawings? What would you think if you'd seen them all those years ago?"

"Kid. Imagination."

"If it was some other kid, maybe. But . . . These were Sally's."

"She's gone."

"I know. But what would you think if you'd found them then? Would it have made you—"

"I did. Find them."

"You found these?" Lucinda said.

"Some. Like them."

"Why didn't I know about this, why—"

"You were a child."

"But . . . What did you think, what *do* you think?"

"They were. Ominous. Gave them to him."

"To who?"

"Jonah."

"Jonah knew about these? Why didn't you keep them, the ones you found, for evidence? I don't understand? They were evidence."

Her father worked his tongue as if trying to rid a hair stuck to the roof of his mouth, making a wet clucking sound.

"Why did you let Jonah have them?" Lucinda said.

Her father mumbled, his head wobbling as if the muscles in his neck were too weak to hold it upright.

"Why did you let him have them?" Lucinda pressed.

"Better. That. Way."

"Why?"

He closed his eyes, his jaw muscle pulsed. Drool leaked from the corner of his mouth. His fingers slackened from around her own fingers, his hand falling into his lap, and he fell into a doze.

"Damn it," Lucinda said. "Damn it."

Dot cleared her throat behind Lucinda.

"Everything all right?"

No, everything was not all right. Nothing was right at all. It was not all right that after twenty-five years someone had been in Jonah's house. An adult and a child. It was not all right that Sally had drawn such violent, disturbing images. It was not all right that a new girl was missing, the date of her disappearance coinciding with that of Sally and her mother. It was not all right that her father had not logged Sally's drawings as evidence. It was not all right that Lucinda was hearing dolls speak and keeping Dale in the dark. "Everything's fine," Lucinda said.

"Could have fooled me."

"I had a doll once," Lucinda said. "Beverly. I never let her out of my sight. I took her everywhere. I cried whenever my mom washed her. Afraid she'd drown. Needed her with me at all times. Now I have no idea where she is. I lost her at some point. You love something so much and can't live without it and then one day you don't even know what became of it. How's that happen?"

"I don't know."

"I think she's in the basement. Or the attic. I thought I'd look. I'm feeling . . . I don't know. Nostalgic. You haven't come across a doll, have you?"

"Never been in the cellar or the attic."

"You wouldn't mind if I looked?" Lucinda said.

"It's your house," Dot said.

It was absurd to ask. Yet, technically, the house was not Lucinda's house. Not yet. It was her father's house. She'd only grown up in it. "It's silly. It's just . . . Something happened today. I saw a doll that looked so much like mine. Like Beverly. It shook me. It's made me sentimental. I feel badly that I don't know where she is. Like I've let down the little girl I once was. And—" It sounded ridiculous, but it was true. Yet only in part. Looking for the doll was also a ruse. If her father had let Jonah keep the drawings, possible evidence to at least establish Sally's state of mind, what else might he have kept out of the light to protect his friend? She wondered if he kept files or other evidence in the house no one else knew about. Looking for Beverly might be a waste of time, but searching for old files or evidence of her father's was not.

"It's not silly," Dot said. "Our pasts are important."

Lucinda patted her father's hand and stood. She kissed his forehead then tried the cellar door. The deadbolt was locked. She went to the cupboard and rummaged until she found a brass key and unlocked the door.

The hinges creaked as she opened the door, and a fungal odor rose as from a shut tomb.

Lucinda tried the light switch but no light came on.

She dug a flashlight from the drawer and covered her nose and held the stairway rail as she slowly descended into the cellar.

The flashlight beam glowed weakly.

The stairs moaned.

At the bottom of the stairs, she looked back. The doorway seemed miniature and far away, the meager light from the kitchen dying halfway down the stairs.

She shone the light around the cellar, a tighter space than she remembered, the ceiling so low she was forced to duck. Cobwebs clotted the beams and pipes above her head, and a cold dampness stuck to her skin as her boots sank into muck, the dirt floor reduced to a swamp from water leaking in from the stone foundation. She sneezed in the fetid air, her body trying to expel the mold spores. She stepped to a bowed shelf, mud water sloshing at her boots.

On the shelf sat a few boxes, cardboard wilted decomposing from dampness. An old lamp and an iron stuck out from one box. One box was marked BOARD GAMES, another GLASSWARE.

Lucinda poked around from box to box. Bric-a-brac. Junk. No stuffed animals or dolls. Or files. A noise in the corner made her jump and swing the light toward it. Nothing. Darkness. Dirt. Mud.

She shone the light on the workbench. Her father's place of escape. She twirled the handle of the workbench vise, remembering the night she'd come down to find him, so upset for his friend, and at his failure to help him or solve the case. How awful, to balance friendship and official duties.

Her father had stopped coming down here years ago, lost interest in his birdhouses.

Lucinda spun the handle of the vise. Socket wrenches and chisels, jars of rusted screws and nails, caked in dust, cluttered the workbench. Lucinda opened a drawer. Bins of nails. Brads and nuts. A staple gun. No Beverly. No files.

In the far, dark corner, a mouse skittered out from under an ancient trunk that sat rotting in a depression of pooled water. The mouse squeezed into a crack in the foundation wall. From behind Lucinda rose a roar. She shrieked and dropped the flashlight and tripped her way up the stairs, heart beating in her throat.

"What is it, dear?" Dot said.

Lucinda waited for her breathing to calm. Then, smiling, feeling foolish, said, "Just the furnace kicking on."

"Find your doll?" Dot said.

"I'll check the attic."

LEAVE

The man stood on the cabin porch, tugged on the waist of his duck-cloth pants. Despite his gut that slopped over his belt and seemed to force him to leave his snowmobile parka unzipped, he possessed the assured posture of a man assessing the value of property—his property—as his eyes roamed over the front of the cabin. It was the man from earlier, the one on the ATV.

"Get out of here," Jonah said.

"You can come outside or I can come inside. I got something you have to hear."

"I don't have to hear a thing from you." Jonah started to close the door.

"*Law* sees different," the man said and sniffed, ran his tongue along the inside of his bottom lip as if to extract a dip of tobacco.

Jonah paused, one hand on the door, one hand on his rifle behind the door.

The man tipped his grubby camo ball cap back off his brow, his skin red and indented where the hat had dug into his flesh. "The

law says I got to deliver you this message in person and make sure
you understand it. Make sure it sinks in."

What was this? Law. Bullshit. Jonah glanced back at the door
to the back room to make sure it was shut and the girl hidden. It
was. She was. For now.

"Here's something for you to understand," Jonah said.

He opened the front door and stood with the rifle aimed at the
man's gut. It was work to keep the rifle level, the effort threatened to sap what meager energy he'd been able to muster to simply
stand at the door.

The man sucked in a breath and stepped back. "Hey," he said.
"Don't—"

"You forget the promise I made you or do you just think I was
full of shit?"

Jonah's thumb worked the rifle's smooth hammer. Cocked it.

The man shoved a yellow piece of paper at Jonah.

"I don't want that," Jonah said.

"This ain't your cabin. You're on private land. A squatter." The
man's voice quavered. "Most these trees are coming down come
spring. This letter tells you that you need to get out come December
one. If not, you'll be escorted out."

Jonah looked at the paper. The visit had nothing to do with
Sally.

If he'd not been bitten by the spider, they'd have been long gone
by now anyway.

"Tell your paper people I'll be as far away from here as I can by
then," Jonah said. "Not because they say so. Because I can't stand
it here anymore. Now leave."

The man backed away, leaving the piece of paper on the porch
rail.

Jonah watched until the man disappeared in the dark trees; then he let out a breath and rested the rifle in the corner, the metal lever action slick with sweat.

He would have shot the man for certain if he had come for her.

He opened the door to the back room.

The room was empty.

The Past Packed Away

Lucinda climbed the stairs to the second floor of the house, the runner rug as worn as an animal trail up the middle of the steep old steps. Photos of herself and her father and mother hung from the stairway wall, each of them staring back at her from past lives. Lucinda and Sally on the tire swing in the backyard, pigtails flying, gap-toothed and laughing. Photos of Sally and her parents with Lucinda and her parents, picnicking, camping, sledding.

Except for Dot dusting and vacuuming the house, no one had been up the stairs in years, her father sequestered in the downstairs bedroom where he'd slept every night since her mother's passing nearly twenty-three years ago.

On the second floor, the air was still and dead. The heat volcanic. Sweat sprouted on her forehead. The path in the rug continued down the center of the hallway.

Lucinda nearly tripped on the top stair tread. Still loose, to this day.

She looked back down the stairs.

Ten stairs.

Lucinda shuddered. She saw her mother now, heaped at the bottom of the stairs. Her father kneeling beside her, weeping as he looked up at Lucinda, aghast with fear. Those who did not believe in the soul had not been beside a body whose life had just departed. Lucinda had just been with her mother an hour earlier at bedtime, laughing in the bathroom as they'd brushed their teeth together.

That is not my mother at the bottom of the stairs, she'd thought. That was not her father, that frightened man who had already started to slip away from the living world after failing to find his friend's wife and daughter, or the person behind their disappearance, and now would disappear more every day, retreat to a place in his mind where no one could reach him.

Lucinda wandered down the hall; her wounded face pulsed with pain.

She stood in her parents' old bedroom.

She'd not been in it for decades.

It was as it had been. Immaculate, tidy. The dark wood floors shone as if freshly shellacked. Pristine white doilies adorned the polished dresser and nightstands. On the wall beside the bureau mirror hung a calendar from Ivers Insurance, the page revealing the image of two kittens tousling a ball of yarn. March 1989. Month of her mother's death.

Lucinda opened the closet door. The scent of old wool irritated her nose, made it itch, yet there was none of the expected astringent odor of mothballs. Each of her mother's winter coats hung from its own hanger, each equally spaced from the other, and bagged in a dry cleaner's clear garment plastic. Lucinda looked at one of the dry cleaner tags. Its date just two weeks ago. Dot saw to it. Scarves and mittens, folded with meticulous precision, sat in a neat stack on a wire rack.

From the closet ceiling hung a string with a ring on the end.
Lucinda pulled it.

A collapsible attic stairway unfolded with the complaint of un-
used springs.

Icy air seeped down from a draft above as Lucinda climbed the
stairs into the attic, shivering at the cold. She reached around in
the dark, pulled a string. A lightbulb pulsed and flickered, lit the
attic, her breath visible in the cold.

The wind shrieked in the eaves sounding like the cry of a
wounded animal.

At the far gable end of the attic, boxes were stacked atop one
another in a haphazard fashion, not the work of Dot. The jagged
sharp points of rusted nails poked through the plywood roof just
above her head, and a ribwork of joists with wide spans between
them ran from Lucinda to the boxes. Beds of pink fiberglass insulation lay between the joists atop Sheetrock that Lucinda's foot,
Lucinda herself, could easily crash through if she put too much
weight on it. She would need to tread with care.

Lucinda ducked beneath the ominous nails and picked her way
down the attic, clutched the beams above her to keep her balance
as she stepped over each expanse of insulation, from one joist to
the next. At the boxes, she stooped, balancing herself on her heels,
and read the black marker on the sides of the boxes. More of the
same, eras packed away, clothes and games, tools and dishes, the
indelible turned untenable. She checked each box, searched for
files and for Beverly. She found neither.

She came to a box marked STUFFED ANIMALS.

She took a deep breath. She opened the flaps and peered inside. There lay Boo Boo Kitty. An oddly flat cat with blue matted
fur and yellow plastic eyes. Lucinda took it out and smelled it. It

smelled as she remembered, an odor of milk and baby blanket. She held it to her, set it aside, and rummaged through the box to find Ducky, Stiff Piggy, Lil Lamb. The sight of each triggered a melancholic ache.

She picked up a small stuffed bear she did not recognize, flooded with shame for having forgotten what the bear had meant to her. If it were here in this box, the bear must have meant something to her at one time, yet she could not recall.

She found no Baby Beverly.

She placed the animals gently in the box and left the flaps open, not wanting to shut her stuffed animals away entirely. Stooping under the rafters, she spied a box marked TOYS.

In it sat a wooden hound dog with a plastic pull leash and felt ears. Snoop 'n Sniff. A xylophone. She tapped a finger on its key and a note rose high and tinny and fell away. A Chatter phone. Stacks of *Mad Lib* booklets. No Beverly. Lucinda's back began to ache.

The last box was marked UNIFORM.

Lucinda placed a palm on it, feeling her breathing catch.

She peeled back the box flaps. A millipede slithered out from the box.

Inside lay her father's old sheriff's uniform, a rigid khaki sheriff's hat atop it. The shirt of the same khaki, pressed and folded crisp, badge pinned to the pocket. The uniform had defined her father. Whenever he worked at the Grain & Feed, particularly Sundays, and wore a flannel shirt and green Dickies, he'd looked odd, out of sorts, his behavior too loose, volatile. His measured voice grew boisterous, and it pitched and swung in sudden ways. It was as if the uniform had kept him contained. In control.

She held the shirt up before her. A broad-shouldered shirt that would swallow his now scarecrow body. Above the badge and shirt pocket, her father's named stitched from stout green thread. She set the shirt beside her and lifted out the pants, made of the same smooth khaki as the shirt, with black piping running down the outer seam of each leg. A button fell from the pants pocket, one her father had likely sewn on the shirt himself after her mother had passed.

She tucked it in her coat pocket, folded the pants and shirt, and placed them in the box. Put the hat on top of them. She took a last long look and folded the box flaps shut.

She did not want to be here any longer. The house upset her. Her failing father upset her. The end of things. A closing in of his mortality, and her own. Each breath burned in her lungs, and her eyes wept, an allergic reaction to the fiberglass insulation.

Lucinda hurried to the stairs and took them two at a time.

Driving down Main Street she saw the lights were still on inside the rectory. She slowed her Wrangler down and pulled over across the street, killed the engine.

She watched the rectory. She pondered telling Kirk about the drawings, about people being in Jonah's house. She needed to abide by the law, the process. Yet she imagined how Kirk might react to her *developments*. Scoff. She could just see, through the parlor window, the back of his head where he sat in the chair. He rose and left the room and returned. Likely to get a beer. He sat again.

Lucinda shivered.

The Wrangler had grown cold as an icebox.

She watched the parlor window for some time then started up the Wrangler and headed home.

HIDING

Jonah stepped behind the trunk to see if she had hidden there. She hadn't.

He went to the window.

It was shut. She couldn't have just left the room without him hearing her.

But the room was empty, and there was no place to hide. Except.

Jonah threw open the trunk lid.

Clothes. Only clothes.

She had to be here. Had to.

She'd be suffocated if she was. Dead.

He tossed clothes behind him, crazed, the trunk seeming bottomless. How could she not be here? Had he dreamed her? Had she been a manifestation conjured in some fever fit when he'd been bitten by a spider, and time had been confused?

How—

There. He thought he sensed movement beneath the clothes and flung more of them out of the trunk. There. On the bottom. Hunkered. Hiding.

Curled up fetal and unmoving.

"Sally," he said.

What had he done, leaving her here alone?

She didn't move.

He shook her. Hard.

"Hey," he said. "Hey."

Slowly, she turned her face up at him and smiled.

"I went away," she said. "I was far away."

"You were here. Hiding," he said.

She shook her head. "I went away."

Strange Day

Lucinda came in through the kitchen door. When Dale saw her wounded face, he stood up from the table. "What happened?" He reached to touch her.

Lucinda eased away. She did not want to explain her ruined face again, lie again. Fatigue had settled in her bones, confusion cobwebbed her mind. What she needed was to think. She wished now she'd gone to the Grain & Feed or stayed in her Wrangler while she tried to sort out all that had happened, all she'd discovered, and tried to figure out what to do next. What any of it meant. "I'm fine," she said.

"That's not fine," Dale said and touched a fingertip to his own face, as if he'd been wounded too.

"I fell. On the sidewalk." She did not know why she was lying to him. Or why she had lied to anyone. Except that what had happened at the house was too tangled in her mind to explain clearly. Some kid's crayon drawings from twenty-five years ago. A talking doll that could not talk. She needed a shower and to get some food in her. A drink.

"This damn town needs to maintain the walks," Dale said, an edge to his voice. "Keep up with the snow instead of plowing after it falls."

"That seems to be the consensus," she said.

She took a jug of milk from the refrigerator, poured milk into a saucepan on the stove, and cranked the burner.

"I can do that for you," Dale said.

"I need to keep busy."

"You've been busy all day," Dale said. "Gone all day."

What was she supposed to tell him, she'd been passed out for hours in Jonah's home? Who would believe that? And even if he did, he'd pester her with concern.

She snatched a bag of dark chocolate chips from the lazy Susan and spilled a handful into the warming milk. Stirred it with a spoon.

"You get the face checked out?" Dale said.

"No."

"Then where've you been?"

"Working."

"You said you were knocking off at the Grain & Feed by noon."

"Working on the missing girl."

"With Kirk?"

"No."

The milk crawled up the side of the pot in a hot froth that spilled over the brim to hiss on the burner. Lucinda killed the burner and poured the hot chocolate and sat with the mug at the table.

Dale sat across from her. "You didn't see him?"

Was he really doing this now? Could he not see the exhaustion on her face, sense her weariness and agitation? "He's the sheriff. I'm the deputy. But no . . . I didn't. I probably should have." She blew on her hot chocolate and peered at Dale. "I looked into a trespassing report. Someone had seen a light in Jonah's old place."

She sipped her hot chocolate, let it warm her insides.

"What is it?" Dale said. "What's upsetting you?"

"I found these drawings. Sally's. I think. They have to be. I don't know. I—"

"What is it?"

Dale seemed to want to talk about everything except the acceptance letter and whether she'd sent confirmation. She could hear the questions—*Did you send confirmation?*—in every silence between his spoken questions. *Are you really just taking off for ten months?* Kirk would have moved out by now, just for her applying without telling him, keeping secrets and lying by omission. Not that he'd put it so diplomatically, *lying by omission*. No. He'd just tell her to get screwed for lying.

"What's upset you?" Dale said.

"Everything," she said. She felt like sobbing, though she would not allow it. She was like her father that way, would not let anyone see her cry. "Strange things happened today. I can't talk about them now."

Dale worked his jaw as if it had locked on him and he was trying to free it. "What was so strange today? You come home with a black eye and tell me *everything* is bothering you but you can't talk about it."

She finished her hot chocolate, rose and washed out her mug at the sink, stared out the window until Dale left the kitchen for the living room. She did not want to take the bait. Dale seemed to want to conflate his anger at her not including him about her application to the Canada dig with his anger or envy toward Kirk.

She took a deep breath and turned around, back to the cupboards, palms planted on the counter edge.

She could see Dale through the kitchen doorway. He sat at his desk, but he wasn't working on one of his cars. He sat drinking a scotch. He finished what was in his glass and poured another drink.

She sat at the kitchen table and spread out the drawings.

She focused on the one drawing that was entirely black. Was it a night sky? What had Sally envisioned? Was Lucinda reading too much into it? Would the drawings give her a sense of disquiet if they had been drawn by another child, or if Sally had drawn them but never disappeared? Sally had been an odd duck with a bent for dark tales and mysteries. Or was it only because Sally had disappeared that the drawings distressed Lucinda? Wasn't context everything, though, to a cop, in a criminal case. Context. Motive. What had motivated Sally to draw these?

Lucinda looked at the next drawing, all black except for a sole evening star in the corner. She considered the drawings of stick bodies severed into pieces and smeared with red crayon.

Lucinda might consider the black drawings as Sally being afraid of the dark. It was a common fear. Lucinda was still afraid of the dark, or what she could not see in it.

Maybe that was all that was behind the drawings: Sally had been afraid of the dark, though Lucinda did not remember her being scared of much else. During sleepovers, camped out in a tent in the backyard, Sally told ghost stories. Sally had no fear of the snakes and bugs in the mucky pit. Sally told Lucinda about the man in the woods without any trepidation, told Lucinda about him as if sharing a curious fact, with no fear that he might harm them. So what had compelled her to draw these? Or were the drawings the equivalent of her scary stories, drawn on paper instead of told as narratives? It could be as simple as that.

No. Something had troubled Sally, and she'd hid it from Lucinda, hid her deepest fears from her best friend, and instead she'd drawn these.

Lucinda sighed. She was making too much of a child's spooky drawings. Chasing ghosts when she had a new girl missing to find.

She wondered who had been in Jonah's old house, and why.

Had it been Jonah? The tire tracks could have been from Jonah's truck, or an SUV. But there were two sets of faint tracks in the snow.

An adult's.

And a child's.

A question leaped to her mind. Was it possible Jonah had the girl? Gretel had disappeared twenty-five years to the day that Sally had disappeared. The similarities between the two girls, age, size, and those eyes, were frightening.

Had Jonah seen Gretel in town previously and been overwhelmed by the likeness of her to Sally? Or . . .

Or was there something more wicked at work that Lucinda had never entertained: that Jonah had been responsible for his wife and daughter's disappearance? Lucinda had never doubted him. Even her father had doubted Jonah for a spell; it haunted her father, that he'd doubted his friend.

But if Jonah had taken Gretel, why would he take her to his old house? Why risk it? When would Jonah have even seen her to know she existed? If it were in town, she'd have been with her foster parents. Would he follow them home, then snatch her? *He was in town the day she disappeared,* a voice said. *And in town at night, when Marnie saw the light inside the old place.*

It was unimaginable.

Demented.

She refused to believe it.

Still. There were two sets of tracks in the snow outside Jonah's house.

An adult's tracks. And a child's.

Whose were they and why were those two people in Jonah's old home?

She felt frayed and uneasy.

Lucinda looked at the drawings. She needed to act. She felt helpless in the house trying to reach conclusions and make connections.

She rolled the drawings up, put on her jacket, and slipped out the kitchen door.

Dale now dozed in his armchair, mouth agape. Lucinda wanted to apologize to him for being so short and easily irritated, but it would have to wait.

FOOTPRINTS

Lucinda got out of the Wrangler and stood in the dark cold night. She did not want to go inside to see Kirk. She did not want to feed his ego with the satisfaction that she sought his insights; whether he actually had any or not would be moot to him. But he was the sheriff, and she was stuck with him, for now.

With the drawings in hand, she walked up the snowed steps. She knocked on the rectory door as she opened it and let herself inside. Even with her coat on and coming from outside, Lucinda felt the chill of the place edge into her, making her shiver. She was surprised she could not see her breath. She wondered if the furnace was on the blink.

She passed two rooms, in which easels still stood, maps of the surrounding woods propped on them. No one was about. The search was over. Already. After just a couple days. It did not seem possible that the matter was now in the hands of the state police, and the town was settling back into its routine when the search for Sally, and the disruption of routine, the calamity of it all, had seemed to go on for weeks. Lucinda wondered if she was exaggerating the timeline in her memory or had exaggerated it then. Or if the search for Sally and her mother had actually gone on far longer because Sally and her mother were from a respectable family, and the sheriff had been their friend.

She found Kirk sunk low in his chair watching TV, beer propped on his lap.

"I have something you need to see," she said.

"Ah. Finally."

She brandished the drawings. "I need your input."

He stood. "What happened to your face? You look like shit."

"I fell on the sidewalk."

"Liar." He nailed it. He knew she was lying and said so, straight out. The others had probably known she was lying, too, but none called her out on it. No one told it like it was. Straight. He called her out, then dropped it. Didn't prod or try to make her feel better because he knew he couldn't, knew that her feeling better was up to her.

She sat at the table and spread the drawings out on it. "Look," she said.

He stood behind her, his hands resting on the chair back.

"Crazy kid drawings," he said.

"Drawn by Sally. Jonah's daughter."

"I thought this had to do with the missing girl."

"Sally's missing too," Lucinda said.

"Sally isn't missing. Sally's dead."

"Even if she's dead, she's still missing. She's never been found."

"Her drawings don't have squat to do with our missing girl. I hope you don't think buggy shit like that."

"I don't know."

"Have a beer," he said.

"Are you kidding, it's freezing in here."

He left the room and came back with two open beer bottles and handed one to her.

He quaffed half his beer at a go.

Lucinda didn't touch her beer. She was exhausted, and her head bogged enough to add to her troubles. "These are ugly pictures," she said. "The woman and girl. They're being killed? Tortured? In the night. Sally drew these *before* she went missing. As if she knew something bad was about to happen."

"Kids are fucked up. That's why I'm never having any." His voice was cold with certainty.

He demolished his beer and got another one, half of it gone by the time he returned with it.

"Drink your beer," he said.

Lucinda studied the drawing. "This is of a mother and a girl."

"Could be anyone. Any sex."

"Sally and her mom vanished. And—" Lucinda nearly told him about the man in the woods, but refrained. She did not want to elicit more sarcasm. Yet she felt a need to share it with someone, to gain perspective. If the man in the woods had been responsible for her friend disappearing twenty-five years ago, and had never been caught, why couldn't he be the one behind this girl too? Were the two men the same? Was the man in the woods Jonah?

"You're talking bogeyman shit," Kirk said. "Sally disappeared twenty-odd years ago."

"Twenty-five. I need to see Jonah about it."

"That old coot would just as soon shoot you as have you on his porch after you were such a bitch to him."

Lucinda pushed the chair from the table and stood. "Jonah's not shooting anybody," she said, though she was no longer certain. "Not me, anyway."

"Don't bet on that."

"I want to check on him, anyway." She wondered again what Jonah had been doing at Ivers Grocery. And the amount of groceries he'd had in his bag. The *kind* of groceries. Sugared cereal. Pop-Tarts. The thoughts chilled her. She willed herself to keep them at bay, yet they persisted.

"You're not his nurse or his mom," Kirk said. "It's none of your business."

Maybe it is your business, a voice said. *Police business.*

"He's all alone," she said.

"He likes to be alone," Kirk said.

"No one likes to be alone."

"I do."

"You're not alone like he is. I think Jonah was in his house the other night. Someone saw a flashlight from outside. I'm sure it was him." Except, she wasn't sure at all. She just didn't know who else it could be, which meant it could have been anybody. The adult's tracks could have been a teenager's. Maybe it was just two kids messing around, a teenage boy and his younger brother. Jonah hadn't stepped foot in that house for two decades. Why would he bother now?

Because of the girl.

The boot print of the child.

"How do you know it was him?" Kirk said.

"I don't know. I guess."

"Stellar work, Detective. You want to go up to apologize to Jonah, is what it is. You're a bleeding heart. Finish your beer."

"I haven't started it."

"So start it."

She made to leave.

He touched her wrist. The tendons of his own wrist taut, his fingers warm.

She took her hand away.

"Have a beer with me," he said.

She picked up her beer and chugged it down, slammed the empty bottle on the table, and marched out of the room.

"Make sure you announce yourself to that old coot," Kirk shouted, "and don't get what's left of what used to be a pretty face shot off when you pay him a visit."

ALONE

Dale dozed in his easy chair. Lucinda watched him breathe. His glasses sat crooked on his nose. In his sleep his slack jaw showed signs of going jowly.

She knelt and touched his wrist. Took off his glasses and set them on the coffee table.

He awoke, confused.

"Let's go to bed," she said.

"You smell of beer," he said.

"I had one while you were sleeping."

He pulled back from her. "We're out of beer."

"I went out for one."

"Where? What time is it?"

"I don't know."

"Where?"

"Come to bed."

"You go."

Lucinda left him and shuffled down the hall and into the bedroom. She lay on the bed alone, listening to the radiators gurgle. She lay there waiting for him to come to bed. But he did not.

She did not blame him.

She wouldn't come to bed angry either. No, that was untrue. She would. Had before, to Kirk's bed. She'd choked down her self-worth for him. When angry with Dale, she stayed angry instead of finding every excuse to forgive as she always had for Kirk. Why did she behave in ways that undermined the person she wished to be, believed she was? It was as if there were two different versions of herself.

When Lucinda awoke at noon after a long night of hectic broken sleep, she knew before she opened her eyes that Dale was gone.

BOOK V

TONIGHT

We go tonight," Jonah said, his voice weak, hoarse, his throat rasped raw. He'd tried to eat that morning but could not even keep down a piece of bread. His legs felt watery and his head clouded, but he planned to leave tonight. He'd time it so they'd head out for the truck in the late afternoon, at dusk, and be driving in the dark. He did not dare enter town in the light. "Tonight. We start again."

"Home," she said.

"Wherever we go, that's our home."

He wrapped his arms around her and kissed the top of her head.

No one will harm or take you away again.

My child.

Business

Lucinda shuffled into the kitchen exhausted, the yeastiness of beer a paste on her furred tongue. She sipped a glass of water and slushed the water around in her mouth and spat it out in the sink.

She called Dale's real estate office, but Dale hadn't been in. She wondered if he would come home today. Or at all. She wondered if she'd come home if she were him. Suspicion was often worse than knowing. More painful. Jealousy's dark imaginings. She lay on the couch, studying the drawings, trying to discern connections before she headed up to see Jonah.

The phone rang. Lucinda shouted, startled awake.

She'd fallen asleep. She felt drugged and addled.

"Hey," she said, "where are you? I—"

"Wherever you want me to be."

"Kirk?"

"Your one and only."

Lucinda had thought it was Dale calling. She was going to say she wanted to apologize.

"Why are you calling my home number?" she said.

"Business," Kirk said. "Come to the office. I'll show you."

She looked around the empty place. She glanced at the clock on the wall. 2:31.

"You and the beau have a spat?" Kirk said.

"No."

"Why don't you know where he is then?"

"I'm not his mother. He's probably at work."

"Come over. We've got business."

"*Business*," she said.

Outside, the tire tracks from Dale's car where he'd backed up far earlier that day were wiped clean by newly falling snow.

Same Old Business

Lucinda shucked her hat from her head and clomped down the rectory corridor, her rubber Mucks shedding clods of slush from their lugged soles.

She found Kirk with his feet up on the desk.

"What business?" she said.

He lifted a beer can from his lap.

"Jesus," she said.

"Judas maybe."

Lucinda turned to leave.

"Hold up," Kirk said and swung his feet to the floor.

"What?" Lucinda said. "If you have business, what is it? Spit it out."

"Personal business." He stood. "Unfinished business."

What a fool she was.

"I mean real business," she said.

"This is real as it gets. The way you let me touch your wrist."

"I didn't let you do anything. I'm leaving," she said, ice in her voice.

He reached for her, got her wrist.

She yanked away. He grabbed tighter.

A button on her coat sleeve popped off and spun on the floor.

Kirk stared at her. His eyes deadened with a cold meanness. She'd forgotten it, the meanness. She remembered it now. His words used for cruelty. Strength wielded for intimidation, bravado masking weakness.

"Relax," he said.

"I am relaxed," she said, though her heartbeat crashed in her chest, her ire steaming.

"Good," he said. Smiling. A fake smile. If he had a real one at all. He tapped his badge with his fingertip. "You don't want to make the sheriff take out his handcuffs."

He reached for her wrist.

She spun, yanked free, and drove the heel of her palm into his nose.

He staggered back, clutched his nose, blood leaking.

SICK

Lucinda drove toward home as fast as the road permitted. She needed to get up to Jonah's, but the snowfall was worsening each second. By the time she got up into the Gore, dark would be gathering, the snow piling up in the mountains. She'd need real snow boots and a good flashlight. *And your handgun*, the voice said as she yanked the Wrangler into the drive to almost smash into Dale's Ford Tempo. He was home. She'd never been so relieved to see his homogenous heap.

She jumped out of the Wrangler, her boots slipping on the drive. Her arms pinwheeled and she clutched her side-view mirror and balanced herself. She ran her hand along the Tempo as she trudged along it up the drive.

She entered the kitchen and called out, "Dale?"

No answer came.

Was he in the bedroom?

Packing?

She trod into the living room where Dale sat at his desk, absorbed in using tweezers to set a seat in the cockpit of the 1930s Tether.

He'd lit a fire in the fireplace. The warmth from it radiated in the room and the orange glow from the flames jigged on the walls and floor. Dale sipped scotch from a tumbler, the amber liquid shimmering and swirling.

"Hey," Lucinda said, winded.

Dale drank down his scotch. "Hey."

"Sorry," she said.

"About?"

"Last night."

"I'm over it."

"I thought—"

"What?" he said and worked his tongue around the inside of his mouth, savored the smoky brined aftertaste of the scotch, the mellow numbness at the tongue, Lucinda knew. At times, he spoke about and described scotch as if he were an art critic deconstructing a Rembrandt; he narrated as he drank. Normally, Lucinda was apathetic toward his fervor for scotch, if not amused. Right then, she found it endearing. Sweet. He brought up the bottle at his feet and poured a good measure, held the glass to the lamplight. "What'd you think?"

"I thought you'd left," she said.

"I did."

"And you're back."

"Where else was I going to go in that mess outside?" he said. "I didn't expect even to be gone long as I was. I went out to Kale's Auto to see about finally getting the snow tires on the Tempo, and they were packed since all the other jokers who waited for the snow to fly were lined up in there with me; so that took a lot longer than I thought, and by then I was hungry, so I stopped in at the Burger Barn and had a burger and onion rings and got to gabbing with a few folks and well"—he shrugged—"it was about time to get back home by then. So here I am."

"I can't tell if you're a good man or just dim," she said.

"Dim," he said and sipped his scotch.

Lucinda stood in front of him, looking into his face. "Why haven't you mentioned Canada. Asked more about it? Been angry?"

"I am angry. But. What's to ask? You'll tell me when you've decided. I hope."

"It's ten months," Lucinda said.

"True."

"A long time."

"I lived thirty-three years before ever knowing you existed. We'll manage."

She eyed his scotch, slipped his glass from his grip, and took a sip. It tasted of peat and stung her tongue, then smoothed at the back of the throat. She shimmered, a liquid warmth in her veins. She needed to get going, to see Jonah, but the warmth of the fire, and the scotch, lulled her. It had been days since she'd known calm. She finished the drink. A vaporous glow bloomed in the brain.

She reached into her coat pocket and took out her deputy's badge. The button from her father's uniform box fell out with it. She set the button on Dale's desk and pinned the badge to his chest. "You are hereby deputized for putting up with me." She breathed on the badge and buffed it with her shirtsleeve.

"What's this?" Dale said, holding up the button.

The scotch was loosening her, swimming in her bloodstream. She peered at the button. "It was in my father's trunk when—"

She stopped. Blinked.

She plucked the button from Dale's fingers and stood with it. Stunned.

She gazed at the button, then at the badge pinned to Dale's chest. "No," she said. She staggered into the kitchen, bewildered. At the sink, she splashed cold water on her face, but the rush of heat pushing through her was too much and she fought the urge to be sick.

Dale put his hand on her shoulder.

"I have to go, right now," she said.

"What is this? Go where?"

"Jonah's."

"You can't go up there now in the snow, it'll be dark soon."

She plucked the badge from his chest and set it and the button down on the table, a sick feeling writhing in her gut like a knot of baby snakes. She vomited in the sink, wiped her mouth with a sleeve, and spat. "No," she said.

"What the hell is going on?" Dale said.

"I have to go."

"You're not going anywhere like this."

"You drive then. Grab headlamps. I need to go. Now."

"Me drive? I've had too much scotch."

But she was already going for the door.

Go

Out in the Wrangler, Lucinda sat in the passenger seat, the badge and button in her lap. She reached over and shoved her key into the Wrangler's ignition as Dale slung open the driver's door. "What is this?"

"Drive. To Jonah's house first."

"That old haunted place?" Dale said.

"Get in, let's go."

Dale hopped in and fired up the Wrangler, backed up fast and headed out of town on Main Street, toward One Dollar Bridge. The snow hurtled at them now, collected on the windshield even as the wipers slapped at their highest speed.

MINE

The Wrangler pulled into the yard in a squall of snow so chaotic and furious it obliterated from sight the house that sat
just a few yards away. For a second, Lucinda was struck with an
odd, eerie sensation that the house was not there behind the fury
of snow, did not exist any longer, had vanished in time, or had
never existed at all, or she had never existed. Did not exist right
then, in that moment, but was living someone else's dream.

The wind rocked the Wrangler, breaking the dark spell that had
gripped Lucinda.

Lucinda tried to open her passenger door, but it resisted against
a howl of wind. She leaned into the door to try to force it open, as
if it were in league with, or under the spell of, the house in trying
to keep her from going inside to investigate her suspicion.

As if to disprove her mad thought of the house and wind conspiring against her, the wind flagged and the door opened in a wild
sweep and she fell out onto the ground. She got to her feet as Dale
came around to her. Dusk was approaching. The house would be
dark with shadows inside. Lucinda strapped on her headlamp.

In the gathering storm, the house lost in a cyclone of snow, they pushed their way toward the house and onto the porch.

Lucinda remembered the night her father had brought her here, the last night she'd ever been in the house as a child. How she'd expected Sally to be home but had also been nagged by a feeling of unease while on the porch waiting for Mr. B. to answer her father's knock, and then again on the couch wondering where Sally was and why she, Lucinda, had been told to stay put.

Lucinda opened the door.

"What are we doing here?" Dale said.

"I want to be sure," she said, but what she really wanted was to be proved wrong.

She crept inside the house, Dale trailing her, his boozy breath at her neck.

"God," Dale said, gagging. "This place."

Lucinda turned on her headlamp. The bulb leaked a drab yellow pulse of light. A pair of silver eyes shone from the couch as a rat slunk away, its naked tail dragging behind it. Lucinda picked her way across the living room and down the hall and entered Sally's bedroom.

The doll lay on the floor where Lucinda had left it.

Lucinda knelt and picked it up, set it on the desk.

She could hear Dale breathing behind her in the doorway as she pulled the badge and button from her coat pocket and set them beside the doll, pulled out the drawings and unfolded them on the desk.

"What is it?" Dale said. Lucinda glanced at him to see he held the doorframe for balance, then turned her attention back to the doll and the other artifacts. She studied the drawing of the stick girl with one button eye and one red X for an eye.

She looked at the rag doll.

One button for an eye.

The other eye: A red x of thread.

A button missing.

She took out the button that had fallen out of the pants of her father's uniform.

Compared it to the button eye on the doll.

"It's not *like* mine," she whispered.

She turned to Dale.

"It *is* mine." She shook the doll at Dale, its stuffing flying from where earlier she'd ripped it open. "This is my doll. *Beverly*." Lucinda fought back a sob; it'd do her no good now to let emotion overwhelm her. "Not *hers*. Mine. The button. And the evening star in Sally's black crayon drawing. It's not a star. I need to get to Jonah. Tell him. I know."

"You're not making any sense. You need to calm down. Wait till tomorrow."

"This is not waiting until tomorrow. It's waited twenty-five years."

INTO THE COLD

Lucinda attempted to study the drawings on her lap as the Wrangler bucked its way up Gore Pass, up beyond the farm fields, up into the Gore, leaving the town far behind as the road disintegrated to what seemed a rock-strewn creek bed, the tempest of snow obliterating visibility beyond a few feet.

Lucinda's head ached as she thought of confronting Jonah.

"Where the heck does he live?" Dale said.

"Keep going, it's up here, somewhere," Lucinda said. She was not certain where Jonah lived. She'd not been this way in years, but she knew roughly where he parked his truck off the road, and that there was a small trail from there to the cabin, though she was unsure how she and Dale would find their way in the snow and near darkness. There were mines up here that would swallow you and never give you up, and she was no longer a girl naive enough to believe herself immune to their dangers.

As the Wrangler lurched upward, the snowfall diminished.

Lucinda stared at her reflection in the sideview mirror. She'd forgotten about her injured face. She looked disfigured. The eye had shut tight as a walnut shell, swollen and tender with fluid. The gash, crusted black with dried blood, would leave a scar. *What karmic forces are at work that I deserve this?* she wondered.

She wrapped her arms around herself, leaning across the seat to lay her head against Dale's shoulder, and the Wrangler shuddered. She was bone-achingly cold, and tired—

As the road crested, she saw through the now gentle snowfall a glint of chrome through the trees.

"Stop!" she shouted. She thrust her finger toward the truck in the trees.

"There?" Dale said. "There's no—"

"Pull in."

Dale cranked the Wrangler steering wheel as far to the left as it would go, the steering column clacking and whining. He eased the Wrangler in toward the trees, branches screeching on metal.

"You're shitting me," Dale said and tucked the vehicle into the trees beside the truck, forced to pull onto a flat, precarious ledge, the Wrangler cockeyed and half off the ground. Lucinda wondered if they'd ever be able to back the Wrangler out, but that could not be a concern then.

Lucinda got out and stood in the small clearing. The snow here was deep, up to her knees.

The dusk woods were quiet and still, and the snow had stopped save the slow sifting of it as it fell through hemlock bows. The world crystalline. Purified with its cold. The scent of the hemlock made her think of the pit. It was near here, wasn't it? Or had they passed it, farther below? They must have gone by it long ago. She and Sally had never ranged up this far. Had they? Perhaps the slow going and the dark had only made it seem she was now farther up in the Gore than she actually was, or perhaps as girls she and Sally had ventured farther up into the woods than they realized. She could not be sure. The woods had changed in the past decades. They were not the same woods. They'd grown all the more dense and forbidding. And she'd never entered them in the dark.

She searched for the path that led to the shack, turned on the headlamp as darkness descended, the light a trifling against the deep black of the woods. She could not locate a path, though she knew one must be there, somewhere. If she could not find one, she'd make her own.

"Now what?" Dale said.

"We hike." Lucinda pointed into the woods, spotting what seemed a wisp of a trail.

"We shouldn't be here in the dark."

But Lucinda was already pushing into a darkness so absolute it now seemed a physical presence, the headlamp beam lighting only the tangle of branches most immediate, the blackness folding in behind her as she passed.

The wind picked up again, screamed in the treetops. Icy snow bit into her wounded face. Several times she stopped, searching for the phantom trail she was sure she'd lost for good. The blowing snow covered their tracks behind them. She picked up the ghost of a trail again and forged on.

She slogged ahead in the deep snow, eyes wet from the cold shearing wind, her hope for finding the cabin fading as her fear of being able to find their way back to the Wrangler intensified.

"We're close," she said, though she had no idea if they were closer or farther from the cabin, or about to fall into a mine shaft with the very next step.

Too Late

The wind cried beneath the tin roof as Jonah seared a steak on the stove and Sally slept on the couch.

She needed to eat so they wouldn't have to stop until they were long gone. He'd wanted to leave earlier, but the blinding snow had come in so fast and hampered him, and he'd decided to wait it out. Despite the few gusts of wind blowing snow now, the storm had passed. It was time.

He laid the rifle on the table, grabbed an extra box of rifle cartridges, and dumped a handful of cartridges into his trouser pockets, to have them at the ready.

He flipped the steak.

What was that sound?

Cries? Voices?

No.

It was the wind.

There it was again.

Voices?

Yes.

Out on the porch.

"Get up," Jonah barked at Sally, who rested on the couch. "Wake up."

He put his hand on her shoulder and gently shook her.

She did not move.

"Wake up," he said.

He shook her shoulder, but she didn't move. She was as limp as a rag doll.

What was wrong with her? Why wouldn't she wake up?

He cupped her chin in his hand and lifted it. Her head lolled, loose on her neck, like a sunflower too heavy for its flimsy stalk.

"Wake up!"

The voices outside rose.

The sound of boots on the porch.

Something was wrong with Sally. She was cold. Too cold.

"*Wake up,*" he pleaded. "Please."

He placed his cheek to hers. It was cool. Waxen.

"*Please.*"

He shook her by the shoulder. Hard.

"Wake up. We're leaving. Going home."

He shook her harder.

She moaned. Thank God.

A knock came at the door.

"No," she said. "No no no."

He looked around as if for help, but there was no help to be had. He was alone.

The knock came again.

Who would come for him in this darkness?

Not the loggers.

The law. They knew. Somehow they knew.

He looked into her eyes, his daughter's eyes.

They were catatonic with fear. "No one will hurt you," he said, "no one will take you from me again."

He scooped her up in his arms and rushed her into the back room, looked around for a place to hide her. Where. Where. There was but one place.

The trunk. Open and empty.

He knelt and set her into the trunk as carefully as he could. She made an odd soft crying sound, barely audible. Then fell silent.

"Shhh," he said. "Shhh."

He started to shut the trunk lid.

"No," she mewled and held up a palm against the underside of the trunk lid.

"It's the only way," he said. "They're here. They've come for you. They'll take you. I know. I know it's dark in the trunk. But it's safe. It's just like closing your eyes. Close your eyes and dream a nice dream and I will be back before you know it."

A fist pounded on the cabin door.

"Please," he said. "We're out of time."

She nodded, a tear leaking down her face.

He shut the lid and stepped to the doorway, looked back at the trunk. The lid remained closed. He shut the door behind him and hurried to the front door as its latch was jostled, and a voice cried, "Jonah!"

Jonah grabbed the rifle from the table and eased open the door a crack to see her standing on his porch. Lucinda, and her man. The collar of her deputy's jacket flapped against her neck in the wind.

"What?" Jonah said.

"How's your hand?" Lucinda said and looked behind him to see into the cabin.

"Better." Jonah lifted his hand to show her.

"That's not better," she said.

"Better than it was. Better than your eye." Her eye, her face, jarred him. It looked as if she'd been struck by a shovel. "Now you've seen it, go."

"I'd like to come inside. Talk."

A noise behind him disrupted his thoughts, but he dared not turn around to see what had made it.

"No," he said.

The noise came again.

Logs settling in the woodstove?

Her?

Had she sneaked out of the trunk?

"We're freezing out here," Lucinda said. She smiled, trying to persuade him.

"That's not my fault."

"I'm not leaving," Lucinda said.

"Sit out on the porch all you like." He made to shut the door.

"Please. *Look. Look at these.*"

She held something out to him, folded sheets of paper.

He looked back up at her. "Leave me be. I told that asshole I'd be gone by spring."

"Why'd you go to your house the other night?" Lucinda said.

How did she know he'd been in his house? Had the police been watching him? Had the ATV man been up here under false pretenses? Had Jonah been under suspicion the whole time? How long had they known he had her up here with him, how long had they planned to move in and take her from him?

A hissing noise came from behind him. The steak, sizzling in the cast-iron pan. Fat melting. Burning. He'd forgotten it. If it got too hot, it would catch fire.

"Please leave." He tried to push her from the open door. But she would not budge.

"Why were you in your house?" Lucinda wedged a boot between the door and jamb.

"I wasn't."

He could smell the butter now. Scorching. Its acrid smoke.

"I *know* it was you," she said.

"So *what*? It's my place. It's my house."

"I found these," she said.

She thrust the papers toward him.

"Everyone's shoving papers at me," he snapped. He eyed her. And her man who stood behind her. Why must she torment him like this? Why didn't she just come in and take her? If she wanted to arrest him, arrest him and get it over with, end it. Maybe she was trying to ease into it, knowing he would not give her up without a fight. Not now. He clutched the rifle more tightly.

"You have no right being in my house. Taking my stuff." His fear of being caught with Sally was being edged by his ire at his privacy being trampled.

"Have you seen these?" Lucinda said. "Please, Jonah, look at them."

For a moment Jonah saw the girl Lucinda had been; the heartbroken innocent girl who'd thought she would stop by to see if Mr. B. wanted to go find his daughter with her in some pit in the woods. Sweet little Lucinda.

"I got a steak burning," he said.

The pan spewed smoke. Any second now, it would erupt into a wild grease fire.

"Look at the damned papers, Jonah!" Lucinda shouted. "Look at them!"

The pan burst into flames.

"Jesus!" Jonah yelled and raced to the fire.

Flames leaped from the pan as he grabbed a pot lid and slammed it down, killing the flames.

A shadow passed at the bottom of the door to the back room.

Or he thought it did.

Damn it.

He wheeled around. Lucinda stood inside the cabin now as smoke hung between her and Jonah. Her man stepped inside, snow blowing in behind him and melting on the floor as he shut the cabin door.

"This has nothing to do with the logging company. This has to do with Sally."

So she knew. His heart squeezed into a rock.

He moved up close to her. Close enough to see her good eye twitch at the corner. He clenched the rifle in his hand.

He bit into the inside of his cheek, tasted copper as blood seeped.

Lucinda unfolded a paper. What was it, a warrant for his arrest?

His thumb worried at the rifle hammer.

"Look," she said, shaking the paper at Jonah. "Please."

Jonah finally looked. Nausea rose in him. The paper was a drawing. A black sky and a silver evening star in it. Stick figures streaked with red crayon.

His own blood rushed out of him as if he'd been gutted.

"Where'd you get these?" he said.

"Her room."

"You have no right."

"I'm a deputy. I got a report someone was in your old place."

"Those weren't in my house." Jonah nodded at the drawings. "Those were not in my daughter's room. I'd know. What are you trying to do? Why are you doing this?"

"They were behind coloring book pages tacked on her bulletin board," Lucinda said.

"I had enough of getting blamed years ago. Arrest me if you're going to arrest me." But he would not be arrested. He would not allow it. He'd gone too far. If it all ended here, so be it. "Leave me be. Or I swear—"

Lucinda laid the drawings out on the table. "She knew. Sally knew or sensed something wrong."

"I know all about the drawings," he said. He lowered his voice, worried she would come out from the back room to see what was wrong. "Not these exact drawings. But I saw some. Your father found them and wanted to keep them. But we knew the state police would use them against me somehow. Twist everything all around. They were dying to pin it on me. Like they used everything against me. So I tore them up. He wanted to keep them, as possible evidence. But he left it up to me in the end, what came of them. He was a friend. The only one I had. Ever had. I don't know what Sally saw to make her draw such things. Or maybe she saw nothing. Maybe they're just a kid's drawings. You two were hiding out in that awful pit. Scaring yourselves."

A shadow passed at the bottom of the door again.

"There's a girl missing," Lucinda said. "The same age as Sally was."

So this was it. She'd been leading up to it. He was trapped. His hands were slick with sweat around the rifle. "I heard," he managed to say.

"And?" Lucinda said. "What do you think?"

"I don't think anything."

He looked at the drawings. Glanced at the door to the back room.

"The girls are the same age. Sally and this new missing girl. Same eye color. They look a lot alike. Could be sisters, or even—"

Not the same eye color, Jonah thought. *The* same eyes.

"There's a lifetime between their disappearances," Jonah said. "It's got nothing to do with me." A shadow seemed to pass under the door to the back room. "Go." He jerked the rifle up at his hip and pointed the muzzle at her gut.

"Hey," her man said, stepping back. "Easy."

Jonah lifted the rifle to his shoulder and squinted down the barrel at Lucinda, at the center of her chest. No missing from here.

His thumb rested on the hammer.

"Easy," her man said again.

Easy was right. Jonah could shoot them both right here. Easy. Hide her Wrangler. The bodies. Drop them down a mine shaft. Never to be seen again. Easy. He'd do it. He would. He'd be gone a month before anyone found Lucinda and her man up here. If anyone ever found them.

"There's no need for that," the man said, backing up more.

"I decide what there's a need for in my home," Jonah said.

He heard a sound behind him. If she came out now, she'd ruin everything. He did not want to shoot them in front of her. But he would, if forced.

He held his breath tight. His trigger finger buzzed against the trigger.

"You were a good girl," he said. "You were my daughter's friend. You knew me. You knew us. We let you come and go as you pleased. You were family. How could you think that I did—"

"*You?* I don't think you did it. Listen to me. Trust me."

Trust. He'd abandoned it twenty-five years ago.

"The star," Lucinda said. "It's not a star. She had my doll. Sally, she had *my* doll. It was Beverly at your house."

Jonah didn't know what she was talking about. Nonsense to distract him. He pushed the rifle muzzle at her.

In his periphery the shadow passed under the back door.

Lucinda's eyes followed his.

"What is it?" she said, staring at the door to the back.

"Rats," he said.

"Luce," her man croaked, "let's go, before he kills us."

"Wise words," Jonah said.

Lucinda stepped toward Jonah, looked him in the eye. "You never killed anyone," Lucinda said. "You aren't going to start now."

"I will."

"Listen to me. I know where your daughter is, I know where Sally is."

Yes, the voice said, *but she'll never take her from us.*

"Sally *and* your wife," Lucinda said.

Lucinda's eyes fell to the children's books stacked on the table. The coloring books. Two place settings. "What is all that?"

"Sally's stuff."

Lucinda stepped closer to it.

"Stop," Jonah said.

"That's a *new* coloring book. New crayons."

Stop her, now, the voice said.

Lucinda flipped through the coloring book.

"They're Sally's," Jonah said.

Lucinda looked at the door to the back room.

"What's back there?" she said

She picked up the backpack. "Are you packing, going somewhere?"

"Leave my things be," Jonah said. Why wouldn't she listen? Why was she making him have to do something he didn't want to do? He thumbed the rifle's hammer, cocked it back, hammer worn smooth.

Click.

Lucinda stared at the rifle. She was trying hard to keep her breathing calm but her chest rose and fell heavily, Jonah could see that. She unzipped the top of the backpack.

Jonah lunged at her and yanked her arm, the rifle barrel swinging wildly. Food and children's books and clothing tumbled to the floor as Dale grabbed at the rifle and wrested it from Jonah's weak grasp, clutched it to his chest awkwardly. The man had never held a rifle, that was clear.

Jonah spun, grabbed at the rifle, but the younger man was stronger than Jonah, who could not wrest it free.

"*Get out of here,*" Jonah shouted. "Get out. Get out. Get *out* of *my home. Get out and leave me be.*"

Lucinda looked at the backpack and children's books. The two place settings on the table, astonishment flooding her face. "What's in that back room, Jonah?"

Jonah reached for the rifle again, but Lucinda grabbed his shoulders with both hands and pulled him back.

"What's back there?" she said. "Who is back there? I can help you sort it out if she's not hurt. I can get you help."

Just like her old man. She knew all along, the liar, the voice said.

Came up here prattling about Sally, baiting you, distracting you. Pretending to be a friend. She knew.

Lucinda strode to the door to the back room.

"*Stop*," Jonah railed. "*You have no right.*"

"We're here to help," Dale said.

"*I've heard that before*," Jonah said.

Lucinda turned the doorknob.

"*Goddamn it*," Jonah shouted and shoved Lucinda as hard as he was able, sent her reeling to the floor. Her forehead cracked against the table edge. Blood came. Goddamn it. Look what she'd made him *do*. Look at it. Good.

"I told you!" Jonah spat as he stood over her, frothing, seething, that ancient rage roaring up out of him as he grabbed her by the jacket and shook her. "Goddamn you, this is my house!"

Jonah grunted as he was slammed into the wall and crumpled to the floor.

Dale stood over him, rifle trained on his forehead, steady.

Lucinda grunted and managed to gain her feet, her forehead torn and dripping blood. She took hold of the doorknob to the back room.

"No," Jonah said. "Please."

"Tell me what's in there," Lucinda said. "Who's in there."

"I—" Jonah stared at the door. He wanted to tell her. That he'd found her. She'd *found* him. She'd come to him. He had meant to take her back, had tried, but the things he'd heard, he couldn't return her to *that*. He knew that life. He knew. The odds of escaping it. So he'd kept her here with him, safe. He'd found her for a reason. She came to him, found him, for a reason. It could not be for nothing. She was his now. His. And he was hers. They were all each other had now.

But he didn't say it. Couldn't. They'd never believe him. They never had believed him.

"Okay," Lucinda said and opened the door to the back room.

The lone trunk sat in the barren room.

Dale stepped behind Lucinda.

Lucinda wiped blood from her eyes, her face pale and grim yet her eyes keen with mistrust as she looked back at Jonah.

"Open the trunk," she said.

"You think I put a girl in a trunk?" Jonah said. "You think I'd *do* that? You lied, told me you know where my daughter and wife are, but you came here because you think I have Sal—, have her, that other girl, up here?"

"Open the trunk."

"You open it," Jonah said. "You want it open so bad, you open it."

Lucinda stepped into the room and stood over the trunk. Blood ran from her wounded forehead.

"We need to get you out of here, to a doctor," Dale said.

Jonah watched helplessly from the doorway as Lucinda lifted the trunk lid open and peered down into it.

She drew a sharp breath and reeled backward, staggered into the doorframe.

"I— I don't know what to say," Lucinda said and put her face in her hands, blood leaking from between her fingers.

Jonah limped into the room, looked down into the trunk.

It was empty.

"I'm sorry," Lucinda said. "I thought. What with the coloring books and the place settings—"

Jonah stared unblinking into the trunk's emptiness.

As empty as his heart. As confusing as his memories.

"The books," he murmured, "and place setting are for my daughter, for when she comes back. I keep them ready for her. Buy her new ones."

He shut the trunk lid to see behind the trunk. Nothing. The room was empty. Where was she?

He turned in a circle. Swooning.

The lone window was shut tight.

The walls breathed.

"No," he said.

The floor fell away.

The ceiling floated.

He heard voices far away, calling, calling.

He lifted the trunk lid again.

"No," he said.

His own voice far away.

Thin and hollow.

Calling from the distant past.

A long ago life.

Another life.

A life that had ended years ago.

He careened back through the doorway and collapsed into a chair at the table. Had she ever been here at all? Old man. Old fool. Had he heard the story on his transistor radio and been bitten by a spider or fallen into a fugue? What had happened?

Lucinda sat in the chair beside Jonah. "I'm sorry," she said.

"She's gone," Jonah said, trying to reason out the past days, untangle his labyrinth of dark thoughts. "My daughter's gone."

"She's been gone a long time, sir," Dale said.

"You don't understand," Jonah murmured.

"No, I don't," said Dale.

"I think I know where she is," Lucinda said, her voice one of sorrow. She put her hand on Jonah's.

"Where who is?" Jonah said, his voice a ghost.

"Your child. And your wife."

"My daughter," he whispered. "I thought—" He hung his head. "I get confused."

Lucinda looked at the coloring books. The two place settings. "It's okay," she said.

"It's just," Jonah said. "I miss them. Still. I know how long it's been. I know what people said. What people say. I know the world moved on. Long ago. I'm not stupid. I'm not crazy."

"Of course not," Lucinda said.

"I just. I miss them. I want them back."

Jonah rubbed his face.

"My *heart* doesn't know they're gone," he said. "It might as well be yesterday. Every door I walk through is my front door, every room I enter is my daughter's room, and every time it's still empty. Every day. Every second is a lifetime. Even up here. I kept waiting. Thinking. Maybe. Maybe. Today. But they never come back. All I want is for them to come back. All I want is to see them again."

"I'm sorry I doubted you."

"I'd doubt me too," he said.

"I think," Lucinda said. "I think news of this missing girl triggered something in you. You saw her posters in town, maybe, or heard it on your truck radio or transistor radio up here, and it brought back memories—it made you want something so badly that you imagined—I'm so sorry."

"No," he said. "My daughter. She went out the window. She's out there in the cold. The dark."

Lucinda touched his cheek. "Your daughter's dead. Sally is dead."

It was the first time she'd said it, because it was the first time she truly believed it. Knew it.

"Yes," Jonah said. "Of course she is. Of course. I know that."

His body caved and his shoulders collapsed as if the wiring from his brain had been cut with a razor. He thought he'd go blind. Mad. He'd thought the pain could be no worse. He'd been wrong.

"Come to town with me." Lucinda placed a hand on his shoulder.

"I can't. I can't leave her. Here," he said.

"Please, Jonah."

"I can't. I can't."

"If I find her, them," Lucinda said, "I'll have things to do. Take care of. So if I'm not back soon, you'll know I've found them."

She patted his hand.

"Where are they?" he said.

"I have to find out for myself before I say," Lucinda said. She squeezed his hand once more. "We'll see ourselves out. But please. Come to town. Jonah. Come back."

Jonah said nothing, stared through the doorway into the room at the empty trunk, the shut window.

An icy wind chilled him as Lucinda and Dale left the cabin.

The door clicked shut against the outside world.

Jonah sat in the pulverizing silence.

He put his head down on the table and wept.

No Answer

Jonah awoke, jarred awake, as if from a Van Winklean sleep.

Dawn bled through the windows.

He pressed his face into his palms and moaned, the sound an ancient wind conjured from deep within him. He stood, unsteady, the room aglow in dawn's slow golden light, the sun's mindless warmth creeping along the floor.

Dust motes turned in the light.

He shambled to the doorway to the back room. A spider skittered across his boot then squeezed itself into a crack in the floor.

Jonah stepped into the room and lifted the trunk lid.

Empty.

Fool.

He shut the lid on the empty trunk.

No. Not empty. Not quite. Something caught his eye. He lifted the lid again. A tiny scrap of paper lay at the bottom. Blank.

No, not tiny. Folded small.

He bent and picked it, unfolded it.

Not blank.

A drawing. Two stick figures. A man and a girl. Sitting on a porch swing.

Had she been here after all? His mind spun with confusion; the fever from the spider bite left his memory opaque. He slipped the drawing in his pocket and went to the window.

It was closed.

No.

Not quite.

It was open, a hair, the width of knife blade. A slice of frigid air leaked into the room.

On the floor at his feet, a droplet of water. Melted snow.

"No." He backed away from the window, his heels striking the trunk.

No. If she were out in the cold all this time. If she'd fled. Again. Fled him. Was alone again. She'd die. Was already dead.

He rushed out of the room and stumbled out onto the porch, looking about wildly, shouting, "Sally!"

He stepped off the porch, the snow a blinding white with the rising sun shattering off of it, trudged around the side of the cabin.

A ruffed grouse busted from beneath a stunted spruce with a spray of fresh snow, startling him.

He continued around the back of the cabin.

Virgin snow. Not a mouse track upon it.

He circled the cabin but saw no tracks.

Had the falling snow covered her tracks? How would he ever find her if she didn't answer his call?

"Sally!"

He'd failed her.

Again.

He traipsed into the woods, his aching legs leaden. Snow cascaded from limbs. He fell, cold snow melting at the back of his hot neck. He cried out for her.

No answer came.

Panting, he pulled himself up, jacket stuck to his back with sweat. He was too lame, too old, and the snow too deep for him to tramp any farther so blindly. He worked his way back to the cabin. Went into the back room to reassess. The cold air leaked under the window, but the droplets of water could have come from snow melted from Lucinda's boots.

He went back out and stood on the porch, listening.

If she'd existed, she was gone now and he'd never find her. She was lost, and a primal grief crowded him. For a moment, standing there, he smelled her, the milky fragrance of her breath. Then a breeze caught her scent and carried it away.

If it had ever been there at all.

The door creaked behind him.

His heart stopped. He dared not move.

The door creaked again.

It was her. She'd hidden elsewhere in the cabin. Somehow.

The door creaked.

By degrees, he turned to see—

The door swaying in the wind. The emptiness within him opened wider.

Home, she'd said.

He sniffed at his shirt collar but no hint of her remained.

There was nothing left to prove she'd ever been there at all.

HOME

Dale eased the Wrangler down Lucinda's childhood street.
"I'll need help with this," Lucinda said, her voice flat.
The horridness of what she was about to do, what she suspected,
made it hard to speak. Her body felt dull and deadened even while
her senses seemed too intense to bear. The sky had cleared over-
night in the valley, and the mean morning sun pierced her eyes.
Her breath raked through the cilia of her lungs. The sound of the
Wrangler's blinker blasted in her ear.

"Help from Kirk?" Dale said as he turned off Main.

"What?"

"You'll need help from Kirk?"

"From you. And . . . the state police." Exhausted from her sleep-
less night, Lucinda thought she might be sick but closed her eyes
and tried to calm herself. She seemed to be vibrating, as if her
skeleton were a tuning fork that had been struck hard against a
rock.

Dale pulled the Wrangler up out front.

"You okay?" he said.

"No." She slipped her hand into Dale's hand.

He squeezed it.

Lucinda stepped out of the Wrangler and stood on the street where she'd learned to ride a bicycle with her father's help. Where she'd played hopscotch, kick-the-can, and hide-and-seek with Sally. Where she'd sat out in Kirk's parked pickup truck after the drive-in, hurriedly buttoning up her blouse and checking her lipstick and trying to hold him off against her own desires before she slipped into the house to find her widowed father asleep on the couch in front of the flickering TV.

Dale got out and put his arm around her and led her to the house.

She was unsteady of feet and of mind, as if she had not slept or eaten in years.

Each step and thought was a precarious labor.

Dale knocked on the kitchen door and a moment later it opened, Dot standing there bleary eyed and puffy faced with slumber.

"Hullo. What brings you so early?" Dot smiled. She pulled the top of her robe tighter around her throat, squinting. "What's wrong?" she said, her smile vanquished.

"We need to come in," Lucinda said.

"What's wrong?" Dot said, opening the door wider to allow them entrance.

Lucinda and Dale stepped into the kitchen.

The clock on the microwave blinked from 6:45 to 6:46.

"What is it?" Dot said.

"It's personal," Lucinda said. "Is he up?"

"He had a rough night. Moaning, agitated, crying out. Worst night he's had in my memory. I gave him something to help him rest. I doubt he'll be awake before noon."

"What was he calling out about?" Lucinda said.

"Nonsense. The stuff of nightmares."

"I need to use the phone."

Lucinda shuffled to the phone on the wall and dialed.

Dot looked at Dale. "What's this about?"

"I can't say," Dale said.

As the phone rang, Lucinda ran her hand along the doorframe to the living room, over the pencil marks that had measured her height over the years. Her mother had been the one to keep track. The last mark's date read: 10/29/87 44¼".

Sally had disappeared a week later.

The phone on the other end rang, and rang.

"Hello," Lucinda said finally. "This is Deputy Sheriff Lucinda Welch in Ivers. I'd like to have a trooper sent to fifteen Maple Street here in Ivers."

Dot stared.

"No, it's not an emergency. Okay, all right. That's fine. Thank you."

Lucinda hung up the phone. She stared at the penciled marks her mother had made to measure her on the doorframe. She tried to stave off the ugly images petitioning her for attention. They came anyway. Her mother at the bottom of the stairs. Her father kneeling at her side, looking with a fear Lucinda had believed was a reflection of the dread he felt for his wife. Now, she wondered.

"Why are you calling the state police?" Dot asked.

Lucinda emerged from her murky reminiscence. A chill ran through her.

"Dot," she said. "I'd like to be alone with my father. In our house. Maybe you could run to the Lucky Spot and get coffee."

"But what's—"

"Dorothy. Please."

"I'll go change," Dot said. "I can't go in my bathrobe."

Dale took some bills from his wallet, handed them to Dot.

"Will you stay here," Lucinda said to Dale, "and wait for them? I need to see him."

"He won't have his wits about him," Dot said as she left.

Dale sat at the table and looked out the kitchen window at the street as Lucinda walked down the hall to the door to the room where now her father lay confined.

She inched the door open and peered into the dark room.

Her father lay on his back in his bed, the rails up at the sides. Three years and more of suffering. Who knew how much was yet to come beyond this life. The balancing for deeds done. He'd never been anything but a good father to her. Never anything but that.

She shut the door behind her, the room going dark save a gash of hurtful morning sunlight at the bottom of the window shade.

She could hear his breathing. A wheeze followed by a protracted silence. Another wheeze. High-pitched and frothy, like air drawn through a collapsed straw at the bottom of a nearly empty glass.

Heeeeeeegh.

"Dad."

She drew closer.

"Dad."

She sat in his bedside chair, her whole life, her past collapsing around her.

He'd lost weight in the past days.

Mouth agape as if he'd stopped talking midsentence.

Let me not ever come to this, Lucinda thought. *Let my end come quick, and with mercy and dignity.*

Not this.

Lucinda leaned close. Kissed her father's forehead.

Whatever he'd done, whatever she might discover, he was her father.

The same man she'd cherished her entire life.

Yet he wasn't.

Cast now in her suspicion, her father gave off an aura before unknown to her. Her nerves crackled with disquiet, as though in his dying state her father's body was preparing to transform, split open to reveal an alien being within. Grotesque and unfatherly. Unsafe. Above all, a child in a parent's presence ought to feel safe. Though he lay there feeble, Lucinda did not feel safe. She felt locked in with an evil she could not rid through denial alone. Would never expel from her blood.

The wheezing and quiet stillness and darkness weighed on her, suffocating.

She gathered her will and kissed his forehead again.

A light knock came on the door.

The door opened a crack.

"He's here," Dale said.

NOT A STAR

In the kitchen, a trooper stood by the door, his hat in hand before him, posture erect and dutiful.

"Deputy." He nodded with a professional camaraderie.

Lucinda returned the nod.

"What is it we have here?" he said.

She told him.

"You're sure?"

"No."

She took the flashlight from the drawer, her fingers weak with terror.

She opened the door to the cellar.

"Down here," she said.

She followed the flashlight beam down into the darkness.

Dale and the trooper followed her lead.

"Careful," she said.

In the cellar, she swam the flashlight beam over the workbench. Screwdrivers and jars of nuts and bolts.

"There."

The beam cut across the cellar to the corner. To the trunk she'd seen when looking for Beverly. The shovel with its broken handle.

Her mind shrieked: *Wake up! Wake up! Run!*

"Under it," she said.

She shone the flashlight on the trooper's and Dale's faces.

Her heart beat loud in her head. A breathless claustrophobia pressed in on her.

"Whose house is this?" the trooper said.

"My father's."

"I see."

Did he see? Could he see what she saw? If so, he could not feel what she felt.

"I want to look in the trunk. But it's locked," she said, noting now the padlock. She shone the flashlight over the workbench, underneath it. Looking among her father's old tools. "There's a bolt cutter there."

The trooper took the cutter and worked it, the jaws nearly seized with rust.

He got the padlock bar in the jaws and squeezed down. Twisted the cutter's jaws. The padlock finally relented and the lock dropped to the wet earth floor.

"You want to open it?" he said to Lucinda.

She handed the flashlight to Dale who shone it on the trunk as she lifted its lid.

Inside the trunk, Lucinda found shoeboxes, stacked as neat as bricks to the top of the trunk.

Lucinda took a box and opened its lid.

Photos. Stacked just as carefully as the shoeboxes in the trunk.

Lucinda picked up a photo. It was of a young teenage girl, of perhaps fourteen. She wore denim Capri pants, flip-flops, and a tank top with a sunflower print on it. Long straight hair parted in the middle. A sixties child.

"Who is that?" Dale asked, training the flashlight beam on the photo.

Lucinda thumbed through the photos. Faded. Dozens. Scores. Some yellowed by time's brush. Others mildewed. The oldest photos black and white, square with sharp edges and a glossy finish, bordered by white. The newer color photos fading faster than the black-and-white photos, their edges rounded with dates in one corner. The star of each photo was the same girl as in the first photo, ranging from about the age of five to her midtwenties, the early sixties to late seventies. In most of the photos a young man was with her. Laughing with her. Hugging her. Kissing her cheek. Giving her a piggyback ride. Leaping hand in hand from the covered bridge into the river. Splashing water on each other in the swimming hole. Making the peace sign together. Sitting beside each other on a Ferris wheel. The boy beaming. Always beaming.

"Do you know these people?" the trooper asked. "Do they mean anything to you?"

Lucinda handed the shoebox to the trooper and took another box from the trunk. Opened it. The same girl. The same boy. An entire childhood and young adulthood caught in faded snapshots. The girl's smile effervescent, her eyes startling, hypnotic. Dark. So dark.

In photos beginning in the early seventies or so, another boy started to appear in the photos with the two of them. A skinny, slight boy who wore grubby, high-water jeans and ill-fitting threadbare shirts.

His face was hacked over with a red marker.

Slowly, as the dates of the photos advanced, the first boy's beaming smile faded, until it was gone, replaced by a smile that was more like a pained wince. A fake smile.

Lucinda looked inside another box.

The same. More photos. Hundreds and hundreds of photos.

She searched through box after box.

The same three youths.

Dale took a photo.

"Who are they?" he asked.

"Mrs. B.," Lucinda whispered.

Dale pointed to the first boy. "But that's not Jonah."

"The other one. The skinny, meek one. His face is marked out with red. That's Jonah," Lucinda said.

The trooper took a photo and looked at it.

"Who's Jonah?" he said.

"My father's friend."

"Who's the young man kissing her cheek, and splashing, horsing around, the one whose face we see? Who is he?"

"My father."

At the bottom of the last box sat a book. She picked it up. A diary.

On the inside cover was written in pen: 1987.

Lucinda flipped through to the last couple entries from late October.

As she read, a sensation of vertigo overcame her, as if a bottomless pit in the earth had opened up before her and she stood precariously at its edge.

She dropped the diary. Mrs. B.'s diary.

Dizzy, Lucinda stared at the depression of earth under the trunk, the one she'd believed was caused by water leaking into the cellar.

She grabbed hold of a handle at one end and dragged the trunk away. She looked around, grabbed an old shovel, and started to dig at the earth, letting out a cry.

"Deputy," the trooper said. He took her arm, then the shovel. "Go sit on the bottom stair there. I'll manage."

Dale helped Lucinda to the stairs and sat with her.

The trooper jabbed the shovel point into the dirt where Lucinda had begun to dig, brought the heel of his boot down hard on it, and scooped earth, tossing it to the side.

Lucinda closed her eyes, tried to shut out the sound of the rhythmic shoveling; the *shooof* of the blade sunk into earth, the grunt of the trooper as he lifted and tossed the dirt, the *hoomph* of the dirt landing softly to the side.

Shooof. Uuumph. Hoomph.

Can't find them. All my fault, her father had said in the kitchen the other morning of Lucinda's visit.

Them.

Failed. All my fault.

Peace. Find. Before. Devil finds you.

Lucinda took one of Sally's drawings out from her jacket pocket.

Black night with a star.

Not an evening star.

A sheriff's star.

A badge.

The Truth

A shadow fell across Lucinda as she sat at the bottom of the stairs.

"I got the breakfast sandwiches," Dot called down from the top of the stairs. "What are you doing sitting down there?"

Dale turned and looked up at her. "Shhh," he said.

"I'll put them on the counter."

Shooof. Uuumph—

"I got something," the trooper said and leaned the shovel against the cellar wall.

Lucinda stood, Dale at her side.

They crept over to the excavation site.

Dale shone the flashlight beam into the hole.

In the dark earth at the bottom of the hole, white protruded from the wet black earth.

The trooper reached down with his fingertips to pick away at the earth around. Earthworms wriggled in the dirt. Beetles scuttled.

"Let me," Lucinda said.

The trooper turned to look at Lucinda.

"Please," she said.

The trooper stepped aside.

Lucinda knelt and with her fingers picked away at the edges to reveal more of the bone. A convex shape materialized, like an overturned bowl.

The cap of a skull.

Without the lower mandible.

"A child's," the trooper said from behind her. "I'd guess."

Lucinda wilted. Dale righted her. "No," Lucinda said.

"We shouldn't proceed," the trooper said. "We need to get a forensic team here right away. Follow procedure exactly." He stared down into the shallow grave. "I have two daughters," he said.

They turned to go up the stairs.

In the doorway at the top of the stairs, Lucinda's father sat in his wheelchair looking down at them.

Then he wheeled away.

Dot was setting out the breakfast sandwiches on the table.

"Help yourself," she said.

"You need to go," Lucinda said.

"There's coffee on," Dot said. "And—"

"Ma'am," the trooper said, "the deputy is right. You need to vacate the premises."

"I don't understand— When should I come back?"

"We won't need you to come back," Lucinda said.

"But your father?" Dot said.

"I don't know how something like this works. Do you know how this works?" Lucinda asked the trooper. "Someone his age? So ill. Months, if not weeks."

"I don't know, Deputy. I don't know."

"Please tell me what's happening," Dot said, going pale.

"Ma'am," the trooper said, "please, if you'll just come with me outside."

"I have personal belongings here."

"We'll see you get them." The trooper turned to Lucinda. "I'll put in the call from the cruiser. Don't go down there again. We don't want to disturb anything more than we have, now that we know."

NOTHING REMAINS

Jonah looked around the cabin.

There was nothing here for him. Had there ever been? He'd sought escape but had escaped nothing. He'd sought a new life but had found only a long quiet death.

He opened the woodstove door. Embers pulsed in a bed of ash. He poked a kindling stick in the coals, got its tip glowing.

He lit a cigarette with it.

Coughed.

In the corner, he found the can of lantern fuel and unscrewed its cap and walked about the cabin tilting it, kerosene burbling onto the floor behind him.

He soaked the couch with the fuel.

Sucked on the cigarette.

He walked to the door, fuel gurgling behind him. From out on the porch he threw the can into the cabin. He looked up at the sky through the swaying treetops. Vultures rode the draft to circle over the beeches down below.

He took one long last deep drag on the cigarette.

It tasted of death.

He stepped off the porch and flicked the cigarette back into the cabin, as far as he could.

The fuel lit with a hollow *whoooop*.

Exploded.

He was knocked back by the rush of flames, felt their hot breath scorch his face, the acrid smoke in his nostrils as he retreated to the hemlocks.

Let the whole cabin burn.

Let it burn to the ground.

VULTURES

Malcolm LeFranc saw the smoke rising. Up toward the old man's place.

"What in hell, Shirley?" he said, looking out through his truck's windshield as he drove up to the Gore. His mutt, Shirley, squatted on the truck seat beside him, whining.

LeFranc parked up off a logging road and got out as Shirley loped behind him. The old man was probably burning his summer's and fall's worth of trash before winter grabbed everyone by the balls.

LeFranc slung his tree-marking sprayer on his back and set off into the woods, picking his way along with familiar ease among the talcum mines and blowdowns.

The snow rose shin deep where it drifted in clear-cuts, yet there was scarcely any at all beneath the biggest beasts of trees. The real lumber. Moneymakers. Two hundred feet tall, two hundred years old. Thousands of board feet per trunk. At each colossal tree, LeFranc was pained to spray an orange X. Trees to be spared. Much as he'd love the money they'd bring, the deal with the feds in order to log the younger trees was to keep these behemoths standing. A trade-off to get at fifteen hundred acres of fifty-year-old trees.

He sprayed an X on a trunk. Kept on.

Up ahead, Shirley barked.

LeFranc smelled the smoke from the old man's burn pile.

Shirley barked.

The logger moved deeper in the woods, working down toward the beeches to mark the stray spruce.

Shirley barked and whined.

Ahead, ravens called in their garrulous gravel voices, and he heard the *whuuuumph whuuuumph* of massive beating wings of vultures lifting off the ground. Glimpsed black bodies stark against the white world. They lifted up off into the trees and sat in the top branches of the beeches clumsy-footed off the ground, gawking down on Shirley, who barked and barked.

"Hey, girl," LeFranc called. "Come on."

Shirley kept barking.

Barking at something.

No getting her away, except to go yank her and get her on a leash.

"Shhh, girl, shhh," he said, taking the leash out of his coat pocket.

He stooped over to hook the leash onto her collar.

She growled and bared her teeth.

"Easy, what's—"

He saw it.

In the snow, next to a pit.

A leg.

A tiny leg.

Half buried under the snow.

Shirley nipped at him.

LeFranc grabbed her by the scruff. "Lie down! Lie down and be quiet."

Shirley hunkered in the snow.

"Sorry, girl. Just. Be good."

He looked into the pit.

It was a leg all right.

LeFranc dug around in the snow.

Uncovered a shoulder.

A face.

A girl's face.

The missing girl.

GIRL IN THE SNOW

Jonah called out in the wild woods; he expected no voice to call back and none did.

Finally, he collapsed in the snow.

He lay on his back, staring up at the branches swimming on the breeze above him. The blue sky beyond.

He closed his eyes.

And heard it.

The bark of a dog. Muffled by snow and trees. But not far off. Not if he could hear it.

He tried to get up. Couldn't.

Tried again, shifting to his side.

He took hold of a tree branch and pulled. Got to his knees. Rested.

A voice now too.

The barking came again.

He used a stick as a cane and lurched toward the voices of the man and dog.

Near the beeches, he leaned against a boulder that had calved away from a cliff high above him.

The voice rose. The bark sounded. Clear. Sharp.

He picked his way, from tree to tree.

Stopped.

There.

Movement.

Just ahead.

Close.

He dipped his head to better see through the whips.

A man. Malcolm LeFranc. And a dog. LeFranc knelt, looking at something, his face a mask of horror.

At LeFranc's knees lay a yellow coat.

She was still as a doll. Still as the dead.

A movement in the trees near LeFranc caught Jonah's eye and he glanced to see the vultures and ravens looking on from their perch in the branches. Waiting their turn.

He backed away and fled down through the trees, mindless, racked with pain.

DOWN FROM THE GORE

Jonah limped out of the woods, got the truck running, and worked his bare hands at the heater vent waiting for the ache of life to return to his fingers.

He needed to find Lucinda. Explain his story. He. What? It confused him, the past days. He'd seen LeFranc kneeling beside her and known she was dead. Because of him. Or was it because of him? Had it even happened, his bringing her to the cabin?

Had he shot her and found her dead a week ago and left her there and slipped into a hallucination? Out of a desperate need for a second chance, had he dreamed of saving her and protecting her? Or had he lived all that he imagined the past days? He'd seen the yellow coat. Hadn't he? How could she get the yellow coat if she'd not been in the cabin? Perhaps it wasn't the same coat. Or perhaps he was imagining that too.

No. All of it had to have happened. And now. She was dead. Because of him.

He needed to explain he'd done what he'd done in order to protect the girl. He would take the consequences. He'd harbored her not out of altruism but out of selfishness. He'd looked for reasons to keep her. Wanted to keep her.

He drove his truck down out of the mountains, past the old house, to Lucinda's place. Her Wrangler was not in the drive. He sat in his truck, waiting. When she did not show, he drove off.

He pulled in front of the Grain & Feed and went in, the cowbell clunking.

A boy Jonah did not recognize sat behind the counter.

"How are you this morning?" the boy said.

"Lucinda around?" Jonah said.

"Nah."

"Know where she is?"

"I'm just filling in for Mr. Baines. She's at her house, I guess."

"Nope."

The boy shrugged.

"Maybe her father's place," the boy said.

Lucinda's Wrangler sat parked in front of the house, along with three state trooper cruisers. *Something's happened to Maurice,* Jonah thought.

Though he had not seen Maurice in many years, Jonah knew of Maurice's failing health.

Except. If something medical had happened with Maurice, where was the ambulance?

He buttoned his coat to the top, smoothed the front of it. A nervous flutter in his chest, like the moment he'd been about to confess his love to Rebecca for the first time, knowing it would change everything, the arc of his life, one way or another.

He went up the walkway and knocked on the door.

No one came.

He knocked again.

The door went unanswered.

He pounded on it.

The door opened and Lucinda stood before him.

"Jonah," she said, and he saw anguish in her eyes, remembered her as a sweet, sweet girl, the friend of his daughter.

She looked out past him, up toward the Gore. He knew she saw the smoke from his burning cabin rising in the distance. He needed to tell her about what he'd done, what he'd seen these past days. Tell her the truth, as he knew it.

"I have to—" he said.

The torment on her face morphed into compassion.

Jonah composed himself, tried to hold Lucinda's gaze. He looked down at his boots. Their leather was worn through at the toes so a dull sheen of steel shone through. His eyes trailed back up her to find her face again.

"We found them," she said, her voice that of a frightened girl.

What Lucinda had prattled on about in the cabin, her believing she knew where Jonah's wife and daughter were, but not wanting to tell Jonah until she was sure.

A star but not a star. She had my doll, Lucinda had said.

The words cleaved him open.

He thought of Sally's drawings that Maurice had found. Not a star. A badge. Maurice's badge. And Jonah knew. Knew what the anguish and compassion in Lucinda's face meant. Maurice had manipulated Jonah into thinking the drawings might implicate Jonah. Tricked Jonah into destroying evidence, not against Jonah, evidence against Maurice.

No.

Yes.

Jonah waited for the old rage to rear in him, prepared to fight against it. Yet it did not come.

Instead, he felt calm. To allow his rage to overcome him, to lash out would only shame his wife and daughter. What was there left to lash out at?

"In the cellar," Lucinda said.

Jonah ran his palm down the front of his coat.

Part of him never wanted to lay eyes on that cellar, to see where his wife and daughter had lain in ignominy all these years, yet another part of him wanted to rush to them, assure them all was well now. They were found and they would never be lost again.

"The state police are handling it," she said. "One of them is speaking to my father now. He's dying. Has been for years."

Good, Jonah thought. *I'm glad it's been a long torment.*

"We're all dying," he said. "The best we can hope is that no one hurries us toward our death. No one decides for us how and when."

He stared at his boots for an eternity.

No matter what he did or where he went, it would never end. Missing them.

"I need new boots," he whispered.

"Jonah, he's my father," Lucinda said. "My father did this."

He looked up at her again.

She was crying. "She was my best friend."

This was not Jonah's pain alone. Her father. Her dearest childhood friend.

He took her hand in his.

She tried to blink back her tears but they could not be stopped. "Do you wish to . . . after they're done, after they take him away . . . just you and them?"

"I'd like to remember them as they were. Before all this."

A state trooper came up behind Lucinda.

"Deputy," he said.

Lucinda turned to address the trooper.

"We'll need to speak to you," the trooper said.

"Give me a moment," she said.

The trooper nodded and walked back toward the kitchen.

Lucinda turned back to see Jonah was halfway to his truck.

"Mr. B.," she said.

But Mr. B. kept walking, opened the door of his truck, shut himself in the cab, and rested his forehead on the steering wheel.

Deputy Welch

Lucinda sat in the kitchen as the troopers performed their tasks, came and went from the cellar carrying plastic bags of evidence. Bones. Scraps of clothing. Photos. The diary.

She'd sent Dale to get food though she wasn't hungry and felt she'd never again have an appetite. She'd only wanted time alone, and he'd known that and respected it.

A trooper stood in the cellar doorway. Lucinda wiped at her runny nose with the back of her hands.

"We're done, for the time being," the trooper said.

"What happens now?" Lucinda said.

"We can process him here. Read him his rights, though in his state he may not understand, making it void. Then have him transported to the hospital." The trooper cleared his throat. "I have other news. That girl, the missing foster girl. She was found."

Lucinda let out a long sigh. "Where?"

"Up in the Gore. If you believe that."

"I was just up there."

Lucinda shook her head at the tragedy of it.

TELL ME

In the living room, her father lifted his shaking hand for her to
hold.

Lucinda sat on the edge of the couch across from him. She did
not take his hand.

He set his hand back down, made a slurping sound with the
corner of his mouth.

The living room was ferociously hot and airless, and Lucinda
felt as though she were trapped in a forge.

She took her smartphone from her pocket, pressed her finger
on the record app. She cleared her throat, sat straight, chin up.
"This is Town of Ivers Deputy Sheriff Lucinda Welch, recording
suspect Maurice Welch, November 12, two thousand twelve, at
ten thirty-five A.M., in the home of Maurice Welch."

Lucinda looked at the photo behind her father on the wall, of
her and Sally on the tire swing, smiling madly.

"It happened here," Lucinda said.

Her father did not speak or nod, but his eyes confirmed the
story the bones in the basement told.

"Please, speak for the record," Lucinda said.

"Yes. Here."

Lucinda did not need his confirmation. She knew it had happened here, right here in her home. Her friend and her friend's mother had been killed in this house, her childhood home, and had been down in the cellar all these years while Lucinda had been stricken with sorrow and bewilderment and fear. In the past hour, Lucinda had read enough of the diary—Mrs. B.'s diary— she'd found in the trunk to piece together the background to the days leading to the disappearances. The murders. The motive and the scenario were clear now in her mind, even as they muddied her soul to think of them, to think this of her father. Know this about him.

"The photos. The faces scratched out, Jonah Baum's face. Jealousy. All this, from jealousy."

Her father shook his head.

"Speak for the record," Lucinda said. "Jealousy was the motive."

"Yes," her father said. "And no."

"Please, clarify. Was it or not?"

"Not jealous. Humiliated. She came here. She and her daughter."

"Sally. Sally Baum. You can say her name. Sally. And her mother, Rebecca Baum."

"Yes. Them."

"Why did she come here?"

"She was upset. Afraid." His breath whistled.

"Of what?" Lucinda knew the truth, knew what, who, Rebecca had become afraid of in those last days.

"Of him. Jonah." Lucinda's father sipped air in tiny gasps. Grimaced.

"The photos. Jonah's face mauled by a pen. You did that. Yet she was afraid of Jonah?"

"You know his temper."

"Tell the truth."

Her father licked his dry, peeling lips. "The truth. She was *mine*. First. I came from the good family. Me. He. Stole her. *She* came to *me*. She was afraid."

"And what happened?" Lucinda steeled herself against the words this man was saying. The lies. This father who'd had a lovely wife and adopted daughter he never treated as anything but his own, with love and tenderness. What had he thought, that he'd just leave Lucinda and her mother, run off to some fairy-tale life? Abandon them and . . . what?

He gritted his teeth, strained to breathe. "You judge. But. You. Kirk. You are always tempted to go back. I see it."

"You don't see anything." How dare he use her as means to justify what he'd done. Her father was manipulating her. She felt it in her belly like the twist of a knife, his lying about the specifics. Shading the truth. She was certain. When did it stop, her being manipulated by men, however calculated and selfish, or unconscious and well intentioned, their attempts?

Her father hacked up phlegm on the cuff of his pajama top, phlegm tainted with blood.

"What did you do to them? What did you do to my friend?"

"She feared what he might do." His voice splintered.

"She did," Lucinda said. *Just not the way you want me to believe it.* "Go on."

"I told her. Stay. I'd take care of her. She got—"

"What?"

"Hysterical."

"Oh, *hysterical.*" Lucinda felt numbed with disbelief, disembodied, and her voice seemed to come from somewhere, someone else.

"She was off her meds," her father said. "She could get . . . She *swung* at me. I—defended. A man can't."

And what did you do to make her swing at you? Lucinda thought.

"I grabbed a knife."

Lucinda could barely find the breath to speak. She felt weak, and so tired. Vanquished. "Sally? What'd you do to my friend?"

"You don't"—he coughed, hacked up phlegm—"want to know."

"The law wants to know. It needs to know who and how and why."

Her father bit his lower lip, drawing blood. He licked at the bead of blood, put a frail fingertip to it. "She started crying. Crazy. Like her mother."

"A girl. Crazy."

"No control."

Lucinda could imagine Sally frenzied, from terror. Lucinda could bear no more. She stood.

"*Accident*," her father pleaded, desperate. "That's the truth."

"Lies," Lucinda said. "Sally's mom was not afraid of Jonah. Not in the way you make it seem. *You*'d begun to hound her."

"Not true, I—"

"I *read* it in her *own words* in the diary from the trunk. The diary you stole. You went back to her house and took it. Where was it?"

"Nightstand."

"Why'd you keep it?"

"It was hers. Her thoughts. Her handwriting."

"Why, after so many years, did you start to hound her? Obsess over her? You were friends. You and her and Jonah. And *Mom*. All of you. Why?"

Her father closed his eyes as if mulling options for answering the question. He opened his eyes.

"Sometimes. An itch. Can't ignore anymore. You scratch. It helps. But. Then. You scratch and scratch and scratch." He shook his head, drool shining on his chin. "It gets raw. Starts to bleed. Fester. Becomes a sore."

"She came here once to reason with you to leave her be," Lucinda said. "Told you to stop. But you made wild threats and spouted terrible things. That Sally should have been your daughter. Your natural daughter. The real daughter you should have had." Lucinda's voice trailed as her words skewered her.

"That's not. I didn't. Mean that. I was—"

"But you backed off that time because Sally had stopped by to see me, let herself in without knocking, as we always did. I wasn't home and neither was Mom, and Sally heard you saying awful things to Mrs. B. before either of you heard her crying in the living room. *That's* why Sally drew those pictures. Because of your ugliness. Because of how much your threats to her mom scared her. Sally and Rebecca were *both* afraid of *you*."

"Yes," her father said.

"You backed down that first time to calm Sally. So Sally wouldn't tell me. Or her dad. You gave Sally my doll to calm her and she took her home. Baby Beverly. You swore Sally to secrecy. Her mom swore her to secrecy. Because she knew Jonah's temper. She was afraid of it, not at it being directed at her. But at *you*. He was suspicious she was seeing someone. His suspicions were taking their toll on them. She swore she wasn't seeing anyone, there was no one for her except Jonah. And it was true. She wrote that in her diary. There was no one else. Despite their problems. But he wasn't convinced, he knew something was off, wrong, felt her tension and secrecy. Because it existed, just not the way he imagined. She couldn't come clean, she couldn't tell him it was *you*. Bothering her. She feared what he'd do and knew it would crush him. She hoped she could get you to see reason."

"Love knows no reason," her father whispered.

Lucinda tried to ignore the lacerating, delusional words.

"When Mrs. B. found Sally's drawings, and forced Sally to tell her about a man in the woods, Mrs. B. came back the morning Jonah left early for campus," Lucinda said. "She brought Sally. I don't know why. Maybe she thought you'd see the damage you were doing if you saw Sally's face. Maybe it was to have a witness there to keep you in check. Maybe because Sally had been feeling sick the day before and was sick that morning. But you were the one who followed Sally in the woods. Her and me. Do I have that right?"

He swallowed, winced, as if swallowing shards of glass. "Yes," he said. "But—"

"But *what*?"

"It was an *accident*."

"And Mom, falling down the stairs. Was that an *accident*?"

"*You*," he barked, his voice so much louder than she'd heard it in years it made her jump. "How *dare you*."

Lucinda turned to leave.

"You're my daughter," her father gasped. "No one else. I was mad. When I said that. I was—"

"I'm not here in the capacity of your daughter. I'm here in the capacity of a deputy sheriff. The state police will handle you from here."

"I want . . . to see him. Jonah."

She spun on him. "Why? To hurt him even more?"

"To tell him the truth. Myself. To his face."

Before You

J onah stood in the dark living room, remembering times when the house was lit and vibrant, raucous with the two daughters' laughs and screams, his and Rebecca's and Maurice and Julia's voices, the fire roaring in the fireplace, its heat warming and its light inviting.

Before him, in the shadows, slumped in a wheelchair and peering up at him, sat the man who had been his friend.

"You confessed," Jonah said.

"Yes," Maurice said. "And. No."

Maurice shook his head, his eyes glassy, pupils seeming to float. "I confessed. But did not tell the truth."

Jonah longed to sit. He felt fragile on his legs, yet wanted to remain standing, looking down on this man.

"Sit," Maurice said.

Jonah refused. He was not sitting for this man as he had at his own kitchen table so many years ago.

"I lied. To Lucy," Maurice said. "I— Loved Rebecca."

"I don't want to hear this," Jonah said and started to leave.

"We both loved her." Maurice sucked in a thin unwell breath. "You. Me. You know that. I didn't hurt Rebecca. I . . . Sally . . . She was starting to look." He swallowed, smacked his dry lips. "So much like her, when Rebecca and I first met as kids. When it was just. Rebecca and me. Before you."

"Stop."

"Never hurt her. Sally. Or Rebecca. I—" He shut his eyes, clacked his teeth together. "I bothered her. Scared her. Both of them. I'm sorry. My fault. But—"

Jonah tried to control his breathing, stem the anger that made him quake. "You're sorry because the truth is out."

"It's not out. The real truth. It would kill Lucinda."

Maurice struggled to sit up straight, look Jonah in the eye. "Rebecca came here. Threatened to tell you about my . . . behavior. I got. Mad. Said things. When you won her over. Betrayed me when I was at academy."

"You were not together. Not an item. Ever. You were friends."

"But you knew. You knew how I felt."

"She didn't feel that way."

"It killed me. You knew. I told you. It killed me. And you. While I was away. I kept thinking. She'd see you. The real you." He gasped for breath, wheezed. "Sooner or later. See the violent boy inside, fear you. Come back to me. I waited. Time passed. She never saw that violent boy, never feared you. He was dead. She killed him."

"You wanted her to come back to you? You were never hers to come back to. All that time, all those years? You were happy. You had a wife and a daughter."

"Didn't matter. All that mattered. Was. One day. She'd look at me. One time. Look at me like she'd looked at *you*. She came that morning. Angry." He sagged in the wheelchair, wheezing, closed his eyes, as if to remember that day. "So angry. Sally with her. Told me. She knew it was me in the woods, stalking Sally. *Stalking.* Said I had to stop. For her, for Sally. For all our sakes. She brought her own daughter, as a pawn."

"So you—"

"No." His chest heaved, his mouth gaped, as if he were about to be sick. "No. Never."

"They're in your cellar—"

"I wasn't home. Was gone. Called out for stolen tractor. It's in dispatch records. I was not here."

"How do you know Rebecca came to see you that morning if—"

"She told me."

Jonah wondered if Maurice were lucid, if he even knew what he was speaking about, or where he was. "How could Rebecca—"

"Julia. Told me," Maurice said. His face turned to stone before Jonah. Not out of anger or fear, but out of restraint, as if every cell of his face was fixed against the tiniest betrayal of emotion. Jonah heard the truth in Maurice's voice, saw the truth in Maurice's stone face, in the torment in his eyes at having said what he'd just said. "I came home, afternoon. Before school was out. She was. Kneeling over them. Mouth open, like a roar. Silent roar. No sound. Eyes wide. Not seeing. She'd been there. Hours. Kneeling over them, rocking, drooling."

"Julia," Jonah said.

"She could not stand," Maurice said. "Even with help. Knotted and stooped from kneeling over them. For hours. She told me. Rebecca came, looking for me. *Demanding.* Refused to leave. Shoved the drawings in her face. Shouted I was stalking Sally. Raving. She scared Julia, like that night at your house. The night Rebecca struck you. It. Scared her. Scared Sally. Julia thought it was Rebecca obsessed with me."

"Don't blame what you did on your dead wife, that's—"

"The truth. Julia tried to get her to leave. Sally got between. Julia shoved her. Rebecca went wild. Swung at her."

"Don't you dare."

"Just. Telling you. Julia. Sally was crying, hysterical." Maurice coughed up bloodied phlegm. "Rebecca pounded her fists at Julia. Julia. Grabbed a knife."

"No."

"When she turned around with it, Sally was there."

"No," Jonah croaked.

"The knife. It sunk deep. Julia dropped it."

"No. No. You're lying. You did it."

"Rebecca fell to her knees beside Sally. But Sally. Was gone. Rebecca was wild. *Shrieking*. Wailing. Julia begged her to stop, begged her to let Julia call an ambulance. She tried to get the phone. Rebecca. Grabbed the knife and lunged. Julia picked up a marble paperweight. Hit her. Once. Just. To stop her. To stop it."

Jonah's legs gave and he caved into the chair behind him, his flesh afire as he buried his face in his hands.

"You," Jonah whispered. "All those questions you had for me, asking if I knew of anyone, a *friend* of Rebecca's, if I had any reason to think it might be someone else, you were trying to see if I knew if Rebecca had told me about you. About you bothering her."

Maurice nodded. "I tried. To keep focus off you. I tried. So you would not be blamed. You would not pay for something you didn't do."

"I paid. All this time," Jonah said. "You let me live with not knowing what happened to them."

"It was too awful. I couldn't—"

"Nothing is more awful than the horrors in my mind." Jonah stood. "You lied and deceived. Went on as if you knew nothing. Kept it from me. All this time. Made me suffer. How could you do that? Cover it up, continue to protect Julia even for years after she passed. You were the sheriff. You were my friend. How could you do that?"

"*She was my wife.*"

Jonah paced in the suffocating darkness and heat of the room.

"Why tell me now, if you wanted to protect her name and memory?"

"You deserve it. But. I want you to keep it to yourself. Lucinda. Can't know."

"Why should I believe any of this? Someone who frightened my wife and child. Betrayed me. Followed Sally in the woods."

"I didn't. Follow her."

"You told Lucinda just now."

"She assumed. I did not correct her. I don't know who the girls saw. If it was a person. Or just imagination. But it was not me in the woods."

"Why should I believe you, about anything? How can I believe you? That you're not just blaming Julia for what you did?"

"Because. I'm dying. And . . . I was your friend. Once."

THE SWING

Jonah pulled his truck up into the yard to stare at his old house, his mind empty ruins.

He got out and stood in the front yard.

In the gray daylight Jonah saw again that the old place was in as much ruin as his mind. He looked again at the tree he'd planted as a sapling those years ago, which had died and fallen and lay now among its own dead and broken branches scattered across the lawn. He stepped around the tree. The rotted wooden porch steps sagged beneath his weight.

The porch swing, its paint chipped and faded, slats caked with dried bird and bat shit, swayed from rusted chains in the breeze. He took hold of a chain, gave it a tug. Tested it. He eased himself down into the swing and sat on its front edge, holding it steady with his feet.

He sat there, with his eyes closed and tried not to think or feel.

An impossibility.

All these years, he'd believed nothing could be worse than not knowing what had happened to Rebecca and Sally; yet being in the dark had given him perpetual if slight hope that one day his wife and daughter might by a miracle return to him. Knowing what had become of them did not diminish the pain or lessen the feeling of absence that carved him hollow. It deepened it. The law needed to know who, how, and why, know the specifics of what happened, but he did not. The answer he'd sought, that he'd lived for, changed nothing. It did not resurrect his wife and daughter, did not bring them back, did not alter a single thing. What mattered, he realized, was not what happened and how, but how he handled himself afterward, what he did with the life his daughter and wife no longer had.

"I let you down," he said. The porch swing creaked.

He hadn't *lived* since that evening he'd fallen asleep correcting papers. He'd never really even woken up. He'd wallowed in a purgatory of anger and loss and absence instead of forging on alone without them but with courage. He'd hidden from the world. Shamed his wife and daughter's memory for not continuing on in a way of which they'd be proud. He'd lived a life of delusion when he had known, deep down in his marrow, as a fact, that his wife and daughter were dead.

There were no miracles.

This godless world.

He was alone in a life he'd refused to live.

He thought about how consumed and beleaguered he'd felt those years ago before the disappearance; the money issues, his stalled teaching career, and parenting doubts had strained him, seemed so singular to him and so unnavigable and insurmountable. The future so remote. He'd lived with the fear that with a single wrong word or decision, his world would disintegrate. How young he'd been, and how unremarkable his and Rebecca's trials.

He saw them now for what they were, a phase of a young married couple, of young parents, a phase his wife and he would have managed and overcome, eventually, if given the chance.

He opened his eyes and looked out at the valley and the mountains beyond. A thread of smoke unspooled from the forest up in the Gore. He'd not told Lucinda what he'd gone to her father's house to tell her. That he'd found the girl, kept her, and this had led to her death. He would tell Lucinda. He would confess. He would not wait to be on his deathbed to account for it. He could not live with keeping it to himself. But he could live keeping Lucinda from ever knowing what her father had said about her mother. He did not know if what Maurice had told him was a lie or the truth, and he did not care. It did not matter who was responsible. Not to him. Not anymore. But it would matter to Lucinda.

He leaned back in the swing.

He watched the smoke, a smudge in the morning sky, a sky as blue as ever it had been or ever would be.

Slowly, he began to move the swing with his legs. The chains squeaked but there was an oil can in the shed, sitting on a shelf with the gasoline cans for the mower. Oil did not go bad with the years. He'd oil the chains and they would fall quiet again.

There would be time for that.

Rest

The whole town showed for the burial of his wife and daughter, save the two ghouls who'd masqueraded as caring foster parents, and Lucinda's father.

Jonah stood graveside, hands clasped before him, head down, solemn and aggrieved yet moved by the presence of the many who'd come. He forgave each of them their past gossip and suspicion. What good would it do to cling to his tired anger in the face of their showing of support? What point would it prove, or purpose would it serve, except to isolate him? The solace of forgiveness warmed his blood. Loosened his knotted soul.

As he turned from the graves, a hand rested on his shoulder.

Lucinda.

Snowflakes piled on the shoulders of her black wool coat as they had that day at the pit. He searched her eyes now for that frightened little girl but he could not find her.

The two stood there, saying not a word, the snow gently alighting on them.

The crowd disassembled, and folks departed with silent nods

and glances, murmurs of condolence, not a few faces shaded with regret and guilt for their own failings toward him.

Jonah worked loose the knot of his tie at his throat.

"They found her," Lucinda whispered. "The girl."

Jonah looked off toward the Gore. He knew they'd found the girl. He'd watched LeFranc uncover her body in the snow.

"She'll be okay," Lucinda said. "Considering."

"She's—" Jonah said.

"Alive."

A keen and desperate longing to see the girl welled in him; he wanted to know more about her, ask Lucinda how this was possible, that she was alive, that she even existed. But he did not dare show interest in her. He'd planned to confess today about the girl, confess his part that had led to her death.

"Dale and I have taken her in, for the time being," Lucinda said.

Jonah could not speak.

"She told us about an old man who kept her," Lucinda said. "It hasn't been made public. Yet."

Tell her now, a voice said. *Come clean. Speak the truth.*

"We'd like to find him," Lucinda said.

Jonah unslung his tie from around his neck, the tie so tight he felt it would strangle him.

"We'd like to thank him," Lucinda said.

For a moment the old ugliness of paranoia crept into Jonah's heart, and he knew what Lucinda told him was a trap, to draw him out. A lie to make him feel safe. He wondered what Lucinda really knew and suspected. He'd nearly gotten the girl killed. And they wanted to thank him?

"She'd never have survived that first night if she'd not been found and taken in," Lucinda said. "We deduced that his age and the poor weather impeded him from getting her to town straight-away. There's no indication he was anything but good to her."

Jonah wrapped the tie around one of his forearms.

"If you ever want to stop by my place, say hello to her," Lucinda said.

"Why would I—"

Lucinda took his hand. "She looks so much like Sally. Her eyes. And has her spirit, now that she's coming out of the trauma. I think seeing her, it might do you some good."

Jonah looked back at the two headstones.

"I'll leave you be," Lucinda said.

She squeezed his hand then headed down the hill to leave him with his family.

WHY?

Lucinda sat with Dale on the couch, curled in front of the fire, its heat a comfort as she leaned into him, bone tired, Gretel asleep in the guest room Lucinda and Dale had decorated in a way they hoped comforted and pleased her.

From the other room, Gretel cried out in her sleep.

Lucinda stiffened.

"She'll settle down," Dale said.

"That poor girl," Lucinda said. "What kind of God allows a child to come to this earth only to have her treated as she's been treated? Left without anyone."

"She's with us."

"For now. But the abuse she's suffered along the way. What reason could God have for bringing her into this world and having her treated this way?"

"I don't know." Dale pulled her closer to him. "You send your confirmation email?"

Confirmation. Canada. The dig. She'd forgotten it.

She had one day left to confirm her acceptance or be replaced.

There was so much to do to prepare. And there was Gretel now too. Lucinda wanted to go. Yet she wanted to remain here too. "I think I'm going to call them instead. Explain things. The exceptional circumstances. Maybe they'd let me defer, participate in the next one. I hope they would understand."

"They'll understand," Dale said.

"Maybe. Not everyone's you."

"Or you."

The fire crackled.

Outside, a snowstorm had picked up, buffeting the windows with wind and snow. Inside, Lucinda was warm and safe, if mystified at the wrongs of the world, as sleep claimed her.

SPRING

S pring returned as spring will, and its breeze carried the sweet
and tanged odor of manure turned into fresh thawed earth.

The song of peepers chorused in the swamps.

Rivers rushed, choked with mud, to finally run clear.

Those solemn bears that had slumbered away the winter, lumbered again from their dark caverns to scratch and to blink back
the brightness of the world.

With life insurance funds he'd never before dared touch, Jonah
had bought back his home for a song.

Now, with the help of his neighbors, he sawed up the dead tree
that had fallen in the yard and planted a new tree. He cut back the
weeds, and raked up the sticks, and strew new grass seed. Shutters
and gutters were rehung, and the porch rail and steps repaired. He
oiled the porch swing's rusted chain.

Inside the house, he opened the shades and windows and let
spring's cool air and warm light pour into the house. He swept
and scrubbed the floors, washed the windows and walls until his
bones rang with the ache of work.

On good days, he ambled into town to buy groceries, stopped in the Grain & Feed to sit and have a coffee and biscotti and watch the people pass on the street outside the new bay window. He'd return home and sit on the porch swing, rock idly, and watch kids jump from the One Dollar Bridge into the river as they had always done and probably always would do, their screams splitting the shimmering air.

Sometimes he dozed and awakened much later, frightened and confounded to find the sun at a strange new angle in the sky.

He thought of his daughter and wife, and when he heard the song of their laughter in the house, he let it run over him like river water over stone, giving himself up to it and letting it move him wherever it liked.

And he missed them. More than ever. He missed them.

One summer morning, as he sat out in his swing, he spotted Lucinda strolling down along the sidewalk. With the girl. A gasp escaped him and he felt his heart tighten with nervousness and fear. He'd never gone to visit the girl. Never dared.

Lucinda and the girl walked hand in hand.

He watched them as his panicked heart pounded.

Lucinda waved.

Jonah waved.

Lucinda and the girl walked across the yard toward him, the girl with a small canvas bag slung over her arm. He smiled as they came up the steps. He wanted to stand and wrap the girl in his arms, pull her tight to him and feel her warmth, but he stayed put.

He looked in her face for some recognition of him, worried she might be afraid or confused. He saw none.

The girl had grown. Her hair had lightened to the color of honey and now fell past her shoulders. Her face was pink with health and her fingernails trim and clean.

She wore a yellow dress.

Lucinda sat on a porch rail as the girl sat in the swing beside Jonah, her bag on her lap.

Jonah took a deep breath and exhaled it in a long thin thread. "I like your dress," he said.

"She picked it out herself," Lucinda said.

He thought of the impossibility of his finding her that day.

If he'd not found her, she'd have died. And he'd have died alone.

If he'd not kept her, he'd never have come back here that night with her, to look around his old home for ancient drawings, and Lucinda would never have come here to investigate it and found more drawings—made connections—without the girl.

What should one call such events?

Coincidence.

The stars aligning.

Fate.

Jonah smiled down at the girl and she smiled back.

"Well," Jonah said, his face warm. "It's nice to meet you. What might your name be?"

The girl offered a shy, coy look.

"You know," she said, her voice soft as dandelion tuft.

"Do I?"

The girl nodded.

"Let's see if I do," Jonah said.

He leaned in and whispered in her ear.

She looked up at him.

"Did he guess it?" Lucinda said.

The girl smiled, and her eyes shone deep and dark and bright and lovely.

And Jonah thought of the world's many misfortunes, and of its many miracles.

What came next, God knew.